The Last Merlin

Legends of Avalon
- Book One -

Other Works by this Author
Written as R.J. Pommarane

Darkness in the Art
Halfelfin
The Body Chaotic
In the Memory of David

The Last Merlin

Legends of Avalon
- Book One -

R. Matthew Jocks-Warren

Sunfyre Books, LLC

First Printing: 2015

ISBN: 978-0-9903709-6-3 (paperback), 978-0-9903709-7-0 (eBook)

Sunfyre Books, LLC
PO Box 12024
Portland, OR 97212
www.sunfyrebookstore.com

Cover Art Courtesy of George Hodan, Celtic Myth Podcast, and Pixabay.com
Author Website: www.Jocks-Warren.com

This book is dedicated with love to David Brew:
It was years in coming but it's finally done. I only wish you were
here to see it...

Acknowledgements

There are so many people I wish to show my gratitude. First, I want to thank all those who have inspired this work of fiction, those who came before me: Geoffrey of Monmouth, Chretien de Troyes, Richard Blackmore, John Dryden, Alfred Lord Tennyson, Marion Zimmer Bradley, and Douglas Clegg. All of these amazing people have inspired my work and their voices weighed heavily in the writing of The Last Merlin. I want to thank George Hodan, Celtic Myth Podcast, and Pixabay.com for lending me their artwork for the cover illustrations. My sister, father, and friends have all helped me to find the strength to pursue my writing and for that I will be forever grateful. I want to thank my partner, Kevin, for all his love and support. Without him I wouldn't be able to craft and create my fiction. Most of all, I want to thank my mother who has inspired me to pursue my dreams every day of my life.

Characters

Galahad: *son of Ban and Viviana, Apprentice to the Merlin*
Madoc: *son of Elaine, Apprentice to the Knights of Avalon*
Tristram: *son of Drustan and Daphne, Apprentice to the Guardians*
Morgana: *daughter of Gorlois and Igerna, Apprentice to the Maiden-Healers*
Morgause: *daughter of Gorlois and Igerna, Inhabitant of the Unseen Vale*

Viviana: *mother of Galahad, Lady of the Unseen Vale, High Druidess*
Taliesin: *father of Viviana and Elaine, Merlin of all the Britons*
Ban: *father of Galahad, King of Lodecran*
Drustan: *father of Tristram, King of Lyonesse, Lord of the Cantii*
Uther: *father of Arthur, King of South Whales, Lord of the Silures*
Ambrose: *father of Uther, High King of Britannia and Gaul*
Vortigern: *servant of Mab, former tyrant king of Britannia*
Igerna: *mother of Morgana and Morgause, Queen of Tintagel, Lady of the Dumnonii*
Mordred: *son of Gorlois and Igerna, King of Tintagel, Lord of the Dumnonii*
Gorlois: *father of Morgana and Morgause, Duke of Cornewall*
Lot: *King of the Orkneys, Lord of the Pareisi*

(The Knights of Avalon)
Agrivain: *King of the Metaris, Lord of the Iceni*
Ector: *King of Deva, Lord of the Corvanii*
Cunamaglos: *King of North Whales, Lord of the Ordovices*
Bors: *King of the Armorica, Lord of the Brettanai*
Neithon: *King of Lindum, Lord of the Coritani*
Gwynedd: *King of Carmarthen, Lord of the Dometae*
Gnaeus: *King of Calleva, Lord of the Atrebates*
Mareth: *King of Bath, Lord of the Regni*
Brannos: *King of Corinium, Lord of the Bubroei*
Accolon: *King of Wight, Lord of the Duratriges*
Bedevere: *King of Camboricum, Lord of the Catuvellani*

(The Fey and Gods)
Rhiannon: *mother of Viviana, Elaine, and Igerna, Queen of Faerie*
Oberon: *father of Rhiannon, King of Faerie*
Kernos: *God-King of the Britons, Lord of the Forests*
Brigga: *Goddess of Fire and Life*
Catsubodhva: *Goddess of Silence and Death*
Nimue: *Goddess-Queen of the Britons, Lady of the Earth*
Mab: *Goddess of Shadows, Mistress of Magick*

(The Christians)
Bishop Sebastianus: *leader of the Nicene Church in Britain*
Father Jimellus: *Nazarene abbot of Glastonbury*
Father Fortunatus: *Nicene abbot of Glastonbury*
Brother Jonas: *Nazarene monk, Galahad's childhood tutor*

(The Druids)
Faelan
Gaius
Bodon
Uriens
Orin
Baelig
Ennis macDwyr
Sorin
Haseph
Haman

(The Bards)
Lugubelenus
Tovin
Jareth
Eamon
Dorin
Llewellyn
Ywain

(The Priestesses)
Elaine
Maeve
Asphodel
Elian
Raven
Mora
Kleia
Tamara

(The Maiden-Healers)
Livia
Rowa
Adiane
Varelia
Neywin

(The Guardians)
Leawys
Ortheon

(Fenfolk)
Fishwalker
Stargazer
Slider
Sunstalker

(The Children)
Arthur
Guinevere

Table of Contents

Preface
"Note from the Author"

I want to start by recognizing all the wonderful writers who have tackled the legend of Arthur before me. Inspiration for <u>The Last Merlin</u> came from many sources, most notably authors such as Marion Zimmer Bradley and Douglas Clegg, as well as television representations like the show starring the young Merlin in the early days of his adventures. This work of creative fiction is a blending of many voices into one masterpiece, mixing true history with epic legend.

The trilogy *Legends of Avalon*, of which <u>The Last Merlin</u> is the first installment, takes place in Britannia between the years 462 and 497 AD. The Roman occupation of Britain ended in the year 413, with a complete withdrawal of military forces. Britain was left to its own devices, seeing to its own defense for the first time in three centuries. There is little historical evidence to support events from the retreat of the Romans until the Anglo-Saxon conquest of the early sixth-century, giving rise to multiple postulations about the legendary King Arthur and his Knights of the Roundtable. I will attempt to sift through the legend, to expose true historical evidence before going on to explain the legend of Arthur as it exists in <u>The Last Merlin</u>.

Not all Roman citizens abandoned Britain in 413 AD, though most left the island with their soldiers. The few that remained asserted their diplomatic authority over the native Britons and a short line of Roman Emperors of Britannia and Gaul served for the next dozen or so years. Of these, the most notable were Constantius Chlorus and Ambrosius Aurelianus. Constantius Chlorus was a relative of the Emperors serving in Rome, a devout Nicene Christian, and a formidable soldier. Ambrosius Aurelianus was his chief supporter and ruler of Valentia in his own right. The pair continued to govern Britain for at least two decades before they were forced into exile by a man of the north known as Vortigern, or Vortimer. Vortigern was a native Briton and wished to see the island returned to its indigenous traditions. He also worried about the protection of the island from the Germanic tribes invading Gaul and Iberia. In order to protect his people, Vortigern turned to the enemy and hired a massive army of Saxon Sellswords to fight the other Germans threatening a total conquest of Britain. As payment, Vortigern offered the Saxons a large swath of arable land in Valentia to serve as their own, autonomous agricultural society.

Slowly the Saxons grew in numbers and became a serious threat to the Britons living to the south. By the end of the fifth-century, the Saxons had allied themselves with the Germanic tribes they were meant to combat, the Angles and the Jutes. Together they moved south and invaded the other lands of Britain, displacing the native Britons and forming the roots of Anglo-Saxon society. A large population of the indigenous peoples remained in Cornewall and Whales but the majority of the Britons moved across the straits to settle in Brittany. This marked the end of the Bronze Age in Britain and the birth of medieval society. The legend of King Arthur was born to fill in the gaps in historical knowledge of the native Britons during the interim between the departure of the Romans and the conquest of the Anglo-Saxons and the other Germanic Tribes. All the aforementioned characters make an appearance in this book, which focuses on the Druids and their role in the birth and upbringing of Arthur Pendragon. Ambrosius Aurelianus, called Ambrose, has been High King of the Britons since the deposing of the tyrant, Vortigern. The number of Druids and Druidesses dwindles as the Christians supplant them at home and abroad. Meanwhile, a darkness is rising to engulf Britannia in war. The only hope for the Britons and their Druid leaders rests in the hands of a young man set on a hard road, to rise up from the masses and become the last Merlin…

Britannia

* Marks the entrance to the Unseen Vale

Galahad
Prince of Lodecran

Chapter One
"Britain"

The crossing to Britain was not as hard as my father feared it might be. The Pictish incursions along the coastline were ended and the world fell into that eerie silence present at the end of a terrible war. We moved through the countryside swiftly, mounted on my father's most prized steeds and accompanied by a retinue of soldiers. The old roman roads were in severe disrepair, littered with highwaymen and vagabonds. My father insisted we bring the soldiers for my protection even when I knew he did it for himself. With every mile we rode away from home, my father's disposition soured more and his grimace grew into a scowl, contorting his face into some hideous and unnatural mockery. He made no attempt to hide his opinion concerning the summons we received a fortnight earlier, calling him at once to Londinium, to an audience with the High King Ambrose.

☼   ☼   ☼

I was enduring one of my routine bible lessons with Brother Jonas in the Great Room when Eogan, my father's most trusted friend, came rushing in like his heels were on fire. He hurried passed the large round table hewn from oak that all kings faithful to Londinium housed in their castles as a symbol of their allegiance to the High King. Ambrose's high kingdom stretched across all of Britannia and the Armorica, reaching all the way to my father's tiny kingdom, Lodecran, nestled between the forest of Broceliande and the duchy of Aquitaine. We were a Christian kingdom but my father was a Nazarene and held no allegiance to the ominous Nicene Church of Rome. He still hearkened to the old ways in his own life and always obeyed the will of the High King. Lodecran escaped Ambrose's wars against the Picts, that raged for nearly two years, mostly because my father's soldiers were unfamiliar with the sea. Ambrose required mariners to defeat the Picts, not mounted knights skilled in the use of lance and spear.

My father was standing near the doors leading to the rest of the castle speaking with one of his guards. He was so immersed in their conversation, he failed to notice Eogan until he was practically on top of him. My father always dressed in the roman fashions and wore a bronzed crown atop his head as a symbol of the kingdom he fought hard to build. His brown hair was graying and his beard was nearly white but the fire in his green eyes burned with youth, defying the inevitable pains aging brings to us all. He looked at Eogan with his usual stoic smile as the steward bowed.

"I'm sorry to interrupt, King Ban," said Eogan, "but your brother's here. He sent me in to announce him."

The smile melted from my father's face. The one person in the world I ever saw my father fight was his older brother, Bors. Bors was king of the Armorica. It was by his gift that Lodecran came into being. Once, Bors and father were close, until they had a falling out over matters of faith. Bors refused to accept the Christ and remained devoted to the Old Religion, to the magick of the druids, the way they had been raised. He hated father's adherence to the religion of the Romans and made his opinions known whenever possible. Bors was tattooed from head to foot, shaved his head bald, and wore hides and furs. He was a giant of a man, burly and hairy and tall. I was eleven years old at that time, growing closer to manhood with each breath, but the thought of Bors still frightened me. I felt a chill as the main doors to the hall were thrown open and he marched in with the countenance of a king but the manners of a beggar.

"I welcome you to Lodecran, brother," said my father.

Bors grunted.

"Enough of the pleasantries, Ban," he said, "I come with a message from the High King. We've been called to Londinium to sit in council."

"And what of the Picts?" asked father, "Are they not still raiding the southern coast?"

"Ambrose has succeeded in driving them back into the north. The war is over, brother. We must go and give thanks to Ambrose for saving our kingdoms from the threat of invasion."

"When must we leave?" asked father.

"Now," barked Bors, "and we need to bring the boy."

My father looked from Bors to me with his brow furrowed in curious displeasure. My father went across the straits to Britain often, but never once did I accompany him on the journey. I barely saw my father. My upbringing was in the hands of Brother Jonas while father tended his soldiers and prepared for war, even when the world was at peace.

"Did Ambrose explain why he wishes to see Galahad?" asked father, "What does he want with my son?"

"It is not Ambrose who summons the boy," replied Bors.

"I am King here," snapped my father, "and I obey no orders except those issued by the High King. Who else would dare command me?"

"Viviana," said Bors simply and the opposition within my father melted, his anger giving way to shock and suspicious unease.

☼   ☼   ☼

The ride through Broceliande took almost a week. The wooded kingdom of my uncle Bors was filled with danger and discord but, between my father's soldiers and those in Bors' company, a highwayman would have to be extremely brave or exceedingly stupid to attack us. The Romans cut an avenue through the forest to build a highway from Aquitaine to the coast of the Armorica centuries before. We followed the remains of that expressway before emerging on the rocky coastline overlooking the churning waves the dark blue sea. It was the first week of spring and the water was calm. I had never seen the ocean. I remember how magnificent it looked, the endless water reaching out into the unknown places beyond the edge of the world. As we approached a hill called the Dragon's Mount, the sun rose over the canopy of the forest behind us and struck the ocean with its gentle beams, illuminating the water and warming the air. In that second I swore I could hear the singing voice of a woman rising and falling with the waves.

A small sailboat was waiting in the harbor beyond the Dragon's Mount to take us across the strait. There was a favorable westerly wind that carried us across the water like a stone skipping across the surface of a pond. After only a single night and day, we were mooring in the harbor at Dubrae, the largest of Britain's cosmopolitan ports and one of the first areas conquered by the Romans when their empire stretched over the whole of the known world. The buildings in Dubrae were built from stone and the rock avenues were still in good condition. A land once exclusively occupied by the Britons had become a center of commerce, filled with men from every walk of life, seeking to make their fortunes on the untamed frontier. It was drastically different than Lodecran. I had trouble hiding my excitement as we piled into a carriage and set out for the High King's court in Londinium.

The ride by carriage from Dubrae to Londinium took twelve hours, too long to ride in a single day. After seven hours on the road, our small entourage left Watling Street and turned up a long dirt avenue leading towards an impressive Roman-style villa in the distance. The villa, with its marble columns and open air design stood alone on a hill overlooking the rugged coastline and the strait beyond, like a lighthouse meant to guide ships safely to harbor, or a fortress guarding the borders from barbarian raiders. The familiarity of the structure made me think of Lodecran, of my father's castle-sized villa, the only home I had ever known. I was stricken by a momentary wave of homesickness before a tall red-haired man wearing a white and red toga emerged from the villa with a roman woman and a dark-haired boy my age on his heels. The carriage came to a halt in front of the house and my father jumped out, motioning for me to join him as our knights began offloading our dressing trunks.

"Ban, you old dog, how long has it been? Ten years?" exclaimed the red-haired man.

"Eleven," smiled my father.

"You haven't changed a bit," said the man.

"You got old," joked father before both he and the man burst out in laughter. It was rare for me to see my father laugh. He usually maintained a disposition that bordered on frigid. He never told me he loved me, not once. For him, our relationship was based solely on his desire for me to grow into a capable knight and compassionate king. He also wished for me to follow him into the Christchurch, to be a Nazarene and Christian faithful to the gospels of Arius and Pelagius. Brother Jonas was meant to be my salvation as much as my teacher. But I didn't feel the same way about the Christ as my father. I believed he was a great prophet who challenged men to think about more than just themselves but I was not convinced he was the Master begotten by God as the Nazarenes believed, or the Son of God as the Nicenes taught. Brother Jonas often chastised me for my lack of faith but it did nothing to dissuade my curiosity or damper my inquisitive nature.

"Galahad," my father said to me, "this is my old friend, Drustan, King of the Cantii and of Lyonesse."

I bowed in the direction of the red-haired man.

"And may I present my wife, the Lady Daphne, and my son, Tristram," said King Drustan, motioning for the woman and boy that accompanied him out of the villa to step forward. With the traditional roman custom, Lady Daphne kissed my father on the cheek and then me. Tristram remained silent and nervous. He was a tall, gangly youth, probably only a year older than me, if not the same age. He had distinctly roman features, with a high forehead and hooked nose and his ears were overlarge for his head. He looked like a studious weakling who had never raised a sword or spear once in his life.

"We made up the extra room for you and Bors," Drustan told my father, "and the boy can share with Tristram tonight. Our house-woman has filled the baths with hot water and set out fruit and wine. My house is your house for as long as you're here."

"Much appreciated," replied father as the carriage carrying Bors pulled up in front of the villa and Drustan rushed off to greet him with Lady Daphne in tow. A plump Briton woman emerged from the villa and

9

approached us. She wore a simple gray dress and her dirty blonde hair was pulled tightly behind her head. She kept her eyes fixed on the ground and when she spoke it was clear Latin was not her first language.

"If you will follow me, my Lord," she said.

The house-woman led us into the villa, passed a dozen archways, to the center of the house where a large bath was filled with steaming hot water. There were platters of figs, dates, and grapes sitting on a large table with casks of wine opposite the bath, surrounded by plush couches for the men to lounge on and stiff wooden chairs for the women attending them. Bors came lumbering up behind us and, together with my father, headed towards the bath and drink.

"There's water waiting in Master Tristram's room for you to wash up," said the house-woman in my direction, "and I set out some cakes and honey, and milk. Master Tristram will show you the way."

Tristram sprinted off towards the far corner of the villa, through an archway into a spacious bedchamber with couches, a feather bed, a table, and bookshelves filled with scrolls and parchments. There was a bronzed crucifix adorning the wall above the bed. A pitcher and basin were sitting on the table next to a plate of wild berry cakes, a jar of honey, and a tall cask of fresh cow's milk. I washed my face and hands quickly before diving at the food. I had never been so hungry, or tired. The food tasted better than it probably was and satisfied my appetite. Tristram didn't touch a thing. He sat by the window staring out at the sea. Once my belly was full, I joined him.

"This is a nice place," I said, "it's a lot like my father's castle in Lodecran, except it's colder here."

"This your first time visiting Britain?" asked Tristram.

"Yeah, how did you know?" I asked.

"If you'd been to Britain before you would know it's always cold here, except for maybe five weeks in the summer," said Tristram, "I don't like the cold, or the damp. I like Rome. It's always warm there."

"I've never been," I replied.

"Have you ever been anywhere?" joked Tristram.

"Not really. My father travels all the time but he thinks it better that I stay home and study."

"Sounds like my father," laughed Tristram, "if it wasn't for my mother, I'd never get to go anywhere either. Lucky she has the final say when it comes to us children. My father might be king but my mother is master here. Just don't tell her I said it."

"Why not, my son? Everyone knows it to be true," came the voice of Tristram's mother, Lady Daphne as she entered the room with a fresh dressing robe and pitcher of water. She was an elegant woman, tall and thin, with full hips and breasts. Her hair was the same shade of brown as Tristram's and she had the same distinct features of the Latin tribes.

"Ban sent me in here to make sure you are in bed," she continued, "you leave for Londinium in the early hours of morning and you will need your rest. To bed with you both."

Tristram did has he was told without question, slipping into his own dressing gown and crawling into his feather bed. Lady Daphne handed me the gown she was carrying and nodded at me to change out of my dirty clothes. I obliged, quickly slipping into the gown, acutely aware of my scrawny body and Lady Daphne's eyes examining my naked flesh. I got into bed next to Tristram as his mother poured us each a goblet of water to leave on the table by the bed in case we got thirsty. She was gentle and maternal, something severely lacking in my life back in Lodecran. I couldn't help but feel jealous of Tristram, of having a mother who was willing to stand up against his father to further his best interests. I wanted her to be my mother, to care as much for me as she did her son. But she wasn't.

"Goodnight my sweet boy," she said as she leaned in to kiss Tristram, "and goodnight to you, Lord Galahad."

Lady Daphne blew out the candles as she left, plunging the room into near total darkness. The soft glow of the sliver moon shining in the windows became the only source of light and cast long shadows across the walls. I snuggled down into the covers and closed my eyes, listening to the sound of Tristram's breathing as he drifted off to sleep, thinking about all the wonderful places I had yet to see, and I thought about the woman who commanded my father bring me to Britain, whose name caused him to tremble. Viviana. My mother.

☼　　☼　　☼

I had never met my mother, not once, and whenever I asked my father about her he would get this look of disgust on his face and leave the room without saying a word. I was left to always wonder about her, who she was and where she had come from. Eventually, I resigned myself to the not knowing, at least until a cold winter's night when I was eight years old, when my questions were finally answered.

My father was away on one of his voyages to Britain, leaving me in the care of Brother Jonas and our house-woman, Genovefa. The land was covered with frost and the air was bitter to the touch. A cold northern wind was assaulting the lowlands of Lodecran with its frigid breath and the countryside had fallen silent. Man, woman, and child sought sanctuary by their hearths. The midwinter celebrations of the pagans were drawing to a close while the Christians were cloistered in their churches to celebrate the birthdate of the Christ. Brother Jonas was with his fellow monks, leaving me with Genovefa in the kitchens of our villa. Genovefa was a woman of the Briton Tribes, the Catuvelanii to be exact, and she carried her heritage in her every mannerism, from the way she dressed to the way she spoke. Though Latin was my first and most used language, I could speak Celtic and often would with Genovefa, who didn't like to speak the roman tongue. Genovefa refused to convert but my father was willing to overlook her decision since she had been his employee for over two decades.

"Are you a pagan?" I asked her as she served me a bowl of stew and fresh baked bread.

"I'm not a Christian," smiled Genovefa.

"Do you pray to the old roman gods?" I asked.

I wanted a better understanding of the gods of my ancestors.

"Of course not. I pray to my gods, the gods of my people, your people," she said.

"Brother Jonas says there is only one God and that all the others are false idols. He says praying to them is a sin and that the only fault God will not forgive is accepting any other God but him."

"Jonas has always served the Christ. And he's a Roman. He cannot understand our ways, even if he tried, just as his religion is foreign to me. I could no sooner abandon my gods and goddesses than he could his savior. But it's not Jonas' place to tell you what to believe, or your father's. As you grow older, the decision will be yours alone. I suspect you will choose the ways of your ancestors since the blood of the Old Religion courses through your veins. Your mother's blood."

"You knew my mother?" I asked in shock.

"Every Briton who still follows the Old Religion knows your mother," she said, "even those such as your father, who have turned their back on the ways of their ancestors, know to fear your mother's name, to hearken when called by Viviana, Lady of the Unseen Vale."

"I don't understand. Is she a queen?"

"She is more than a queen. She is High Priestess of the Druidesses, the wisest, most powerful woman of the Britons. It's said that her own mother was one of the faerie people who dwelt in these lands before mankind crossed the eastern mountains."

"And she lives in an unseen vale?" I asked.

"The Unseen Vale of Avalon," corrected Genovefa, "last outpost of the Druids. Curse your father for never telling you. I thought he was waiting until you were old enough to understand, to make your own choices but now I just think he's afraid."

"Of what?" I asked, "I've never seen father afraid of anything. He has a warrior's courage."

"He's afraid of her and of you," she said, "your father used to worship our gods, when he was younger. He knows better than most what the magick of the Holy Isles is capable of doing, of the power Viviana possesses. Only the Merlin has greater wisdom and strength. After your father converted to the Christchurch, his respect for magick turned to fear. He thinks your mother's blood will draw you to her and he fears for your soul. Even the tolerant Nazarenes condemn those who do not accept the Christ to an eternity in their hell. He should know better. He should let you go to your mother if that is what you wish."

"She sounds amazing," I said.

"I hope you will meet her one day," smiled Genovefa.

"I know the Christian God but the Druids have many and I do not know them. Can you tell me who they are?"

"The gods of my religion are called the Dagda and they are many," smiled Genovefa, "Of them, I only know two: Kernos, Lord of the Winter and Holly King and Cernunnos, god of the forests and Prince of the Spring. The goddesses are fewer but no less important. There is Brigga who rules the hearts of maidens and the power of the hearth, Nimue, the goddess of the earth and Queen of Summer, and Catsubodhva, lady of death and dreams. Epona is goddess of animals, Persapona is the Autumn Maiden, and then there's Mab the Malevolent."

"Mab?" I asked.

"We do not speak of her much," said Genovefa, "She is banished. Long ago, she betrayed her sister, Nimue, and the god, Kernos. As punishment, she was deprived the right to manifest in earthly flesh as the others do at will. The only way she can return to this world is by taking a mortal host, possessing someone against their will, to use their body as her own and bring destruction on the world. She was the Mistress of Magick and her sorcery is more potent than any that ever existed. But she has been gone for a long time and I doubt she will return."

"What's going on here?" said Brother Jonas as he returned home.

"I was just talking to Galahad," said Genovefa.

"I know what you were talking to the boy about," said Jonas, "and it is absolutely unacceptable. You are a kitchen maid, not a scholar or priest. Don't you think it best to leave the boy's religious education to those of us who are better equipped? I think King Ban should learn of your betrayal. I hope he is lenient in your punishment."

Genovefa responded by hurrying off to the wood-burning stove with a lump of raw dough but that was not the end of it. Brother Jonas went straight to my father and divulged exactly what he overheard Genovefa telling me. My father visited the kitchens soon after. Genovefa remained in our employ but I was forbidden to see her for nearly a year. Then after that she was not permitted to be alone with me. Every time I took a meal with her or spent evenings warming by her ovens I was accompanied by Brother Jonas. She never again spoke of the Druids or the Old Religion and if I dared to ask her a question, Brother Jonas would chastise me with stern warnings and cruel words. My relationship with Genovefa was never the same.

☼　　☼　　☼

We set out for Londinium before sunrise the next day. The house-woman came to rouse me from bed with my freshly laundered clothes and ushered me out to the carriage where my father was waiting with Eogan. I settled into the seat near the window and stared at the countryside silently as our journey resumed.

The Watling Road ran directly from King Drustan's estate to Londinium. We arrived at the city after five hours on the highway and I was shocked at the scene I was witnessing. I expected the city to be a glorious metropolis with cobbled streets and wondrous stonework buildings in the likeness of Rome, situated proudly along the banks of the River Thames. What I saw was a ruined city, the skeleton of a once thriving cosmopolitan center renowned throughout the Romanized world. The city walls were crumbling and the streets were in severe disrepair. Many of the buildings had collapsed in on themselves and the stonework cathedral at the heart of town was nothing but rubble. Our carriage moved swiftly passed the throngs of peasants crowding the streets, begging for food and coin. The only magnificent structure left was a large fortress positioned on the eastern banks of the Thames and even half of it was decaying and condemned. We pulled up directly in front of the rampart leading into the fortress and my father threw open the door to exit the carriage with Eogan beside him.

We stayed at the home of the High King Ambrose in Londinium for six long, uneventful days. While my father attended council meetings every day before retiring to the city pub to drink the night away, I was locked away in a small corner of the fortress with a servant woman named Lierna, a young woman of the Tribes with fiery red hair and freckles who barely spoke two words to me as she served my food and drew my baths. I was made to attend Mass every morning since there were no Nazarene presbyters in Londinium. My father saw the Nicene Priests as better than nothing and ordered Lierna to make sure I went to chapel on time, dressed in my finest tunic and breeches. Then I would spend two hours practicing my Latin, alone in an abandoned courtyard, before returning to my temporary Londinium home. I wanted nothing more than to ride out into the countryside, to see the villages and meet the people. And I daydreamed about my mother. If she commanded that I come to Britain, it must have meant she intended to meet me, and I would finally get to look on her face.

Even in Lodecran we heard tales of the raw beauty of the British countryside with its monolithic stone circles, rolling downs, and thousands of rivers. The damp cold that entered into my bones at night subsided during the day as the sun cast its spring warmth on the world around me. If I wasn't stuck in the middle of a dying city half burned by the Picts seeking to conquer the land, I might have enjoyed the experience. I was used to never seeing my father but I was rarely alone. Between my studies with Brother Jonas, my martial training with the soldiers, and my nights with Genovefa, I was never lonely. Lierna barely looked at me. I tried talking to her in Latin. She wouldn't respond. I spoke to her in Celtic. She still didn't respond. I got the feeling she was disturbed by my presence, that she was afraid to approach me or engage me in conversation. I thought it strange that she wore the tattoo of a crescent moon upon her brow and dressed in gray wool robes drastically different than the Roman styles worn by everyone else I had seen in

Londinium. Perhaps she was some kind of nun and had taken a vow of silence to fulfill her obligations to her God.

"Why don't you like me?" I asked Lierna one day in Celtic, hoping she would finally find it in her heart to speak to me.

She remained silent.

"Does my presence bother you?" I asked, this time in Latin.

Still nothing.

I wanted to crack her over the head with a mallet. It was utterly frustrating to try to connect with someone who ignores you completely. Then, on the last day of our stay in Londinium, the question of Lierna was finally answered when my father and Eogan came to visit me. As they entered the bedchamber serving as my home, Lierna was busying herself with gathering soiled laundry. Eogan saw her furtively glancing in my direction and decided to speak.

"Does the Druidess not find you to be pleasant company?" he asked me dramatically as Lierna rushed away to another part of the room.

"I would never have agreed to allow a Druidess to serve as Galahad's wash-maiden," said my father, "If she hadn't taken a vow of silence. At least she won't be filling his head with any of their nonsense."

"Wise decision," said Eogan, though he didn't looked pleased. He almost looked offended by my father's words, about the hypocrisy of his beliefs. He was a Nazarene Christian, one who valued peace, but he despised the Old Religion to which he used to belong. He decried the complete façade of the Druid mystique but he had a son with the High Druidess. Eogan was also a Christian but he didn't harbor any resentments towards the Druids. In many ways, he stilled followed them. In an attempt to change the subject and ensure my father would not be angered by the presence of Lierna I asked him a question I knew he was eager to answer. It had been seven days since we came to Ambrose's fortress and father was anxious to return to our home in faraway Lodecran.

"Is the council over, father?" I asked eagerly.

"Yes," he replied, "pack your things. We leave at once."

"Where are we going?" I asked.

My father looked tired and pale. He didn't want to look me in the eye and seemed determined to make me feel like an insolent child. He hesitated for a moment and then, without looking at me, he said in almost a mixture of a whisper and whimper.

"I'm taking you to the Unseen Vale."

Chapter Two
"The Isle of Glass"

We rode hard along the Welsh Road for three days. We left the carriage and my father's knights in Londinium to enjoy the few remaining markets and brothels. Only Eogan and two soldiers, Tiberius and Lucianus, rode with us. We spent the first night at an inn in the town of Calleva, a smaller, more maintained version of Londinium but with standing buildings and fortified walls. I had my own feather bed and relished in the warmth of the nearby fire. Like the day we left Dubrae, we rose before the sun and continued on our way, crossing from the interior of Britain into the western half, coming closer to the great ocean with each passing hour.

The second night we slept inside tents on the side of the highway. The town of Aquae Solis was only a few miles down the road but we continued down the Fosse Way without stopping. My father took to his tent early and, the sounds of his snoring ensured he had gone straight to sleep. I stayed up by the fire, wrapped in furs, as Eogan sang and played his flutes. Eogan was a Nazarene but he maintained a love of the old songs. He sang of the people across the great ocean, on the Isles of the Beakers, how they brought the knowledge of the ancients across the waters to Britain and founded the priesthood of the Druids on the Raven's Mount. It seemed to me that, as he sang, images appeared in the smoke and flames of the fire, silhouettes of dragons and griffins, of wizards and priests. Eogan noticed as I blanked out staring into the fire and stopped playing his flutes.

"Have you ever seen shapes in the flames?" I asked him.

"To me they are only flames," replied Eogan, "but I am not the son of the Lady of Avalon."

"You know about my mother?"

"Your father told me many years ago," said Eogan.

"Are you frightened of the Druids?" I asked.

"No. I may not share their beliefs but I respect them. The Druids were the teachers and priests of our ancestors. Their time in the sun might be waning but their place in my heart remains. That's why I still sing the songs of the bards, out of respect for my ancestors. I don't think God minds if we remember where it is we came from."

"Do you think I'll like her?" I asked.

"I have no idea, Galahad. It is your choice to accept or reject her. She may command your father's heart but she does not hold such sway over you. Your future is yours to write. Make the story your own. Now I am off to rest. Knowing your father, we will be setting out early."

☼   ☼   ☼

We left the Fosse Way sometime around midday and rode down a narrow dirt road leading through a thick glade of hawthorn trees for nearly two hours, until we emerged on the banks of a high water marsh. There was a tiny cluster of thatch-roof huts forming a village several yards away. Just beyond the village I could see seven hilly islands rising up amidst the reeds and brackish backflow like pillars holding up the weight of a marble ceiling. The island nearest to the village was only a few hundred yards offshore but there were no visible avenues or causeways leading to it by land. On that same island there stood a large wooden longhouse with a steeple surrounded by little wooden cottages shaped like octagons with shingled roofs. The air was filled with the smell of saltwater and I felt a strange tingle vibrating up my spine, as though I was standing on the string of a harp being plucked by a master musician.

My father dismounted just as a strange looking, short young man emerged from one of the huts in the village on the banks of the fens. He was maybe five and a half feet at most and his skin was darker than even the bronzed complexion of the Romans, with a strange, slightly reddish hue. He had no hair on his body, except for the silky black locks growing atop his head and his wide-set black eyes darted from me to my father, to Eogan, and then back to me.

"You need passage to island of monks?" the man said to my father in broken Latin.

My father responded by nodding and then waving at me and Eogan, signaling us to get off our horses and follow him. We walked passed the little village, where other men and women that looked like our guide were busy stacking wood, drying fish, and repairing nets, continuing on to a tiny dock with flat pole-barges tied to it. We filed onto the largest barge with my father sitting at the bow, me and Eogan in the middle, and our guide at the rear, standing with a long pole to maneuver the boat. We glided out across the water with ease and were soon approaching the lower slopes of the island with the longhouse and wooden cottages.

"It's called the Isle of Glass," said Eogan, sensing my confusion as to where exactly we had ended our travels, "in the summer and early autumn, the waters of the fens are low enough to reach the island on foot by crossing a narrow land bridge connecting it to the village. But in the winter and spring, most especially at high tide, the only way on or off is by boat. Thank the Master for the Fenfolk. They know these waters better than any man, Roman, Gael, or Briton."

"Is he one of the Fenfolk?" I asked, pointing to the man poling the barge towards the Isle of Glass.

"He's a Fen Hunter," replied Eogan, "We call him Skipper. I'm not sure what his name is in their language. I've never met a Briton who could speak their tongue. They don't speak Latin very well either but they're better at Celtic or Gaelic."

"You sound like you've met this man before," I said.

"I have. Many times," replied Eogan, "your father and I come to the Isle of Glass whenever we're in Britain. This place is close to God."

"Wait. You mean this is a Christian commune? I thought we were going to see the Druids," I said.

"You only see the Druids here if they wish to be seen," Eogan replied.

We docked on the side of the island nearest to the little community and my father led the way up to the longhouse with the steeple. A group of men with their hair tonsured, wearing brown robes and large wooden crosses, were congregated near the entrance to the building, talking amongst themselves. When they caught sight of us, they fell silent and the oldest of their ranks walked forward to greet us, leaning heavily on a cane as he hobbled over.

"My Lord Ban," he said with a wheeze, "what a pleasant surprise. And Master Eogan. Always a pleasure. Who is this?"

The monks question was directed towards me.

"This is my son, Galahad," said father.

"It can't be. He is so grown," replied the monk before turning his attention towards me, "last time I saw you, you were still in your swaddling clothes. How the years fly by. Welcome back to Glass, Master Galahad. I am Father Jimellus and this is our holy house."

He pointed to the longhouse with the steeple as the other monks coming closer to investigate.

"It isn't much but it's home," continued Father Jimellus, "Will you be staying with us long?"

"Not sure," replied father, "we are not here of our own volition. We were summoned."

The smile on Father Jimellus' face wavered for a moment and it seemed his knees might buckle. Then he regained his countenance and began leading us towards the other monks.

"I see," he said, "Well, as long as you are with us, you may shelter in Brother Nicodemus' cottage. He is assigned to guarding the Holy of Holies for the next two weeks and his bed will be empty at night. We take our morning meal with the rising sun and our evening meal when the sun sets. We don't have much to spare but you are welcome to anything we have to offer. Knowing you, my Lord, you will wish to fast but your son looks to need some meat on his bones. Perhaps Brother Benedictus would be willing to bake some sweetbreads."

"I think that can be arranged," said a portly little monk.

My father spent that whole night in the church praying. I ate the sweetbreads prepared by Brother Benedictus and some honey cakes I brought along on the road from Londinium. Then I slept. I had never traveled before, let alone such a great distance and, despite my nervousness at the prospect of meeting my mother, I was still a child on the edge of puberty and required a lot of sleep. I didn't hear Eogan come in or when Brother Nicodemus returned from his guard duty. My father came in around dawn and woke me with a nudge to my shoulder.

"Get up," he said.

Without another word, he led me out of the cottage and passed the longhouse church towards the incline leading to the top of the hill. It was clear there had once been a path twisting up the hillside but it was overgrown and neglected. The air was fresher at the top and it smelled like apples. As we approached the summit, a single monolithic stone came into view, rising fifteen feet into the air like a giant sentinel guarding a precious treasure. It seemed the sky grew lighter and the countryside more silent as we approached the stone, as though we had entered an invisible bubble amplifying the light of the sun and blocking out the sounds of the world. My father walked straight over to the stone and placed one hand on its cold and rough gray surface.

"Viviana," he said, "Viviana, I'm here and I brought the boy."

There was no response.

"Don't play games with me Viviana. I am here with our son."

Still nothing. My father jerked his hand away from the stone in anger and stomped away, clearly unamused. I stayed there, taking in the spectacular view of the fens below. It was a clear day and I could see all the way to the Summer Sea. For a place that had once been a center of pagan learning, the fens were sparsely populated. Aside from the Fenfolk village and the Christian settlement, there were no signs of life on any of the seven mounds forming the marsh islands. The water was lower than it had been the previous night, exposing little strips of land amidst the reeds. I was sure that, when the water was at its lowest levels, it would be possible to traverse the seven islands on foot. I thought about running off and finding a boat to explore the other islands but the church bells started to ring, snapping me out of my daydream and bringing me back to reality. With another look at the distant Summer Sea, I stood and ran down the hill.

The monks were chanting hymns in the church by the time I reached the commune. My father was nowhere to be seen, probably praying in the church with the monks. Eogan was down near the edge of the water casting a fishing net out into the marshes with a couple of the Fenfolk. I thought about joining them but didn't relish the idea of wading into the water after snagging the net in some reeds. Instead, I found a nice shady place under a lonely white birch tree growing near the back doors of the church. I was intending to take a nap until the peaceful silence was interrupted by the shaky steps of Father Jimellus.

"I see you found our tree," he said, "it's our pride and joy. It came from the Holy Land, you know, carried here by the man who founded this commune 350 years ago. It was nothing but a little sprig then. Now it's the tallest tree in the fens."

"Was it him who raised the stone at the top of the hill?" I asked.

"You mean the Tor Stone? No, the stone was not constructed by him, or the hand of any Christian. It was raised by the Druids in the days before our Master walked the earth. We leave it alone to honor those that were here before us. The Druids and the Fenfolk."

"And now they're gone," I said and for some reason, I felt sad. I had never known any Druids and yet it felt like I was missing out on something important, some long hidden knowledge worth knowing.

"They're still here," said Father Jimellus, "and they'll show themselves to you in time. The Druids are a mysterious people and they work at their own pace, in their own time."

"I don't understand. How can they still be here?" I asked.

"That, my Lord, is a lesson for another day."

☼   ☼   ☼

The days turned to weeks and the weeks to months. We remained at the Christian commune through the rest of spring and through the early summer. Every day, my father would climb the Tor and place his hand upon the stone, calling to my mother. She never came.

After a week, our status as guests gave way to a more permanent place in the community. My father, being a king, was not expected to contribute to the commune and spent his days in the church praying. We remained sheltered in Brother Nicodemus' cottage, while he began living with Brother Benedictus. Eogan started working with the younger monks in the gardens and I was assigned to shepherding the goats. We attended services on the Lord's Day and observed the Sabbath in the Nazarene tradition. My bible studies were continued with Father Jimellus. I even started learning the hymns the monks chanted daily for the three hours leading up to dinner.

In my free time, I took to exploring the Isle of Glass and, one day I crossed the western ridge of the hill and stumbled upon another structure I hadn't noticed before, a longhouse larger than the church with a vegetable garden growing beside it. There were figures tending the garden. They were dressed all in black and their heads were adorned with white veils covering their hair. I knew without getting any closer what kind of people they were. They were nuns. We had many nuns in Lodecran but they wore the traditional habit of the Nicenes. The clothing these women were wearing was simpler and more practical. Since the monks on the island were Nazarenes, it stood to reason the nuns were from the same sect. I took to herding the goats up the hillside and over the western ridge so I could watch the nuns as they bustled about their cloistered grounds, tending their plants and caring for their cattle.

After three months of the same routine, I was finally spotted. I was sitting on a rock on the ridge chewing on a blade of grass and watching the goats graze when a woman emerged from the nearby orchard of apple trees. She was tall and thin, with dark skin like the Fenfolk and the bright blue eyes of the Gaels. She wore the black robes of a nun but her head lacked the white veil. Her reddish black hair fell wildly down her back in droves of curls and braids. Judging by the wrinkles around her eyes and mouth, she was somewhere in midlife. She wore a stern expression on her face but when she spoke her voice was calm and kind.

"Have you enjoyed spying on us all these weeks?" she asked.

I didn't know how to respond.

"I don't suppose you've done any harm but you're really not supposed to be here," she continued. I was intrigued that she chose to speak to me in Celtic and not Latin. Maybe the nuns were more in touch with the language of the Tribes and less with the roman lifestyle favored by the Britons living in the cities.

"I'm sorry," I said.

"You've done no harm but do not go any closer to the convent. The nuns do not have contact with men, not even little men like yourself."

"Aren't you a nun?" I asked.

"Of sorts," she said, "What brings you to the Isle of Glass? Are you here to take vows as a monk? You seem a little young to make such a serious decision for your future. But it's not unheard of. Father Jimellus was only eleven when he took his vows."

"I'm not here to be a monk," I said, "I'm visiting the monks with my father. He's a Nazarene."

"And you're not?" asked the nun as she sat beside me.

"I don't know what I am."

"I'm sure you will in time and whatever choice you make will be the best one for you. I'm sure, if your father is a Nazarene as you say, you are well-versed in the gospels but do you know any of the pagan tales of this land, of these isles?"

"Not really," I replied.

"Pity," she said, "every Briton should know the stories. Even those who choose to follow the God of Abram. Many years ago, the Seven Isles were covered by shrines and sanctuaries. This very island was home to a stone circle built in the likeness of the Henge on the Summer Plain, and to the House of Healing where the Maiden-Healers practiced their wortcunning and their medicine."

"And that island there," she continued pointing to the kidney bean shaped island facing the Isle of Glass, "it is known as the Isle of the Font. There is a spring there that runs with water as red as the blood spilled when the Christ was nailed to the cross. The Priestesses of Nimue dwelt there and tended both the spring and the shrine to the goddess both day and night. The High Priestess of all Druidesses kept her home in a dwelling hewn into a tall tower, near the Blood Well and the Font."

The nun continued to describe each of the isles in great detail with stories about the men and women who lived on them. The isles in the fens were scattered across a few miles but all could be seen from the top of the Tor on the Isle of Glass. Westward across the fens about a half-mile was the Isle of Birds, where the Crones serving the goddess Catsubodhva lived out the last days of their long lives, eating vision-inducing mushrooms and gazing into their Cauldron, divining visions of the future they seldom shared with those with many days left to live. The Isle of Oak was separated from the Isle of Birds by a narrow channel of the River Sabrina. It was covered by a thick grove of ancient oak trees and was home to the Druids and Bards, who dwelt at the heart of the little forest and kept the fires of the god, Kernos, burning through the cold half of the year. Near the exact center of the fens was the tall and imposing island called the Watch Hill, once home to a large village of Fenfolk. The far end of the Watch Hill, where it leveled out to meet the waters of the marsh, was home to the pastures of the horsemen serving the goddess, Epona. On the far side of the fens were the two twin islands, one sitting on the edge of the Summer Sea, the other just to the landside of its sister. The one nearer to the land was known as the Isle of Stone and was the place where the Guardians dwelt, protecting the secret treasures of the druids. The final island was called the Crossroad. It was where the druids and priestesses gathered for the high celebrations of Beltane and Samhain to be closer to Kernos and the goddess, Nimue.

"There's something I don't understand," I said to the nun, "you talk about the Holy Isles as though they are a thing of the past but I thought they were still here. Isn't there still a Lady who rules over the Druidesses and the Holy Isles, and a Merlin who guides men of the Tribes towards the Old Religion and away from the Christ?"

"When I say they used to be, I mean that they were once fully a part of this world but they long ago vanished. Some of the Nazarenes believe they were destroyed by the Romans, during the days of dread. There are others who say the Holy Isles were lifted from this land by the King of Faerie and set in the realm of the Unseen, just beyond our earthly perceptions but, not so far removed to be free from the passage of time."

"Have you ever seen any Druids here?" I asked.

"I have," she smiled, "but not for a long time. I think they come to this land less and less. As the Tribes turn towards the Christ and away from the Old Gods, the Druids grow more inclined to remain in the Unseen and tend to their own needs in the manner that befits them."

The nun and I met every day for over a week and she told me all the tales of the islands. Then she stopped coming. I waited and waited, seated on the rock on the western ridge, but she never came. Eventually I stopped going to the ridge and stayed in the grazing grounds nearer to the monastic commune, disappointed at the loss of my first British friend whose name I had never even asked.

☼   ☼   ☼

"We are leaving in the morning," announced my father as he finished his evening meal, "we have been here four months now and still my calls to the boy's mother go unanswered. All this while, Lodecran has been without its king. My messengers bring word of Germanic barbarians raiding the countryside of Aquitaine. I must return to my duties."

"If that is your wish, my Lord," said Eogan, "I will make us ready for the road."

My father and I were sitting at a table outside the church where we took to eating our dinner. The monks were busy running from one edge of the commune to the next with bowls filled with holy water, which they spritzed on the ground as they bustled about. The sun was creeping towards the horizon and the half waxing moon was already shining brightly in the sky. The monks looked stern and serious, focused solely on the task at hand as they muttered prayers under their breath. They seemed to be in a panic, to be afraid of some unseen force threatening their way of life and the peace of the island. My father noticed my confusion and decided to explain.

"Tonight is the night of the dead," he said.

"It is Samhain," said the voice of a woman. I turned around to be greeted by the nun I'd spent a week with on the western ridge. She was wearing the same black habit but this time bore a white veil over her reddish black hair. My father's eyes narrowed as she approached and, when the monks saw her, they looked frightened. I expected them to run to their cottages and lock the doors at the sight of a fairly attractive woman. But they stood their ground, crossing themselves fervently and chanting their prayers louder. Father Jimellus approached the nun slowly with soft steps and then bowed deeply, as though she were a mighty queen calling on a lowly band of peasant priests. It was then I understood she was no nun. I suspected, on all those afternoons, that she might not be who she claimed she was. She was too knowledgeable about the Druids. I thought she might be a Druidess in disguise but, never in my wildest dreams, did I expect her to be the woman she turned out to be.

"How may we serve you, my Lady?" said Father Jimellus.

"It's time for me to take the boy," she replied with a voice absent any real emotion.

I was confused.

"There will be others," she continued, "keep them here and keep them safe. I will come for them as well in their turn."

I was still confused and my father noticed.

"Galahad," he said, "may I present the Lady Viviana. Your mother."

Chapter Three
"Lady Viviana"

My mother smiled and she was instantly transformed. The wrinkles disappeared from her face, her eyes grew brighter, and the red hues of her black hair began to shine like firelight reflected in a mirror. The white veil atop her head vanished and her hair fell in wild curls to the small of her back. The black habit melted away to reveal robes dyed a deep, midnight purple. Upon her forehead there appeared a tattoo in the shape of the crescent moon. She was more regal than any noblewoman I'd ever seen. She seemed taller and more elegant as she approached my father, but even as she stood over him, he refused to meet her gaze.

"Always playing games, Viviana," he sneered.

"The Glamour is not a game," replied my mother curtly, "these are dangerous times. It is far safer to appear as a nun than a druidess. The sisters of the convent do not mind when we take their likeness to travel to and from the Unseen Vale."

"There is no danger, at least not anymore. The war is over, or has that news not yet reached the isles beyond the veil?" asked father curtly.

"Ambrose's battles with the Picts may have come to an end," said my mother, "but the war is far from over. A darkness threatens to engulf these lands and return them to the fear and violence not felt since the days of Vortigern and his Saxon Sellswords. We are all at risk. The safest place now is the Unseen Vale, which is why I sent for the boy."

"About that," replied my father, "nobody said anything to me about you taking Galahad. I brought him here because I thought you finally wished to see your son. I did not agree to leave him here. With you."

For a brief moment my mother looked angry, like a madwoman on the prowl for an unsuspecting victim to attack.

"Galahad is a child of the Holy Isles. He was born within the Circle on the Tor," said my mother.

"He is a Christian," interrupted my father, "the heir to the kingdom of Lodecran, and my only son. You are not taking him. Not today, not tomorrow, not ever."

The atmosphere around us was at once utterly changed. The air was filled with a charge, as though it were whirling into one contained burst of wind powerful enough to topple the Church and send us flying. My mother grew taller and more imposing, and it seemed the glow of the evening moon had been funneled into a spotlight shining only on her. Her hair grew even redder than it was seconds before and her eyes shined silvery blue. When she spoke, her voice was filled with authority and decisiveness, causing my father and the monks to look away in fear.

"You will not deny me my son, Ban of Lodecran," she said, "his destiny is far greater than that of King or Christian. I will not be denied. Another child comes even as we speak this night. He will arrive in two days' time. When he is here, I will come again. Galahad will leave with me then."

In a flash, my mother transformed back into the middle-aged nun I'd spent so many days talking with on the Western Hill. She looked at me with a wink and then walked away back into the darkening twilight.

☼   ☼   ☼

I was in shock knowing I had met my mother, that I'd spent multiple days talking with her like a student with a teacher. I was angry but also relieved, relieved to know she was just as magnificent as I imagined her. I would be lying if I said I wasn't excited at the prospect of living with her in the Unseen Vale. I was not a Christian, at least not in my heart. I respected the Christ and the Nazarene monks but I was called to a deeper wisdom, to the ways of my Briton ancestors, to magick. My mother was the most powerful woman in all Britannia and I was going to be taught at her side. My father could see the astonishment in my eyes and he grew colder towards me as a result. The next two days he avoided me entirely, withdrawing into the Church for sober prayer and reflection. I knew he was praying for me, for the safety of my soul and the future of his namesake in Lodecran. I wanted to give him space but at the same time I wanted to confront him, to make him give me his blessing and permission. He was my father. I loved and respected him, despite his cold distance and natural detachment. I understood he was a king and not able to give me the affection other parents gave to their children but I still needed his respect. I wanted to know he would be okay on his own, that he would find a way to forgive me for leaving him without a son and heir.

The evening before my mother was due to return I found the courage to enter the Church and confront my father. At home, I would never dream of interrupting his prayers but under the circumstances I was sure I'd be forgiven. He was kneeling at the altar at the front of the empty church with his head in his hands. I could tell by his body language he was tired and weary. He'd been fasting and his body was weak and fatigued. He heard me as I shuffled up the aisle between the pews and struggled to his feet.

"Don't run away from me," I said as he made his way towards the archway leading to Father Jimellus' rooms. He stopped in mid-step and turned around to face me, a stern expression contorting his face.

"I would say the same thing to you," he replied, "but I know it would do no good. You have always been your mother's son."

"How's that father? I only just met her," I said.

"You don't have to meet your parents to be like them. I was twenty before I met my father and found myself to be strikingly like him. I saw her the moment you were old enough to walk and talk, in every question you would dare to ask the monks, in your mannerisms, even in the way you eat your meals. I feared the day would come when she would call for you and I knew you would never turn her away. You want to go, don't you? Even now I see that same defiance in your eyes. The same unbridled determination that drives your mother in everything she does."

"I'm sorry if I disappoint you father."

"What disappoints me is that you would willingly turn your back on your faith, on the faith of your family."

"Christianity is your faith, father. Not mine."

My father looked as though he'd been punched in the stomach. He curled over and screamed, clutching at his abdomen like a frantic cat trying to claw its way out of a box. At first I thought he was crying, that my choice had driven him to the point of breaking down. Then I realized something was wrong. He was sweating and pale as he stumbled over and hit the floor. I ran out of the Church and to the nearest cottage, where Eogan and Father Jimellus were studying the Bible. I screamed for them to come, that my father was sick but by the time we reached the Church nothing could be done. He was already dead, lifelessly slumped against a pew with his vacant eyes staring absently at the altar.

I stayed by my father's side the whole night, watching as the monks washed his body and wrapped it in a clean burial shroud of white linen. They placed him upon the altar and sang somber hymns in glorification of their God while I was torn in two. A part of me felt it was my fault that he died, that I'd placed too much of a burden upon his weak heart. I felt compelled to return to Lodecran, to take up my father's seat as king, to become Christian and act always in defense of my people. But then there was the calling within my soul to cross into the Unseen Vale and leave the mortal world behind forever. I desired the unknown and I wanted my mother. She was the only blood I had left. I cried and cried. I was still just a child of twelve and, though I was mature for my years. The thought of death was still terrifying. Father Jimellus and Eogan did their best to comfort me but I was inconsolable. The grief hit me like a hammer hitting an anvil.

As dawn came the next morning I left the Church and went to sit on the Western Hill overlooking the tiny convent of nuns. I had no more tears left to shed and my sadness was replaced by anger. I never got what I wanted from my father, I never heard him say that my choice to go to the Unseen Vale was okay. He only chastised me for my desire to follow the Old Religion. His last words to me implied that I brought shame on the family. I screamed in hatred, enraged by a lifetime with a father whose cold distance and religious fanaticism had kept him from knowing me and from showing me love.

"Your father did care for you, Galahad," said Eogan as he mounted the hill to join me, "but his heart wasn't strong enough for him to stay in this world. He's been sick for a long time. He made me keep his secret."

"He told me I reminded him too much of Viviana," I said, "I think that kept him from loving me."

"I won't lie," said Eogan, "Your look and nature is so much like your mother's, gentle yet fierce. Ban didn't like that about you but not for the reasons you think. Did you know you're father grew up here, in the Fenfolk village as an orphan?"

"No," I answered.

"His parents sent him here when he was younger than you to keep him safe from the tyrant, Vortigern. He stayed until he was twenty, when he finally met his father and took his place beside his brother, Bors, as heirs to the kingdom of the Armorica. By then he'd already met and fallen in love with your mother. She was pregnant with you when he got word that his father was dying. He begged her to go with him, to become his queen, but she refused. She chose her faith over their love and he never forgave her. They saw each other a few more times over the years and once they even briefly rekindled their love. But Viviana is the Lady of the Unseen Vale, chief servant of the goddess, Nimue. She could never choose your father. It drove him mad with anger, to the point that he abandoned the Old Religion and embraced Christianity in an attempt to find relief. That's why he always pushed you away. You reminded him not only of your mother, but also of the religion she chose over him."

I didn't care what Eogan said. My father treated me more like a ward than a son and I was having trouble forgiving him. I sat there staring down at the marshy fens stretching out towards the Summer Sea, contemplating the future. I was scared. Like any twelve year old, I longed for the safe embrace of my parents but my father was dead and my mother a stranger. Eogan was the closest thing I had to a father and our house-woman, Genovefa, was the only mother-figure I ever had in my childhood. A part of me wanted to sail home to Lodecran, to run into the kitchens and seek the warm embrace of Genovefa. The other part of me wanted to go with my mother, to discover the destiny she mentioned, and to explore the ways of the Druids.

"What should I do?" I asked Eogan, "I don't know what to do."

"Yes you do," he replied, "You will go with your mother. There's nothing left for you in Lodecran. There's nothing left for me there either."

"What do you mean?" I asked.

"I've decided to remain here and take the vows of a monk. It's time for me to lay down my harp and renew my faith. And I want to stay close, in case you have need of me."

I wanted to cry, not from sadness but from gratitude. On some level Eogan knew I was afraid. He wanted to calm my fears by letting me know he would remain nearby. I resolved I would return regularly to the commune and see him, to let him know all that was happening in my life. Then I thought of Genovefa and my heart again grew sad.

"What is it?" asked Eogan.

"I'm just wondering what will happen to Genovefa," I replied, "Will she remain at the villa in Lodecran?"

"Most likely. It's a good place for her. She will be safe and cared for, of that I'm sure. Now that your father is gone and you have chosen to go to your mother, the crown of Lodecran will pass to Bors. He'll happily claim it but he won't go to live there. He'll appoint a Duke to rule Lodecran on his behalf. That man will live in the villa and will be Genovefa's master. If I had to guess, I would gather Bors will appoint his friend, Dagony, to rule your father's kingdom. Dagony is a good man. He'll treat the servants with dignity and he'll keep your people safe."

"I guess it's settle then, I'll go to the Holy Isles," I said.

"That is your only choice," said Eogan.

Eogan and I continued to sit there on the hill in silence, watching the light intensify around us as the sun rose to herald in the day. I was still staring out at the fens when I noticed a barge floating across the reedy, brackish water. It was the Fenfolk medicine man, Skipper, poling three passengers to the commune on the island. They were close enough for me to make out their features. The first was a boy a few years older than me, with golden blonde hair and fair skin. He was thin and athletic and seemed to be going through the change to manhood. His eyes were roaming across the water as though he were a scout sent to strategically mark a field before a great battle. The second was a tall woman with the same reddish-black hair as my mother, the same dark skin, and the same classic feminine features. The third passenger had a familiar face. It was the same boy I met at the estate of King Drustan. It was Tristram of Lyonesse.

☼   ☼   ☼

The passengers were exiting the barge as Eogan and I arrived at the docks. The woman, whose regal nature outshined even my mother's, was helped from the boat by Father Jimellus, who bowed his head and spoke with a soft, reverent voice.

"Lady Elaine," he said, "this is a pleasant surprise. Are you here to visit your sister?"

"I am here to stay, Jimellus. Viviana sent word for me to bring Madoc at once to Avalon. My son goes nowhere without me. If he is to remain here, on the Holy Isles, then so shall I."

I knew this woman was my mother's sister even before her exchange with Father Jimellus. The family resemblance was striking. What I hadn't considered was that the blonde boy was my cousin. Madoc of Logres, nephew of Lot of the Orkneys. The confident teen who'd been surveying the landscape from the barge was no longer present. In his place was a shy, retiring young man who refused to meet my gaze. In stark contrast, Tristram leaped off the barge and ran towards me, wrapping his arms around me as though I was his long lost relation. I could tell he was afraid and took comfort in knowing I would be there with him. In a strange way, his presence brought me relief as well.

"This must be Galahad," said Lady Elaine as she approached me. Her eyes were as blue as mine but more piercing and inquisitive. She was about the same height but, up close, her beauty was greater than my mother's, younger and more vibrant. She smiled as she gazed down at me before placing her fingers under my chin.

"You have your mother's bearing," she added, "Where is your dad?"

I could not answer.

"He is dead," answered Eogan, "his heart failed him in a moment of stress after battling a secret illness for years."

"Pity," said Elaine, "he was a good man. Is he here? We will go and offer our prayers in respect."

"He's in the Church," said Eogan, "I will show you."

Together, Eogan, Elaine, and Madoc walked away towards the longhouse serving as the Church where my father's body was still lying upon the altar. Tristram and I remained behind, by the edge of the fens, looking out at the black swans swimming amidst the reeds.

"I'm sorry about your father," said Tristram.

"Thanks," I said.

"I didn't know you'd be here," he said, "my father informed me I had to go on a trip with Lady Elaine and that I wouldn't be back."

"You were okay with that?" I asked.

"I'm ready for an adventure."

I was ready for an adventure. I was ready for all the sadness and loneliness of my childhood to melt away and reveal a new, meaningful path. As the others returned from the Church, I realized I was ready to face whatever laid in front of me and stood with confidence, walking over to join the others with Tristram on my heels. Lady Elaine was speaking with Father Jimellus and Eogan, while Madoc stood behind them silently staring at the ground and twitching his leg nervously.

"I just can't believe he's gone," said Elaine, "he was always so strong and healthy. Who would've thought his heart would give out during the prime years of his life."

"His heart didn't fail," came a familiar voice as my mother walked up behind us, as though she had risen from the waters of the fens like an otter seeking the warmth of the sun. This time she wasn't veiled in the visage of a nun. She appeared as her true self, with her purple robes and fiery black hair. Madoc and Tristram looked like they'd jump out of their skin at the sight of my imposing mother while Elaine walked over to kiss her sister lightly upon the cheek. Eogan and Jimellus bowed slightly.

"He was murdered," continued my mother, "by the darkness. It has come already to the isle of the Christians, sooner than I expected. We mustn't linger here any longer. I sense you will be joining us, sister."

"I won't be leaving Madoc," said Elaine.

My mother quickly surveyed our small group, passing over Madoc, Tristram, and me before stopping at Eogan.

"You are welcome to join us," she said to him, "I can feel your love for my son. You wish to protect him."

"I do, my Lady," replied Eogan, "but I am a Christian. I would find no comfort beyond the veil. I will remain here and take vows to join Father Jimellus' brotherhood of Nazarenes."

"Your choice is commendable," replied my mother, "I wish you all the best. I know Jimellus will treat you well."

Without another word my mother began to walk off towards the Tor with the single monolithic stone at its summit. Elaine followed her and Madoc instinctively trailed after his mother. Tristram and I glanced at one another as if to say so it begins and then ran off to join them. The sun was now fully visible over the eastern horizon, casting its radiant glow across the green knolls of the hillside as we mounted the Tor. Viviana and Elaine never wavered as they continued marching upward, despite the sheer incline of the hillside. Viviana looked to be in her mid-thirties and Elaine wasn't much younger but they moved with the youthful grace and determination of twenty-year-old maidens as they reached the summit and circled the Tor Stone. For a moment my mother looked like she might waver, that she would give into some abiding sadness and turn away. Then, as though she were forcing her true feelings deep inside, she regained her regal but slightly apathetic demeanor.

"Place your hands upon the stone," she said.

Without a word we each stepped close to the Tor Stone and put one of our hands on its smooth, cold surface. For a long minute it seemed nothing would happen. Then a strong wind rose up from nowhere and blew across us with gale force. The light of the sun became muted, as though it were shining through a silk blanket, and the earth began to shake softly. As sudden as a clap of lightning the Christian commune that had been my home for months melted away to reveal another world more wondrous and unique than I could've imagined.

Chapter Four
"Beyond the Veil"

In many ways the Seven Isles that laid before me were the same as those which had been my home for months but, in most ways they were different. We were no longer standing with our hands on a single monolithic stone, rather we were within a Stone Circle, a miniature replica of the Henge on the Summer Plain to which the Druids once flocked on their Holy Days. There was a processional way zigzagging down to the more subtle slopes of the Tor, where the cottages and Church of the Nazarenes stood in the other world. In their place was a massive stone roundhouse with a thatch roof and a series of raised gardens producing herbs of various shape and color. The water of the fens was higher than I'd ever seen it, creating a full brackish lake reflecting the soft shimmer of the sunlight. There were half a dozen young women dressed in gray woolen gowns flitting about the gardens, some watering, others harvesting but all ceased their labors when they caught sight of us standing in the Stone Circle. My mother quickly led us down the processional way towards the roundhouse as the young women lined up in a row to greet us.

"Lady," the young women said in unison, bowing deeply in the direction of my mother.

"Children," said Viviana, "these are the Maiden-Healers who serve the goddess, Brigga. They tend her gardens and also the fires on the night of the Beltane Rites. Take a good look. You will not see them again until you are either ready to reenter the outside world or to take vows as a Druid Priest, Guardian, or Bard."

Without further explanation my mother waved the Maiden-Healers back to their duties and ushered us towards the lowest point of the island, where the waters of the brackish lake lapped at the green grasses and lush apple trees. A familiar barge was waiting with a young Fenfolk man manning the pole. Tristram, Madoc, and I sat at the front of the barge with my mother and Aunt Elaine sitting directly behind us.

"There are Fenfolk in the Unseen Vale?" I asked no one in particular as the young man pushed us away from the dock and out into the open waters of the brackish lake.

"As I told you in our meetings on the hill above the convent," said my mother sternly, "there is a village of Fenfolk upon the Watch Hill, along with a clan of horsemen who worship the goddess, Epona. That's the hill just over there."

As we inched passed the tip of the Isle of the Font, just opposite the Isle of Glass, I could see the imposing hill at the heart of the Fens and, upon its southern shores, were a few dozen poled huts built in the fashion of the Fenfolk. I saw no signs of another settlement and assumed the Eponi clan must've dwelt on the other side of the island. The young Fenfolk man switched from a pole to an oar and paddled us westward towards what I knew to be the Isle of Birds and the Isle of Oak. The Isle of Birds was covered by a thick glade of willow trees but a steady stream of black smoke was billowing upwards through the inner canopy of the trees. The Isle of Oak was very similar, except that it was home to a grove of massive oak trees, growing like towers reaching out to touch the heavens. Amidst the massive trunks of the trees, I could make out three stone roundhouses similar to the one on the Isle of Glass, sitting side by side at the eastern edge of the grove. The barge veered towards the cluster of roundhouses and soon we were docking at a shallow point in the water.

"Come along," said my mother as she stood and exited the barge, disappearing briskly up a narrow stone path leading inland towards the trees. By the time we caught up she was nearing the largest of the three roundhouses from which a tall older man in white robes emerged. He was fair of complexion but his skin was riddled with sunspots. His white hair was growing passed his shoulders but his beard was even longer. He seemed a wise old philosopher and this time it was Viviana who bowed.

"Master," she said softly, "the boys are come."

"I see," said the old man with a smile. He shakily walked over to us and examined us with his eyes one by one, as though he was sizing us up, to see who might be the fittest. When he reached me he paused.

"You're all fine looking lads," said the man, "you'll do well here."

"Taliesin," yelled a young man in faded blue robes from the doorway of the second of the third roundhouses, the one nearest to the docks where the barge let us out. The old man, Taliesin, smiled and turned away to go join the younger man but not before he said.

"Welcome to Avalon."

As Taliesin began to enter the roundhouse with the young man, a teenager a few years older than me came running up from the thickest part of the oak grove. He was tall for his age, and extremely skinny, but he was attractive in his own way. He has soft, Gaelic features, with freckles and long red hair but it was his emerald green eyes that were captivating, as though he could mesmerize the most defiant soul into peaceful stillness. He was wearing an undyed woolen tunic that hung down to his ankles and he carried a pitcher of water in his hands.

"You must be the new guys," he said to me, Tristram, and Madoc, "I'm Uriens. I'll be your warden while you're in the House of Initiates."

"I'm sorry, what?" I said in confusion.

"Uriens is Prefect and Senior Initiate here, on the Isle of Oak," said my mother, "it's his duty to teach the new initiates how to behave. This is the House of Initiates."

My mother pointed to the roundhouse furthest from the docks, closest to the thickest part of the oak grove. Then she pointed to the one nearest to the dock.

"That is the House of Bards," she said and then pointed to the roundhouse standing between them, "and that is the House of Priests."

"I don't understand," said Tristram, "we are to stay here? But we're not Druid initiates...I'm a Christian."

"And I thought I'd be staying with you, mother," I added.

My mother looked at me with an empty face, as though she was a legendary general sizing up her troops before leading them into battle.

"While in Avalon you will address me as Lady," she said sternly, "and the first lesson for you to learn is one you already know well. In Christian communities the men and women live separately. It is the same here. The Druids live on the Isle of Oak, the Maiden-Healers on the Isle of Glass, the Crones on the Isle of Birds, and the Guardians on the Isle of Stone, and I live with the priestesses on the Isle of the Font."

Without another word, my mother turned on her heel and marched away towards the dock and the waiting barge with Elaine at her heels, leaving me, Tristram, and Madoc with our new warden, Uriens.

☼   ☼   ☼

Days turned to weeks and weeks to months. Before I knew it, nearly a year had passed. I celebrated my thirteenth birthday modestly, with a rye cake in the House of Initiates baked by Tristram. Tristram, Madoc, and I grew really close those first days in Avalon. We were best friends. We were brothers. Tristram was not much for studying with the Druids and proved himself incapable with a sword. He was a gentle soul who loved listening to stories, dying fabrics, and cooking. His personal qualities were in stark contrast to his roman features. Romans were supposed to be the fiercest warriors, shrewd strategists with an eye for discovering weaknesses. Tristram was none of those things but Madoc was all of them. Madoc proved that a sword was indeed the fiercest weapon at only fifteen years of age. He was also exceedingly intelligent when it came to formulating plans. His raw muscles provided him ample strength and he spent his days exercising, herding, and practicing with sword, knife, or spear. I discovered I had some talent with a blade but I preferred learning with the Druids over combat or the more cultured traditions observed by Tristram.

Uriens took me under his wing and taught me everything I needed to know about living as an Initiate on the Isle of Oak. There were seven of us sharing the house: Uriens, Tristram, Madoc, and myself. Then there was a boy a year older than me but two years younger than Madoc named Ywain, a boy the same as Uriens named Ortheon, and a boy a year younger than me and Tristram named Orin. Orin and Ywain joined Madoc in his martial pursuits. Orin excelled in the uses of a spear and shield. Ywain was skilled in the use of a battleax and all three were formidable hand-to-hand fighters. Ortheon was like Tristram but with more interest in the harp, leading the bards to think he might one day join their order. Uriens was preparing to enter the priesthood. He knew all the secrets of the Initiates and showed great power within the Sacred Grove.

The men and women of Avalon only came together twice in the year, once at Beltane in the spring and again at Samhain in the autumn but Initiates were not allowed to attend the celebrations. The only woman we saw was an old Fenfolk boatwoman who brought us provisions from the other islands on her rickety barge. I was not allowed to leave the Isle of Oak. I spent my days studying the stories with the bards, my evenings learning about the Mysteries from the priests, and my nights sleeping restlessly on a straw mattress with Tristram snoring in my ear and Madoc elbowing while dreaming of adventure and intrigue. Life was simple and I enjoyed it.

I had two teachers on the Isle of Oak. One was the portly, bald little bard named Lugubelenus and the other was a strikingly tall middle-aged Gael named Faelan. Lugubelenus was the head of the bardic order. He taught me the Ancient Songs of the Beakers and how to play the harp and flute. But my true passion was in studying the Mysteries with Faelan. He would take me into the depths of the Sacred Grove, to where a large stone statue stood in honor of the god-king, Kernos. An altar sat at the statue's feet and it was part of the duties of the Initiates to make sure tha altar was filled with fresh fruits, bread, and wine in supplication to our patron god. The Druids believed that Kernos ruled the world of man from Samhain to Beltane and that the goddess, Nimue, ruled from Beltane to Samhain but on the Isle of Oak the altar of Kernos was always filled, no matter the season, whether he was reigning as king or sleeping in the Otherworld.

Three months after my birthday, and ten months after my arrival in Avalon, Faelan and I were sitting on the stones near the altar to Kernos and he was teaching me about the fundamentals of elemental manipulation but I wasn't listening. I was curious about another matter. In all the months I'd been in the Unseen Vale, I knew of only one person who had left and no one new had arrived. The old man, Taliesin, who greeted us that first day we came to the Isle of Oak had soon after departed. No one explained where he was going or if he would come back, leaving me to always wonder. I couldn't take it anymore and so I decided to ask Faelan about him.

"I don't mean any disrespect to your lesson, master," I said, "but I was wondering if I could ask you a question?"

"What is it?" said Faelan.

"I was wondering about Taliesin. Where did he go?" I asked.

"Wherever he pleases," said Faelan, "Taliesin is the Merlin and the Merlin answers to no mortal man or woman."

Taliesin was one in a long line of Merlins dating back to the days of the Beakers. The Merlin wasn't like other men who live and die, taking their memories and experiences with them. When one Merlin died, all the things within his mind transferred to the next Merlin. Taliesin held within his head the culmination of dozens of lifetimes, symbiotically merging into one ultimate font of wisdom and power. Even my mother bowed to the Merlin and honored him for his wisdom.

Faelan turned the conversation back to the day's lesson when suddenly a loud ringing filled the air, as though someone standing in the hills beyond the isles had struck a gong with a wooden mallet. As soon as it started, the sound faded away, returning the island to the quiet serenity of water lapping at the banks and birds singing in the trees. Faelan noticed curiosity once again taking a grip in me and decided to preemptively respond to my impending questions.

"Whenever someone passes through the fabric separating the Unseen Vale from the rest of the world it makes that sound, the sound of a bell ringing out to warn us of possible intruders."

"Who do think it is?" I asked.

"Only Viviana and Taliesin go forth to walk between the worlds," replied Faelan, "it must be one of them."

☼   ☼   ☼

The following morning, Elaine arrived on the Isle of Oak with an invitation for the Druids and Initiates to attend a feast in the Fenfolk village on the Watch Hill. The feast was a celebration honoring my mother but I had no idea why she was due any more honor than she was already afforded as Lady of the Unseen Vale. The feast would begin at sundown and we were instructed to wear our finest garments, soft linen robes dyed sky blue and used mostly for ceremonies involving the Mysteries, a stark contrast to our bland, undyed work robes of gray wool.

We did as we were commanded and arrived on the Watch Hill in mid-evening. The Fenfolk had several tables set up at the center of the village, near a roaring bonfire creating heat to ward away the chill of the cold autumn night. The Maiden-Healers and Priestesses of Nimue were already present, sitting at the table with an assortment of foods and wine. At the head of all the tables sat my mother dressed in a gown of midnight purple and cradling her full belly in her hands. She was full-term with a baby. When she caught sight of us she struggled to stand with the help of two young ladies bearing a striking resemblance to one another. One was my age, with brown hair so dark it was almost black, falling wildly down to the crest of her buttocks. The other was a few years older with bright red hair of the same texture and consistency as the other girl. Once they had helped Viviana to her feet she waddled over to greet us.

"Thank you for coming brothers," she said to the Druids. Then she turned to speak directly to me, "Welcome, my son."

"Lady," I replied with the customary bow without taking my eyes off her heavy, protruding belly. She was not unaware of my fixation and decided to address the proverbial elephant in the room.

"I am with child, as you can see," she said, "I am come to term but still have not dropped for labor. I feel like it might be a girl, a daughter to carry on in my place when I am gone."

"Who's the father?" I blurted out without thinking.

My mother's smile faded and she looked as though she would knock me over the head for my impudence.

"This child's father is the same as yours," she said, "three nights before his death, Ban sought me out on the Tor Hill. I brought him into Avalon and we spent a night together. His cold exterior and anger thinly masked his desire for me. He begged me to leave Avalon, to journey to Lodecran with him, and you. When I refused his anger was renewed and he fled my bed. But not before he left me with this gift."

I was disgusted. I'd grown to forgive my father for his cold distance and disapproval of me but I was still angry with my mother for bringing me to Avalon and then leaving me with the Druids without coming to visit me even once. I was her only son, her only child yet born, and she treated me like any other Initiate. I was a supplicant and she was my Lady. I almost yelled out at her to tell her how much she disgusted me but I caught myself and went to sit at the table without saying a word. Tristram joined me while Madoc ran off to sit with his mother. Faelan and Lugubelenus were seated with some of the senior priestesses and Uriens was sitting alone beneath a tree strumming his harp. I was conscious of the movements of everyone and there was one person I expected to see but who was absent.

"Where's Taliesin?" I asked Lugubelenus as he walked passed on a journey to refill his cup with wine.

"Not here," he grunted.

"I thought he came through the veil yesterday," I said.

"You mean the ringing? That was Lady Viviana bringing the girls over there to Avalon," said Lugubelenus, pointing to the girls attending my mother as she ate.

After everyone had eaten their fill and imbibed enough wine to loosen their tongues and feet, the Fenfolk struck up a vibrant brand of their folk music and everyone began to dance. I wasn't much of a dancer but even I felt compelled to stand up and sway to the rhythm of the drums and the mystical melody produced by all the flutes. Hearing the veracity of the Fenfolk music reminded me of when I was living with the Nazarenes in their commune on the Isle of Glass. Sometimes, in the darkness of the night, it seemed we could hear strange music rising from the waters of the fens. The monks believed it was the devil attempting to lure them out into the treacherous marshes, where they would likely lose their footing in the darkness and be dragged down to the watery depths by the weeds. But the music wasn't a device of the devil, it was the music of the Fenfolk on the Watch Hill, music so powerful it could breach the veil and reach the isle of the Christians.

I felt the music wash over me and soon I was dancing around the bonfire with the Fenfolk children in my loincloth. I had thrown my robes to the ground in a moment of primal passion, shedding my rational coil to experience freedom in a way I had never known. For a few precious moments I transcended my body. I became one with the music, with the fire, with the Watch Hill itself. Everything around me was blurred into a golden haze and I could hear a voice singing in perfect harmony with the Fenfolk music, a woman's song in a language I couldn't understand. I thought it might be my mother but she was sitting casually at a nearby table conversing with Faelan. I didn't care where it was coming from. It was beautiful and I was mesmerized into endless tranquility. The other children and I moved faster and more intensely as the rhythm of the music shifted. Madoc joined us in his loincloth and he and I gyrated against one another in primal heat.

"You can really dance," said the girl with dark brown hair who'd been attending my mother. She had come to join us in our movements around the fire. Her words snapped me out of my trance and returned me to sensory reality. The people around me came back into focus and the sound of the music became softer and more distant. The girl was looking from me to Madoc and back again. I felt a sudden boyhood inclination to push her away, for fear of catching some parasite only carried by girls.

"What?" I said defensively.

"Just looking," she said.

"At what?" I complained.

"I think you two are my cousins," she said, "you're Galahad, and you, you're Madoc."

"And you are?" said Madoc.

"Morgana," she replied, "Morgana le Fey."

Chapter Five
"In the Cauldron"

"I've never heard of you," I said to Morgana as the Fenfolk concluded the festivities with one final song.

"I've heard of you," she smirked, "the Lady is your mother, and Madoc's mother is Elaine. They are both my aunts. Their younger sister, Igerna, is my mother. That's my sister, Morgause, over there."

Morgana pointed to the redheaded girl a few years older than us still tending to my mother's needs.

"Mother insisted we come here to live with the healers because the High King is sick and the people are starting to look for a leader in their own clans. Mother thinks there will be war. But I think she's overreacting. I mean, everyone knows Ambrose wants my father to be the next High King."

"Who's your father?" asked Madoc but I already knew the answer. If her mother was my Aunt Igerna then her father was Gorlois, the Duke of Cornewall. My father spoke of Gorlois often, though I had no idea he was my uncle-by-marriage because I didn't know about Igerna. I learned of Igerna from Faelan and of her marriage to Gorlois. Next to my father, Gorlois was the greatest military commander in Britannia and had the favor of the High King's ear regularly since he also resided in Londinium.

"Let's not talk of such things this night," chastised Lugubelenus who'd come to stand behind us without us knowing, "the druids are working spells to aid the High King with his maladies. He is still alive and there is still peace in the land. Be grateful."

The music had come to an end and the Druids were beginning to gather at the base of the Watch Hill, where several barges were waiting in the Brackish Lake to carry them back to the Isle of Oak. I knew I had to go with them but a part of me longed to remain behind, to stay in the company of my mother and the other priestesses. To get to know Morgana better and to meet her sister, Morgause.

"It's time to go," said Lugubelenus to me and Madoc. I smiled at Morgana as if to say it was nice to meet you then turned around and sprinted down the hill with Madoc on my heels.

☼   ☼   ☼

Weeks passed before we saw the women again. I remained preoccupied with my studies and tried not to think about my mother. It was clear she would've given birth to her baby just days after the celebration on the Watch Hill. I hoped she came through the birth unscathed but I was worried since we'd received no word. As much as it concerned me I tried to put it out of my mind and focus on my lessons with Faelan.

It was an exciting time in my life. I had finished my book studies and was ready to start learning magick from Faelan. I was a full-fledged Initiate and would one day be a bard or priest, pledged to the service of Kernos and the other Gods of the Dagda. The last vestiges of my Christian upbringing were erased as I embraced the Mysteries of the Old Religion. The magick permeating the Holy Isles had entered into my soul. I knew there was no turning back from my chosen path and I didn't care. I would be a Druid. Faelan respected my determination and drove me not only to succeed but to excel in every lesson, every challenge.

"All things in nature possesses guardian spirits and it is those spirits that we entreat when we work magick," said Faelan as we stood in an open field between the Oak Grove and the Brackish Lake. It was a warm late autumn morning. The waters of the lake were calm and the air was still. There was not a cloud in the sky and the light of the sun was hot. Faelan was teaching me how to summon the elements, not by calling to the element itself but by supplicating their guardian spirits.

"We have spells that speak to such creatures," continued Faelan with a stern expression.

Faelan walked a few feet away towards the Brackish Lake and raised his hands above his head, as though he were reaching up to pull the sun from the sky. When he spoke, his words were foreign. It sounded like Greek but I couldn't be sure. I could speak Latin, British, Gaelic, and a little of the Fenfolk language but I'd never learned to speak the ancient and classical Hellenic tongue. Faelan's voice reverberated off the water and echoed through the vale like thunder erupting from above.

"Kaló ta pnévmata ston ánemo," he said, "Eímai gnóstis tis archaías sofías kai egó diatázo na fysíxei tóra."

Suddenly a gale-force wind whipped up from nowhere, churning the waters of the lake and bending the boughs of the oaks with its juggernaut force. I was knocked to the ground from the impact of the air but Faelan remained on his feet, untouched by the raw power of the deadly gust. After a split second, Faelan spoke again.

"Erchómenos tóra sto drómo tis fýsis kai ton kópo mas óchi perissótero."

At once the wind died down and the calm autumn warmth was returned to the island. I stood and marveled at Faelan's power as he walked over to join me.

"That was amazing," I said.

"It is only the beginning," replied Faelan, "calling the elements is a Druid's first and most readily available tool. But it is only the first of many lessons for you to learn."

"Why was the spell in Greek?" I asked.

"It was not Greek," said Faelan, "though to the untrained ear it sounds very similar. There are more than one Hellene dialects and all originate from the one that forms our spells. It is the language of the Beakers, brought here by those who founded the Old Religion. Our dialect bears more resemblance to the language of the Trojans then the modern Hellenic tongues. Both our tongue at that of Troy are considered to be dead languages and ours is kept secret. It is the foundation of the Ogham, the spell-tongue of the Drowned Lands. You understand?"

"I understand," I said but in truth I didn't entirely. I knew the stories of the Beakers from the songs of the bards. Long ago, before the rise of the Hellenic Armies or the Roman Empire, there existed an ancient and advanced civilization across the sea in a place the Druids called the Drowned Lands because it was believed the waters of the sea rose to engulf the land centuries ago. According to the songs, the Pendragon ruled the civilization of the Beakers but it was the Merlin who held the real power. When the civilization became undone by greed and malice and the Pendragon fell to darkness it was the Merlin who tried in vain to save their holy civilization. None more so than the one called Talkannon.

Talkannon was the first Merlin, the one who brought the secret knowledge of the Bakers to Britain before journeying on to found the golden city of Troy. Legends tell that Talkannon returned to Britain in the last days of his life and bound himself to the land with a Blood Oath so that all the Merlins that came after would be born in and tied to Britain. He saw our land as bearing the greatest potential for sustaining the ancient wisdom and using it to fashion a civilization in the likeness of the fallen realm of the Drowned Lands. All the Merlins have been tied to the Britons, serving to preserve the balance and keep the people in touch with the spirits of the natural world. I was entranced by the story, driven to believe in the cause of the Druids because I knew that the stories were true.

"Before you can attempt to call the elements, you must learn the language," said Faelan, drawing me back into the moment, "if you are serious about entering the order, you must know the tongue. Since you have foresworn to keep your lessons a secret, I have no qualms in giving you this."

Faelan produced a scroll bound within a leather holder from his sack laying in the grass and handed it to me. It was very old, formed from papyrus, and smelled of mold.

"Study the characters. Learn how they flow into one another. The tongue will reveal itself to you if you spend time with it. We will not meet again until you've mastered the language. It could take months, or even years if your mind is not focused on the task at hand.

Faelan left me there in the meadow with the scroll. When I unrolled it I found more than thirty characters of a foreign alphabet which resembled hieroglyphs more than letters. Latin was a simple language with a familiar alphabet. This was completely different. I had no idea how I was going to learn the language by myself, without someone helping me with pronunciation and with conjugation. I rolled the scroll back up and sheathed it in its case with a sigh. I was panicking about what I was being asked to do, to learn an entire language alone.

"Another tough lesson," said Madoc as he appeared from the edge of the oak grove, a longsword in his hand.

Madoc was starting to fill in with masculine features. He was almost three years older and his body was more mature than mine. He was already on the path from boy to man and it showed in his strong movements and deepening voice. Madoc and I had become great friends since arriving in Avalon. I thought of him as my protector and he called me his priest. As Tristram drifted towards Ortheon in his scholastic pursuits we grew further apart. Madoc was there to fill the void. I felt comfortable telling him my secrets and he was open to hearing them. We weren't just bound together by friendship, we were bound together by blood, cousins through our mothers. He was a stable and central part of my life and I relished any time we could spend together, however rare or brief.

"It's more like an impossible task," I said, "How am I supposed to learn an entire language without a teacher?"

"You can do anything you put your mind to, Galahad," said Madoc with a smile, "You're the smartest person I've ever met. You're smarter than Faelan and he knows it. That's why he put this task to you. It's a chance for you to show your worth."

"You think he wants me to fail?" I asked.

"I think he wants you to struggle," said Madoc, "Faelan is next-in-line after Taliesin in the hierarchy of the Druids. He doesn't want anyone threatening his position. Not even you."

"How can I threaten his position?"

"You still don't get it. We're not just children they brought here to protect from the outside world but to protect the world from us. No one's told you about our grandmother, have they?"

"No. I didn't even know about your mother, or Morgana's, until I got here," I said.

"Our mothers are the daughters of the Queen of Faerie," said Madoc, "The fey lived here before man and disappeared when the Beakers arrived in their ships. They vanished into the realm beyond the Unseen we call Faerie. Some people don't believe they exist but the people here know better. They've seen them, wandering in the mists at the Crossroad. And then there was our Grandmother Rhiannon."

"One day during the years when Vortigern ruled these lands, Rhiannon walked out of the mists and joined the Priestesses of Nimue," Madoc continued, "she brought with her the great magick of her people and the wisdom of the arts practiced even before the Beakers founded their civilization in the west. It was only natural that, in time, she become the Lady of the Unseen Vale, that she lead the Priestesses and Maiden-Healers. Now, the fey don't age, at least not like us, but they do conceive children in the same manner. Rhiannon took many lovers and had five daughters. The two oldest died when they were young, leaving Viviana, my mother, and Igerna, all half-man, half-fey, with the same extraordinary magick and physical attributes as Rhiannon. When Rhiannon wandered out into the mists, she left Viviana in charge. Viviana had you, my mother had me, and Igerna had Morgana, Morgause, and their brothers. We are quarter fey, each of us has the same power coursing through our veins. Who knows what damage we could do if we were left untrained. Here, we have a purpose, we are fulfilling our destiny, a warrior, a healer, and a mage."

I had no idea we were different from other men. No one ever told me about Rhiannon or even about the realm of Faerie. I was about to ask for more information about the fey from Madoc when the air filled with the sound of a bell, signaling someone passing from the outside world into the Unseen Vale. A few minutes later, Lugubelenus came running into the meadow with a look of dread on his face. It was apparent something was terribly wrong.

"The High King is dying," he cried, "We are all doomed."

☼   ☼   ☼

Lugubelenus, Madoc, and I arrived on the Watch Hill just as the barge carrying the High King pulled up to the dock. Ambrose was a frail old man, with wrinkled, sagging skin and hair as white as snow. There were still flecks of red in his beard, the only remnants of a once vibrant and courageous man renowned for his battle skills. He was emaciated and pale as a group of Fenfolk men pulled him from the barge and carried him into the village, to the sweathouse used by the Fenfolk for their purification rituals. The Maiden-Healers and Priestesses were already gathered at the sweathouse, as were the Druids, except for Faelan, who was conspicuously absent. My mother was at the head of the Priestesses. She was again thin and tall and full of life. I wondered about the baby. I wanted to run to her and ask about my brother or sister, to know if they were healthy and unharmed but I kept my distance. It was she who approached me, Morgause and Morgana on her heels.

"I'm glad you are here, Lugubelenus," my mother said.

"I would be nowhere else," replied Lugubelenus before running off to join the Druids.

"What can I do?" I asked my mother.

"You and the other children will go to the Isle of Birds," she said, "You must carry a message from me to the Crones. Ask them to look into their cauldrons and tell me who will follow Ambrose to the throne. We must know to whom we must pledge our support. Go now, a barge is waiting to carry you across the water."

Madoc, Tristram, Morgause, Morgana, and I went at once to the barge that poled us silently across the Brackish Lake to the Isle of Birds, home of the mysterious and isolated Crones. When a Priestess reached the age of fifty it was customary for her to retire from the outside world and join the

Crones, to spend the rest of her days in quiet contemplation, staring into the cauldrons at the heart of the willow grove serving as their home. The island was known as the Isle of Birds because of the number of ravens found in the willows. Ravens are the heralds of Catsubodhva, the goddess of silence and death to whom the Crones pledged their service.

The barge let us out in a quiet inlet on the west side of the island, near the perimeter of the Willow Grove. Morgause looked intrigued at the prospect of meeting the Crones and Morgana was also very curious. Madoc put on a brave face but I could tell he had trepidations. Tristram looked outright scared, clinging to me like a child seeking the protection of a caring mother. I was strangely relieved as we started into the willow grove. I had always wondered about the Crones and my mind had convinced me they were something I knew they were not. That night I would prove to myself that they were just old women seeking answers from the only goddess still willing to give them her favor. Brigga and Nimue were goddesses of youth and the living. An older woman passed her prime was no longer the concern of the Great Healer or the Protectress of the Earth. It was only Catsubodhva who cared for the aged and the ailing.

"Do you think they'll be all warty and stinky and gross?" asked Morgana as we ventured into the woods.

"I think they'll be jaded old women with a bad attitude," said Morgause in her usual pretentious way. Morgana was pledged to the Maiden-Healers, a perfect place for an inquisitive girl with a penchant for illustrating every point with a thousand words. Morgause was unpledged. She was rapidly becoming a woman and cared more for her looks and her station than the Mysteries or the traditions of our forbearers. Whenever she showed the slightest inclination to learn the Mysteries she was shot down by my mother. She resented having to serve my mother constantly and made it clear she wanted to return to the outside world at the first possible moment, leaving Avalon and the Unseen Vale behind forever. As we ventured into the woods, I couldn't help but satisfy my curiosity and ask Morgause and Morgana about my mother's baby.

"Did my mother have a boy or girl?" I asked.

"A little girl," said Morgana, "she named her Guinevere."

"Guinevere," I repeated. It was a familiar name to me. It was the name of my father's mother.

Morgana grabbed on to Madoc and held him tight as we ventured into the darkest glade of the willow trees. The sun was still hanging in the sky but it was making its final descent towards the western horizon and its rays had trouble penetrating the thick eves of the willows. It was cool and damp and smelled of moss. Tristram latched onto me and we led the way with Morgause on our heels and the other two behind her. Morgause was unaffected by our surroundings. She was too preoccupied with not tearing her dress or mussing her hair.

We crossed a babbling brook near the heart of the grove over a tiny man-made land-bridge before finding ourselves standing amidst a half-dozen thatch-roof cottages falling into disrepair situated around a massive iron cauldron sitting atop of a fireless hearth. The air was still and the village silent, aside from the soft crowing of the ravens perched in the trees above us. It looked as though the village was deserted decades ago. We were just about to give up, to turn around and return to the barge, when a twig snapped in the distance and four old women appeared from the trees carrying wood. They were each no less than seventy years old, with gray or white hair and faces as wrinkled as the nose of a pig. They were wrapped in black rags, their hands were gnarled, and their backs were bent from arthritis. I was surprised they could walk without canes, let alone carry bundles of wood under their arms. All but the shortest woman were blind and she only had sight in one eye. They were gnarled and haggard, like the kind of green-skinned witches found in children's stories.

"Aela, Eilan, Nerwa, we have visitors," said the short woman with the one good eye when she saw us standing at the edge of the village.

"Of course, of course. Remember Oonagh, they were sent by Viviana," said the one called Nerwa.

"She needs us to gaze into the cauldron," said the one called Aela.

"And find a weapon to combat the darkness," said the one called Eilan as she piled tender in the hearth beneath the cauldron. Aela pulled out a flint-stone and began striking it with a knife. Soon the tender was aflame and the women were heaping wood atop it to create a large, hot fire. In mere minutes the water in the cauldron was boiling and a thick, dark smoke was rising up from the depths of the iron pot. The women each took a position around the rim of the cauldron and gazed into its depths with their lifeless, blind eyes, rocking back and forth as they were overwhelmed by a trance.

"The dragon will rise again in the west," said Nerwa.

"And another in the north," added Eilan.

"One red, the other white," said Oonagh, "Both hungry for the Crown, eager to rule the men of the Tribes."

"The Henge will run red with the blood of the one born unto the Christ," said Aela, "He will be struck down by the man who will rule for sixteen years before the True King rises to claim the crown."

"But he will need your help," said Eilan, "Mage, Healer, Warrior, and Scribe. Four souls bound together by fate and one who will bring doom upon the land. Be wary of Morgause. She will be your undoing."

Morgause looked shocked as the old women began to come out of their trance. She was not the most selfless individual but it was hard to believe she would one day be our enemy.

"One more thing," said Oonagh, "Galahad. You must go at once to the Crossroad and seek out Oberon. He holds the key to your destiny."

Chapter Six
"Oberon"

We returned straightaway to the Watch Hill to deliver the news of what we learned to my mother. She was sitting at the bedside of Ambrose. He seemed to breathing deeper. The color had returned to his face and he snored lightly as he slept. When my mother saw us she put her finger to her lips, commanding us to be silent, before standing and exiting the sweathouse. The other Priestesses and the Maiden-Healers were already on their way back to the Isle of the Font and the Isle of Glass. The Druids remained on the Watch Hill, sitting in a smoke circle at the edge of the water in a state of meditative introspection. The Fenfolk were in their beds, except for the village medicine-woman who remained in the sweathouse tending to Ambrose's needs. We told my mother everything we had learned and she listened intently. When we were finished with our tale she stood and brushed off her purple gown before walking back towards the sweathouse. Just as she disappeared through the doorway she turned back to us.

"Go now to your beds," she said to us, "you've done well. Galahad. You will remain here with me."

The others made their way to the docks while I joined my mother in the sweathouse. The Fenfolk medicine-woman was putting more water on the hot coals, causing steam to billow forth and drench us in its humidity. It was hot but Ambrose was still covered with furs. He was sweating out the sickness that nearly claimed his life while the Druids prayed in their smoking circle just outside. I could hear the Fenfolk elders in one of the nearby huts, chanting in their native language, and I knew the Priestesses were back on the Isle of the Font praying to Nimue for the High King's quick recovery. Nobody wanted Ambrose to die and everyone understood the significance of what his death would mean. The darkness of which Viviana had spoken many times over the years was threatening to destroy our land, that much was clear from the prophecy of the Crones. Tristram, Madoc, Morgana, and I had a part to play in the coming years and, from what the Crones foretold, Morgause would be our enemy.

"There's something I don't understand, Lady," I said to my mother as we sat down next to the High King.

"There are many things you don't yet understand," she said.

"If Morgause is our enemy, why do you let her stay here?" I asked.

"Morgause is not our enemy," replied Viviana, "at least not yet. The Crones may have seen her commit crimes against us in the waters of their Cauldron but those events have not yet come to pass. Morgause is arrogant and selfish without an inkling of shame but she's not evil. She's my sister's daughter and I will keep her safe for as long as the Goddess grants me breath, just as I will protect you and Madoc and Morgana and Guinevere."

"Should I go to the Crossroad right away to seek out this Oberon?" I asked my mother.

"No you will not," she replied, "It is forbidden for you to step foot upon the Crossroad until you have been formally initiated into the Mysteries which cannot happen until you've learned the Ogham."

"I don't know that I can learn the Ogham without a teacher."

"And therein lies the ultimate test. If you want to be a Druid bad enough, you'll find a way. Now, you should be off to bed. Try not to worry about the prophecy of the Crones. None of it will come to pass as long as Ambrose lives and, thanks to the Maiden-Healers, and the Fenfolk's medicine, the High King will return to Londinium and the throne."

"Just one more question," I said.

"Yes?" replied my mother.

"Is it true that your mother is fey?" I asked.

"It is true," she said, "my mother was fey but she is long since dead, passed into the Otherworld as we all must at the end of our days. And that is all you need to know."

"What about your father? Is he still living?"

"Yes, though he's now very old," smiled Viviana, "but don't tell him I said so. He would never let me hear the end of it."

"I know him?"

"Everyone here knows him. My father is Taliesin."

She smiled again and I saw something in her I'd never seen before, something emotional, almost human.

"Now to bed with you," she commanded and I did as I was told.

☼   ☼   ☼

I tried to do as my mother commanded and focus on learning the Ogham. I spent weeks pouring over the scroll Faelan gave me, trying to decipher the meaning of each symbol without success. I couldn't get the prophecy of the Crones out of my head and resolved I would steal a barge and visit the Crossroad without telling anyone.

Whenever we were in need of transport from one island to the next we would call upon the Fenfolk to pole or row us to our chosen destination. On the other isles, the ones in the outside world, one could conceivably walk between the isles in the summer at low tide if they knew the way but here, in the Unseen Vale, the water did not ebb and flow according to the tide and was always high enough to form a lake. The only way to reach the Crossroad was by boat and the only boat readily available on the Isle of Oak belonged to Faelan. Stealing it wouldn't be easy. I had to wait weeks, until the last days of autumn when the air cooled and the fog rolled in off the sea. I slipped out of the House of Initiates while everyone was still sleeping and made my way to the docks where Faelan's canoe was tied. I untied the knots binding the boat to the dock and slipped inside, taking up the oar and paddling silently, determined not rouse the priests sleeping in the nearby House of Druids. I had butterflies in my stomach thinking about being caught by Faelan. If they realized I was visiting the forbidden isle without being initiated I would probably be ejected from the Isle of Oak and the Unseen Vale altogether. Avalon was a place of rules and breaking the rules always carried severe and unbendable consequences carried out by the Council of Senior Druids and Druidesses.

The water was choppy and a strong wind was blowing off the ocean, causing me to shiver and a thick fog was obscuring my vision. I had to navigate the canoe from memory but I was confident I knew the way. I visited the island called the Crossroad many times in the outside world. It was the last isle in the Brackish Lake, lying on the edge of Avalon where it reached out to meet the cold western ocean. I was able to paddle faster and stronger once I was safely away from the Isle of Oak, though my heart was still pounding. If I were to come across a Fenfolk out rowing, he or she would surely stop me and ask me questions, leading to my apprehension and return to the stern Druids. I kept to the borders of the lake as much as possible and, within a half-hour I was in sight of the Crossroad.

It was a strangely shaped mound rising slightly above the water and covered by ancient trees. There was a narrow gulley on the opposite side of the island just big enough for a little stream to run down from the top of the hill. In the outside world, the Christians had a tiny chapel in the gulley next to a cemetery where they buried their dead. I had no idea what I'd find in Avalon and the fog prevented me from finding out until I moored the canoe and went ashore. There was no dock and the water became so shallow I was forced to anchor the boat and wade to shore where I found a convenient set of stairs carved into the side of the hill, leading up to the gulley. I bundled myself in my furs and started up the steps until I came to the small stream and the gulley beyond.

The gulley was filled with apple trees that filled the air with the smell of blossoms. There were no buildings or manmade structures that I could see but the whole expanse was one giant garden of roses, lilies, irises, and other beautiful flora pleasing to the eye and nose. I was confused by the lack of people as I entered the garden but that was soon rectified when I heard the voice of a man from just ahead. He was standing in one of the aisles between the flowers with a pair of sheers dressed in the plain brown habit of a Nazarene monk. His brown hair was tonsured and his middle-aged face was wrinkling. He closely resembled the Fenfolk but I'd never met one of their people who was a Christian. As I approached him the fog receded and the sun warmed the garden around me.

"Not often we get visitors out here," said the man.

"You live here?" I asked.

"I do," replied the man, "sometimes."

"But you're a Christian."

"I am a man of many religions," he smiled, "Is there something in particular that brings you all the way out here?"

"I'm looking for someone, maybe you've heard of him," I said, "his name is Oberon. I was told to seek him out by the Crones after they looked into their cauldron."

The man stopped clipping the rose bush he'd been tending.

"Oberon doesn't live here," he said, "but he comes to visit from time to time. Why do you need to see him? Something magical?"

The man stowed his sheers in a small wooden tool tray and picked it up, walking off towards the interior of the garden. The fog parted as I followed him, revealing the true splendor of the lush flowers and apple trees. It also revealed a structure that I had yet to notice, a stone funeral pyre positioned at the heart of the garden, next to the stream. Atop it was the body of a woman with black hair and dark skin, a woman of the Fenfolk by the look of her features, preserved by some magick so that, though she was dead, she looked to be asleep. The color had not drained from her skin and there were no signs of bloating or rigor. She was dressed in the purple robes of a priestess of Nimue and wore a tattoo of the crescent moon upon her forehead. The priest walked right up to the pyre with me on his heels and set his tool tray down in the grass. He stared down at the woman's body with a sad expression and then folded a single, thornless white rose he'd harvested from the garden into her hands.

"This woman has laid here for more than twenty years and receives only two visitors each week. Me and the Lady Viviana. Elaine and Igerna don't even come. It's a shame they can so readily forget their mother. She would not have forgotten them if their roles were reversed, no matter what they might say on the subject."

I was stunned. Madoc told me that our grandmother, Rhiannon, had walked out into the mists to return to Faerie. Viviana had said that her mother was dead. This seemed to confirm that Viviana was telling the truth, that there on the funeral pyre laid the body of my grandmother. As I gazed down at her I began to see the familial resemblance. She had the same reddish hue to her hair that my mother possessed and her nose was identical to Elaine's. She was tall and thin like both her daughters I had met thus far and she had the same high forehead. The only distinct difference was the shade of her dark skin. Viviana and Elaine looked like women of the Tribes. Rhiannon was clearly a woman of the Fenfolk.

"She gave everything to Avalon and Avalon has forgotten her already," said the man, "but I will never forget. Men turn their minds now towards the Christ because he sacrificed himself for their sins. Rhiannon sacrificed herself to save the Holy Isles, to keep the Druids alive and safe. She deserves no less praise and veneration, yet here she lays without sanctification. Without praise."

"Did you know her?" I asked.

"Know her," said the man, "She was my daughter."

"But she was a Queen of Faerie," I said in disbelief.

"And I am its king," replied the man who was at once transformed. As the glamour he'd been wearing dissolved he was revealed to be a tall, lean young man with long black hair twisted into a hundred braids. His clean-shaven face was unchanged but his green eyes shined like emeralds. The Christian habit vanished, replaced by a leather loincloth and a bear fur draped over his shoulders. His hairless chest and stomach were exposed and his dark, olive skin glistened in the sunlight. On his forehead was tattooed the symbol of the sun that all Druids wore as a symbol of their devotion. I could tell without speaking that he was indeed the King of Faerie. I had stumbled across something I was not expecting and it sent rapid chills down to the base of my spine.

"You were searching for Oberon," said the Faerie King, "and it is Oberon that you have found."

I couldn't speak.

"The Crones sent you to me, Galahad, because they understand that you are one vital piece in a game for the survival of our ways. Faerie even now feels the strain of the darkness pushing against our walls. If it succeeds, we will disappear, the gods will disappear, and the land will be cursed by the blood of the Britons. We must act before everything is irreparably damaged. It begins with you."

I still couldn't speak. Being in the presence of the King of Faerie had forced me into a stunned silence.

"You are the Mage," continued Oberon, "and your cousins are the Healer and Warrior. Your friend is the Scholar and together you will prepare the world for the coming of the True King. You can no longer live apart, and waste no more time learning the Ogham. I command that the four of you take up residence here in the Crossroad. Build a house to keep you warm and learn from each other. It is vital that none of you are corrupted lest the balance be destroyed. Go now back to the others and carry my message to Viviana. Tell her I will not be ignored."

"Will she heed your request?" I asked, finally able to speak.

"I am the King of Faerie," he laughed, "She will have no choice."

Oberon turned back towards Rhiannon, resuming his loving gaze at his fallen daughter. I took it as my cue to retreat back to the canoe. As I moved out from the center of the garden the fog returned, wrapping me in its chilly embrace. I waded back out to the canoe and had started to paddle back into the open waters of the Brackish Lake when Oberon appeared next to me from out of nowhere. He was standing on the water like a man stands on the edge of a road and I could see the invisible silhouette of a halo circling his brow. He was smiling. He reminded me of the Saints venerated by the Christians as he hovered there in mirthful glee.

"I have a gift for you," he said and then he bent down and kissed me on the forehead.

In mere seconds the entirety of the Ogham was unlocked in my mind, every symbol, every nuance. I would be returning to the Isle of Oak with a mastery of the language of our Spellcraft, ready to enter the order of the Druids and begin my initiation into the mystical wonders of our ancestral magick. But I wouldn't be returning alone. As I paddled I heard the sound of another boat moving across the water in the fog. Moments later, it emerged from the mists and its course was one to intercept me. At the bow of the boat was standing my mother and she did not look pleased.

☼   ☼   ☼

I was taken directly to the Isle of Glass where the leading Druids, Priestesses of Nimue, and Maiden-Healers were gathered together in council. When we arrived the councilors stood and bowed to my mother in reverence. My mother took a seat on a chair at the foot of the tallest stone in the circle while I was instructed to remain standing next to the altar stone at the exact center of the circle. I knew right away I was in serious trouble. The Druids wore stern expressions of apathy and Faelan refused to meet my gaze. The Priestesses were softer but still admonished me with their eyes. The Maiden-Healers stared at the ground and my mother pursed her lips like a scornful woman berating a misbehaving dog.

"Do you know why you're here?" asked the Senior Priestess of Nimue, a middle-aged woman called Asphodel.

"I think so," I replied.

"You are accused of trespassing upon sacred ground without the consent of the elders or the proper station of an avowed member of the Old Religion," said Faelan scornfully.

"Can you tell us why you would so flippantly break one of our most ancient laws?" asked the oldest of the Maiden-Healers, a mature roman woman named Livia.

"The Crones told me to seek out Oberon," I said. I was determined to be defiant.

The Druids looked at the Priestesses and the Priestesses looked at the ground while my mother narrowed her eyes in suspicion.

"The King of Faerie has not appeared in the Unseen Vale for over a hundred years," said Faelan, "The Crones were mistaken. Their visions are not always accurate. You should have consulted one of the elders in order to understand the severity of the crime you committed."

"I asked my mother," I said, "She denied knowing who Oberon was and told me not to go to the Crossroad. But she knows you he is. He's her grandfather, father to her fey mother, Rhiannon."

"How do you know this?" asked Livia.

"He told me," I replied, "Oberon told me who he was to me. He showed me Rhiannon on her pyre and he commanded that I come to live on the Crossroad with Tristram, Madoc, and Morgana. He said Viviana wouldn't dare ignore his commands."

Many of the councilors shifted in their seats as I spoke and it was clear they were divided as to whether or not I was telling the truth. Faelan, who was by nature a skeptic, looked at me as though he was compelling me to tell the truth while my mother scowled like a banshee come to claim a soul for Catsubodhva.

"It matters not what the boy claims," said Faelan, "he has broken the law of our ancestors and the proscribed punishment is clear. He must be ejected at once from the Unseen Vale. Send him back to Lodecran and let us be rid of his insolence."

I was suddenly overwhelmed by a fiery desire to run furlong at Faelan and rip him from his chair. To hold him above my head with the strength of the fey coursing in my veins, to tear him limb from limb and offer his heart to the dark goddess called Mab. I opened my mouth to defend myself and instead words of the Ogham billowed forth, filling the air like a note strummed upon a harp, echoing down the Tor and out across the calm waters of the Brackish Lake.

"Den miloún gia ména san éna város géros ótan ítan esý pou mou dimiourgíthike gia na apotýchei," I said with the voice that was not my own.

It was as though Faelan had been punched in the stomach as the color drained from his face. The other Druids' eyes were as wide as a palace archway and the hair on the arms of the Priestesses was standing on end. The Maiden-Healers stared at the ground, covering their ears, and my mother stood from her chair in anger.

"How dare you utter the Ogham without training," she barked, "Our language is sacred. You seem not to care about anything we hold dear, child, and I will not allow your rebellious attitude to go unchecked. You cannot stay here. I thought you were the hope of the future but you're just like your father, a failure and a fool."

The other councilors feared to speak as Viviana loomed over me. Her slap was hard and cold. It stung as my face was contorted and my neck jarred. I refused to cry even though I was still a child and the pain was something foreign to me. Viviana's rage subsided as quickly as it appeared and she regained her usual stoic countenance. She looked at me with hateful eyes and then returned to her seat.

"I have made my position known," she said, "but it is not by my will that judgment is passed. Let the Council vote as it always does and let the verdict be swift in coming."

The councilors rose as Faelan produced a bronzed pitcher and Livia two marbles for each councilor, one red, the other black. The councilors took their marbles, concealed them in their hands, and returned to their seats. When everyone was again reseated Faelan first put a marble in the pitcher, one of the two he'd been given and a color I couldn't see. He then stood and walked around the circle to each councilor who likewise deposited one of their marbles in the pitcher. The last person to cast their vote was my mother, visibly placing a black marble in the pitcher. I assumed the black ones were a vote for me to be exiled and the red were for me to stay. There were eleven councilors in the circle meaning six votes would constitute a majority and assure my fate one way or the other.

It was Asphodel who counted the votes. Seven black and four red. It was decided. I would be exiled immediately from the Unseen Vale, sent back to Lodecran in shame, forced to join the Nazarenes and live out my days as the obscure ruler of a distant kingdom. I was shocked and bewildered. I made up my mind I would do no such thing. They might be able to force me out of Avalon but they couldn't make me leave Britain. I would stay on the Isle of Glass with Eogan.

"You are banished," said my mother.

"Send him at once to the Isle of Christians and let us be done with this," barked Faelan.

"I agree," said Livia.

"As do I," added Asphodel.

"But I do not," said a voice from the entrance to the Stone Circle, the familiar voice of Taliesin, Merlin of all the Britons.

"Forgive me, Master," said Faelan, "but the boy has broken the law and the votes have been cast. Not even you have the authority to veto the ruling of the Council of the Round Stones."

"You're right, I do not. But I know someone who does," replied Taliesin as he came to stand beside me in the center of the circle. He placed his hands in the sky above his head and opened his mouth to speak, filling the air with his magnanimous voice.

"In éla tóra patéras tou neráides ston kýklo tis génnisis sas," he said with a terrifying tone.

There came a sound like thunder clapping and the earth beneath us shook. The councilors were knocked out of their chairs, sinking to the ground from the force of the tremors. Only Viviana remained seated and untouched, extending her own powerful aura into the air around her to protect her from the mystical onslaught. When the event subsided, there was a third figure standing in the center of the circle with me and Taliesin. It was Oberon, the King of Faerie, arrayed in all his supernatural glory, with light emanating from his naked flesh and his head wreathed in a golden halo so blinding I was forced to look away.

"The boy stays in the Unseen Vale," he commanded, "He will live on the Crossroad with the Healer, the Warrior, and the Scholar. I will not be disobeyed in this, Viviana. You are my daughter's daughter. The blood of the fey courses through your veins, a blood that bends to my will as surely as the sun rises in the east."

My mother looked from her father to her grandfather and then back at me. The other councilors had returned to their seats as my mother rose from hers. The Priestesses of Nimue stood and followed her as she made her way to the entrance of the Stone Circle. They were, in turn, followed by the Maiden-Healers but the Druids remained sitting. Just before she started down the processional way, Viviana turned back and sighed.

"The boy stays," she commanded, "but he is your responsibility, father. Let him and the others go to live where Oberon asks but, they will do so alone, without the support of Avalon."

Chapter Seven
"Taliesin Speaks"

"The boy will not be alone," said Taliesin as my mother began down the processional path, "I will take him as my student and apprentice and he will one day take my place as Merlin."

"As you wish, father," said Viviana before she disappeared down the slope of the processional way.

"Follow me," Taliesin said to me and he led me out of the Stone Circle and down the Tor Hill towards the docks. We stopped at the House of Maidens and got Morgana and then the three of us boarded a barge and set out across the lake to the Isle of Oak. Tristram was reluctant to come but Madoc was more than willing and Morgana was thrilled that Madoc was coming along. It was obvious she had a crush. Together with Taliesin, the four of us were rowed to the Crossroad. We scaled the steps and followed the stream into the garden.

"This is where I will leave you," said Taliesin, "I will return soon to begin your training."

Taliesin retreated back down the steps while Tristram, Madoc, Morgana, and I continued into the garden. I showed them the pyre with Rhiannon's body on it at the heart of the garden and tried to call Oberon but he would not come. We decided to explore the rest of the island and eventually came upon a small clearing at the top of the hill, near the headwaters of the stream running down into the gulley and beyond to the Brackish Lake. It was a cloudy day but it was clear the sun was beginning to fall behind the distant horizon so we decided to split up, each with our own task. Tristram went to gather firewood, Madoc started building a shelter, Morgana started breaking out the food and stores we brought with us in the barge to cook a meal and boil water, while I set to work gathering moss and underbrush to make beds. We decided that night as we sat around the fire that we would build our home there by the headwaters looking out across the Brackish Lake at the other Holy Isles, at the life we were leaving behind for Oberon, and the prophecy of the Crones.

☼   ☼   ☼

It took us nearly five months to build a small four room cottage with a stonework hearth and thatch roof to serve as our home. In all that time we never saw any of the Druids, Priestesses, or Maiden-Healers. They were reluctant to disobey a command from Faelan and Viviana. The Fenfolk were not so reticent. They were not vowed to serve the Gods and Goddesses and thus were not under the jurisdiction of the Druids or my mother. They came to the island regularly with food and provisions. Taliesin also came often, as did Elaine and Morgause. The four of us soon fell into a routine to ensure our survival alone at the Crossroad. Madoc assumed the role of leader and provider. He would fish and take the boat to the other islands to hunt small game. Morgana was the gatherer, finding fruits and nuts and turning them into jams and butters. Tristram tended the fire and washed the clothes and dishware in the stream. I cut firewood and kept the cottage clean but I spent most of my time with Taliesin, learning the Mysteries and the magick of our ancestors. Taliesin had chosen me as his apprentice. It was his duty to ensure that I complete my training, take the vows of a Druid, and go on to become his successor as the Merlin.

Taliesin picked up where Faelan left off. Now that I had been imbued with the knowledge of the Ogham by Oberon I was ready to start learning how to conjure the elements by invoking the power of the elementals. At first I had trouble concentrating. My mind would drift and I'd think about my mother or Oberon, Morgana, Madoc, or Tristram. Taliesin sternly chastised me many times for my inability to focus. For nearly three months we worked without any success until, at last, I called a mighty wind from the west and then caused a spark to grow into a bonfire. I still couldn't cause the earth to quake and water only responded minimally to my spells but Taliesin was impressed enough to move on to my next lesson.

Taliesin explained there were five principles of magick that every Initiate must learn before taking vows to become a Druid: how to conjure the elements, how to Glamour, how to call a Spell of Protection, how to cast a Hex, and how to cross through the Veil back to the outside world. Since I showed adequate advancement in controlling the elements we spent the following weeks focusing on the Glamour. Glamouring required the practitioner to bend the light around them so that they might alter their appearance in subtle yet convincing ways. I'd seen my mother and Oberon using the Glamour so I thought I'd be able to master it quickly. I was completely misguided in that thought. My focus had improved but, just as I found a new level of devotion to my studies I was faced with a new challenge. I started puberty. I was nearing my fourteenth birthday. My voice was cracking, my body developed a strange odor, and I started growing hair in the manly places. I was also distracted by thoughts of sex, not sex with girls, but sex with other men. I was attracted to other men and I knew it but I kept it quiet, a secret I shared with no one for fear of what it would mean to my future and my friends.

Madoc and I were best friends and our friendship with Tristram had also been renewed since we came to live on the Crossroad but I feared what they would think if they knew about that part of me that desired them in a lustful way. Just a few weeks before I started going through the change, Madoc finally gave in to Morgana's advances and they made their relationship official. They shared the larger of the two bedrooms in our cottage, while Tristram and I shared the smaller. I wasn't attracted to Tristram so our cohabitation was relatively easy. It was not so easy to convince Taliesin that I was still committed to my learning. He saw my focus slipping and knew there was something on my mind. As my grandfather as well as my teacher, he decided to talk to me about what my feelings meant.

"What in damnation is wrong with you, boy?" asked Taliesin after my millionth failed attempt at trying to Glamour.

"I've just got a lot on my mind," I replied.

"You're going through the change. It's natural for you to be preoccupied but you need to buckle down and learn this. You're about to be fourteen, only two years from manhood, only two years from your vows. If you haven't mastered the five principles, you cannot become a Druid. You understand that, right?"

"It's you who doesn't understand," I snapped.

Taliesin smiled a crooked grin.

"I was a boy once, believe it or not," he said, "I know where your mind is wandering. You're thinking about girls, about what you could do with one if you were given the chance."

"Not exactly," I said.

"It's boys then. Doesn't matter, it's the same principle. Men who let themselves give into their sexual urges are not good for much else. All they want is to rut and rut again. That's why Druids take a vow to only experience carnal pleasure on the night of the Beltane Rites. At all other times we remain chaste, unless called directly by the Gods and Goddesses to break our vow. Kernos sees no distinction between men who lay with women and those who lay with other men. We are all called to the same discipline."

It was good to hear that I wasn't a freak, that Kernos didn't think less of me for my urges. Taliesin gave me the confidence I needed to refocus on my studies. I didn't stop thinking about intimacy with other men but I forced the thought to the back of my mind. In the following days I mastered the Glamour. I transformed myself from myself into a roman soldier, dressed in armor and holding a spear. My face essentially remained the same, though my jaw became more pronounced and my eyes darkened to a chocolate brown. My hair turned brown and my nose hooked at the bridge. I hardly recognized myself when Taliesin held up a looking glass for me to examine the results of my spell. Then, with a shake of my shoulders, the illusion melted away and I was myself again. Taliesin asked me to enact the same disguise three more times that same afternoon before declaring that I was ready to begin learning the third principle, how to call a Spell of Protection to keep myself and those around me safe, to extend the energy of my aura outward and form a barrier of magick energy.

☼　　☼　　☼

Another year passed without incident and I found myself almost fifteen. We were still living on the Crossroad. Morgana and Madoc were still hopelessly in love, Tristram was still a bookworm, and I was still learning magick from Taliesin. The only key difference was that Morgause had come to live on the Crossroad alongside us, an inconvenience I was barely able to tolerate given her attitude and behavior.

Morgause was seventeen and ready to go out into the world to find a husband but my mother refused to take her through the veil, just as she had refused to allow Morgause to become a Priestess or Maiden-Healer. She made no qualms about hiding her desire to learn magick. She was lustful for both men and power and I could see in her the enemy the Crones had spoken of in their vision. She made me uneasy, as did her unnatural ability to control Morgana. Morgause convinced Morgana to give up her training as a Maiden-Healer and turn her attention towards earthly pleasures. Morgause was constantly running off to the Watch Hill to bed down with men of the Eponi or young Fenfolk of both genders. I was starting to despise Morgause and she had no love for me. It was rumored amongst the Fenfolk that Morgause was learning dark magick in the service of the goddess, Mab, but no one had proof and disbelieved someone could serve the sinister darkness secretly within the Unseen Vale.

"I just don't understand why Viviana won't let me leave," complained Morgause as she sat with me, Tristram, Morgana, and Madoc at the table just outside our cottage. We were having a simple breakfast of eggs and biscuits in the fresh air of a cool summer morning. Morgana and Madoc were intertwined together and the sight of them set Morgause off on one of her typical tirades.

"I'm sure Viviana has her reasons for keeping you here," I said.

"Like you'd know," spat Morgause, "I mean she doesn't even talk to you…your own mother. Our mother has a husband and sons to tend. If she didn't she'd be here with us…that is certain."

Morgause's words stung. I felt like an orphan in so many ways. My father was dead, I hadn't seen Eogan or Genovefa since coming to the Unseen Vale, and my mother treated me like a criminal instead of a son. If it hadn't been for the kindness of my Aunt Elaine I would've felt like I had no family whatsoever. Morgana, Morgause, and Madoc were my cousins but we weren't raised together and they felt more like friends. At least Morgana and Madoc did. Morgause was more of an enemy.

"All I wanted was to be a Priestess and she wouldn't let me," continued Morgause, "Now I'm a woman. I want to go out into the world and find a good husband, one that recognizes my needs. A rich, handsome duke or king with a penchant for showering me with gifts."

"Like that'll happen," joked Morgana, "there isn't a prince out there who could put up with your attitude."

Morgause glared in her sister's direction and Morgana became silent at once. Morgana liked to poke at Morgause but Morgause was the dominant sister. She had a way of forcing Morgana to do things she wouldn't otherwise think to do and often shirked the blame onto Morgana when the pair of them would be caught and punished. Morgana idolized her older sister and, without their mother and brothers, she was her only true family on the Holy Isles. They never grew close to Tristram and kept me at arm's length but both viewed Madoc as a living god, fawning over him like peasants bowing to kiss the feet of their king. Madoc had grown exceedingly attractive, with long blonde hair and fair, flawless skin. His muscles rippled and his smile could melt an ice cube in the middle of a subzero snow storm. Even I found myself thinking of him in a sexual way, wondering what it would be like to touch his chest, to feel the nape of his neck with my tongue. I thought there could never be a more beautiful specimen of burgeoning manhood but I was bound by my service to Kernos. I would not lay with man or woman until after taking my vows and then only at the Beltane Rites.

Madoc was the one thing that Morgana refused to relinquish to her sister and they occasionally fought when Morgause would be consumed by her usual jealousy. Aunt Elaine would intercede and protect her only son from the jackals she saw Morgana and Morgause to be. That same morning Aunt Elaine arrived as we were finishing our breakfast and made quick work of Morgause's sour disposition.

"Complaining is very unbecoming of a lady," said Elaine, "you will never find a worthy husband, Morgause, if you drone on incessantly about how unfair life has been. Try to be more like Galahad…I don't think I've ever heard the boy complain. Speaking of, walk with me child, there's something I want to talk to you about."

Elaine and I walked downstream towards the gulley where my Grandmother Rhiannon was laid upon her pyre but we avoided her remains. Elaine refused to see her mother. Instead, we stayed with the stream until we came to the tiny waterfall where the stream's water cascaded down to meet the Brackish Lake. Elaine chose a nice grassy spot to sit down and together we watched two male black swans swimming with a gaggle of cygnets, splashing happily amidst the reeds. Once, after I told Elaine I preferred the company of men, she told me a story about the black swans. Sometimes a male black swan will take another male as their partner for life. They would couple temporarily with a female and then, once she'd laid her eggs, they'd kick her out of the nest and raise the cygnets themselves. Elaine showed me that all things in nature follow their true selves. It was comforting but that morning she didn't want to talk about swans.

"I hear you've already mastered four of the five principles," she said, "I think my father was wise to choose you as his apprentice. You'll be an excellent Merlin."

"You're preparing to try and cross the veil, right?" asked Elaine.

"My final lesson before I take my vows," I said triumphantly.

"I need you to do something for me, Galahad," said Elaine in a serious tone, "I need you to carry a message to someone in the outside world. His name is Accolon. I need you to take this to him."

Elaine produced a small scroll from the pocket of her gown, sealed with the emblem of the Orkneys. I took the scroll and put it in the pocket of my gray robes before asking Elaine a question.

"Can't Viviana or Taliesin take your message to this Accolon next time they visit the Christian monks?" I asked.

"They cannot know about this, Galahad. Promise me you won't say anything to anyone," said Elaine.

"I promise," I replied and I meant it. Elaine had been the kindest woman to me since coming to the Unseen Vale. This was a way for me to repay the favor.

☼　　☼　　☼

It was six days after Elaine handed me her message that Taliesin took me to the Isle of Glass so I could try and transport myself across the veil and back into the outside world. It was the first time I'd left the Crossroad in almost two years and I was amazed I'd forgotten the beauty of the rest of the Holy Isles. A Fenfolk man I didn't know paddled us to the Isle of Glass. I expected to see a gaggle of Maiden-Healers out tending their gardens but there was no one to be found as we disembarked from the barge.

"They were warned of your coming," said Taliesin as we walked toward the processional way and the Stone Circle above. He was referring to the order from my mother forbidding any Priestesses, Maiden-Healers, or Druids from having contact with me or the others. After two years, Viviana was no less inclined to forgive me than she was the night Oberon forced her to concede to his demands. I tried to ignore the obvious pain I felt from the realization that my mother would likely never forgive me for going to the Crossroad and for looking on the remains of her dead mother. I knew that's what her anger was about; it wasn't that I broke the law, it was the fact that I intruded on a private space shared only by Viviana and her mother.

The sky was cloudy and it was drizzling rain as we entered the Stone Circle at the top of the Tor Hill. A foggy haze had set in below, obscuring the other Holy Isles and casting a dull gray across the landscape. Taliesin stood at the entrance and I moved to stand at the tallest of the monolithic stones forming the Sacred Circle. I put my hand on its cold surface and closed my eyes, focusing on connecting my essence with the powerful energy coursing through the stones.

"Remember," said Taliesin, "Picture this world dissolving as you speak the incantation, focus on the other islands, on the Christian commune you once called home. Think of familiar faces there that can anchor you to the outside world as you make the transition."

I did exactly as Taliesin commanded. I pictured the Stone Circle vanishing with only the stone I was touching still standing, just like in the outside world. I thought about the little octagonal huts of the monks strewn around the longhouse they called their Church, and I pictured the little convent across the Western Hill with its gardens and statues of the Virgin and the Apostles. I wished for Eogan, to see his face, to recall his voice, and I remembered Father Jimellus with his gravelly voice and tonsured hair, preaching about his Master and the good virtue of all true-hearted Christians. I was never a follower of the Nazarene Church but I understood its value, counterbalancing the harsher, more hardline theology of the Nicene Christians across the Straits in Gaul and the roman interior. Then my mind turned to my father, to the last time I saw him, and my heart was filled with sorrow. I almost let my thoughts wander to a point of distraction until Taliesin spoke and reminded me of my intentions.

"Now is the time, Galahad," said Taliesin, "speak the incantation and be moved now from this world."

I took a deep breath and recalled the Ogham words meant to open the door between the worlds and deliver me to the other Isle of Glass.

"Anoíxte tin pórta metaxý ton kósmon kai epitrépste mou na perásei mésa," I said.

As my voice echoed across the veil the world around me melted away and I was at once taken back to the place I once called home. I was still standing with my hand on the tallest stone but the other stones of the circle had disappeared. The processional way was gone and down in the small grassy glade sat the little Christian commune. The waters of the Fens were low, exposing trails and muddy pastures where monks were busy gathering algae and other medicinal plants. Another monk was standing near where I appeared tending a small white birch tree growing near the stone monolith. When the monk caught sight of me he smiled and came running. It was only when he was a few feet away that I recognized him. It was Eogan.

"By the name of God the Father," smiled Eogan, "I was beginning to think I'd never see you again."

Chapter Eight
"Knights of Avalon"

"You've gotten so tall," said Eogan, "and your hair is so long. Come, come. We will catch up over some tea by the fire."

If felt like I'd never been gone, like I had only dreamed my years in Avalon but now was awake and returning to my real life amongst the monks. The only reminder that it was real was how much Eogan had changed. He was starting to ebb away from his youth and it showed in the light wrinkles around his eyes and in the graying of his hair. He wore with pride the brown robes and wooden cross of a monk and I knew he'd made good on his promise to join the Nazarene commune after I left. He was grinning from ear to ear. Somehow I knew he'd been happy.

Eogan led me to one of the octagonal cottages on the outskirts of the commune which I assumed was his home. He invited me inside and I sat at a little table while he stoked the fire and put on the tea. Once the tea was finished, Eogan put it on the table with two wooden cups and a plate of biscuits. He sat across from me and sipped from his cup, looking me over from head to toe like an authoritative headmaster ensuring his pupils are adhering absolutely to the school dress code.

"So, how has life been in the Unseen Vale?" asked Eogan, "Tell me everything."

I spent the next half-hour recounting my studies and adventures in Avalon. I told him about living on the Crossroad and about my grandmother's unchanging remains on the funeral pyre at the heart of the garden. I spoke of Taliesin and his decision to name me his apprentice and I told him about my lessons to call the elements, use the Glamour, call a Spell of Protection, how to cast a Hex, and, of course, how to cross the veil between Avalon and the outside world. Eogan listened intently the whole time, sipping his tea and nodding occasionally to ensure me I had his undivided and enthusiastic attention.

"Now tell me about you?" I said to Eogan after I finished telling my long and descriptive tale. For a moment he looked as though he might cry as he stared out the little window next to his stove, fixating on some far away point, not on the horizon but within himself.

"The darkness your mother spoke of the day you left. It has arrived," said Eogan with sadness, "I think it was here when your father was murdered in cold blood."

"My father wasn't murdered," I said, "You told me it was his heart. That it gave out from the stress of coming here and seeing Viviana again."

"That's what I thought at the time but one of the monks here, his name is Varis, he used to be a physician in Rome. After you left for the Unseen Vale he examined your father's remains and found clear signs that your father was poisoned. Jimellus ordered an investigation, hoping the murderer was still on the Isle and could be rooted out but then…"

Eogan stopped speaking and looked at the ground.

"Then what, Eogan?" I asked.

"Father Jimellus died the same way as your father," he said, "and the Fenfolk medicine man, Slider, examined Jimellus. He said it wasn't poison…it was witchcraft. Dark magick, the kind practiced by the followers of the dark goddess, Mab."

"Jimellus is dead?" I uttered.

"Unfortunately he is, and we are lost. No sooner was Jimellus laid to rest than a new Father arrived to take control of the commune. He calls himself Fortunatus, though I doubt that is his true name. He is a Nicene Christian, a Roman Catholic, and he abhors the Nazarene way of believing in the Christ. Most the old brethren are gone, replaced by angry Nicene monks who mutilate their flesh and starve themselves for the sake of piety. If I hadn't sworn to remain here and keep watch for you, I would've left for Lodecran with the others. For nearly two years life here was utterly unbearable. If the Knights didn't come when they did, my wits would've been lost along with my faith. But that's enough of that. I am so glad to see you, Galahad, glad to see you are well."

"There are Knights here?" I asked, my interest peaked.

"They arrived six weeks ago," said Eogan, "they have a camp near the Fenfolk village. They say they felt the darkness and were called by Kernos and Nimue to return to the Holy Isles, but no one has come to bring them to the Unseen Vale and so they wait."

"Are they Ambrose's knights?" I asked.

"No, dear boy. They are the Knights of Avalon."

☼   ☼   ☼

Eogan took me across the marsh back to the mainland, where the small Fenfolk village sat on the edge of the Fens. Nearby were a dozen tents around a large fire pit with a cooking pot hanging over the flames on a tripod. The Knights were gathered around the fire awaiting their afternoon meal. Each was dressed in the leather and furs favored by the Picts. There were eight in total, some old and some young. The oldest of them sat at the heart of their group like a massive bear waiting to consume a rabbit. He had tribal tattoos across his arms and face. His dirty blonde hair was clumped into thick dreadlocks as was his lengthy beard. As we approached he stood and came to greet us sword in hand.

"We've had enough of your monks comin' here and tryin' to convert us to your bloody religion," he said gruffly to Eogan.

"Stand down, Brannos," said another Knight, "that's my brother's son. I'd know him anywhere…looks just like his mother, that one."

The man who spoke was seated closest to the fire with a hood pulled over his head. It wasn't until he pulled the hood down that I recognized him. It was my father's brother, my Uncle Bors, King of the Armorica. He looked exactly as he had three years before when we parted company at the home of King Drustan, Tristram's father, burly and bald with red freckly skin.

"We don't want Christians here," reiterated Brannos.

"Do I look like a Christian," I said confidently. I was dressed in the gray robes of an Initiate. My skin was dark from constant exposure to the never-ending sunlight in Avalon and my reddish black hair fell in hundreds of braids to the middle of my back. I looked like a man of the Tribes, of the Fenfolk, in almost every way. Brannos looked me over once and then twice before deciding I wasn't a threat.

"You'll have to forgive old Brannos. He's not too fond of the Christians and their talk of damnation," said another of the Knights, a tall, broad chested blonde seated closest to where we were standing.

"I understand," said Eogan, "I too grow weary of the Nicene talk of hell and purgatory. I am not like them, brothers. I was born a Briton and I will die a Briton. My devotion to the God of the Nazarenes does not keep me from remembering the old ways. Once I was one of you. I was a bard, a master of the harp and flute. I know what your devotion means to you."

"Then you know our lives are in jeopardy," said another Knight, a smaller, thin man with a long wiry beard and black hair.

"Let me introduce you to the Knights," said Bors, "the muscly guy with the blonde hair is Cunamaglos and that black-bearded fool is Neithon. You know the old guy is Brannos. Then there's Ector, Gwynedd, Gnaeus, and Mareth. The other two are out scouting for food. I'll save their introductions for when they return."

Ector was a fat redheaded man who looked like a living juggernaut and carried an enormous battleax. Gwynedd was also red-haired but he was thin and effeminate in his features. Ector was in his late forties, Gwynedd was barely twenty. Gnaeus was very Roman in his looks, with a hooked nose and olive skin but he wore the garments of a Briton warrior and carried a golden scythe as his weapon. He was probably in his forties but he had a youthful look about him which made him attractive and appealing. The final man, Mareth, had the same reddish black hair as me but his features were fair and freckled like the Gaels. He wore roman armor and carried a pair of gladius swords. All the Knights were big, strong men, but they were mostly middle-aged and strangely outdated.

"Why are you here?" I asked Bors as we settled into a couple of seats by the fire and the other Knights ate their rabbit stew.

"War is upon us again," said Bors, "the Saxons are rallying in the north, behind black banners adorned with a white dragon. The soothsayers have prophesied it is Vortigern risen from the dead to reclaim the throne of the Britons and usher in a thousand years of darkness. We are come to seek the guidance of Kernos and Nimue that they would show us how to combat the looming shadow and save our people."

I stared at Bors in shock and was suddenly overwhelmed by an unnatural chill. My body shook and buckled as I fell to the ground, convulsing in pain. I would've thought it poison but the only thing I ate or drank was the tea prepared for me by Eogan in his cottage. My stomach started to burn and I erupted in sweat. Bors' eyes went wide with alarm and the other Knights dropped their bowls, jumping to their feet and huddling around me as I writhed on the ground in agony. I was sure my life was over, that I was being called to the doors of death by Catsubodhva for some grievous sin I had yet to commit. Eogan stood there staring at me in shock, knowing the symptoms I was enduring all too well. It was the same manner in which my father died. My head was aching like I had a fifty pound stone sitting on my brow and my heart was racing, threatening to stop at any moment. Just as I was sure I was meant to take my last breath the Fenfolk medicine-man, Slider, pushed his way through the Knights and forced a cool tonic down my throat. The fire in my stomach immediately subsided and seconds later I stopped shaking. I sat up with the help of Eogan and looked at the Knights in a delirium.

"What the hell was that?" demanded Bors.

"Boy was poisoned," replied Slider, "Man give boy holly berries and yew. He die if not given antidote in time."

I was fatigued and dizzy but the worst of it was over. Eogan helped me to my feet and then suggested that I take some rest in his cottage but Bors was determined to protect me and insisted that I take a nap in his tent instead, where he could keep a watchful eye on me. Bors inquired as to whether anyone present knew how to cross the veil and seek out the assistance of Viviana or the Merlin but I was the only one and in no shape to even attempt to open a doorway between the worlds.

I rested for almost six hours. When I awoke it was the middle of the night most the Knights were asleep in their tents. Only Ector, Mareth, and Bors were still up. They were sitting at the hearth, where a fire was roaring, wrapped in thick furs. The air was chilly and thick with dew. I felt like returning to Bors' tent and wrapping myself in his blankets but I wanted to eat something, regain my strength, and then open the doorway so that the Knights and I could enter Avalon. Bors stood when he caught sight of me, as though he was a concerned mother jumping up to assist her beleaguered son in his moment of need. He took me by the arm and sat me in his seat then poured me some broth from the cauldron hanging over the fire. The food was a welcome sight. I ate as much as my stomach could handle and felt the warmth of the broth instantly rejuvenating my body, making me feel more alert and refreshed.

"I think I can lead you into Avalon now," I said after finishing my third helping of broth.

"I don't think so, boy," said Bors, "Eogan told me it was your first time opening a doorway. You haven't even taken the vows yet. You don't know enough magick, you don't have enough strength to carry us all into Avalon. I don't doubt your dedication but I won't risk any of the Knights' lives with an Initiate."

"Then I'll go back and tell Taliesin to come and get you," I replied.

"You'll want to wait until the sun rises into the sky," said Eogan as he walked into camp, "Druids channel the energy of the sun to work their magick, just as Priestesses use the power of the earth, and the Maiden-Healers the power of the moon."

"I never knew you were a bard," I said to Eogan as he sat down next to me by the fire.

"I was in another life," he said longingly, "I think you should wait until morning to pass back into the Unseen Vale. Tell the Merlin that the

Knights of Avalon are here waiting for an audience and he will come back and retrieve them."

"That would be best," added Bors, "besides, our other two men haven't come back from their scouting mission yet."

"What are their names?" I asked, curiosity taking ahold.

"The older one's name is Agrivain," said Bors, "he's old Brannos' son. The other one is just a spell older than you. He isn't even a Knight yet, not really. He's Agrivain's only son, Brannos' grandson, so we couldn't just leave him behind. His name's Accolon."

As Bors spoke the name Accolon I remembered the scroll buried deep in the pocket of my robes, the one given to me by Elaine with the instructions that I hand it off to someone named Accolon with the utmost secrecy. I returned to bed that night with every intention of fulfilling my promise to my aunt and delivering the scroll upon Accolon's return. I wasn't sure what she wanted from the man but I was determined to find out.

☼   ☼   ☼

I was up with the sun the next morning. It was warm and the air was still as I emerged from Bors' tent to find him sitting in the same spot where I'd left him. He never went to bed, keeping watch all night just as he had promised. Bors was always protective of his blood and we were family. He was cooking some prime cuts of bacon and eggs brought by the Fenfolk. He held a plate up for me as I approached but I waved it away. I had business to tend to and I didn't want to wait any longer than necessary before returning to Avalon.

"Have the scouts returned?" I asked as Bors stuffed his face with the food on the plate meant for me.

"They got back just before sunrise," he replied between chews.

"Where are they?" I asked.

"Agrivain's in his tent getting some sleep," said Bors, "and Accolon is down at the water washing up."

"Thanks," I said, leaving behind the fire and the little encampment to make my way down to the nearby banks of the Rive Sabine where it flowed out to mix with the brackish backflow of the Fens. Several Fenfolk men were out on barges fishing for sturgeon while their women were on the banks of the Fens scrubbing linens. It was the perfect day for outdoor activities, the sun was warm and the water was calm. The air was still and the smell of blossoms filled the air.

Then I saw him out in the shallows of the river and the rest of the world stopped moving. He was seventeen or eighteen and he was the most beautiful thing I'd ever seen. He was naked and every muscle from his biceps to his chest to his buttocks was perfectly formed, taut and smooth. He had the fair alabaster skin of the Britons but he was tanned from many days spent in the sun. His torso was hairless and wet and made my loins growl and my manhood grow. His hair fell in chocolate brown waves to his shoulders and his face was like the face of a god amongst men. I found myself staring incessantly, hinking about tearing off my own clothes to join him in the water, to latch myself onto his beautiful body and never let go. He saw me as I approached the edge of the water and came splashing up like a playful otter investigating a curiosity on the shore with a smile on his face that would melt even the coldest heart.

"Are you a Druid?" he asked unexpectedly and I found myself at a loss for words. I clearly looked the part of a Druid. An unlearned man would not know the difference between a vowed member of the order and a lowly Initiate. I felt myself blushing which only made him grin more intensely. Clearly he was used to my reaction and relished in the acknowledgment of his masculine beauty.

"Did you need something?" he asked and I was finally snapped back to reality, remembering my mission.

"I have a message for you from the Lady Elaine," I said, pulling the sealed scroll from the pocket in my robes.

"Never heard of her," replied Accolon as he waded out of the water and wrapped a leather loincloth around his privates. He shook off his hair and then reached out to take the scroll. He broke the seal and unrolled it, looking intently at the page in utter confusion

"I can't read this," he said handing the scroll back to me. I looked down at it and immediately recognized the lettering as the Ogham. Without thinking about the fact that the scroll had a spell written upon it, I read the words aloud.

"Apó ti theá kai tin eroméni tou magikoú káno," I said, "Dýo kardiés mas gia pánta nikísei os éna."

As suddenly as I spoke the words I regretted it, but it was too late. I felt a flutter in my heart and instinctively grabbed my chest. Accolon did the same. My trained eyes could see a golden aura expanding outward from Accolon and also from me, blending together like two primary colors forming a complex hue. I could think of nothing but Accolon. I wanted to touch him, to feel his flesh beneath my fingertips, to know his manhood with my tongue. He was staring at me with lustful eyes and started to advance towards me, his arms outstretched to wrap me in a tight embrace. I didn't resist as he tangled his arms around me and pulled me into him, forcing me to know every muscle of his body and to feel his breath against my cheek. I wanted to kiss him, to pull him into me and never let him go. I would've done exactly that if it hadn't been for a sudden interruption.

"What have you done?" said a stern woman's voice and I turned around to find my mother looking down at us from the nearby path leading back to the Knights' encampment.

"It is not his fault," said Taliesin as he appeared behind Viviana, "It is not once but twice that Galahad has been attacked in the last twelve hours. He was first poisoned by the villainous hand that murdered his father and then tricked into casting this dark magick. Do not show him your fury, daughter, show him your forgiveness."

"I don't understand," I said even though my mind was still fixed on lustful thoughts of Accolon.

"You have enacted a forbidden spell, a curse meant to falsely bind two hearts together and drive them into insanity thinking about one another every waking hour of every waking day for the rest of their lives," said Viviana with a harsh tone.

"You'll never be able to finish your training now, let alone take your vows," she continued, "learning magick requires intense concentration. You'll never think about anything but his man again."

"Who gave you that spell?" asked Taliesin.

I was reluctant to confess because of my promise but Taliesin compelled me to tell the truth with his familiar stare.

"It was Elaine," I said.

Chapter Nine
"Shadow in the Flames"

"Elaine?" said my mother, "Elaine did this?"

"We don't know that it was Elaine," said Taliesin, "the scroll could've been switched after Elaine gave it to Galahad or she could've been forced against her will to participate. Never jump to conclusions, Viviana, for often you will find you are wrong."

I was barely listening. I was staring at Accolon's chest and he was fixated on my groin. We were only seconds from tearing into each other, exploring each other's bodies with all of our senses but Taliesin drew us back into reality with a snap of his fingers, a sound that echoed across the River Sabine and beyond with the power of his magick intent. My insane and uncontrollable desire for Accolon subsided a bit and allowed me to return to a rational state of mind. I was weeks from my fifteenth birthday but my training has made me mature beyond my years. I understood what I was feeling for Accolon was not real, it was a spell, a falsity cooked up by some dark witch or warlock for the purpose of distracting me and preventing me from realizing my destiny as the next Merlin.

"Even if Elaine had a conscious hand in this game, she could not have been the one who poisoned Galahad last night," said Taliesin, "There is another, one who even now watches us from just out of sight. Come forth and make yourself known."

Taliesin waved his hand as though he were instructing someone to approach him and suddenly a man was yanked out of the nearby bushes as though he were a dog and Taliesin was holding his leash. I was mortified when I realized it was Eogan. He was wearing his brown habit and large wooden cross but he was anything but pious as he stood there with a devilish look on his face, a fiendish criminal finally caught in the act of perpetrating a heinous and calculated murder. He struggled against Taliesin's invisible grip but no matter how hard he fought he couldn't break free.

"This can't be," I said in shock, "I have known Eogan all my life. He's not a murderer. He's kind and gentle and caring."

"He is all of those things," replied Taliesin, "but he is not himself. He has been hexed. A powerful hex meant to make him an extension of whomever is pulling his strings. The mastermind of all this is looking through his eyes right now, hearing with his ears. Let them hear this..."

Taliesin nodded to Viviana and together they pointed their hands at Eogan, reciting a spell in unison inside their minds that caused Eogan to fall over unconscious. Taliesin and Viviana were advanced enough in the practice of the Druids that they no longer needed to speak their spells aloud unless embarking upon a great act of magick which required them to vocalize their incantations. Meanwhile, Accolon ran back to the encampment and moments later the other nine Knights were present, surrounding Eogan with their weapons drawn.

"There is no need for violence," said Taliesin, "Sheath your weapons. You are in the presence of the Lady of the Unseen Vale."

"And the Merlin of all the Britons," I added.

The Knights did as they were commanded and put away their weapons before dropping to one knee and bowing their heads in Viviana's direction. My mother was greater than any queen to the men of the Tribes who still followed the ways of the Old Religion. Viviana acknowledged their reverence with a wave of her hand, signaling them to rise to their feet.

"Brothers," she said, "We were sent no word that you had arrived here. The darkness that brought Eogan to dark deeds has also disrupted the barrier between this world and Avalon. Our Sight cannot see into this world anymore. But we are here now and we will take you at once with us back into the Unseen Vale."

"Thank you, Lady," said the Knights in unison.

Gwynedd and Mareth picked up Eogan and we all made our way back to the Isle of Glass and up the hill to the monolithic stone. I went to place my hand on the stone and say the incantation to open the door between the worlds but Viviana pulled my arm away.

"That won't be necessary," she said.

Viviana raised her hands above her head and brought them suddenly down to her waist, as though her arms were wings and she a bird trying in vain to fly away. The second her hands reached her waist, the outside world faded and we were standing in the heart of Avalon, within the confines of the Stone Circle, all of us, including the Knights and Eogan. Eogan was still unconscious but he was beginning to twitch, as though he was allergic to the energy of Avalon. His body began to break out in hives and rashes and he moaned incoherently. I worried about his wellbeing. I knelt down beside him and put my hand on his forehead and was overwhelmed by a searing pain stretching up my arm. Viviana pushed me away, severing the connection and relieving the agonizing throb.

"Do not touch him," she snapped, "whatever festers in his soul could easily infect you."

"Go and seek out Elaine, daughter. I will handle this," said Taliesin.

Viviana looked at me with her usual glare and then rushed out of the circle with the Knights on her heels. Accolon hesitated for a second, staring at me with loving eyes but I fought against the urge to run to him and remained focused on Eogan.

"Leave the circle," said Taliesin as he picked up Eogan like a child lifting a ragdoll off the ground and laid him on the altar stone. I did as commanded and moved outside the circle of stones, but I stayed on the Tor Hill, close enough to see what Taliesin was doing. I trusted Taliesin but I feared for Eogan. If he was possessed by a dark curse, exorcising that magick could kill him in a heartbeat. Taliesin pulled his ceremonial dagger from its sheath on his belt, a blade that Druids carry all the time to serve their magical needs. He pointed the tip of the blade at the stone to the left of the entrance of the Stone Circle and then drew a line around the perimeter, stopping when he again reached the stone by the entrance. Once the circle was closed it seemed Taliesin grew younger in appearance. He stood taller and his hands no longer shook. Eogan also looked different, uglier and more seditious, like a psychotic miscreant lurking in the shadows waiting to strike down an unsuspecting victim. When Taliesin spoke, his voice was full of power generating an invisible shockwave that permeated the interior of the circle with its fiery essence.

"Apokalýpsei ton eaftó mou ousía tou skótous," commanded Taliesin. Eogan writhed like a lobster in a pot of boiling water and then suddenly became calm, locked in a forced state of paralysis by the power of Taliesin's potent incantation.

"Who are you?" demanded Taliesin.

"The one whose power you are using this very moment," said Eogan with a voice not his own, "Every drop of magick manifested in this world comes from my pool in the Otherworld, fed by the cosmic waters of the Divine Creator. You have no power over me, Merlin."

"Maybe not," replied Taliesin, "but I have power over the mortal body which you are infesting with your hatred and malevolence."

Taliesin pointed his dagger at where Eogan laid restrained against the altar and spoke with a billowing echo.

"Na fýgei apó aftó to sóma," said Taliesin, "Anevaínei san to smínos kai na epistrépsoun stis aíthouses tis katadíkis."

The cursed presence inside of Eogan laughed maniacally before Eogan began to choke and gag, sputtering foam and bleeding from his eyes. He convulsed and screamed in agony as the altar stone vibrated like a tuning fork beneath him. His face was contorted with a mixture of agony and pleasure and the air within the circle swirled with light. A deep, slow humming rose from the ground, growing louder and louder as it drowned out the natural sounds of the birds and the wind. I almost covered my ears to escape the haunting sound piercing my soul and filling me with dread. Then, just as soon as it started, the humming stopped and Eogan laid lifelessly on the altar, his bloody eyes staring vacantly at the stars. I wanted to run to him, to hold him in my arms and tell him I was sorry for everything he'd endured at my expense. It was almost as hard as losing my father. Eogan was my father's closest friend and confidante. I'd known him all my life and now he was dead. All traces of my life in Lodecran were gone.

"I'm so very sorry, Galahad," said Taliesin as he exited the circle, "We will return his body to the Christians so that he can be buried with a mass and celebration according to his beliefs."

I barely heard Taliesin as he spoke. I was too busy being consumed by sadness. My heart was breaking.

☼　　☼　　☼

"Our enemy is Mab," said Taliesin as he and I arrived at my mother's tower on the Isle of the Font.

"You're sure?" replied my mother in disbelief.

"I would know her voice anywhere," replied Taliesin, "and she still poses a serious threat. Eogan was not her host. She was using the Curse of Commandments to control him, to fill him with the darkness and make him her servant. The darkness was so entrenched inside him that it cost him his life. I fear for the one who is truly afflicted with the burden of carrying Mab's spirit inside of them. Where is Elaine?"

My mother looked as though she might crack from the pressure of the day's events before regaining her composure with a stoic hardening of her aging face.

"The Knights cannot find her," said Viviana, "they fear she has somehow slipped back into the outside world unnoticed but I have assured them it is not possible. Is it, father?"

"Not without alerting me," he said, "even if she crossed through when we were in the outside world I would have known."

"Then she's still here," said Viviana.

"Perhaps she is hiding with the Eponi," said Taliesin, "she has grown close to them in recent days. I've heard whispers she's bedded down with the greatest of their warriors, Gurdik the Tall. If she cannot be found, she is likely hiding within his cottage."

"The Knights searched every house, every stable, she is nowhere to be found," replied Viviana, "I need to consult the fire. Perhaps visions will guide me to the truth of all this."

Taliesin nodded and then looked at me.

"What of the boy?" he asked, as though I weren't standing there, "Shall we send him back to the Crossroad."

"No," said Viviana, "He will stay with me. As long as his mind is clouded by thoughts of the young Knight to whom he is now bound he will be a danger to us."

"Agreed," said Taliesin, "You go to the Fire Pit and I will go and join the Knights. Perhaps with my assistance they will find more answers."

☼   ☼   ☼

The Fire Pit was on the Isle of Stone, one of the forbidden isles I had never visited. It was home to the elusive and mysterious Guardians charged with protecting the sacred treasures of the Druids hidden in the catacombs stretching out for miles beneath the Unseen Vale. I could see four maybe five stone houses built against the sheer incline of the jagged cliff forming the rocky island and thought I could make out a cave entrance amidst the homes. We waited in Viviana's Tower until the sun began to set and then loaded into one of the larger barges of the Fenfolk to make our way to the Isle of Stone. Three of the Senior Priestesses came along but they refused to speak to me or look in my direction. It was clear the shunning ordered by my mother was still being enforced. I was only there because my mother couldn't trust I wouldn't run to Accolon at the first chance and throw myself into his arms. She was right not to trust me. All I could think about was Accolon's naked body glistening in the water of the River Sabine.

We made our way quickly up the staircase cut into the rocky hillside as the quarter waxing moon rose into the heavens above us. Each of the Priestesses was carrying a basket full of different herbs and my mother had anointed herself in oils of jasmine and myrrh. Unlike her normal stately attire, she was wearing nothing but a plain white linen gown. She was barefoot and without jewelry or makeup. She'd removed her braids so that her hair fell wildly down her back like a primal warrior princess leading her people into battle.

The Fire Pit was a large hole dug into a rocky plateau about fifty feet above the waters of the Brackish Lake. The hole was lined with flat river stones and was long enough that someone could lay down inside it and be buried. There was a single Fenfolk man standing near the pit. He had already filled it with kindling and had a stack of firewood piled next to him. Viviana looked intensely at the pit and the kindling erupted into violent orange flames licking at the sky. The Fenfolk man threw firewood into the pit, intensifying the flames into a large, roaring fire. Viviana muttered something under her breath and then removed her white gown, exposing her naked body. I was embarrassed and looked away. She was my mother and the thought of seeing her in such a state sent shivers down my spine.

"Seal the circle," said my mother.

The Priestesses set down their baskets, producing their sacred daggers and drawing a circle just like Taliesin had done when exorcising Eogan, except that this time I found myself inside the circle. Any magick that was conjured would affect me just as much as the Priestesses, my mother, and the Fenfolk man tending the fire. Once the circle was complete, the Priestesses returned to their baskets and began throwing generous amounts of herbs into the flames, causing a thick gray smoke to rise into the air, obscuring the light of the stars and filling the circle with the smell of red sage, monksfoot, and elderberry. My mother stepped up to the edge of the Fire Pit and placed her hands out like she meant to touch the flames before tilting her head back and speaking to the heavens above.

"Alláxete aftés tis flóges apó kókkino se prásino," said Viviana, "Epitrépste mou na doúme ti prépei na dei."

With a violent flicker, the flames of the fire changed from orange to green and rose higher into the sky. Viviana took a deep breath and then stepped into flames. I gasped, expecting her to scream out in agony as the fire burned away her flesh but she was unharmed by the flames. She smiled and then laid down in the pit, disappearing amidst the coals beneath the green tower of flames. The Priestesses took their places at the edge of the Pit and began singing an ancient song in Ogham about the goddess, Nimue, and her love for Kernos. Then a voice rose above the song, the voice of a woman emanating from the flames.

"The tides are turning as the dragons rise to battle," said the voice, "I cannot stop what has been set in motion by my sister. My power even now wanes to its weakest. I am a prisoner in my own palace beyond the veil of the living. Look not to me for your salvation but to my champion. He will come on the wings of a red dragon and bear upon his brow the mark of the True King. Know him well for he will lead you from the darkness into the light everlasting."

"And what of the darkness?" asked one of the Priestesses, "Does it come through the Lady Elaine? Where can she be found?"

"She is here," said another voice from within the fire, one wholly unlike the first. I looked around in shock for Elaine but she was nowhere to be seen. The circle was still closed with only four of us inside and my mother laying in the heart of the Fire Pit.

"She is everywhere," continued the voice, "and she will have her vengeance. I will have my vengeance. I have waited a hundred years to rise from the prison of your making, sister. It is time for you to know what it feels like to be imprisoned and abandoned and watch as I destroy everything you love, starting tonight."

The air grew heavy and cold as the circle broke with a sound like glass being trampled by elephants. The fire flickered and the flames changed from green to orange. Viviana tried to escape but she was held down by an invisible hand. She screamed as the fire bit at her skin like ticks burrowing for blood. The Priestesses were thrown backward to the ground by an intense wind that rose and then died in the blink of an eye. I couldn't think what to do and my heart sank listening to Viviana's cries. Instinctively I stepped forward and put my hands out commanding fiercely in Ogham.

"Echo entolí ti fotiá gia na pethánei," I said with a powerful voice.

For a second I thought my incantation worked as the flames began to dim and flicker but then, in mere seconds, they renewed their ferocity. I tried again and then again but no matter what I did the fire would not release my mother, imprisoned within its destructive web. There was nothing else I could think to do. Luckily, a more competent savior arrived. One of Knights ran passed me and jumped into the pit, dragging my mother out before collapsing on the ground, rolling to put out the flames chewing through his leather breeches and coughing from the smoke. I ran to my mother and breathed a sigh of relief to find her relatively unburnt. She had a few red abrasions on her shoulders and her face was disfigured by intense, scalding burns and blisters. I tried to wake her but she wouldn't regain consciousness. Her eyes were open, staring blankly at the horizon in some bizarre state of catatonia and they had been drained of all their color. Her irises were as white as a mountain peak covered in snow.

"Is she alright?" asked the Knight as he stood and I saw that it was Accolon. I ran to him and wrapped my arms around him. He pulled me into him and returned my embrace with a gentle touch I didn't expect from a warrior and soldier of war.

"What do we do?" he asked as we stood there in each other's arms.

I could think of only one thing.

"Taliesin se chreiázomai," I said in Ogham.

Accolon continued to hold me in his arms as we stood there and listened to the sound of the owls in the nearby trees and the bats flying over the water looking for an evening meal. I wanted to cry but I couldn't. I cried for my father, I cried for Eogan, but I wouldn't cry for Viviana. I was beginning to think I was incapable of shedding real tears for the mother I both hated and loved.

"I don't think she's dead," said Accolon reassuringly.

"She yet lives," said Taliesin as he appeared at the top of the steps leading to the Fire Pit.

"What's happened to her?" I asked.

"Mab has cursed her," replied Taliesin, "She is trapped between this world and the next, imprisoned on the far shores of Faerie."

"Then there's hope," I said.

"Not for you," said a voice from the shadows and my Aunt Elaine stepped into the light. Her face was strangely vacant and she bore deep cuts all across her face. She pointed a twisted finger at me and then spoke with a rasping, demonic voice.

"Ton steílei sti mitéra tou sti gi anámesa stous dýo kósmous," she said and her curse hit me like a brick to the face. Taliesin tried to counter the spell but it was too late. I felt myself falling to the ground as my head throbbed and my vision blurred. With one final breath and a plea for help, I closed my eyes and the world went dark.

Chapter Ten
"Land of Everlasting Twilight"

When I awoke I was lying behind a calm meandering river on a bed of clovers. The air smelled of honey and I could hear frogs croaking in the distance, calling out for a lover in the heat of their lust. I thought about Accolon, about how much my heart was drawn to him. I knew that we were bound together by a spell, that the love burgeoning between us was likely a falsity induced by magick but I hoped somewhere deep inside our feelings were real. I sat up and clutched my hands to my head, expecting to feel unbearable pain from the force of Elaine's curse but I was surprisingly unhurt. I was somewhat lightheaded as I stood to look around, wondering at the simplistic beauty of the strange landscape. I tried to get my bearings by locating one of the Holy Isles but they were nowhere in sight. The Brackish Lake was gone as were the hills and ravines surrounding it. I could see nothing but green rolling hills for miles. There were no signs of life, just the sounds of birds, frogs, and water rushing over stone. I figured my best option would be to follow the river until it brought me to a town or harbor. I turned around to face the water and was startled to see Viviana standing in front of me, unburnt and alive.

"Don't bother trying to find your way home, Galahad," she said, "We are no longer within the confines of the mortal world. We are on the distant shores of Faerie."

Faerie was the world between Avalon and the Otherworld, a place where the spirits of the dead linger to dance and sing while their ethereal bodies are being prepared in the beyond. It was also home to the fey, the supernatural people of my mother's mother, Rhiannon. I expected to see spirits and fey all over the countryside but there was no one, no signs of civilization, and no suggestion of a way home. The last thing I remembered was Elaine's curse hitting me square in the face then falling lifelessly to the ground and I knew why I was there.

"I'm dead," I said in almost a whisper.

"We are not dead," replied Viviana, "at least not yet. Our bodies still endure in Avalon but our spirits are trapped here. The longer we are separated from our flesh, the more likely we will perish. But there is no way to judge time here. A second in Faerie can be a hundred years in the mortal realms, or a minute in the mortal realms can be months here. Time has no meaning in this place but as long as the Maiden-Healers tend our bodies we may yet survive."

"There must be others here," I said.

"There are many others," said Viviana, "but Faerie is vast. We could travel for weeks and not come upon another soul."

"That's what we are here, right? Souls," I said, "But we are still made of flesh and blood."

"You see a body because it is familiar," she said, "in truth we are no more than the vibrational essence of our spirits. If we were truly deceased and lingered here we would start to see ourselves differently, as more light than flesh. As it is, we are not dead and still require that which we can understand. We still need to eat and drink and sleep so I suggest we find shelter, build a fire, and try catching some fish."

☼   ☼   ☼

We found an old fallen tree a mile downriver and decided to use it as the foundation for our shelter. We built walls out of twigs and moss and placed fern fronds down as bedding. Viviana fashioned two fish baskets out of wicker branches and dropped them in the river while I foraged for firewood at the edge of a nearby grove of yew trees. I came across a small orchard of apple trees and picked as many as I could carry before returning to camp to work on starting the fire. I thought I could just use magick to spark a flame in the hearth I fashioned from river stones but, no matter how many times I recited the incantation and focused my mind, I couldn't get a fire to erupt amidst the kindling stacked in the hearth.

"That won't work," said my mother as she approached with three healthy sized whiting caught in her baskets.

"Why not?" I asked in frustration.

"Only fey magick works in Faerie," she said simply.

"But aren't you half-fey?" I asked.

"Yes, and you are a quarter, but neither of us has been trained to use magick in this place. The best we can do is pray and hope Nimue hears us from wherever she has been imprisoned by Mab."

My mother set to work cleaning and gutting the fish while I made a bow fire starter and started rigorously running it across another piece of wood in the hopes of generating a spark. After nearly twenty minutes I succeeded in starting a fire and Viviana placed the fish on the stones at the edge of the hearth to cook. She also fashioned cups out of a couple hollowed out branches and filled them with water from the river. This was the most I'd seen my mother in two years and, though we were in fact only spirits, it was comforting to have her there. The anger I felt for her abandoning me on the Crossroad and banning the other Druids from speaking with me melted away as she sat there tending the fish. Perhaps in another life she would've been a good mother. She might have held me in her arms when I was scared and cared for me when I was sick. I would've been able to turn to her in times of need and seek advice when I was feeling lost. I think she realized what I was thinking as she caught my gaze.

"I'm sorry this happened to you," she said, "I have only ever wanted for you to be safe."

"Is that why you abandoned me as a baby?" I asked.

"I did not abandon you," she said, "I left you with your father so that you could be free of this life, of this burden."

"If that's true, why did you send for me three years ago?" I asked.

For a moment Viviana looked like she might cry, like something had broken deep inside her.

"I had another son," she admitted, "and he died. He was meant to be a Druid and you a King. After he passed away I needed you to become a priest of the Old Religion. It's tradition in our family for the firstborn girl to become Lady of the Unseen Vale and the firstborn boy to be a Druid."

I never knew I had a brother. As I sat there I realized there was a lot I didn't know about my mother or her religion. There were two voices that rose from the Fire Pit before Viviana was burned, the first was a wholesome and kind woman, and the second was a woman full of scorn and envy. I was pretty sure I knew their identities. The first was the goddess Nimue, the second was the goddess Mab. What I didn't understand was why Mab called Nimue her sister and why she was so intent upon destroying her, imprisoning her somewhere in the Otherworld with the immense power of her godly magick.

"Is there something you can clear up for me?" I asked Viviana after we had eaten our fish and settled down into our shelter for the night.

"What's that?" she replied.

"When you were in the fire, Mab told Nimue she would make her suffer by watching our world be undone. Why does Mab want to hurt Nimue so much? Aren't they both goddesses?"

"They are," replied Viviana, "but they are also sisters, both the daughters of Catsubodhva. They weren't always enemies just as Mab didn't always exist in the darkness. Once the sisters were very close and all things were at peace. Then Kernos came into the world and attracted the attention of the sisters. Mab was mistress of magick and Nimue the guardian of the doorway to the Otherworld but both wished to take Kernos as their consort and thus become Queen of the Earth, destined to rule from Beltane to Samhain. Kernos was King from Samhain to Beltane and recognized as the greatest of the gods by all the others. And he lusted after Nimue in such a way that his passion could not be bridled. Mab was outraged at being rebuked by Kernos and swore she would have vengeance upon Nimue for stealing the heart of the man she loved. She disappeared into the shadows with the desire to turn all the world to darkness. Kernos and Nimue had their children: Brigga, Epona, Erastus, and the King of Faerie before the first sunrise and have since lived apart, sleeping during the other's reign only to return again when the year is renewed."

"Has Mab ever come close to getting her revenge?" I asked.

"Once, about half a century ago," said Viviana, "Mab chose a Pictish man called Vortigern to be her champion. The Romans had just withdrawn from our shores and there were many men eager to rise. Mab imbued Vortigern with great strength and supernatural powers and brought him thousands of Saxon Sellswords to serve as his personal army. None of his competitors stood a chance. Everyone with a claim to the Throne of Britain was executed or exiled until Vortigern stood alone and supreme. He placed his black banners emblazoned with a white dragon upon the walls of the Great Hall in Londinium and declared himself High King. For twenty years, the Tribes endured his tyranny until, at last, we ushered in the return of the sons of Constantius and they drove Vortigern away."

"And Ambrose was one of them," I said.

"He was the younger. The older was Constans. He only lived a few short years as High King. Ambrose has ruled since, under the standard of the Roman Eagle and the banners of Avalon."

My mother closed her eyes to go to sleep, wrapping herself in some fern fronds and quieting her breath. The sun never really rose or set. Faerie remained locked in an everlasting state of twilight, with a soft yellow glow falling from the heavens to envelope the land in its subtle warmth. I wanted to let my mother rest but there was one thing more I needed to know.

"What will happen when Ambrose is gone?" I said.

Viviane opened her eyes and looked at me with a serious expression. I was aware that someone was rising to lead the Saxons in the north behind the same white dragon banners once used by Vortigern and I also knew Morgause and Morgana expected their father, Gorlois, to become High King after the death of Ambrose but I wanted to know what my mother thought. She was the greatest druidess in the world and had a perspective very few could attain in life.

"I think there will be trouble," she said, "The Crones were not wrong when they spoke of the two dragons rising to battle each other for supremacy but they failed to see a third player: the eagle. The Knights fear that Vortigern has risen from the dead to reclaim his place as High King but I don't put a lot of faith in bodies rising from their graves. When we are dead we are dead, at least in this life. I think it is Lot of the Orkneys who has raised the white dragon in the north. It is he who is in league with Mab and seeks to drown the world in darkness. Meanwhile, Ambrose publically favors Gorlois as his possible successor. Gorlois stands beneath the eagle of Rome and would carry on the legacy Ambrose has fought hard to build. But there is a third player, one largely unknown but equally as important. The red dragon, master of North Wales, Uther of the Silures. There are few who know the significance of Uther's claim. I am one such person. He is Ambrose's morganatic son. But our concern should not be who will rise to claim the Throne, rather who will ensure the darkness remains at bay."

Viviana shut her eyes again and within minutes she was asleep, snoring gently and twitching slightly as if we were simply camping on the Isle of Stone instead of separated from our bodies, cast to the distant shores of Faerie. The river before us marked the boundary of Faerie. To cross the river would be to enter the Otherworld, the realm beyond the living and a one way journey. It amazed me that Viviana would even wade in the water given the potency of its energy. I had misjudged her. She wasn't a cold and unfeeling authoritarian. She was doing her duty as High Priestess of the Druidesses and Lady of the Unseen Vale. Hers was a powerful calling as mine would be one day, if I truly was to become the Merlin. I wasn't sure of anything. I hadn't been since meeting Accolon and falling under Elaine's love spell. There was not a minute that went by when I wasn't thinking of him and the distraction would surely be a detriment to my future as a Druid. I also thought about my friends back on the Crossroad. Given the information I'd just learned about what to expect after the death of Ambrose, I worried it might undo our friendships. Morgause and Morgana were the daughters of Gorlois and would surely support him if he went to battle to claim the Throne.

Madoc was Lot of the Orkneys' nephew. He might just feel obliged to stand with his father's family under the white dragon banners. Then there was Tristram, a prince of the Cantii. The Cantii were a junior branch of the Silures. He would probably side with Uther.

I was just about to doze off when a voice arose on the air, the familiar voice of the King of Faerie, rolling off the wind as though the air was his very breath. He was speaking in Ogham and his words caused the earth around us to quake. Viviana woke up with a start and looked around, as though she expected to be assailed at any moment by vicious barbarians.

"In érchontai píso ston kósmo ton zontanón kóri tis kóris mou," he said and with a blink and a breath Viviana was gone.

☼   ☼   ☼

I expected to vanish myself, to be pulled back into the living world, back to my body but I remained exactly where I'd been for hours, sitting on a floor of fern fronds next to the river in Faerie. I tried to conjure my own spell but it didn't work. I got up and left the shelter to see if maybe my mother had been transported outside for some reason but she hadn't. She was gone. I understood in that moment that she had indeed been recalled to her body in Avalon and I'd been left behind.

I tried to keep myself busy with fishing and tending the fire as the days began to pass by like a galloping horse. The longer I stayed in Faerie the lighter I began to feel. I needed less water, even littler food, and had stopped sleeping completely. I often sat there at the edge of my camp and stared up at the eternally twilit sky. The stars were barely visible beyond the cloudy, orange haze, and I pondered whether the constellations were the same. I turned my thoughts inward to question exactly what I wanted from life, if I ever returned to the land of the living.

I never really stopped to think about it before that moment. I was thrust into biblical studies when I was barely old enough to walk and hated every minute of my education at the hand of Brother Jonas. I made the choice

109

to go to Avalon but I hadn't taken a breath since starting my druidic training to ponder whether or not that life is what I truly wanted. Perhaps I wanted a life with Accolon, to go back to Lodecran and live out our days quietly in the countryside or stay with the Eponi on the Watch Hill and shepherd sheep. Then I thought about Taliesin's faith in my abilities, how much he wanted me to succeed, to become his heir, and continue the legacy of the Merlins. I wondered what Viviana would say if she was still there with me but I knew the answer. She would tell me to do my duty.

My duty had been decided for me the day Viviana's first son died. She never told me his name or even who his father was and I contemplated the possibility there might be more children of Viviana, other than me and Guinevere. If there were more sons, they'd be younger, since I became heir after my older brother's death and there couldn't be other daughters or else Viviana wouldn't be training Morgana as her successor. Guinevere would've been the more likely choice to succeed our mother as Lady of the Unseen Vale but Viviana expressed Guinevere was meant to become a warrior and a queen dedicated to the Old Religion but positioned amidst the people of the Tribes.

When the days turned to weeks I decided I might just wade across the river and disappear into the Otherworld. I felt abandoned and alone. The land of the dead would be better than remaining in Faerie forever forgotten, like a ragdoll left in the back of the closet by a girl growing into a woman. Subtle contemplation soon gave way to absolute determination as I resolved, if I remained in Faerie for one more day I would forsake the land of the living altogether and cross the river between the worlds.

The following morning I left the shelter after not sleeping and found I was still alone so I set out for the shores of the river. I was already barefoot and the water was refreshingly cool on my feet. I was about to jump in headlong and swim away before deciding to take one final look at the sprawling fields of Faerie where I caught sight of a familiar face on the horizon. Oberon, the King of Faerie and my great-grandfather, was walking towards the river dressed in his usual furs and loincloth. I rushed back to shore and went back to the shelter to wait for him to arrive but, by the time I got there, he was already seated by the fire eating a few clovers and looking at me like a dolphin staring at a shark. For a moment I thought he expected to be alone, that he'd forgotten I was in Faerie until he smiled, reassuring me he had come to be my salvation.

"Are you ready to go home?" he asked.

"I was ready weeks ago," I replied curtly.

"Then let's not doddle," he said.

Oberon led me away from the river towards the hills in the distance. Viviana and I never lost sight of the river and went no further than the grove of yew trees near our camp. The rest of Faerie looked the same as what I had already seen. There were glades covered by forests of different kinds of trees and large grassy fields stretching out for miles. There were many kinds of birds, including the black swans of Catsubodhva, and also various kinds of small forest creatures but there were no deer or predators. The air always smelled of honey and it never grew overly cool or warm. Faerie was clearly a place of tranquility and calm equality. The radical polarities of the living world weren't present in the land of everlasting twilight where the fey went about their enchanted lives unnoticed and invisible.

The only source of water seemed to be the river at our backs, at least until we'd been walking for hours. Then, as we came around a corner and went down a sharp incline we arrived at another river. This one had a simple wooden bridge crossing from one bank to the other with a locked gate on our end. Oberon produced a key, seemingly from thin air and placed it in the lock but he hesitated. Before he turned the key, he looked at me with genuine concern, reminding me he was my grandmother's father. Most his features were otherworldly, from his sparkling eyes to his reddish skin, but the way he looked at me was completely human. He seemed to know what it meant to be mortal, to be born, live, and die in a world of suffering. I thought about the days when the fey lived in the mortal world. I wanted to ask Oberon if he was alive then, or if the fey were always immortal.

"Listen to me, Galahad," he said seriously, "Many things have changed since you've been here. I want you to be prepared."

I looked at him as if to say prepared for what. I couldn't understand what he was trying to imply but I was overtaken by fear, fear something happened to my body, that I'd be returning to a hollow shell incapable of walking, speaking, or seeing.

"Since you have been in Faerie a year has passed in the living world," he said, "and war has come to Avalon."

Chapter Eleven
"Loyalties Divided"

"He's awake Lady," I heard a familiar yet strangely different voice say. My head was throbbing as I opened my eyes to see Morgana and Morgause standing over me, Morgana with a wet rag and Morgause with a basin of warm water. I was laying in one of the Priestess' cottages. I could see the Blood Well, central monument on the Isle of the Font, through the open doorway. The air was hot and sticky and I was covered with a simple linen sheet, meaning it was the dog days of summer, the roman month of August, just days from my birthday. Morgana was smiling at me and the first thing I noticed was how much older she looked. I was lost in Faerie for a year. Morgana was fifteen years old and immensely beautiful. Her skin was smooth and flawless and her almond-shaped eyes were large and alluring. Her almond brown hair was shiny and flowing freely down to the small of her back. She had breasts and her boyish frame had blossomed into a full, feminine figure. She was dressed in the blue linen gown of a Maiden-Healer and bore the mark of the crescent moon on her forehead. On the other hand, Morgause looked strikingly similar to how she appeared the last time I saw her, with her fiery red hair and permanently scowling face. She was wearing a revealing red gown and had her hair pulled up into a roman style knot above her head. Morgana and Morgause no longer looked like twins with different colored hair. Morgana was clearly the more striking beauty.

There was a third person in the cottage, a blind old woman with graying hair seated on a stool near the stove. She had burn scars across most of her face and her scarred eyes were staring vacantly at nothing in particular. She was wearing the purple robes of a Priestess and was holding a long cane in her right hand. I was in shock. I couldn't believe this shell of a woman sitting before me was my mother, the famed Viviana, Lady of the Unseen

Vale. I tried to sit up but my body was weak and my constitution frail. I looked down at myself and saw I was emaciated and atrophied.

"You will be weak for some time to come," said my mother without standing, "You are lucky to be alive."

"I don't understand how it's even possible," I said as my voice cracked and my throat burned from stomach acid.

"You could breathe on your own," said Morgana, "but we had to feed you with a straw and change you when you soiled yourself. It was horrible. Just watching you lay there in a coma, growing weaker and weaker by the day. I really didn't think you'd recover but I'm glad you're back."

"Where's Accolon?" I asked as my mind drifted immediately to the man in my dreams.

"Gone to war with the other Knights," replied Viviana.

"And Taliesin?" I asked.

"With the Knights," confirmed Viviana, "but he will return now. He will know that you've awoken and will want to resume your training. Madoc is training to be a Knight, living on the Watch Hill with the Eponi, and Tristram has taken the vows of a Guardian. He lives in isolation on the Isle of Stone. Everyone is healthy and as happy as can be given the circumstances of the trials we now face."

Oberon told me Avalon was at war but I didn't know exactly what that meant. It had something to do with the High King and the man raising the banners of the White Dragon in the north but beyond that I was at a loss. I wanted to ask more questions, to find out exactly where Accolon had gone and to know he was safe but I found myself relaxing back into the pillow in exhaustion. Viviana rose from her stool and took Morgause's arm.

"Take me to fetch some more water and wine," she said and Morgause led Viviana out of the cottage.

"I'll go get you some stew," said Morgana, "Maeve just made some for our afternoon meal. You need to eat something solid."

Morgana returned moments later with a bowl filled with steaming hot stew. She lifted me into a sitting position and propped me up with pillows but I had no interest in eating. I felt too weak. She gave me a stern look and then picked up the spoon and started gently pouring the warm liquid down my throat. Chewing the vegetables was as hard as breaking rocks with a chisel. The whole endeavor was an exhausting ordeal and, while I felt better once I finished, I was glad it was over.

"It'll take time but you'll be back to normal soon," smiled Morgana.

"Did you take vows to Brigga?" I asked her, referencing the blue linen gown adorning her body.

"Yeah," she said, "after me and Madoc broke up I was pretty listless. Then Viviana woke up and reminded me of my purpose. I'm meant to be her successor, first to serve Brigga as a healer, then Nimue as a Priestess. I never gave Madoc my maidenhead so I am still pure in the eyes of the goddess of life and bounty. Madoc and Tristram aren't the same either, Galahad. You've been gone a long time."

"What about Elaine?" I asked, remembering it was through her that Mab had cast her curse in the first place.

"She's here," said Morgana, "and she wasn't Mab's host. Mab was using her just like Eogan. Viviana thinks Mab has not yet taken an earthly vessel, that she still works her magick from the Otherworld. Elaine barely survived the exorcism but she made a full recovery and then she took the vows of a Priestess. She now serves Nimue."

"Even with a husband?" I said.

"Madoc's father is dead," she said, "for almost a year now. Madoc took the news pretty hard. He threw himself into his martial studies to avoid his feelings. He grew hard and abusive. It was clear our relationship was over after he started visiting the outside world and talking about the coming war and the superiority of his Uncle Lot's claim to the throne, even after Ambrose named my father as his chosen successor. Lot has brought his Saxons down upon us because of Ambrose's choice. He refuses to recognize the legitimacy of my father's right to rule and he thumbs his nose in the face of the authority of the High King. He's just like Vortigern, he even uses his banners when marching into battle."

"The white dragon," I said.

"Exactly," she said.

"And your father marches under the standard of the Roman Eagle," I stated to myself.

"Yes, in the name of his High King and his faith he has chosen to take the Eagle as his banner."

"What about the red dragon?" I asked.

"Not yet risen," replied Morgana.

"That's enough," interjected my mother as she reappeared in the doorway on the arm of Morgause with a pitcher of honeyed wine in one hand and a cask of water in the other.

"Leave us now, girls. Galahad needs to rest," said Viviana as she settled herself down onto her stool. Morgana grinned at me and Morgana glared as they both left the cottage. I looked at Viviana again and felt sad at the misshapen, grotesque remnants of her burned, blind face.

"Do not pity me, child," she said, as though she could feel my eyes probing her face, "Pity those who now stand with swords drawn, fighting to claim the souls of all the Britons."

☼ ☼ ☼

My sixteenth birthday came and went as I laid in that bed recovering. Morgana brought my meals every day and kept me current on all the comings and goings in Avalon. Viviana only came on Sundays but she would stay the whole day, encouraging me to speak Ogham and to recall the techniques employed to enact the five principles. In Taliesin's absence she was my teacher and she was determined that I fulfill my destiny as the next Merlin. The hostilities between us melted away after our time spent in Faerie and she showed me the kind of affection I always yearned for from my mother. Morgause didn't come again but Madoc visited a few times a week to fill me in on his training with the Eponi swordmasters. He was adamant he would become a Knight in the next year and ride out to convince the world that Lot of the Orkneys was the True King to which the prophecy of the Crones referred. He was dedicated to his uncle and all remnants of the boy I once knew were gone. I almost wished he wouldn't come to see me, that he would stay on the Watch Hill and focus on his own future.

"Does Morgana come to see you?" asked Madoc on one of his visits.

"Every day," I replied.

"Is she still angry with me?" he asked.

"I don't think so," I said, "I think she understands what losing your father did to you. It made you realize your potential and turned you into a man. There's nothing wrong with that."

"What are you talking about?"

"You and Morgana broke up because of your father's death. It's alright. She told me."

"I don't know what she told you but that's not what happened," said Madoc, "I mean I was affected by my father's death but it wasn't enough to break apart our relationship. It was Morgause."

"Morgause?" I said.

"You know Morgana and I were really young when we started courting each other and, in the beginning it was really good, but when I started to change from a boy to a man, I started having strong feelings, sexual feelings, and I wanted to fulfill them with Morgana. She refused, again and again and again. Morgause didn't."

"You slept with Morgause," I said, realizing then why Morgana had been so quick to end a relationship she yearned to see come to fruition for months if not years.

"And Morgana walked in on us. She was furious, not at Morgause, but at me. She stormed out and I haven't seen her since."

"Do you love Morgause?" I asked.

"No," replied Madoc, "but I don't love Morgana either. I don't think I've met the one to share my life yet. When I do I'll know it. Until then, I'm going to focus on becoming a great Knight, the warrior of strength the Crones saw in their Cauldron. What about you and Accolon?"

Accolon's naked body flashed through my mind at the mention of his name and I felt a strong desire stirring in my loins.

"There is no me and Accolon," I said, "The only reason we have feelings for each other is because of Mab's curse. I am a sworn Initiate of the Druids and the future Merlin of all the Britons. I am forbidden to know another person sexually."

"At least until you take your vows," smiled Madoc, "You can't tell me you wouldn't jump at the chance to disappear into some shadowy place on the night of Beltane with your strong-armed lover."

In truth, I saw my fixation on Accolon as a severe detriment to my development as a Druid. If I couldn't get him out of my mind, I would never be able to regain the focus needed to pass the Five Trials and enter the order as a sworn Druid Priest.

"I think I'll be leaving soon," said Madoc, "I've learned everything I can from the Eponi Swordmasters. I even have my own blade, forged from true silver and emblazoned with enchantments. I call it Eregolan. It means Mighty Hammer in my people's language. Eregolan was blessed in the waters of the Blood Well and touched by the hand of Kernos, now I want to take it forth and have it sanctified by the Christians. A weapon touched by the hand of three faiths will surely be deadly against our enemies."

"I will take your word for it," I said, "I know nothing of swords."

Druids were forbidden to raise a weapon of violence. In the old days, the Priests of Kernos and Priestesses of Nimue were afforded such prestige that no man would dare bear a naked weapon in their presence. Those days were long since passed but the forbiddance of keeping a weapon as an Initiate remained. Sometimes I dreamt about being a warrior but, even at my best I was never built for it. I had grown taller than any of my friends even before being banished to Faerie and my body was lithe and lean. I didn't have a great deal of upper-body strength but I was fast, like a rabbit being pursued by a limping dog.

It took me over four months to regain the muscular strength to leave the cottage. I took evening walks with Morgana and each day we went further and further until I was convinced I was back to what I had been and so much more. While I was in Faerie, my body went through the change, my voice was deeper, my chest and chin were sprouting hair and I got an erection at least eight times a day. My mind was consumed with sexual thoughts about Accolon and I woke up more than once in an accidental sticky mess. I was growing into a man with every passing day. I should've already been declared an adult and entered the order of the Druids. I wondered if they would honor my right to enter even though I'd been in a coma for the last year of my life. I was ready to resume my training with Taliesin but he hadn't returned to Avalon yet.

☼   ☼   ☼

"I want to go back to the cottage on the Crossroad," I said after months of being cooped up inside one of the Priestess cottages on the Isle of the Font. I was thankful for everything the druidesses did to heal me and help me to regain my strength but I was tired of living with the women. I didn't desire to live with the men either. I wanted to be alone.

"Out of the question," said my mother as she stood in the doorway holding onto the arm of a young Priestess named Maeve.

"There's no one on the Crossroad anymore, Galahad," added Morgana, "and it isn't visited often. Lady Viviana goes there from time to time and the Samhain Rites are celebrated in the apple orchard by the stream. Aside from that, the island is completely isolated. You aren't strong enough to be all the way out there by yourself. What if something happened?"

Taliesin was still in the outside world with the Knights, aiding the Britons in their fight against the Saxon Sellswords attempting to migrate southward and annex all the territories they crossed as their own, encouraged by Lot of the Orkneys, servant of Mab. Madoc was blind to the reality of his uncle's true nature and I feared he would fall to the darkness if he were permitted to leave without the guidance or protection of a Druid. I wanted more than anything for him to become the person I once knew again.

Morgana refused to speak about her breakup with Madoc or to admit to the truth. I didn't see Morgause again but I heard she was living with the Maiden-Healers on the Isle of Glass. She had softened some but was still angry and irritated that she was not yet married. She was eighteen years old, three years older than when most noblewomen took a husband. Morgause was particularly interested in finding a highborn husband, one of the clan kings or Lot of the Orkneys if he were to succeed in winning his battle against her father. Either way, Morgause could find a way to further her ambition, either as a princess or as High Queen. Her ambitions knew no bounds and she was adamant she was destined to become a great woman with immense power. I didn't doubt her.

"I would still prefer to return to my home," I continued, "I will wait for Taliesin there, and I won't be alone. Oberon comes to the Crossroad often to visit Rhiannon's grave."

"I don't know that you should count on Oberon for guidance," said Viviana, "My grandfather is a great being. He is the son of the Gods, but he is also shortsighted and temperamental. He may be helping you today but he could just as easily turn on you tomorrow. It's a lesson you need to learn, Galahad. He can't be counted on."

"He rescued us from Faerie," I replied, "Did he not do so to save our lives, without thought of reward?"

"Oberon rescued us because he believes you have an important part to play in the coming days," said Viviana, "If the Old Religion disappears along with the men of the Tribes then the fey will fade into the mists, forced back into Faerie and exiled there eternally. The fey, just as the gods and goddesses, require the devotion of mortal men in order to walk freely or wield power in this world."

I wondered for a moment about my mother's words, about the truth behind her statement. Oberon was King of Faerie, holding dominion over the eternal realm of the land of everlasting twilight. There were probably thousands, if not millions, of fey and countless mortal spirits on their journey from life to the Otherworld. Why would he care if he could no longer pass through the veil and into the mortal world? Even as a blind woman, Viviana's senses were extremely acute and she could tell what I was thinking before I opened my mouth to speak.

"Oberon is not the ruler of Faerie," said Viviana, "It is his consort and bride, Sulis, who holds power there. He comes into the mortal world to gain followers, to encourage men to worship his name. Long ago, he had a great cult that venerated him in the east but they have been gone many years now. He is desperate for adoration and he won't stop until he receives it again. He is like Mab in many ways."

"Viviana speaks the truth," said a voice I never expected to hear again as my Aunt Elaine entered the cottage wearing the purple robes of a Priestess of Nimue. I recoiled when she attempted to hug me as terror overwhelmed my senses and fear entered my heart.

"Do not be alarmed, Galahad," said my mother, "my sister was under the control of Mab. She would never hurt either of us in her present state of mind. She is now protected by Nimue. Mab cannot take her again."

That made me feel better but I still didn't want her touching me, let alone wrapping her arms around me like a mother greeting a wayward child. She understood and backed away, taking her place next to Viviana so that Maeve could return to her duties.

Viviana went to wrap her hand around Elaine's arm but the second she made contact with Elaine's flesh she was overcome by some unknown force. She began shaking and sweating like she'd been sitting out in the sun for too long without food or water. I thought she might've been poisoned or cursed and I looked to Elaine as if she were guilty. Elaine looked back at me in alarm and I could feel her innocence. She was a new woman and it was my duty to forgive her, after ensuring my mother's deliverance from her present crisis.

Viviana looked as though she might vomit, her skin turned green, and she was feverish. I wanted to ease her pain, to help her recover. Fortunately, none of us had to intervene. As soon as the sickness set in, it was over. Viviana stood there with a vacant expression and uttered words with a voice that was not her own, as though someone was using her as a speaker to broadcast their message from across the void between the worlds, a mighty goddess reaching down to bring us urgent news.

"Ambrose is dead," said the voice, "and the red dragon is risen."

Chapter Twelve
"A Sleeping Viper"

"Uther has moved his warriors to Calleva," said Faelan, now High Druid in Avalon, second in authority only to Taliesin. It has been ten weeks since the voice carrying the message of Ambrose's death came through Viviana in the cottage. It turned out to be the voice of Viviana and Elaine's other sister, Igerna, mother to Morgana, Morgause, and their four brothers and wife of Gorlois, Duke of Cornewall. She was Queen of the Dumnonii in her own right through the line of her father who was not Taliesin but the late King Aeryn of Tintagel. Igerna was still learned in witchcraft and knew how to send a message across great distances when the need arose. The news of Ambrose's death was not a shock but the sudden appearance of Uther of the Silures was a surprise. Viviana wasted no time in calling the Council in the Stone Circle to discuss where Avalon should be steered and behind whom they should stand. Viviana, Elaine, and Maeve were present representing the Priestesses of Nimue, Morgana was there with two other Maiden-Healers, Rowa and Adiane, while the Druids were represented by Faelan, Gaius, and a bard called Bodon. Neithon and Ector were also present to represent the Knights of Avalon. Taliesin was still conspicuously absent.

"Uther and his men will stay in Calleva," said Elaine, "it is winter now. We often forget how harsh the season can be because the snow and frosts do not come to the Unseen Vale but, in the outside world, it would take a very brave or foolhardy man to brave war in such weather."

"I agree," said Viviana, "The war will cease until spring comes again. Gorlois will remain in Tintagel with his sons and Igerna. Lot will slink back into the north to winter with his men beyond Hadrian's Wall. Even Mab has not the power to make him come south again in the ice and cold. We must take advantage of the few months of peace and work to rebuild our ranks.

There are fewer Priestesses on the Isle of Font than there has ever been and the Druids dwindle in numbers daily."

"The people are turning towards the Christ," said Neithon, "at least those living in the cities. The men in the countryside still pray to Nimue and Kernos but they're growing to be a small minority. I don't think we can rebuild your numbers anymore. The Old Religion is dying."

"But it is not dead yet," said Viviana sternly.

"The question tonight is not how to increase our numbers but to whom we should pledge our allegiances," said Faelan.

"One thing is clear," said Elaine, "We cannot back Lot of the Orkneys in his claim. He serves Mab and she is our enemy, the enemy of Nimue, and of Kernos. If we wish to entreat favor from our god and goddess, we must do everything in our power to see Lot fail in his designs."

"Then it is either Gorlois or Uther," said Ector.

"Gorlois is a good man but he is a Christian and a Roman," said Bodon, "I doubt very much he will have any sympathy for our plight once he has taken the throne. He will encourage the young Britons to follow the God of Abram, to turn their backs on their traditions."

"That is not true," said Morgana defiantly, "My father is not a bigot or a hateful man. He is a Christian but he is married to a daughter of the Holy Isles, a daughter of Rhiannon. He has never forced my mother to take his faith and two of my brothers follow the Old Religion. He would be a good High King. He knows the British people and he understands what it takes to keep us safe. Can the same be said of this Gaelic nobody, Uther?"

I looked at my mother, expecting her to say something about Uther's true heritage but she just sat there staring blindly into space.

"He isn't a nobody," I said.

"Silence," said Viviana, "You are not a member of the council and not permitted to speak. You are here to observe because it is what Taliesin would want, not because we seek your opinion."

"I still think it wise to support Uther," said Faelan.

"I agree," added Maeve.

"All who wish to support Uther in his claim make your choice known now," said Viviana and everyone in council besides Morgana and Ector raised their hand into the air. It was settled. Avalon would do everything within its power to make Uther the next High King.

☼   ☼   ☼

It was as Faelan believed. Each contender for the throne remained in their corners through the winter. The weather in Avalon was always temperate and the harshness of the cold remained at bay but, in the outside world, the arctic winds billowed and the snow fell in droves. The whole countryside was encased in subzero frosts. It was hard enough to feed and warm their massive armies. The three claimants were stuck.

Taliesin returned to Avalon just before the worst of winter and took me back to the Crossroad, to live in my cottage with him and renew my studies. He looked older and weaker, holding tightly to a tall oak staff to keep him steady as he walked but his mind was still sharp. As always, Taliesin avoided the funeral pyre with Rhiannon laying upon it. I'd never seen him go near it or look on her face, something I found strange since they were once lovers and shared two daughters between them. We kept to the narrows by the stream where my cottage still stood untended but unharmed. I asked Morgana if she wanted to return but she declined. She was a vowed Maiden-Healer and belonged on the Isle of Glass. Madoc offered to come with me but I expressed a desire for him to continue focusing on his studies. The truth was he had become someone I didn't recognize or respect. His opinions were brash and his demeanor brazen. He turned up his nose at the authority of the Druids and Priestesses, choosing to turn to an absence of faith in favor of reason. Then there was Tristram. We were very close before I became lost in Faerie. Since my return I hadn't seen him once. He was a Guardian on the Isle of Stone and forbidden from interacting with anyone other than the other Guardians. My soft, slightly effeminate friend chose to live the hardest most austere life of any in the Unseen Vale and I had a really hard time understanding why. He was completely transformed from a mild-mannered boy into a gallant man.

Taliesin spent the first few days of our reunion reviewing the five principles and ensuring I still understood the Ogham. I proved to not only be proficient but exemplary in all the above but I had a hard time focusing on my studies. I was busy thinking about Accolon. He hadn't returned to Avalon from the warfront. It had been a year since he'd seen me awake. I wondered if he thought about me as much as I thought of him and Taliesin was quick to intercede.

"You must get him out of your mind, Galahad," he said during one of our last performance reviews.

"I know but it's hard," I said, "Isn't there some way to break the curse? To make me forget all these feelings and thoughts? You are the Merlin. Can't you do something?"

"I'm afraid not," he said, "You were cursed by a goddess, and only a spell of equal measure can undo what has been done."

"How do you not think about Rhiannon?" I asked him and he reacted like I had punched him in the stomach. The color drained from his face and he gripped his staff extra tightly to prevent his knees from buckling. I was sure he'd react in anger but he actually looked sad.

"I remember how much she hurt me," he said, "and it helps to forget how much I loved her, at least most of the time. But you cannot do the same. What you feel for Accolon is not real. He is a good-looking warrior and anyone like you would desire him but that is where it would've ended if Mab had not cast her curse. You must fight against your desires and take your vows. After that you can bring life to your feelings with him beside the Beltane Fires, if that is your wish, but not a moment before. Now, where were we? Yes, that's right. Recount for me the nine common hexes and their practical uses."

I could recall each hex with ease. The hexes were little works of magick which could accomplish a variety of feats, from putting another person temporarily to sleep, to causing a latched door to unlock. They were cast with a simple Ogham command and a point of a finger but could easily be ineffective or rebound if not cast with the utmost focus. Taliesin was satisfied that I was still in control of my magical knowledge. He could see that, despite my obsession with Accolon, I was determined to become a priest of Kernos, to be a Druid in the likeness of my grandfather, to fulfill my obligations to my bloodline.

"Your next challenge will be one that requires the utmost discretion," said Taliesin and I was taken aback. Secrecy was of paramount importance to Druids but they weren't in the habit of asking their Initiates to participate in their secretive activities. I was still far away from my induction into the order and below such knowledge.

"You need me to keep a secret?" I asked.

"Something like that," he said, "I am departing Avalon again in the morning. I know I just returned but I sense the tide is on the brink of changing and, if there is no one there to guide the current, I fear we may all be washed away. While I'm gone I need you to act here on my behalf."

"I don't understand," I said.

"Viviana and the others believe that the darkness is gone from Avalon, that it left when Elaine was exorcised two years ago," he said, "but I am convinced the evil one still resides here, hiding in plain sight, right beneath our very noses."

"Wouldn't Viviana know if Mab had taken one of her priestesses as a host?" I asked.

"I didn't say anything about a priestess. I need you to keep an eye on Morgause. She has been here as long as you and was present on the Holy Isles when you were cursed both times. We expected Mab's host to be Elaine and that Elaine might be controlling Morgause, teaching her how to work dark magick but now I fear it was the other way around. Morgause is the host now joined with Mab, joined with the evil one's lifeforce and seething with her dark magick. If there is no one here to keep a watchful eye I fear the sleeping viper will rise up and poison everyone with her venom before they even knew who it was attacking. You cannot let that happen."

"Me?" I said, "I'm not even a Druid yet. I don't know enough magick to stand against Mab. How do you expect me to fight a goddess, let alone the mistress of magick?"

"I'm not asking you to instigate a fight," said Taliesin, "I want you to watch Morgause, nothing more, but I will teach you how to use magick that will allow you to enter Morgause's mind, to overpower her within the confines of her own thoughts. Entering the consciousness of another is a magick known only to the Druids and it will take the utmost concentration on your part to be able to master the technique."

The power to enter someone else's mind required me to begin by staring intently at Taliesin, so hard that I felt my eyes would pop out and my head would split open. Then came the difficult part. As I stared at Taliesin with the utmost focus, I was meant to shift my gaze from my sensory eyes to my third-eye, the chakra located on the forehead and responsible for intuitive awareness and psionic experiences. I tried for days to accomplish the transition from physical awareness to cognitive awareness and finally managed to allow myself to relax into the technique. Seeing with the third-eye allowed me to distinguish the aura of Taliesin, emanating around him like a golden cocoon waiting to birth a glorious butterfly. At that stage, the key to entering Taliesin's mind was expanding my own blue aura outward to mingle with the yellow hues of his. Once the essence of our spirits was locked together, I could see into his mind, as though his head was a window exposing the secret transgressions of a dysfunctional family.

"Good," said Taliesin, "I can feel you inside my head. Now, issue a command with your mind. Tell me to do something you know I wouldn't normally spend my time doing."

"Laugh," I commanded with my thoughts.

Suddenly Taliesin burst out in the most raucous laughter, though he did not look like he was enjoying the experience. The effect only lasted seconds and then Taliesin's usual detached and stoic demeanor returned. I smiled at the success of my little joke and Taliesin grumbled a series of profanities under his breath.

"Not what I was expecting," he said, "but effective nonetheless. Keep practicing and, should Morgause try anything, enter her mind and shut it down. Command her to lay down and die. It is the only way Mab will be expelled from within Morgause. The only way to protect Avalon."

Taliesin left that same night, left me there to wait and watch with the directive that, should anything occur that warranted such action, I was to murder my cousin, Morgause.

☼   ☼   ☼

The winter passed without incident and soon the warmth of spring was upon us. To better achieve my mission of spying on Morgause, I decided to leave the Crossroad and live on the Watch Hill with the Eponi where Morgause had a small house. I despised having to be so near to Morgause as much as was needed. She was a snobbish, unfeeling woman with entitlement issues and a generally bad attitude. It was a far reach to think that Taliesin was right. Morgause was the human host of Mab's dark spirit, though it seemed outwardly her only aspiration was consorting with men in extreme and undeniably morose ways.

In the five months I lived on the Watch Hill, I saw Morgause with no less than fifteen men, young Eponi horse masters looking for a ride with an unbridled woman or Fenfolk fishermen using their boats as a floating brothel to satisfy their carnal lust with a willing Morgause. Even the Knight of Avalon, Agrivain, would come to Morgause's cottage whenever he visited the Holy Isles to noisily couple with her. The home I was sharing with Madoc was only a few feet away from Morgause's cottage and we were made privy to her numerous, nightly affairs whenever she would scream out in ecstasy or one of her lovers would grunt louder than a boar being chased by a hungry bear. A part of me was jealous that Morgause was able to experience something I would never be allowed to pursue, completely unrestricted sexual exploration with another man, preferably the beautiful man haunting my waking dreams.

Completely contrary to Morgause's behavior, Madoc seemed to have lost interest in the opposite sex altogether, focusing intently only on his martial studies. He rose before dawn and returned home after dusk every single day, taking his sword, Eregolan, out into the fields between the Eponi encampment and the Fenfolk village to practice his technique and refine his abilities in mock combat situations. He was more determined than ever to leave Avalon and join Lot of the Orkneys in the north. He had a traveling trunk packed and was hoarding gold under the floorboards in his bedroom, just waiting for the day when he could leave us all behind and start his life anew. I wondered if Morgana had something to do with his desire to run. Maybe his loss of interest in women and his urge to flee were both caused by the pain of losing his one true love to the call of the gods. On one of the nights when Madoc and I sat by the fire drinking mead and remembering the days of our childhood, I inadvertently triggered the power of my third-eye and heard what was transpiring inside Madoc's head. What I heard was intense and horrifying.

"You will serve only Lot of the Orkneys. Your sword will belong only to his command. You will help him to fulfill my call and raise my lover from the grave."

The voice was not Madoc's, it was Mab's and it was chanting the same phrase over and over again. It was like Madoc was asleep inside his own head, trapped in the deep recesses of his mind while the psionic commands of Mab drove him to abandon his home to serve a distant relation he'd never even met. I wanted to run to Viviana that moment and demand she free Madoc from Mab. Instead, I reached out to blend my aura with his and said inside both our minds.

"You are not a pawn of the evil, you are a child of the light, born of the blood of Faerie. Cast out the darkness and reclaim your mind as your own."

For a moment I thought I heard Mab's voice quietly screaming in rage and then Madoc's mind was silent. He fell backwards onto the floor, as though he'd been hit in the face and dazed by the realization of having been possessed by Mab. He stared around frantically trying to comprehend what was happening and where he was. He looked at me for a moment as though I were a perfect stranger. Then his features softened.

"What's happening?" he asked.

I tried to answer, to explain all that had transpired but just as I opened my mouth to speak our cottage began to shake and quiver. The wall behind us was ripped away, like an invisible giant decided on a whim to assail our home. I swung around on the defensive, searching for an enemy amidst the dust and rubble while Madoc instinctively reached for his enchanted sword, Eregolan. It didn't take long to discover who was behind the attack. Morgause was standing at the opening torn into the side of our home, her face contorted in rage and her eyes filled with malice. Morgause was always an unfeeling woman but her present disposition made the normal Morgause look like a Good Samaritan. She glared at me with those unblinking, angry eyes as she waved her hand, causing Eregolan to fly out of Madoc's grip and impale itself in the nearby chair. With another wave of her hand Madoc was lifted into the air and then slammed back into the ground so hard it caused his arm to snap and knocked him unconscious.

"You really shouldn't have meddled in our affairs," said Morgause with a maniacal voice.

All I could think to do was try and cast the Spell of Protection around me and Madoc to prevent Morgause from doing us any more harm. I threw my arms out in front of me and channeled the power of my aura outward around me, spilling forth to fill the room with its unseen indigo radiance before speaking the sacred incantation.

"Megáli Theá Mitéra," I yelled, "Mas prostatéfsei apó tin apeilí tou skótous kai tou kakoú aftá."

I repeated the incantation twice more to build upon the energy growing around us. The untrained eye would see nothing and would presume there had been no change. Those who could see through the third-eye chakra, like myself, would see a thin veil of luminescent blue energy growing like a bubble to encase me and Madoc. Morgause watched as the protective barrier manifested between her and us, laughing the whole time like a madwoman deprived of her wits. At first I thought the spell was successful until Morgause stepped through the veil of energy as though it were nothing more than a curtain separating two rooms. She was wearing a twisted smile as she raised both her hands and caused me to fly across the room and become pinned against the wall near my bed. I couldn't move a muscle as I hung there at the mercy of Morgause, who was once again laughing maniacally.

"You're supposed to be Mab's greatest foe?" she said, "Pathetic. You're no mighty Merlin. You're a dead man."

Chapter Thirteen
"Death of the Eagle"

Morgause drew a long dagger from the inside of the black cloak covering her shoulders, concealing her provocative red gown. The blade of the dagger was curved and the handle was bejeweled with rubies and pearls. She dragged the knife across one of her fingers to show how sharp it was and to imply she meant to run me through but she never got the chance. When she was just a few steps away Morgause suddenly froze in place like she'd been turned instantly into a living statue. I fell to the ground with a thud as her supernatural grip on me was released.

"Are you alright?" said my mother from where she had come to stand behind Morgause. She was alone, holding onto her walking stick and gazing in my general direction.

"I am," I said, "but I think Madoc is hurt."

"Take him and leave," said Viviana.

"I can help you," I said.

"Take Madoc and get out of here now," she said forcefully.

I did as I was told. I pulled Madoc up off the floor with all my might and threw him over my shoulder. Morgause was beginning to twitch, fighting against Viviana's hex even before we were clear of the cottage. I took Madoc to the edge of the Eponi encampment and then retreated quietly back to the demolished cottage to make sure Viviana was alright. I hid in the bushes just yards from the ruined house. My mother was still standing behind Morgause but Morgause was breaking free and slowly turning around to face her attacker, to look at Viviana with her evil eyes, glaring a stare of pure, unadulterated hatred.

"You are not welcome here," said Viviana forcefully, "You are trespassing on hallowed ground."

"You may be the daughter of Rhiannon but your magick is no match for the power of a goddess," laughed Morgause.

"I am not only the daughter of Rhiannon," replied Viviana, "I am also Lady of the Unseen Vale. Do you think that only a title? You should know better, Morgause."

Morgause didn't wait for Viviana to finish. She lunged forward with her dagger raised with the intent of stabbing my mother in the heart but, just as Morgause came within arm's length, Viviana swung her walking stick with the efficiency of a fighting master, hitting Morgause square in the jaw. Morgause was thrown to the ground and, for a moment, it seemed she'd been defeated. Then she rose like a stringed marionette being animated by a puppeteer, her face contorted into an inhuman monstrosity. She looked like a demoness risen from the pits of hell, her eyes emblazoned with red and her mouth furled into a snarl. With only a twitch of her eyes Morgause caused a large boulder nearby to fly through the air furlong towards Viviana's head. Viviana remained calm. As the boulder threatened to collide with her skull, my mother touched it with the tip of her walking stick and the rock exploded into dust. Morgause didn't wait for Viviana to counter her attack. She began chanting in Ogham, calling for the dark spirits that lurk in the shadows to come forth and assail my mother with their insidious energy. I saw no demons or ghouls but I saw a change in Viviana. Her skin was turning green and she seemed as though she might vomit. She crumpled over and braced herself with her walking stick to prevent from losing her balance. Still, she found the strength to raise her free hand into the air and speak her own powerful incantation.

"Avalon apomakrýnei to skotádi," said Viviana as though she was holding a megaphone to her lips.

Morgause looked like an escaping inmate caught in the prison floodlights. She started to sputter and wheeze and her arms and legs shook violently. She threatened to collapse at any moment and the more she writhed the more intent Viviana became. The color had returned to my mother's cheeks and she was again sound on her feet but she looked five years older and a new streak of white appeared in her hair. Morgause almost passed out but she wasn't beaten yet. She regained enough composure to conjure an enormous fireball and hurtle in towards Viviana. Viviana looked perplexed, not from fear of the fireball which she turned into a puff of black smoke with a wave of her hand. It was something else.

"You are not the host," said Viviana in astonishment.

"I never implied I was," spat Morgause.

Viviana pointed her walking stick at Morgause and she was lifted off her feet, thrown twenty feet, and then slammed against the wall of one of the cottages adjacent to mine and Madoc's home. Morgause cried out from the pain but Viviana did not relent. She held Morgause there, frozen in shock, trying without success to break free from Viviana's control.

"In whom does the spirit of Mab reside if not within you?" asked Viviana forcefully.

"I'm not telling you anything," spat Morgause.

"I don't need you to divulge your secrets," replied my mother, "The asking was a courtesy. I can enter your mind and wrench the truth out of you one bit at a time before I break Mab's curse and free you from her control."

I could tell from how eerily silent Viviana and Morgause became that Viviana had entered Morgause's mind. The battle would recommence on another level, in the abstract places of Morgause's consciousness where Mab had likely imbedded her curse, taking control of my demented cousin. I thought about using my third-eye to join my mother inside Morgause's head but I figured I was not skilled enough yet to face off against the power of an angry goddess, even if that goddess' spirit wasn't actually in residence within Morgause. For nearly five minutes, Viviana stood there like a statue and Morgause remained pinned against the wall, staring blankly out into the night air, locked in an unbreakable trance. A slight twitch in Viviana's left arm indicated she found what she was searching for and, with a deep breath, she returned to her own body.

Morgause resumed her attempt to break free of Viviana's control but she couldn't find the strength to counteract Viviana's spell. Viviana stood there as still as a stone in the desert while Morgause filled the air with curse words and profanities.

"You are not under Mab's control," said my mother, "You pledged yourself to her service of your own free will. Why?"

"Because I hate you and I hate Avalon," spat Morgause, "I have tried to escape this place for years, to go out into the world and find a husband with power and prestige but you, you have held me prisoner, unwilling to let me go, unwilling to let me join the Maiden-Healers. I yearned to know the secrets of magick but you wouldn't teach me. So I found someone who would. Someone more powerful than you will ever know."

"You're wrong," said Viviana, "I do know Mab's power. I have seen it. Felt it. And I know it is my mission to destroy it, for the greater good of Avalon and the outside world."

Viviana had heard enough from Morgause. With a sigh, she raised her hand and spoke a powerful incantation.

"In ýpno tóra," she said and Morgause was rendered unconscious, falling hard to the ground in a state of unbreakable sleep.

☼　　☼　　☼

"I think you were right, father, Mab has not yet manifested fully in this world. She has no living host but operates from the edges of the Otherworld," said Viviana to Taliesin as they sat at the table in Viviana's tower on the Isle of the Font.

Taliesin had returned to the Unseen Vale the day after Morgause and Viviana's magical battle. The armies of Gorlois and Uther were battling at the foot of the Cotswolds, just outside the town of Vindogladia, while Lot of the Orkneys was preparing a large invasion force of Saxons and Picts that would imminently set sail down the eastern coast of Britannia with the intent of laying siege to Londinium. The lands of the outside world were in turmoil since the death of King Ambrose. The Tribes required a High King in order to work cohesively together and, with the throne unoccupied, chaotic pandemonium was setting in across the lands of the Britons, causing undue violence and panic the likes of which hadn't been seen since the days of Vortigern's tyranny.

"I looked into her mind and one of Mab's motives was made clear to me," said my mother, "she wants Galahad dead. She knows you are old and frail and will likely not survive many more winters. Galahad will be the next Merlin and that frightens her. She knows your power, the power you will pass to Galahad with your last breath. If there was no Merlin, there would be no one left with the strength to oppose her except for me and I barely survived my battle with Morgause."

"What of Morgause?" said Taliesin, "What should we do with her? She can't remain suspended in dreamless sleep forever."

"She can't be freed," said Viviana, "If we let her go she will continue serving Mab and seeking to destroy us. We will wake her but we will keep her here, locked in this tower until she decides to give up serving the darkness or dies from old age."

It seemed that would be the end of the discussion until Morgana appeared in the doorway of the tower, her face contorted with rage, her skin red with anger. She stormed into the room and I half-expected her to haul off and slap Viviana across the face but she held her composure. She looked at me as though she meant to chastise me for allowing anything to happen to Morgause. Then she turned on Viviana and Taliesin, her fury boiling over into unbridled rage.

"How could you?" she yelled at Viviana, "You would do this to your own blood? After she did so much for you?"

"You don't understand, Morgana," said Taliesin, "Morgause is sick. Her mind has been invaded by the darkness. What Viviana did she did for your sister's own good."

"I don't care," screamed Morgana, "Wake her up."

"I won't," replied Viviana, "at least not yet."

"You will wake her or I am done here," said Morgana forcefully, "I will recant my vows to the goddess Brigga and leave Avalon without its future Lady. What would you do without me here to take over when you are dead and buried?"

"You and Morgause are not the only daughters of my mother's bloodline," said my mother, "If you decide to abandon your vows then Guinevere will take your place when she is old enough."

"You told me once you had seen Guinevere's future in your mirror and that she could never succeed you as Lady," said Morgana.

"There is Elaine," said Viviana.

"She's too old," sneered Morgana, "I am the only one left who can follow in your footsteps. I'm begging you, Viviana, give me back my sister."

My mother looked compassionate, turning her kind eyes in the direction of Morgana and frowning from the insurmountable sadness of the previous night's events.

"I didn't take her from you," said Viviana softly, "If you wish to be angry, be angry with Mab. She has reached out from the Otherworld to corrupt your sister's soul, to twist her mind towards dark and selfish ambitions. She now serves Mab and no other."

Morgana was about to say something, to go on the defensive on behalf of her comatose sister but they were interrupted when a small raven flew through the window near the hearth and perched itself on the table next to Taliesin. It squawked a few times and then commenced to preen its feathers. I would've thought it only one of Taliesin's pets except that Taliesin's demeanor was immediately changed. It was as though he'd been hit in the groin by a stray ball. Even without her sight, Viviana could sense something had changed and Morgana looked at me quizzically, as if she expected me to explain the significance of the bird. Taliesin looked from Morgana to me and then back to Morgana before deciding to speak.

"It seems Uther has murdered your father," he said to Morgana, "and he's claimed your mother as his new bride."

The color drained from Morgana's face and she fell to the floor in shock. She never spoke of her father but I knew she'd been close to Gorlois but she was even more attached to her mother, my Aunt Igerna. Viviana shifted in her seat in disbelief and my jaw dropped thinking about what this tragic news would do to Morgause's anger. There would be no hope of saving her from the darkness with this fresh kindling to fuel her rage.

"What about my brothers?" cried Morgana. "Mordent, Morevain, Moreth, Mordred. Please tell me they are safe."

Taliesin looked at the floor.

"Only the youngest was spared," he said sadly, "Mordred is the only one who still lives."

Morgana screamed a blood-curdling, heart-wrenching wail that would've made even the most unfeeling tyrant drop to his knees and sob. My mother stood and tried to wrap her arms around Morgana but Morgana pushed her away and pulled herself to her feet. She looked changed. The sadness was drilling into her heart, blackening her otherwise innocent spirit with the devastating feeling of loss. In one day she had lost nearly everyone in her family. Her father and older brothers were dead, her younger brother was still alive but from what Taliesin said, he was missing. Morgause was in a coma because of her betrayal and Igerna was the prisoner wife of Uther of the Silures. My heart was breaking for Morgana.

"This isn't over," hissed Morgana before rushing out of the tower with her teary eyes cupped in her hands, her robes flailing behind her like the wisp of a ghostly gown caught in the wind.

Viviana returned to her seat while Taliesin pulled out a pipe and started smoking a fragrant weed called Arichouá. He used the herb primarily to induce visions but it also had the side effect of causing relaxation and euphoria. Taliesin wasn't much for mead but he had a passion for the Arichouá that kept him sedated and mellow. Viviana wasn't the same when it came to alcohol. She retrieved a cup and bottle of mead from a nearby shelf and commenced to drown her sorrows in drunkenness. The pair of them were in shock. It was understandable. The raven strutted across the table and then flew away but not before it let out one final series of squawks.

"There's more," he said.

"What else?" said Viviana with a dismal tone.

"Lot has launched a fleet of 200 ships bound for Londinium," said Taliesin, "I must go at once to join the Knights, to do what I can to drive Lot back to the Orkneys where he belongs."

Taliesin stood to leave but Viviana rose from her chair to cut him off.

"What about Morgause? This hasn't been settled," said Viviana, "If nothing else, it shows Avalon is no longer safe. I'm worried about the children staying here unguarded."

"What do you propose?" asked Taliesin.

Viviana took a few moments to breathe, pondering exactly what needed to be done to ensure the safety of those she most cared about. Taliesin tapped his foot in impatience and threatened to walk out if she didn't speak. Just as he was about to leave, a lightbulb went off in Viviana's mind and everything was made clear.

"Morgana will never leave without Morgana but the others should be taken away from here when you leave this very day," she said, "Galahad can accompany you on your travels. He is your apprentice after all. Madoc wishes to join the Knights and he's come of age. He might as well be allowed to fulfill his dreams now. There might not be a tomorrow. Tristram will be reluctant to abandon his post on the Isle of Stone but he must for his own safety. Keep him with you until you find a proper place to leave him, maybe back with his family. And I want you to take Guinevere."

I was astonished that my mother was willing to part with her beloved daughter. While I had been sent to live with my father in Lodecran nearly at the moment of my birth, Viviana kept Guinevere by her side all the time. She was nurturing and caring in a way I had never known. A part of me was jealous but I cared deeply for my two year old little sister and that love outshined any contemptuous thoughts I might've entertained about her and my mother's relationship. Taliesin was reluctant to agree but Viviana wouldn't take no for an answer. She was just as stubborn as her father, if not more so, and he knew arguing with her would do no good.

"Where should I take her?" he asked, "She is too young and fragile to live on the road with me."

"Take her to Glevun," said Viviana, "There is a woman there named Aelis who runs a fish market with her husband, Rugar. I have known Aelis a very long time. She can be trusted to keep Guinevere safe. Rugar is a Saxon but he is a follower of the Old Religion and assimilated into the Tribes by his marriage to Aelis. They will give Guinevere a good home, a place for her to grow into her destiny."

☼   ☼   ☼

The group of us left the Unseen Vale that afternoon and, for the first time in years, I found myself in the outside world, away from the familiarity of the Druids and the safety of Avalon. It was also the first time I'd seen Tristram since my year in a coma. I was surprised at how attractive he'd become. The gangly roman boy with a big nose and odd features had given way to a tall, broad-shouldered beautiful man with the beginnings of a smart beard and captivating eyes that could pierce the heart with their honesty and intrigue. Madoc was always the good-looker in our crowd and he still had strong, handsome features, but the exotic uniqueness of Tristram overpowered any of Madoc's attractive qualities. Madoc looked gallant in his leather armor, with Eregolan sheathed in a scabbard at his side, but Tristram looked like an otherworldly monk in the black robes of a Guardian and the mystery of his duties added to his allure. He seemed a mysterious magician from another world, come to teach me his secrets.

Taliesin led us through the veil to the Fenfolk village near the Christian Isle of Glass where we retrieved horses and supplies for our travels. The road would take us northeast along the Fosse Way for a matter of hours and then a quick ride up the Welsh Road would take us to Glevun. Guinevere was riding with Taliesin, her little legs barely dangling passed the edge of the saddle. Taliesin was careful and kind with Guinevere, ensuring she was changed and fed when needed but the presence of a toddler slowed our travels and we found ourselves camping overnight near where the Fosse Way and Welsh Road intersected.

Madoc built up a roaring fire and we all huddled around it for warmth. Guinevere was nestled in the folds of Taliesin's robes, quietly snoring, while Tristram and Madoc slept on the other side of the hearth. Taliesin was smoking Arichouá and staring into the fire while I gazed up at the stars wheeling slowly around the earth as it grew later. The moon was new and so the landscape was wreathed in darkness. The only real source of light was the fire itself and we made sure to remain always within its glowing ring of protection.

"So are we supporting Uther now in his claim to the throne?" I asked and Taliesin shifted his gaze to meet mine.

"We will support the True King," he replied.

"And who's that?" I asked. I knew the prophecy of the Crones. I was there when they spoke it but they never said who the True King was, or when he would come. Until then, our choice was clear. Gorlois was dead. It was either Uther or Lot.

"The True King will be revealed in time," said Taliesin, "You mustn't doubt what you feel is true in your heart. I know we now face perilous times and all Britons are in danger of being eradicated. I also know these dark days will pass and the light will return. The Crones have never been wrong, not since their order was established centuries ago. Their Cauldron may obscure their visions but it never shows them falsities."

"You didn't really answer my question," I said.

"Until the True King arrives it is our duty to support the one who supports us," he said, "I think you already know who that man is."

"Uther," I replied, "but he murdered Gorlois in cold blood and took Igerna as wife against her wishes. Is he really the man to save Avalon?"

"The white dragon and the red," I said softly.

"What's that?" asked Taliesin.

"Uther marches behind banners with a red dragon and Lot behind banners with a white dragon. Gorlois was the eagle but the eagle is dead. Now the dragons will fight relentlessly to claim the throne and begin ruling according to their own designs."

"Not just the throne," admitted Taliesin, "the man who emerges triumphant will also claim the title of holy ruler of the ancient Britons and master of the lands of Britannia, Valentia, Whales, and Caledonia. Avalon can no longer be without a leader if we hope to endure but only the True King may bear the name Pendragon."

I barely slept that night. The comfortable safety of Avalon was no longer there. I was in the outside world, a place of violence and fear with highwaymen and vagabonds ready to assault travelers on the roads in order to line their pockets with gold. Taliesin fell asleep moments after our conversation ended and snored loudly. Madoc and Tristram didn't stir until the sun was rising into the sky, heralding in the dawn. Madoc rushed off to hunt down some breakfast and Tristram began restarting the fire. I stretched and rubbed my eyes, hoping to massage away the exhaustion with every swipe of my fingers. Guinevere was wandering around chasing a butterfly and Taliesin awoke demanding water from Tristram. Madoc succeeded in catching two healthy size whiting from the nearby river and we cooked them on the fire quickly. After eating and packing our provisions onto our horses, we resumed the road to Glevun. The journey took only three hours, a straight shot down the Welsh Road, passed the Dunland Hills and down into a narrow valley near the River Sabine.

The town of Glevun was little more than a village enclosed with walls of timber. It was situated on the banks of the River Sabrina and accessible only by a narrow roman bridge, crossing the tumultuous rapids of the rushing waterway below. Taliesin knew I would be saddened parting with Guinevere and so he insisted I say my goodbyes on the near side of the bridge. I hugged my little sister and kissed her on the forehead but she didn't understand. Taliesin allowed me to hold onto her longer than I expected before turning his horse around and trotting across the bridge, into the town. He didn't return for an hour and when he did his face was solemn and bereaved. I wanted to ride into Glevun and make sure Guinevere was happy, that she would be safe with her new family but I couldn't. Taliesin would insist against it and force us to carry on.

"Now that Guinevere is safe we must ride with all speed," said Taliesin, "Some of the villagers confirmed Lot is already nearing the channel. We must make sure he doesn't reach the Thames."

"Where are we going?" asked Madoc.

"To join the Knights in Camulodunum," said Taliesin, "The last battle for the throne is about to begin."

Chapter Fourteen
"The Perfect Storm"

The ride from Glevun to Camulodunum took twenty-five hours at a gallop. We only stopped to rest the horses and replenish our water stores before continuing our swift journey through the lowland countryside along the Welsh Road. The road led us through the towns of Corinium and Calleva and through the city of Londinium. The city was just as I remembered it, with its ruined avenues and crumbling architecture, but the people on the side of the streets seemed more beleaguered and less lively. Since the death of Ambrose, the city had been abandoned by the aristocracy who retreated to their country estates to weather the storm brewing between Uther and Lot, waiting to see which man would emerge victorious. Then they would return to the city and pledge their fealty to the new High King.

We didn't stop but continued on to Camulodunum, another six hours' ride passed Londinium. Camulodunum was the seat of power for all the Britons before the Romans conquered the land. It was an ancient city fashioned in a design by some forgotten civilization, filled with Celtic artwork and Beaker ornaments. It was a fortress city with stone walls and ramparts, the only one of its kind west of the Channel. There was only one entrance to the city, crossing the River Menos, with an iron gate that could be sealed with the severing of a single rope. We rode right into the heart of the city, to the castle built against the northeastern wall, on a rocky ledge overlooking the ocean. Taliesin led me, Tristram, and Madoc into the castle, to a great hall with granite floors and walls held up by massive pillars adorned with intricate Celtic braids. At the far end of the room sat a large throne wrought from white marble and adorned with gold, set before a round table of granite with eleven chairs around it. All the Knights were seated in these chairs: Agrivain, Ector, Cunamaglos, Bors, Neithon, Gwynedd,

Gnaeus, Mareth, Brannos, Accolon, and a teenaged boy with brown hair I'd never seen before. My eyes drifted immediately to Accolon and he met my gaze with a loving expression that overflowed with yearning. The primal part of me wanted to run to him, strip off his clothes, and take him right there on the stone table in front of the other Knights but the rational part of me overpowered my yearning so that I could maintain my composure in front of Taliesin and the others. I forced myself to stop looking at Accolon, focusing instead on the newcomer.

"Galahad," said Bors, "It's good to see you, nephew."

"We were beginning to think you'd never arrive, Taliesin," said Ector, "The raven we sent to Avalon never returned. We weren't sure if you received our message or not. Who are these?"

Ector was not referring to me but to the other two boys.

"This is Tristram of Lyonesse and Madoc of the Holy Isles," said Taliesin, pointing to one and then the other. Ector and the other Knights acknowledged them with a nod of their heads. Taliesin was clearly also unfamiliar with the brown-haired teenager seated at the table and he demanded to know the newcomer's name.

"I'd forgotten you had yet to meet our newest member," said Ector, "This is Bedevere of Dubrae. He has come to join us in fighting against Lot of the Orkneys and the return of the darkness to the Tribes."

"Nice to make your acquaintance," said Taliesin, "What news of Lot's fleet? Are they within sight?"

"Our scouts spotted them just off the point of Icenorum late this morning," said Gnaeus, "with a favorable wind they will pass by Witch's Point tomorrow just after first light."

"If left unchallenged Lot's fleet will come to the mouth of the Thames by the time the moon rises tomorrow," said Agrivain, "We don't have enough ships to battle Lot at sea. If we are to have any success, we must warn Uther and have him march his army into Londinium straightaway."

"Uther's forces are still in Cornewall," said Accolon, "It would take them at least two days hard marching to reach Londinium. Lot is only a day from the city. He'd have no problem fortifying the city against invasion long before Uther's armies arrived. We have to count on our ships. They may be few but they're strong with resilient sailors."

"We will not risk our few ships," said Taliesin, "Order them to retreat south this very night. Nor will we send for Uther. I will go before first light to Witch's Point and take care of Lot's fleet."

"Alone?" asked Mareth in disbelief.

"I will take Galahad with me," said Taliesin.

The Knights looked unsure of Taliesin's plan. They were all faithful to Avalon and the Old Religion but they had little experience with magick. To them, magick was something esoteric with no relevance in the real world, best left to fey and gods. Agrivain was the most uneasy. He kept shifting in his seat, as though he wished to speak but he remained silent. None of the Knights had the clout or fortitude to question the Merlin. Any opposition that may have arisen was rendered obsolete as the room went silent. Ector, Bors, Neithon, and Brannos looked like they'd seen a ghost. I turned around to see what they were staring at and was shocked to see the ghostly image of my mother standing in the archway leading into the room. She was nothing but a shade, a transparent specter floating there like a dandelion spur traveling on the wind. Taliesin was the only person in the room who wasn't alarmed at the sight of his daughter.

"Father," said Viviana's image, "I have grave news. Morgana awoke Morgause without my consent in the night. I tried to stop them, to put her back to sleep but Morgause overpowered me. She took Morgana and together they fled Avalon. They are in the outside world and they are very dangerous. Keep Galahad safe."

Just as soon as she appeared, Viviana vanished, leaving the Knights to wonder if what they'd just witnessed was a trick of their senses or a real occurrence with serious implications. Accolon was aware of the meaning behind Viviana's message because he knew Morgana. The other Knights were in the dark and Taliesin meant to keep them that way.

"What was that?" asked Ector.

"None of your concern," snapped Taliesin, "Keep your mind focused on the task at hand. Galahad and I will go before first light to face the threat of Lot's fleet. You must remain here and fortify the city. If we fail, Lot will take Londinium. Camulodunum will have to serve as the center of resistance to his rule. Make the city safe and beseech Kernos and Nimue to show us favor in our endeavors."

✶　　✶　　✶

Taliesin insisted I try to get some rest and showed me to a small bedchamber in the corner of the castle overlooking the sea. There was a large feather bed covered with furs, a wooden chair, and a table with a basin filled with water, as well as a small hearth in the corner where a fire was lazily burning, filling the room with warmth. I was utterly exhausted. We'd been riding nonstop for well over a day. My backside was sore and my legs were stiff. I wanted a warm bath but would have to make do with a quick wash with a rag and a full night's sleep.

"I will return early, I suggest you take some rest," said Taliesin and then he retreated from the room, leaving me alone to wash up and rest. I slipped out of my robes and set them by the hearth. I was hoping for a fresh change of clothes for the morning but I knew it wouldn't happen. The best I could hope is for the smoke from the fire to leave my robes with a rich, oaky fragrance. I was glad to be rid of the smelly, heavy fabric. I ran the washcloth over my body and then jumped onto the bed like a weary child in need of rest. I furrowed into the blankets, my naked body tingling from the sensation of the fur on my skin. I was just about to drift off when there came a soft knock on the door.

"Come in," I said, covering my loins with the blanket.

I expected Taliesin to walk through the door because he forgot something. I was shocked when it was Accolon that walked through the door. I nearly jumped out of the bed before remembering my present state. He stood still by the door for a second, staring my lithe, lean body up and down with his masculine brown eyes, as if compelling me to throw back the blanket and show him the most private parts of my body.

"You shouldn't be here," I said in alarm.

"I know," he replied, "but I don't care."

"Well you should care," I said defensively, "I don't know if you being here has any negative consequences for you but for me it would be the end of everything I've worked for since I was a little boy. I am meant to be a Druid and Druids do no not have sex."

"That's not entirely true," smiled Accolon.

"Don't do that," I snapped. He was using his unique brand of charisma to entice me into relenting. I didn't know how long I'd be able to fight against the temptation.

Accolon didn't even pretend he was concerned with my discomfort. The more nervous I became the more he seemed to enjoy himself. He sat down at the edge of the bed and pulled lightly on the edge of the blankets with a grin, staring towards where the furs were covering my groin. I couldn't help but turn my head and blush.

"It's only fair for you to show me yours," said Accolon, "Since you already got to see mine."

I couldn't forget that day by the river when Mab's love spell was enacted. The first thing I noticed as Accolon ran up to the shore was his large, well-formed member, how it bobbed and swayed with each stride. Its perfection only added to the overall splendor of Accolon's beauty and, from that day forward, all I could think about was finding an opportunity to touch it. I was once again falling under the sway of the love spell as I relented, pulling back the covers to expose my cock. It wasn't as large or pleasing to behold as Accolon's but it was above average in length and bore a sizable girth. I had no real complaints about my body. I was long and skinny but my muscles were tight and my face was symmetric. I looked like one of the fey or Fenfolk, Accolon looked like the god of love.

I tried with all my might to resist him but I couldn't, especially as he stood and removed his own clothes. He crawled across the bed like a panther stalking its prey before pouncing. He lowered himself gently on top of me and began to kiss my neck as I ran my hands back and forth down the muscled contours of his back. I grew hard and so did he as we laid there, our flesh entwined into a single passionate creature intent on nothing but satisfying our sexual desires.

"This isn't real," I said, thinking about Mab's spell driving our lust so that I would ruin my future and any chance of becoming the next Merlin. Accolon stopped grinding himself against me long enough to look up into my eyes and smile.

"I think it is," he said, "I was attracted to you even before you read that spell on the shore of the river. I know you were attracted to me too. I could see it in your eyes the second you spotted me in the water."

I didn't know if I believed him and I didn't care. I pulled him back down on top of me and kissed him again and again, forcing my tongue down his throat as though I was a child trying to lick up the last traces of ice cream from the bottom of a sugar cone. In that second, I was willing to give up everything I'd worked for. I would've done anything to put my hands on Accolon, to know the secret places of his body, shared with no one else but me. I felt important, wanted. Accolon licked at my chest, tracing his way down the muscled road leading to my groin before slurping up my manhood into his mouth. I sighed in ecstasy as he moved up and down, back and forth, taking my tumescent manhood down his moist throat. I was about to explode in orgasmic passion when he detached himself from me.

"Not yet," he said before turning me over and burying my face in the pillow. He kissed me on the back of the neck as if to say I'm sorry if I hurt you and then thrust himself inside me. I thought for sure he would tear me open as the pain cascaded through my body, overwhelming my senses and causing me to scream. I felt like pushing him off and running to a corner to cower but I bit my lip and allowed him to continue. Soon the pain gave way to a more intense pleasure than I'd ever known. My screaming became filled not with pain but with contentedness as Accolon raced towards climax. He let out a primal grunt as he released his seed inside me and then collapsed onto the bed, using the furs to wipe away the sweat on his brow. I put my arm around him and nuzzled my head into his chest as he ran his fingers through my hair, gently massaging my scalp.

"Tell me about yourself," I said softly as Accolon shifted beside me.

"There's not much to tell," he replied, "I've been a Knight of Avalon since I was fifteen, when my father died. He was Acron, Clan Lord of the Belgae and King of the Isle of Wight. He was murdered by a Saxon brawler. Then I became King. But I don't want the office. I ran away from Wight to join Ector and the others without looking back. My cousin Anaris macUna will likely become King when the Belgae elders finally decide to depose me. Other than that, there's nothing. I'm good with a spear, better with a sword, and I believe in Kernos and Nimue. And I am completely falling for you, not because of some spell, but because I knew you before I met you. I saw you in my dreams."

I replied with a deep, passionate kiss.

We made love twice more that night, each time better than the prior, and I felt myself falling for him too. I would love the man taking away my innocence and virginity. Instead of giving myself to Kernos, I was giving myself to Accolon. I didn't want to forsake my future as a Druid but I also didn't relish the idea of being without my warrior. I resolved I wouldn't worry about it until something was found out. I would keep the affair a secret and hope against hope no one would be the wiser. Taliesin was good at seeing into the minds of others but, perhaps if I kept the secret buried deep in the dark recesses of my mind it would never come to light. There would be no turning back and, what's more, I didn't want to. I set my course that night, with Accolon thrusting himself into me again and again. I would walk on both roads: the road of love and the road of devotion. If Kernos or Nimue were displeased with my actions, I would count on them to descend from the Otherworld and chastise me themselves. As the night grew increasingly late, moving swiftly towards the first light of morning, I made myself a promise. I would be the next Merlin and I would also spend the rest of my life with my lover, Accolon.

"You have to go," I said after Accolon finished ravaging me a third and final time. He winked and then kissed me as if to say he understood, then stood, dressed and left the room.

☼ ☼ ☼

Taliesin arrived at my bedchamber within an hour of Accolon leaving. He waltzed in without knocking and, to my relief, carried a freshly laundered set of robes. I quickly slipped into them without speaking. I felt intensely guilty about what I'd just done with Accolon and I tried desperately to hide the truth in the deepest part of my mind, to forget about the immense passion of our sexual experiences before Taliesin could sense there was something different about me. Luckily for me, he didn't.

We left Camulodunum while it was still dark. It was just the two of us as we abandoned the road, walking across hilly fields towards a distant point northeast of the fortress city. Within an hour we came to a flat ledge at the edge of a sharp cliff overlooking the sea over a hundred feet below. It was still dark but the sun was inching its way up over the watery horizon and the sky had turned a dull shade of blue. The flat stone stood out against the granite of the cliff. It was limestone and was artificially mounted to the ground beneath it. The surface was completely flat and smooth, as though it had been held under the water of a river with a fast current and shaped over thousands of years. At the far edge there was a railing attached to hundreds of steps leading down the edge of the cliff and into the calm waters of the sea. I expected there to be a small terrace below, situated at the edge of the water, but the stairs just led down into the deeps.

"What is this place?" I asked Taliesin as we came to stand atop the strange limestone platform.

"Witch's Point," replied Taliesin with his eyes fixed on the distant horizon, darting across the water like a cat following a feather. He was looking for Lot's fleet of ships but there was no sign of them yet.

"What are the stairs for?" I said.

"Almost 3,000 years ago the sea was much lower and the channel didn't exist," said Taliesin, "the stairs led down to a road that stretched from here to the continent and beyond. The Beaker Road, built by the ones who brought the wisdom of the ancients here, to the Isles of Tin. When the waters rose, the road was washed away, but the stairs remained. We left them there as a tribute to those who came before us, to imbue this platform, this place, with great power like that of the Henge on the Summer Plain."

As I stood there I could feel the energy surging through the stones and into my feet, especially as the sun rose fully over the horizon, enveloping us in its radiant warmth. I expected Taliesin to be drinking in the warmth and heralding the rise of the sun with an Ogham prayer but he remained completely still, staring out over the water. I followed his line of sight and what I witnessed sent chills down my spine. Lot's fleet had just become visible as they sailed around the point. First a dozen, then fifty, 200, 500. I lost count after that. They looked like a swarm of water-skippers flitting across the calm water, each flying a black banner adorned with the image of a white dragon. Taliesin worked quickly. He pulled his ceremonial dagger from its sheath within the folds of his robe, an ornate bronze knife with a gold-inlayed handle.

"Whatever happens, Galahad," he said, "Do not interrupt the spell. It does not matter if I live or die this day as long as Lot's fleet is sent to the depths. Do I have your word you will do as I say?"

"What's going to happen?" I asked but, after the look Taliesin gave me, I said, "I promise."

Taliesin stood tall, facing the sea, and ran the dagger sideways across his left wrist, then his right, spilling his blood onto the limestone platform, not just a drop or two, but a steady pool. He looked sickly and weak but he remained standing there, his eyes staring at the sky above.

"Anemos ourliachtó kai tin ánodo ton ydáton," said Taliesin.

Suddenly the wind began to howl across the water, causing it to rise up in choppy waves that crashed against the cliff.

"Skouraínei ton ouranó kai afíste ti vrochí," he said.

The sky filled with dark clouds, as if they appeared from nowhere, blocking out the sun and intensifying the violence of the sea below. Taliesin wavered as he continued to gush blood from his wrists but his resolve was clear as his voice echoed across the water.

"Férei tin astrapí," Taliesin continued.

Thunder clapped again and again, shaking the earth and sea, before hundreds of bolts of lightning descended on Lot's fleet, striking each boat and causing their sails to burst into flames.

"Afíste i thálassa katapínoun olóklira," screamed Taliesin before collapsing on the platform in the pool of his own blood. I ran to him, to help him to his feet and take him to help, but not before I watched the tumultuous storm shepherd the waters of the sea into a mighty whirlpool which swallowed the majority of Lot's fleet, leaving only a single ship bobbing amidst the violent waves with incinerated sails and the banner of the white dragon flying upon the mast in flames.

Chapter Fifteen
"The New High King"

Taliesin barely survived the ordeal at Witch's Point. He was tended by the best physicians in Camulodunum but they feared he would slip into a coma and then quietly fade away. He didn't. He remained alive and even regained enough lucidity to call for the Knights and instruct them to send for Uther and his armies. Taliesin paved the way for Uther to stand unopposed in his claim for the throne now it was time for him to be crowned. Taliesin also asked an envoy be sent to Avalon to invite Viviana and the other senior Druids and Druidesses to attend the coronation before he slipped back into a near perpetual state of sleep. The Knights did as they were commanded. Ector and Neithon rode for Uther's encampment in Cornewall while Cunamaglos and Mareth made their way for the Fens and Avalon.

I spent the days that followed in the company of Bors and my nights with Accolon. Bors taught me about our family's history, about the long line of kings from which I was descended. There had always been a king of the Armorica and I was directly related to each. Lodecran was a new kingdom, given to my father by his own, but it would no longer be ruled by a member of our ancestral house. I was the last of my line and forsook ruling my patrimony in order to join the Druids, a commitment I wanted to take seriously but, each night that I laid with Accolon drove me further away from that choice. I actually decided to learn how to wield a sword and, while Taliesin slept, Bors taught me the proper uses of a roman gladium, a Saxon longsword, and a claymore, weapon of the Scotii. I began to understand why Madoc was so fond of his blade, Eregolan. Bors thought I had the makings of a good warrior and Accolon encouraged my studies while we laid together each night in bed. Away from Avalon I was experiencing a world I was never allowed to know and I found it alluring. I very nearly decided to abandon my training as a Druid altogether, until my mother arrived at Camulodunum with an entourage of Priestesses and Druids.

"We need to talk," said my mother. Those were the first words she spoke to me after her arrival. She took my arm and I led her away to the gardens near the heart of the fortress city, a ghastly array of untended rose bushes and grapevines.

"I know what you've done," she said once we were seated on a bench overlooking the heart of the garden and I suddenly felt like I might throw up. I didn't know how but she'd learned of my affair with Accolon. She was going to berate me and then eject me from the order of the Initiates. I'd be exiled from Avalon and never again have the chance to follow in Taliesin's footsteps as the next Merlin.

"It is not an unforgivable offense to hold a weapon of war," she said, "But we are forbidden to do so nonetheless. If you were already a sworn Druid, you might be expelled from the order for learning to use a sword. As an Initiate, you can be forgiven, but only if you promise me to never touch a sword again. You are meant to wield a power far greater than any earthly weapons forged by the hand of man."

I wanted to tell her that I wasn't going to stop training, that I was going to be a warrior, not a Druid, but I didn't. I was destined to follow in Taliesin's footsteps. No matter how much I tried to run, seeing my mother reminded me of my commitment to learn the ancient ways of magick and mysticism. I was set on my road and, though I'd deviated from the path with Accolon, I resolved I would see my training to its end.

"I promise," I said, "I won't use a sword anymore."

"Good," she said, "Now we need to prepare to greet Uther. His army was behind us. They should arrive within the hour. Where is my father?"

I recounted for Viviana what Taliesin had done, how he'd sunk Lot's fleet with a powerful spell. She insisted on seeing him at once so I took her to his room and then returned to the courtyard to wait for Uther. I was curious to see the man who emerged victorious over Gorlois and Lot. Morgana and Morgause were devastated when Uther murdered their father in cold blood and took their mother, Igerna, as his captive bride but the rest of the people of Avalon felt Uther was the only chance to restore the ways of the ancients and save the Britons from total ruin.

I sat there for just over an hour before I heard the sound of a horn blowing across the river, just beyond the main gate leading into the fortress city. In five columns, Uther's soldiers marched into Camulodunum like roman legionaries forming a phalanx to sack a mighty city. At the heart of their ranks rode a man and woman, each mounted on their own horse. The man was broad-shouldered and stocky, with ruddy skin and calloused hands. His dirty blonde hair fell in dreadlocks down his neck and his beard was twisted into three braids. There was nothing overly spectacular about this man. He wasn't even good to look at. The woman at his side was the exact opposite in every way. She was tall and fair, with an olive complexion and hair of reddish black. She was nearing her midlife but was still filled with vibrant energy that made her seem much younger and her smile was warm and filled with congeniality. I didn't need anyone to tell me I was looking on the face of my Aunt Igerna, mother of Morgana, Morgause, and their four brothers, three of whom were dead.

A large mass of people emerged from the castle in the corner of the city and rushed towards Uther. At the head of the column was the High Druid Faelan with Viviana on his arm and my Aunt Elaine beside them. Behind them were half-a-dozen Christian priests clustered around a bishop dressed all in white. The Knights were behind them with several other men and women of the Tribes, waiting to see the man who would be their savior. I thought it foolish when the real hero was Taliesin. It was by his power that Lot was turned away and the land made safe. Why were they so accepting of Uther? Because he murdered Gorlois and his sons. I wondered about the only surviving son of Gorlois and Igerna, a boy of nine named Mordred. He wasn't with his mother amidst the ranks of Uther's army. Perhaps he was back in Tintagel beyond the Cornewall, or he'd been rescued by Morgana and Morgause. A strange feeling washed over me as I thought of Mordred and I thought I saw a shadowy silhouette looming in the corner of my eye.

"Welcome, my Lord Uther, to Camulodunum," said Faelan with a bow as Uther dismounted from his horse. Uther turned to help Igerna from her steed before deciding to respond to the High Druid.

"I'm glad to be here," he grumbled, "I hear I have the Merlin to thank for this victory. Where is he? I'd like to show him my gratitude."

"I'm afraid, my Lord, that Taliesin is teetering on the edge of death," said my mother, "He invoked the Blood Oath to drown Lot's army at the bottom of the sea so that you could rise to become the High King that Avalon knows you will be."

"I will try not to disappoint," said Uther.

"And we also wish to welcome you, sire," said the bishop dressed all in white, "I am Bishop Sebastianus, head of the Nicene See of Britannia. I hope you will allow us the privilege of advising you as we did Ambrose."

Uther only grunted. He seemed wholly disinterested in the Christians. His attention was fixed on the Knights of Avalon standing behind them. He was particularly interested in Ector. He swooped passed those gathered between them and pulled Ector into a massive bear hug. Everyone was at a loss for words.

"You old fool, I never thought I'd see the day," laughed Ector.

"You always were a skeptic," smiled Uther, "I didn't know you were serving the Holy Isles. When did you decide to leave the north?"

"A few years ago," replied Ector, "I was recruited by Brannos."

Ector pointed to the oldest of the Knights.

"Come, let us drink and recall the old days," said Uther, "I want to hear all about your lad, what's his name? Percival, wasn't it?"

Ector nodded as he and the other Knights followed Uther back into the castle and out of sight. The Christians, who looked thoroughly displeased at the way they had been cast aside, stormed off towards the gates to the city, leaving Faelan, myself, Tristram, and Madoc in the company of my mother and her two sisters. Igerna walked over with her hands clasped to her stomach and spoke with a proper tone.

"Sisters, it is good to see you," she said blandly.

"Igerna," grumbled Elaine.

"How are you, Igerna?" asked Viviana, clearly concerned about what her youngest sister had witnessed in Tintagel, the murder of her husband and her three eldest sons. Igerna didn't seem phased in the slightest by my mother's question.

"I am with child," smiled Igerna, "Uther is anxious. It will be his first. I think it will be a boy. What do you think sister?"

Viviana was used to people asking her to divine the gender of their unborn children but she was never pleased to be addressed as though she were a simple fortune teller and not the greatest of all druidesses.

"I'm sure it will be healthy, whatever it is," replied Viviana.

Igerna glanced over towards the retreating Christians and then ran off to retrieve them, calling them back to join Viviana, Faelan, and the other representatives of the Old Religion. The air grew so thick with tension it could be used as a blanket.

"I apologize for my husband's manners," said Igerna to Bishop Sebastianus, "He doesn't have much experience with civilized men. Welshmen are so barbaric. I want you to feel at home here, Eminence. If there is anything I can do for you, don't hesitate to ask."

"Thank you, my Lady," smiled Sebastianus in astonishment and then, with a bow, he retreated into the castle with his priests at his heel. Viviana looked and Elaine and Elaine looked disapprovingly at Igerna, as if to compel Igerna to explain herself, like a stern warden examining a violent prisoner of war.

"I'm a Christian now," said Igerna and then, without explanation, she strode off towards the castle. Faelan, Tristram, and Madoc followed Igerna and soon it was just me, my mother, and my aunt standing in the courtyard. Viviana was leaning heavily on her walking stick and she seemed to be lost in thought. Elaine shook her head dramatically to illustrate her constant and longstanding disapproval of their younger half-sister. Rhiannon was the mother of all three but, in the majority of matters, Igerna seemed to favor her father in both temperament and disposition.

"She hasn't changed a bit," said Elaine, "Still as self-absorbed as ever. She just lost three sons and a husband and she's acting like it never happened, like the man who has now planted his seed within her is a gallant hero and not a cold-blooded murderer. Are we really going to support Uther as High King in these lands?"

Viviana was slow to respond.

"For now," she said, "But I have a feeling it won't be long before the True King reveals himself. I can't help but feel he is here, somewhere nearby, as is a shadow I cannot place. It might be Mab."

"What do we do?" said Elaine urgently.

"Remain vigilant. The darkness will make itself known at the opportune moment," said my mother, "and we'll be ready."

☼   ☼   ☼

Uther's coronation ceremony took place the following morning. All the lesser kings and dukes of Britannia were gathered in the Great Hall of the castle in Camulodunum, along with Bishop Sebastianus and his priests, my mother, Faelan, and the Druids, the Knights of Avalon, and various other notable noblemen and warriors invited to witness the crowning of the next High King of all the Britons. Uther was seated on the large stone seat at the head of the roundtable where the Knights of Avalon were seated when I arrived in Camulodunum with Taliesin. He was dressed in a pristinely embroidered red tunic with black breeches and looked every part the king, except for his disheveled beard and dirty hair. Igerna was seated next to him on a small wooden stool with her hand resting on the arm of his throne. She was wearing a matching red gown and, around her neck, hung the crucifix of the Nicene Christians. The banners of Avalon were hanging alongside the banners of the red dragon on the wall behind the throne and a large golden cross was sitting in a stand on the side of Uther opposite where Igerna was regally seated. I was under the impression Faelan would be placing the bronzed crown upon Uther's head but, to my surprise and the astonishment of the crowd, Taliesin appeared on the dais beside the throne, completely recovered and carrying the bronzed crown with a matching ruby-encrusted tiara on a velvet pillow. These were newly fashioned replicas of the crowns worn by the Pendragon and his consort during the days of the Beakers.

"Friends and fellow Britons," said Taliesin, "We are come here today to witness the rise of a great man, a leader to push back the darkness and ensure the lands remain at peace. All the kings and dukes of Britannia are gathered here today to swear fealty to our new High King, Uther of the Silures, King of South Wales. Stand now and address your subjects."

Taliesin stepped aside as Uther stood and straightened his tunic. He seemed nervous and it was clear he was not a natural public speaker. It took him a few moments to gather his strength and look out at those gathered to call him High King. His voice was shaky as he spoke and he kept his nerves in check by twiddling his thumbs. He was a great bear of a man, a barbarian warrior capable of striking down a dozen men without breaking a sweat, but in that moment he seemed nothing more than a meek student put on the spot by a callous professor.

"I am not a man of many words," said Uther, "I am man of action. I hereby forswear as long as I sit upon the throne, I shall act in the best interest of you, my people. I will not allow Lot to bring his Saxon barbarians down upon us without giving him one hell of a fight. We know his ship survived the storm and limped back to the safety of the faraway Orkneys. Let us who are gathered this day agree here and now to ensure he stays there. Who's with me?"

The crowd responded with a mighty roar. The lesser kings and dukes held their fists high in the air, a sign of fraternity and fealty, while the other noblemen and ladies howled in agreement. Bishop Sebastianus and his priests remained skeptically silent and my mother remained still, as did the other Druids. Once the crowd calmed down, Uther returned to his throne and Taliesin stepped out in front of him, raising the bronzed crown above his head in a ritual gesture signifying his authority as Merlin of all the Britons to anoint and appoint the ruler of Britannia.

"Do you, Uther, son of the Silures, swear to always defend the rights of the Tribes, the Wulds, and the Welshmen?" asked Taliesin.

"I swear," replied Uther.

"And do you swear to uphold the ways of the Old Religion in the face of all opposition?"

"I swear."

"If necessary, will you swear to lay down your life for the benefit of your subjects?" asked Taliesin.

"I swear," repeated Uther.

"Then I hereby proclaim you, Uther, son of the Silures, High King of Britannia, Valentia, Wales, and the Armorica. May all men here act as witness and make their consent known with a shout."

All the lesser kings and dukes in the crowd shouted again with their fists in the air as Taliesin lowered the bronzed crown onto Uther's head. Uther's expression was unchanged as the crown came to rest upon his brow. He didn't seem to feel more important or involved. He was strangely detached and yet present in the moment at the same time. Taliesin moved to stand in front of Igerna and raised the ruby-encrusted tiara out over her head as he had Uther but before he could speak, Igerna pushed the crown away and stood, passing Taliesin to address the crowd.

"I wish to say something," she said, "As many of you are aware, I was not so long ago married to Gorlois, Duke of Cornewall, herald of the Roman Eagle. Gorlois was struck down, not in cold-blooded murder as you've been led to believe, but on the field of battle. Uther proved to be the greater man and I do not hold any animosity towards him, my new husband, for what he was forced to do in the heat of war. I lament the loss of my sons but I cannot allow their deaths to mar the greatness of these events. I want you all to know that I am now with child. I bear Uther's child and, with God's grace, it will be a son and heir, a boy who will be pledged to serve the people of this land and also the God of Abram. My son, and any sons that follow, by my request and the consent of your High King, shall be raised Christian, christened into the Nicene Church of Rome."

This time it was Sebastianus and his priests who exclaimed merrily with shouts and praises and soon the better half of the crowd had joined in their mirth. Taliesin looked at Igerna with his brows furrowed and my mother seemed to tighten her grip on Elaine's arm. The Knights remained silent as well. They were vowed to the protection of Avalon and the preservation of the Old Religion. Accolon was looking at me as if he was waiting for me to walk over and provide him with an explanation to my aunt's actions but I was just as confused. With a sheepish smile, Igerna returned to her stool and nodded at Taliesin, giving him permission to resume the coronation.

"Do you, Igerna, daughter of Rhiannon, swear to aid the High King in all his duties as his dutiful consort and wife?" asked Taliesin.

"I do here swear," said Igerna hotly.

"Then I proclaim you our anointed High Queen," said Taliesin and he placed the tiara atop her head before retreating from the dais to join the other Druids in the crowd. It was the conclusion of the coronation but the crowd was unable to leave. Igerna stood once again and raised her hands into the air to signal the crowd to remain where they were.

"Just one last thing before we go and feast in my husband's honor," said Igerna, "I would invite the wives of the Knights of Avalon to remain here in Camulodunum to serve as my ladies-in-waiting. I would like very much to begin bridging the divide between the old ways, the traditions of our ancestors, and the word of God. It will begin with you."

The crowd cheered again and Bishop Sebastianus looked like he might start dancing a jig. Viviana looked like a mother who'd been betrayed by her favorite daughter and the dissatisfaction on Elaine's face illustrated her ever-present disgust. Taliesin was looking at me and I was staring at Accolon. The crowd was degenerating into jubilant chaos but, just as they began to quiet, there came an eerily familiar voice from the back of the great hall, a voice that sent me into a state of panic.

"Wonderful speech, mother," she said and everyone turned around to see Morgause and Morgana standing behind the Druids. Next to them stood a boy of nine with reddish black hair and pale, alabaster skin. He was staring at the floor and I could feel an overwhelming sense of sadness emanating from his aura. It was the last son of Gorlois and Igerna. It was Igerna's last son, Mordred.

Chapter Sixteen
"The Cup and Sword"

"What's wrong, mother, aren't you happy to see us?" asked Morgause with a sneer. Morgana kept her eyes fixed on the floor and Mordred looked frightened.

The entire crowd was in shock, most of all the dazed Igerna seated upon her stool. Word of the demented Morgause had spread throughout Britannia and everyone present knew she was a servant of the dark goddess, Mab. The noblemen and ladies rushed to the corners of the room as though Morgause was a raging fire threatening to burn them alive. The Bishop and his priests dropped to their knees and crossed themselves, muttering Latin prayers to their God under their breath. The Knights of Avalon drew their weapons and the Druids stepped between the dais and Morgause, to defend their new High King with whatever magick they could muster. The whole time Morgause was laughing maniacally like a sociopathic murderer taking twisted satisfaction in inflicting brutality upon others.

"Morgana," said my mother gently, "Morgana, you don't have to do this, you don't have to stand with her. Come back to us, child. Return to your place with the Maiden-Healers, where you belong."

"She belongs with me," sneered Morgause, "our father is dead and our mother has betrayed us. We only have each other, me, Morgana, and Mordred. How does that make you feel, mother? Do you feel proud of yourself with that crown on your head?"

Igerna didn't respond. It was Uther who stood in defense of his wife, his arms crossed and his eyes filled with rage.

"You have no business here, witch," he spat, "This is my kingdom and you are not welcome. Be gone before these Knights cannot be restrained and set upon you with their swords and spears. I did not murder your family.

Your father and older brothers were casualties of war. If you want evidence to support that claim, look beside you. If I was the cold-hearted brute you believe me to be, why would I let Mordred live?"

"Liar," screamed Morgause and the force of her wailing caused the great hall to shake.

"Enough," said Taliesin with a voice like thunder, "I do not wish to harm you, Morgause, but I will if I must. Leave this place and go back to the shadows with Mab."

"I'm not leaving until I say what I came here to tell my mother," said Morgause, "I have a prophecy to pronounce. You, Igerna, daughter of Rhiannon, have forsaken one son for another, for the one growing in your belly. It is only fitting that the forsaken son one day rise up and destroy the chosen son in the name of Mab. Mark my words, dear mother, from the day of his birth that unborn child will know only suffering, only pain. Desmévoun mágia mou sto skotádi, afíste tin ánodo skiá."

Taliesin began rushing towards Morgause, as though he meant to grab her by the neck and ring the darkness out of her but, as he came nearer, she threw something on the floor that erupted into a billowing plume of black smoke. When it cleared, Morgause, Morgana, and Mordred were gone and Igerna was lying unconscious on the floor.

☼   ☼   ☼

The Knights rushed out of the great hall in pursuit of Morgause and her siblings while Uther scooped Igerna up off the floor and placed her in her chair. He slapped her a couple times on her cheek and she slowly came around. She was dazed and confused but quickly realized what just transpired and clutched her hands to her belly, looking at Uther with sad eyes and a guilty face. For a moment Uther looked as though he might raise his hand and bring it down hard across Igerna's face but he resolved to bottle up his anger, at least in the company of the spectators still gathered in the great hall. Bishop Sebastianus commanded one of his priests go and retrieve a basin of warm water and a washcloth before approaching Igerna and resting his hand on her shoulder.

"Are you alright, my queen?" said Sebastianus.

"I feel sick," replied Igerna as sweat began to pour from her brow and her skin turned the color of milk.

It was apparent something was dreadfully wrong. The curse uttered by Morgause was a killing curse, I recognized the words in Ogham and felt the depraved energy of the spell as it left Morgause's lips. Morgause may have intended for the unborn child within Igerna's belly to survive, to face the harsh reality of her prophecy, but it was clear she meant for her mother to die. Igerna was almost full-term. The Christian physicians could likely save the child by cutting it from Igerna but this would surely mean death for our newly crowned queen. The priests took Igerna under her arms and pulled her up from the stool, leading her out the back entrance of the great hall and towards the bedchambers beyond. Lady Viviana nodded to Elaine who took my mother's arm and led her down the passage behind the priests. I decided I too would follow. By the time the priests laid Igerna in her bed she was fading in and out of consciousness, rambling incoherently about Tintagel and Gorlois. She was speaking to Bishop Sebastianus as though he were her recently slain husband, confessing her sins in a vain attempt to absolve her of her involvement in his murder.

"Forgive me, Gorlois, forgive me," she said, "I never meant to hurt you. Or our sons. Oh God, our sons. Mordent and Morevain, Moreth and Mordred. Our blessed sons, all gone, all dead. If I had known, if I'd only known, I would never have opened the gate for Uther. Never."

Igerna began to sob violently and then gave in to a coughing fit that threatened to constrict her throat and strangle the life from her. She nearly fainted before resuming her incoherent rantings.

"And this child, this poor child," she said, "I have condemned this child to damnation before its first breath. If only I'd loved my daughters the way I loved my sons. Morgause is so much like me, so full of rage, so discontented with her life. I can't blame her for what she's done. To never know the love of a mother is to live a life of barren sadness. I know. My mother never loved me either."

Igerna stopped suddenly and began frothing from her mouth, white foam forming at the edges of her lips. She looked dehydrated and feverish and was stricken with intermediate muscle spasms that caused her to shout out in agony. The curse released by Morgause was doing its work quickly. I doubted Igerna would survive the night. My mother pushed passed the Christian priests huddled around Igerna's bed and put her hand on her youngest sister's brow, muttering something in Ogham under her breath which had little to no effect. Elaine was standing beside me praying to Nimue to deliver her hated sister from the clutches of death. I could see something pure in Elaine in that moment. From what I could see, there was some deep-rooted anger between Elaine and Igerna and yet, in that moment, Elaine was willing to put aside their differences.

It wasn't long before Igerna lost consciousness completely and, by the time the sun began to set, the whole city was in a state of silent vigilance, praying to whatever god or gods they saw fit for the safe deliverance of their queen from her present crisis. My mother never left Igerna's side and neither did Bishop Sebastianus and his priests. They remained on their knees, praying to the God of Abram, while one of their ranks who was also a physician continuously examined Igerna. It was just before midnight when Uther entered the bedchamber to seek a report from the physician on the state of his wife and unborn child.

"How is she?" asked Uther.

"Not well," replied the physician priest, an elderly middle-eastern man named Hasir.

"I fear we are losing them both," continued Hasir, "We must act quickly if we wish to save the child but there is little hope that our queen will ever recover. She is dying."

"You must let Father Hasir cut the baby from the queen's womb," interrupted Bishop Sebastianus, "it is the only way to ensure that the child will have a chance at life."

"There is another course we may take," said my mother, "We must take Igerna to the Unseen Vale. If she is able to survive the journey, I can save them both. There is ancient magick in Avalon which has the power to bring even the most lifeless person back from the brink of death."

"Out of the question," snapped Sebastianus, "Queen Igerna is a Christian. I will not allow you to take her into that realm of devils and tricksters to sell her soul to Satan so that you might control her. I know your magick, we all do. We have just witnessed its darkness. I implore you, sire, do not allow this charlatan to subject our queen to her perversions."

Uther stood there in contemplation for a moment before he rendered his indisputable decision, a choice which would anger the Christians but, in that moment, Uther didn't care.

"The Queen will go to Avalon," he said, "Make the necessary preparations. We leave at once."

☼   ☼   ☼

The road to the Unseen Vale seemed longer and more taxing than when I left with Taliesin to journey to Camulodunum a few weeks prior. Bishop Sebastianus and his Christian priests remained in the fortress city, as did the lesser kings and dukes of Britannia. The Knights of Avalon accompanied us on the road to protect Uther and the dying queen, all except for Brannos who remained behind to train Madoc. Tristram also came along, insisting that he be allowed to return to his duties as a Guardian on the Isle of Stone, regardless of the imminent danger. I was glad Accolon had come along on the journey. With all the commotion of the coronation and the queen's declining health, Accolon and I hadn't been able to have any of our secret meetings in the dead of the night to satisfy our carnal desires against the laws of the Druids and the code of the Knights of Avalon. We were both putting our futures in jeopardy but we didn't care. It was our destiny to be together, just as it was my fate to follow in Taliesin's footsteps as the next Merlin of all the Britons.

Igerna barely survived the journey and, when we arrived at the Isle of Glass, her life and the life of her unborn child were teetering on the brink of death. Uther began to question his decision to bring her so far along the Fosse Way, so far from the heart of his dominion. He grew irritated with Viviana, telling her she better be right about her promise of healing both mother and child or be ready to face the consequences. It was a bold move for Uther, a newly crowned king, to threaten the Lady of the Unseen Vale but she did her best to ignore his complaints as we neared the Christian commune on the Isle of Glass with the single stone monolith rising upon its hill, the gateway into the Unseen Vale.

As the Fenfolk man named Sunwalker poled us to the docks on the Isle of Glass, we were met by dozens of Christian monks led down the field by Father Fortunatus. They were armed with pitchforks and shovels and looked more like a ravenous mob of discontented peasants then pacifistic men of the cloth. Many of them were hissing slurs under their breath as my mother and the others offloaded Igerna from the barge. Uther and the Knights were in a half-dozen barges behind us, allowing Fortunatus the opportunity to register his opposition to our arrival.

"You are not welcome here," barked Fortunatus, "Leave at once before we beat you senseless."

Viviana only smiled at their threats, causing one of the more ignorant monks to rush forward brandishing a shovel, as though he meant to knock my mother over the head. Fortunately, before he could succeed, the monk was knocked off his feet, flying several yards through the air before landing on the ground with a thud. It was as though the monk was a fly hit hard by an invisible swatter. Taliesin marched forward, with his oaken staff held high in front of him, and it was apparent it was he who caused the monk to be thrown off his feet. Father Fortunatus glared at Taliesin but he remained frozen where he stood.

"Keep your threats to yourself," said Taliesin, "These lands are more sacred to us than they are to you. The Old Religion has used these Isles as hallowed ground for thousands of years and, in your insolence, you dare to think you have the authority to revoke our safe passage here. Step aside of your own accord, Fortunatus, or I will force you out of our way."

Father Fortunatus' face was contorted with hatred but he did as he was commanded and we carried Igerna passed him and his monks unopposed. By that time, Uther and the Knights had arrived onshore and were edging up behind us quickly. We reached the top of the Tor Hill as the sun rose to its midday apex, though it was overcast and drizzling lightly. The whole area was covered in a dense fog and a chill hung in the air. Viviana reached out and touched the monolithic stone after the whole of our entourage was gathered nearby. We at once slipped from the outside world and into the Unseen Vale. The single monolith became the sacred circle of stones and the House of Healing appeared in the field below. The Maiden-Healers rushed out from the house towards us, sensing the urgency. I was surprised at how few of them there were. When I came to live in Avalon a few years before, there were no less than twelve Maiden-Healers residing on the Isle of Glass. Now only six remained. They were led by the familiar face of Livia, head of the House of Healing, who came to stand in front of Viviana. She bowed slightly and then turned her eyes towards Igerna.

"Take her at once," said Viviana, "and make sure she, and the baby, stay alive until I return."

Livia and the other Maiden-Healers took command of the gurney with Igerna resting atop it and carried her quickly down the hill, back to the House of Healing, with Uther and the Knights on their heels. Taliesin and Elaine remained standing in the circle with me and Tristram as my mother started to walk away down the hill. She was only a few feet off when she turned around and looked at Tristram.

"If you wish to return to your duties on the Isle of Stone, Tristram, now is the time," she said, "and you will come too, Galahad."

I did as I was told and followed Tristram and my mother down the Tor Hill, passed the House of Healing, to the dock jetting out over the high waters of the Brackish Lake. My mother let out a strange whistle that sounded like the song of a hummingbird and a small barge appeared from the nearby brambles rowed by a Fenfolk woman of the Watch Hill village by the name of Birdsong. Birdsong smiled at Viviana and bowed low as the three of us boarded the barge. She poled us out as far as she could before switching to an oar to paddle through the deeper places of the flooded fens. We made our way with haste to the Isle of Stone, near the Crossroad and the estuary of the Rive Sabine. The weather in the Unseen Vale had its usual temperate and calm air with a cloudless sky. We offloaded at the edge of the Isle of Stone, at the jagged steps leading up to the Fire Pit where my mother was burned and blinded in the flames a year and a half ago.

Instead of following the trail to the Fire Pit, Tristram led us with my mother on his arm towards the jagged cliff overlooking the lake, where five stone cottages stood like piles of rock freshly harvested from a nearby quarry. Just as we came within a stone's throw of the homes, an elderly man with a wiry white beard and bald head emerged from the nearest cottage, brandishing a scythe like a weapon.

"Be still, Leawys," said my mother and, at the sound of her voice, the old man dropped his scythe to his side and bowed dramatically in the direction of Viviana.

"Apologies, Lady," he said coarsely, "Had I known it was you I would never dared come forth with my weapon drawn. Please forgive me."

"You are forgiven," smiled my mother, "I have brought Tristram. He is eager to resume his training with you, if you are willing. And this is my son, Galahad. He will accompany me into the catacombs."

"As you wish," said Leawys, "Tristram. Go and fetch them a torch from your cottage."

Tristram returned minutes later with a torch in his hand, which he gave to me as Viviana took hold of my arm.

"Fotiá," I said as I waved my hand over the torch and it suddenly burst into flames. Viviana tugged on my arm, pointing at a small opening in the side of the cliff just passed the stone cottages. I led her along and soon we were walking deep underground in a myriad of dark caverns. The air was hot and humid while the cave walls were covered in moisture. The torch flickered and fluttered as an air current produced a gentle updraft from some place deep below us. If the torch went out we would be plunged into total darkness and I wasn't sure I could relight it under that kind of pressure. Not that it would matter to my mother. Her blind eyes were used to the darkness, it was all she could see, though her other senses had become heightened and she still had the use of her third-eye. I would be completely blinded and likely stumble into a dangerous situation.

"It's said that the fey used these caverns to flee to Faerie when man came to the shores of Britannia," said Viviana as we made our way deeper into the earth, down the main causeway of the catacombs which descended in a gentle slope.

"I have never fully explored these tunnels," she continued, "but there were others before me who dared to investigate the fullness of their complexities. None of them were ever seen again. Perhaps they became lost and starved to death, or were struck down by a loose boulder. Or perhaps they found their way into Faerie and still reside on those distant shores with the fey peoples. Before I retire to the Isle of Birds to join the Crones, I think I might return here and try my hand and finding the secret places within the deeps of the caves."

"I don't understand," I replied, "How can you join the Crones? You won't be the Lady of the Unseen Vale for the rest of your life?"

Viviana gripped my arm a little tighter.

"No, I will not," she said, "Though I may remain on the Isle of the Font longer than I should. Without Morgana, there is no one left of our bloodline to take my place. Elaine could manage but she is only two years my junior and her service would be brief. Maeve might be a better choice but she was not born of the blood."

"I know you've explained this before but what about Guinevere?" I asked, "She is your daughter."

"And she has a far different future in store for her," said Viviana abruptly, "I have my reasons for keeping Guinevere from this life and it's not just because I've seen what she is to become. The sacrifices made in the service of the goddess are great. I would not burden anyone with such a future if it weren't absolutely necessary."

We suddenly came to a dead-end where the main cavern split off into three tunnels. Viviana pointed to the one furthest left and I proceeded. The floor settled into a sharper decline and the air grew even hotter. If I didn't know better I'd think we were near the everlasting fires at the heart of the earth, being bombarded by their intense, unrelenting heat. I wanted to strip off my robes and continue in only my loincloth but I figured that would be inappropriate considering my mother was on my arm.

"Why is it so hot?" I asked.

"The waters of the Blood Well begin their journey here, deep within the caverns," said my mother, "There is a spring near the heart of the earth where the waters boil, forced upward by the pressure of their steam. As the water travels it collects rare minerals and metals from within the catacombs before erupting from the Font and cooling in the Meres. That is why the water is red like blood and such a good tonic for healing common maladies. Unfortunately the byproduct is the heat. It will only get warmer. No one but myself and the Merlin is permitted to traverse these caverns unaccompanied, partly because they could easily become overheated and succumb to dehydration."

My mother was correct about the heat. As the floor of the tunnel leveled out I started to sweat uncontrollably. I had no choice but to stop and remove my robes. I was glad in that moment my mother was unable to see my semi-naked body. I was not ashamed of my physique and had come to appreciate the form and function of my muscles during my sexual forays with Accolon. It was the fact that my mother was my companion in the caves and her presence made me feel embarrassed about my body.

Soon we came to a maze of tunnels. Every few yards the current passageway would end abruptly and there would be three, four, sometimes five different tunnels breaking off. Each time we came to one of these points, Viviana pointed out the way so we would not be lost amidst the endless labyrinth of superheated caverns. We spent nearly an hour traversing the catacombs before we finally emerged into a wide cavernous space with a high roof. A crack in the far wall seemed to reach all the way back to the surface as a shaft of sunlight illuminated the interior of the space enough that we no longer needed the torch. Nearly the whole space was filled with boiling hot water and steam billowed upward in swaths of white, obscuring the opposite side of the cave. A narrow path weaved its way across the water and into the steam, a path which Viviana urged us onto without hesitation.

"Careful, Galahad," she said as we entered the cloud of steam, "these pools are hot enough to melt gold. If you fell in you would be instantly burned alive. Follow me."

Viviana detached herself from my arm and stepped in front of me, slowly traversing the pathway through the dense pillow of steam obscuring our vision. I found it hard to breathe as we moved further along our course and the cool air wholly gave way to unbreathable vapors. I almost passed out from the heat before I refocused my mind and, with a burst of adrenaline, I continued to follow Viviana. It didn't take long for us to emerge on the opposite side of the cavern where a tiny archway had been carved into the rock, exposing a small passageway leading to a small antechamber artificially hewn by the hands of man. I breathed a sigh of relief as I entered the passageway and felt a cool breeze blow across my face. It was cooler than I'd been since we entered the catacombs. I almost needed my robes and shivered as my body adjusted to the new temperature. I soon discovered the source of the cold air. Several vents had been cut into the rock to supply a steady supply of breathable oxygen to those who were able to make it through all the obstacles of the catacombs and emerge victorious at the endpoint. Viviana had mentioned only she and Taliesin were permitted to enter the catacombs and didn't doubt anyone else who dared to try would become lost and perish as a consequence of their blind adventure.

The small antechamber was lit by a shaft similar to the one in the main cavern and at the far end stood two statues, one of the goddess, Nimue, and the other of the god, Kernos. The statue of Nimue wore a tiara of silver while the statue of Kernos was adorned with a golden crown. But it was not the statues themselves that drew my eye, it was what they were holding. The statue of Nimue held in her hands a beautiful cup of silver adorned with diamonds and etched with Ogham symbols that read: "Let this be Tara, the Cup of Life." Meanwhile, the statue of Kernos was gripping a longsword the likes of which I'd never seen before in my life. Its blade had an iridescent metallic sheen and the handle bore a massive ruby in its hilt. On the blade were Ogham symbols like those on the cauldron, only these read: "Let this be Caliburn, the God-Killing Sword."

Viviana rushed over to the statue of Nimue and retrieved the Cup of Life. It seemed to burn her hands slightly when she touched it. She quickly folded it into her robes to protect her hands with a barrier of fabric. Then she started to retreat back the way we came until she sensed I was transfixed by the beauty of the sword. I wanted to reach out and take it, to claim it as my own. I would have if my mother hadn't grabbed me by the shoulder with a fiercely strong grip.

"Leave it, boy," she said, "That blade is as much of a curse as it is a blessing. Many have tried to harness its power and all have failed. The ancients called it Caliburn, the God-Killing Sword, but to the Druids it is known by another name. Excalibur the Cursed."

Chapter Seventeen
"Rise of the Pendragon"

By the time we arrived back at the House of Healing with the Cup of Life, Igerna was a breath away from death. Her heart had slowed dramatically and the Maiden-Healers were concerned the baby within her would soon expire if there was no change in her condition. Uther was fuming with rage, pacing back and forth and pointing his fingers at the Maiden-Healers with authoritative anger.

"Damn it, I am your High King and you will listen to me," shouted Uther, "You must save the child. Igerna is lost to us but I will not allow my son to die alongside her."

"We can do nothing without Lady Viviana's consent," replied Livia while standing over Igerna with a warm washcloth.

My mother swept into the room and passed Uther without a word, placing the Cup of Life on the table next to the bed where Igerna was lying. She put her hand on Igerna's forehead and closed her eyes, focusing on peering deep into her youngest sister's being, to stare at her soul. She stood there silently for nearly five minutes before breaking her trance and looking at Livia with teary eyes.

"She is ebbing away," replied Viviana, "but there is still a chance we might save her. Go now with all speed to the Isle of the Font and bring me a pitcher of water from the Blood Well."

Livia ran from the room like a little girl racing through a field. Uther looked like he wanted to pick up my mother and throw her against a wall but he reluctantly maintained his composure. It was clear he was worried more about the life of his child than that of his new wife. I know he would've preferred they both be saved but, given a choice between one or the other, it was clear which he would choose. Viviana ignored Uther's angry energy as she sat by her sister's bedside, praying to the goddess, Brigga, for her sister to return fully to the world of the living.

Within a quarter of an hour Livia returned with a pitcher full of the red waters from the Blood Well. Igerna's breathing was extremely shallow and she had a death rattle from the saliva gathering at the back of her throat. It was hard to listen to her. I felt like running from the room, back to the Isle of Oak where my journey in the Unseen Vale began, to pretend the prior three years were nothing more than a bad dream but I stood my ground. I was determined to be strong for my mother. Taliesin and the other ten Druids still alive in the Holy Isles were gathered near the water singing ancient chants, entreating Kernos to intercede on Igerna's behalf and prevent her spirit from crossing into Faerie and then the Otherworld.

Viviana filled the Cup of Life with the water from the Blood Well and then produced a small, sharp pin she used to prick one of Igerna's fingers so that a few drops of her blood fell into the cup. Viviana instructed Livia and the other Maiden-Healers to use the remaining water from the well to bathe Igerna with fresh cloths. Viviana held the Cup of Life above her head and spoke a powerful incantation in Ogham, drowning out the sound of the Druids singing outside.

"Brigga, Nimue, Catsubodhva," said Viviana, "Enónontai kai na angíxei aftó to neró me to therapeftikó fos sas, kai evlogiméno."

Viviana tilted Igerna's head back and poured the contents of the Cup of Life down her throat. Igerna sputtered and choked as the liquid dripped down her throat and it seemed there was no change. Uther was rapidly boiling over and punched the wall in frustration. He was about to grab a knife from the nearby table and cut the baby from Igerna's belly himself when Igerna's breathing steadied and the color returned to her face. She stopped sweating and her heartbeat grew stronger. With a slight cough, she opened her eyes and looked at Viviana, then at Uther. Uther was smiling wide in astonishment and vocally praised the name of Kernos as Igerna sat up in the bed and clutched at her stomach, searching for any indication that her child had been harmed by Morgause's curse.

"The child is fine, Igerna," said Viviana, "The waters of the Cup have healed him, just as they have you."

Igerna smiled for a second and then the joy in her face faded.

"This changes nothing, Viviana," she said, "My child will be raised a Christian and I don't care what you say to try and make me give in. I will not allow this baby to be a part of your insidious world."

"That's enough," barked Uther, "Your sister just saved your life and the life of our baby. Is this how you show your gratitude? Well, if she can't say it, then I will. Thank you, Lady. Thank you for saving my child and my wife. If there is anything you ever need from me, do not hesitate to ask. I am in your debt and that debt will be paid."

Viviana bowed slightly towards Uther and then briskly left the House of Healing, the Cup of Life cradled in her arms. I knew without asking that she was on her way to return the Cup to its resting place, deep within the catacombs beneath the Isle of Stone. I was relieved she didn't ask me to come with her. I feared I would not be able to resist the call of Excalibur a second time. Elaine also departed, followed by Uther. As I emerged from the House of Healing onto the field leading down to the Brackish Lake, I saw Elaine boarding one barge and Uther another. Elaine was likely bound for her home on the Isle of the Font while Uther was making his way to the Watch Hill where he and the Knights were being housed in the Eponi encampment. I was left alone with Igerna and the Maiden-Healers. I saw it as my opportunity to slip away and I made my way down to the water to follow Uther to the Watch Hill.

I arrived as the moon rose high into the night sky. The stars were shining brightly and the air was warm. It was the last days of summer, nearing my seventeenth birthday, but I didn't care about turning another year older without taking my vows. I was exhausted. After reaching the Eponi encampment on the Watch Hill, I located Accolon's tent and slipped inside. He was sleeping, snoring softly, his naked body nestled into a pile of furs. I stripped off my own clothes and slipped into the bed beside him. Without really waking up, he put his arm around me, pulling me into his chest, into the warmth of his body. I felt safe as I drifted off to sleep to dream about a simpler life.

☼   ☼   ☼

The two weeks that followed that miraculous night of Igerna's deliverance from death were spent with Taliesin. Taliesin insisted I continue my training in the uses of magick since we were returned safely to Avalon and the war in the outside world was over. Uther and Igerna remained in the Unseen Vale since Igerna was full-term and likely to begin her labor at any moment. I saw Uther every day but I didn't interact with him. He spent his time with the Knights, mostly Ector, talking about military strategies and the importance of fraternity amongst soldiers. Meanwhile, Taliesin took me to the Crossroad each afternoon.

I was ready for the five trials which would indoctrinate me into the order of the Druids but it didn't seem like Taliesin was in a hurry for me to take my vows. I wondered what the holdup was but I didn't ask. Taliesin encouraged me to focus on learning the next fundamental of magick: telekinesis. Unlike elemental control, spells of protection, hexing, glamouring, crossing between the worlds, and telepathy, telekinesis required a new level of control I wasn't sure I possessed. I had little faith in my abilities since I was not fully a part of the Mysteries detailing the beliefs and traditions of the Druids and I was beginning to doubt I would ever be. My indoctrination into the order was indefinitely delayed.

"Telekinesis requires a lot of imagination on the part of the practitioner," said Taliesin. We had been working on telekinesis for nearly two weeks and I was not any closer to accomplishing my goal than on the day we started the lesson.

"I'm trying to use my imagination. It's not working," I said in complete frustration.

"No excuses," scolded Taliesin, "You are nearly seventeen years old, Galahad. It's high time you take responsibility for yourself, and that includes your failings. If you have not yet accomplished this feat, it's not because you cannot do it, it's because you don't want to."

There was some truth to what Taliesin said, although I didn't want to admit it to him at the time. Instead I focused my mind as hard as I could on a nearby stone. I pictured a giant invisible hand stretching out from my own fingers to wrap itself around the stone and lift it off the ground. I thought it might actually work but, no sooner had my invisible hand wrapped itself around the rock, then my mind drifted to Accolon and the unbridled passion we were experiencing together. The rock didn't move. Taliesin grumbled a curse word under his breath with a look that made me cower. He was not the type of man to be physically violent but he didn't have to raise his hand to make his point clear.

"Again," he barked.

I gave it another go and then another. Twice turned to ten times, ten turned to twenty with no progress of any kind. Finally, Taliesin decided to give up. He refused to take me anymore to the Crossroad and barely looked at me when he was in my company. I began to think he might've looked into my mind and seen my guilty secret. I grew paranoid and elusive, even dodging Accolon whenever he was around. Isolation became my ultimate goal. I sat by the Brackish Lake every day and stared across the water at the Isle of Oak, wondering at the sudden insecurity of my future.

"I think I know what's been on your mind lately," said Taliesin as he appeared behind me on the banks of the Brackish Lake. He seemed to be in better spirits than the few days prior, though I still felt like he was ashamed of my lack of progress using telekinesis.

"You do?" I asked, hoping he was wrong.

"It's Accolon," he replied and my heart started pounding.

"What do you mean?" I said, hoping he was not going to admit he knew about our affair, that I would be ineligible to be the next Merlin.

"Mab's love spell still plagues your mind and your thoughts drift to him when you're least expecting it," said Taliesin, "I have to admit, I didn't think it would be this bad but, since it's become such an issue, I will commit myself to finding a way to break the spell and allow you to be free to pursue the rest of your studies, before it's too late and you do something you will regret for the rest of your life."

"Like what?" I asked.

"You know what," replied Taliesin, "If you had sex now, with man or woman, it would jeopardize everything."

I felt ashamed but I hid my feelings as deep as I could bury them for fear Taliesin would catch on. Lucky for me, he didn't. He decided he was no longer angry and that we should return to our lessons. We journeyed to the Crossroad and I tried again and again to move a single small rock with the power of my mind. I couldn't. I was afraid Taliesin would get angry again and throw a tantrum but he remained patient.

"It's alright, Galahad," he said, "The time will come when you can lift an entire palace as though it were little more than a feather. You just need to believe in yourself, in the strength of your own dedication. The more you try, the easier it will become."

I don't know what happened but somewhere deep inside a light switched on and I understood what I needed to do. If I didn't learn to use telekinesis, Taliesin would continue looking for a way to break the love spell binding me to Accolon. I didn't want to lose Accolon. The desire to continue my affair fueled my determination. I again reached out with my invisible hand and wrapped it around the rock. This time the rock shook and then sprang up off the ground to hover for a moment in midair. Taliesin clapped loudly at my accomplishment.

"I knew you could do it," he said, "All it took was a little determination. Now you've learned everything I can teach you without entering the order of the Druids."

"When will that be?" I asked.

"When indeed," replied Taliesin.

"I'm almost seventeen, master," I whined, "When will I be entering the order? I thought I would become a Druid when I woke up from my year of exile in Faerie."

Taliesin looked at me with a stern expression.

"Faelan feels it would be unwise to indoctrinate you into the Mysteries," he said, "He has always been opposed to my choice of you as my successor. He's distrustful of Viviana and her sisters. He always has been. And he thinks the apple won't fall far from the tree."

"Why does it matter what Faelan thinks?" I grunted.

"Faelan is the High Druid here, Galahad, and his opinion matters a great deal, especially now that there are so few of us left."

"But you're the Merlin," I said, "Can't you make him let me take the Five Trials? You're like the King of the Druids. They have to listen to what you have to say."

"You will take the trials when the time is right, without my interference," said Taliesin, "Faelan will come around."

☼   ☼   ☼

It was the day after my seventeenth birthday that I was called to the Isle of the Font to bear witness to the birth of my new cousin. Igerna began her labor pains the night before and it was impossible to move her from Viviana's Tower to the House of Healing so the Maiden-Healers came to her, along with the Fenfolk medicine woman. I could hear Igerna shouting from the docks near the House of Priestesses. She was clearly enduring a particularly painful bout of contractions. This was her tenth pregnancy and seventh living child. I expected the process to be easier with each child but Taliesin assured me it was not.

"How do you know?" I asked while we sat outside the tower with the Knights and Uther.

"You are aware the living Merlin carries all the memories of the past Merlins within him," he said, "those Merlins were not always men. I can remember being a woman and having no less than a dozen children. Men are strong and proud but, even the greatest of us would crumble if put in the position of giving birth. Trust me."

"So, when you're gone and I am Merlin, I will remember being you?" I asked between Igerna's screams.

I kept glancing at Accolon as he sat by the door of the tower with his sword in his lap. The Knights feared Morgause would attempt to bring harm to Igerna in her susceptible state. There had been no sign of Igerna's dark children but Morgana knew how to cross between the worlds. If they wished to, they could come to Avalon. The Holy Isles were no longer safe from the evil of the outside world. The Knights were keenly aware of this fact and remained vigilant throughout the whole night, patrolling the isles aboard barges rowed by Fishwalker and Slider.

"Do you think they'll come?" I asked Taliesin.

"Even if Morgause convinced Morgana to bring her here," said Taliesin, "They would face the full force of the Druids and Priestesses of Nimue in their own element. They wouldn't stand a chance. Avalon was crafted to amplify the powers of light. With two dozen practitioners here, even without the Merlin, the scales would be tipped favorably in our direction. With me here, there is no chance they'd succeed. Only Mab herself could hope to defeat us here but she'll stay away for now."

For the first time since I'd come to Avalon, storm clouds began to roll in overhead, blocking out the light of the evening sun and casting long shadows over the landscape. There was a clap of thunder and then a flash of lightning as raindrops began cascading down from the heavens in droves. Taliesin, Uther, and I retreated into Viviana's Tower while the Knights remained outside on guard. The interior of the tower was cozy and warm. Igerna was upstairs in Viviana's bedchamber while Viviana was seated by the hearth in the far corner of the room with Elaine and a woman I'd never seen before, with deep auburn hair and a strong Saxon jaw. She was strangely foreign, as though she belonged on the deck of a dragon ship instead of seated with the Lady of the Unseen Vale. As we approached, the woman looked up and stared directly at me, locking her magnificent blue eyes on mine and smiling a radiant grin. Then she was gone.

"Did you see that?" I asked Taliesin.

"See what?" he replied, obviously oblivious to the woman who was there a second ago. I had the strange feeling I'd seen her somewhere before but I couldn't place her face. She looked like a Viking Princess descended from Odin, the God of War. I wondered if she might've been a fey spirit checking up on Igerna. Whatever she was, I didn't dare ask my mother. She looked tense as she rocked back and forth in her chair, staring vacantly towards the little fire burning in the hearth.

"How's my wife?" bellowed Uther as he sat down in a large wooden chair across from Viviana.

"She is well, all things considered," replied Viviana.

"Is there a child yet?" asked Taliesin.

"Not yet, but it will come soon," said Viviana, "Elaine and Livia are with her. They are convinced she is through the worst of it."

Outside the drizzle became a downpour and the wind began to howl. Lightning flashed in the distance and it felt like the tower was shaking. It was the strangest thing. The calm, temperate weather of Avalon was coming unraveled, giving way to a chaotic storm the likes of which many of the Druids hadn't seen since abandoning the outside world.

"What's with the weather?" I asked.

"The veil between the Unseen Vale and the outside world is growing thinner," said Viviana, "Every day that Morgause serves Mab, the balance is undone. Avalon will soon become one with the world again."

There was a terrible scream from above our heads and Uther nearly jumped out of his skin. Elaine came rushing down the stairs in a hurry and approached Viviana in distress. Igerna had suddenly taken a turn for the worse. She was growing too weak to continue pushing and it seemed we would find ourselves with the same choice we faced when she nearly died from Morgause's killing curse. They might have to cut the baby from Igerna's belly, at which point she would surely die. Then, as though the universe was ready to grant us a sudden reprieve, a baby started crying loudly. Elaine rushed back upstairs and then returned a few minutes later with a swaddled bundle in her arms.

"Uther, I would like to introduce you to your son," she said.

Uther looked down at the pale face of the little boy in Elaine's arms and I thought for a moment he would start to cry.

"Welcome to the world, Arthur," he said.

There was a sudden clap of thunder and a powerful gust of wind that threw the doors of the tower open and extinguished all the candles, plunging the room into darkness. Baby Arthur began to cry as lightning flashed just outside the window but it was not his wails, or the suddenness of the lightning that frightened me. The Viking woman had reappeared only inches in front of where I was sitting. She leaned over and, with a voice like an angel, she whispered into my ear.

"Behold," she said, "The Pendragon is risen."

Chapter Eighteen
"The Five Trials"

Uther and Igerna remained in Avalon for a month after the birth of Arthur. They wanted to be absolutely positive Arthur would survive the long journey from the Unseen Vale to Camulodunum. Igerna was restless and disapproving the entire time, preferring to remain isolated on the Watch Hill, away from the Priestesses and Druids. She erected a small altar in her cottage and took to spending hours every day praying to the God of Abram for safe deliverance from what she called the land of the demon fey, which was ironic since she herself was half-fey, like Viviana and Elaine. Uther, on the other hand, preferred the company of the Druids and spent many of his afternoons on the Isle of Oak speaking with Faelan or Gaius about matters of the spirit and the importance of the Britons continuing to follow the Old Religion, as a matter of tradition and culture. Arthur remained at his mother's side and we barely saw him, though it was enough to say with certainty he was a healthy and handsome baby boy who took after Uther in his coloring but Igerna in his look and features.

Just after the birth of Arthur, I was called back to the Isle of Oak to live amongst the Druids again, in preparation for the Five Trials before taking my vows to enter the order. Accolon remained on the Watch Hill and our nights together became intermittent. It was only when I was sent to the Watch Hill by the Druids to speak with the Fenfolk about various matters that I was afforded the luxury of seeing my lover. But those nights we'd spend together were all the more passionate because of our long bouts of estrangement and I grew to love Accolon more deeply with every moment spent in his strong arms. There were times I felt I'd never be able to let him go, nor would I be willing to allow my obligations to the Druids outweigh our love. I would walk the fine line between spiritual devotion and earthly passion, regardless of the consequences to both, and I would do so without anyone knowing my secret.

I was surprised, when I returned to the House of Initiates, to find it completely empty. Uriens and Orin were now vowed priests, living in the House of Druids. There had been no new initiations since. I was all that was left of the ancient system that once produced thousands of Druids and Bards. Ortheon had gone to the Isle of Stone to become a Guardian alongside Tristram and Madoc was back in Camulodunum becoming a Knight of Avalon. What's more, most of the bards were gone from the Unseen Vale, going out into the world to try and reclaim the Tribes for the Old Religion. Only six bards remained: their leader, Jareth, and five juniors, Tovin, Eamon, Dorien, Llewellyn, and my old acquaintance, Ywain. Meanwhile, only ten Druids remained on the Isle of Stone: Faelan, Gaius, Bodon, Uriens, Orin, Baelig, Ennis macDwyr, Sorin, Haseph, and Haman. These were all that remained of the ancient priesthood, a meager band of misfits fighting to maintain their place in the world. I kept mostly to myself, locked within the House of Initiates or doing my chores, avoiding Faelan and his constantly disapproving remarks.

Towards the end of the month following Arthur's birth, Viviana came to the Isle of Oak to seek out Uther. He and Ector were debating military strategy with Faelan over lunch and it was my duty as the only Initiate to serve them. They were dining on a simple meal of mutton stew, strawberries harvested from our gardens, and bread baked by the Maiden-Healers in their kiln. The mead was brought in from the outside world and the water was harvested from the springs feeding into the River Sabine. Faelan was in an especially jovial mood, laughing at Uther's crude jokes and comments about women. When Viviana entered the small gazebo serving as their lunchroom on the arm of Elaine, Uther stood and bowed. Faelan looked annoyed by their presence. Ector gave his seat to Viviana but she declined to accept his meal. She allowed the others to continue eating and remained silent until she was sure they were finished, sipping water and staring off vacantly into space.

"Now, is there something we can help you with?" Faelan asked Viviana abruptly.

"I came to speak with Uther," she replied, "I understand he will be leaving soon. I didn't want to miss this opportunity to say what I need to say and be done with it."

"What's on your mind, Lady?" asked Uther.

"I've heard you mean to return to Camulodunum instead of making your way to Londinium," said my mother, "Is it correct for me to assume you will declare the fortress city your seat of power?"

"Yes," replied Uther, "Londinium has been the center of the Briton world for four centuries but it is a roman city with roman streets and roman buildings. Ambrose was a Roman and had no problem continuing to observe their traditions and customs. I am a Welshman and I mean to make it clear I will observe the traditions of my ancestors, not the roman way. Even the name Camulodunum is a roman word. I will use the ancient fortress city as my seat of power but it will not be called by a foreign name. It will be as it was before the Romans. It shall be known from this moment forward as it was in the days of the Beakers: Camelot, the City of the Sword."

"I am glad to hear such tidings," said Viviana, "and it warms my heart to know a man of the Old Religion has become High King. Yet, there is something troubling me. It's about Arthur. Remember the night he was born? You said you would grant me any request, no matter the cost."

"I remember," said Uther.

"I want you to make sure Arthur is brought up in the Old Religion, as a follower of Kernos and Nimue," said Viviana, "I know Igerna wishes him to be raised a Christian but she has not seen his future, his fate. He will be the True King, the one to bring the people back to the old ways. I know you will be a great King, my Lord, and I want you to make sure Arthur will be even greater. Please."

Uther sat there for a moment with his hand on his chin, as though he was straining to form a proper thought, racking his mind like an imbecile attacking a math problem.

"I promise to do everything I can to see Arthur understands his people and his place amidst our ancestors," said Uther, "And I will keep Igerna from corrupting his mind with her talk of devils and saints."

Uther, Igerna, and Arthur left the Unseen Vale the next day with most of the Knights of Avalon. Accolon, Cunamaglos, and Bedevere remained on the Holy Isles at the behest of Viviana but the others were sent back to Camelot to sit in council with the High King and ensure he would keep his promise to Viviana and the Old Religion. In a way, I was sad to see Uther and the others leave but I was too consumed with my own duties I barely had time to think about it. As Uther left, I was preparing to finally take the Five Trials which would herald the start of my life as a Druid.

☼　　☼　　☼

I began the Five Trials three days after the Autumnal Equinox, when the Druids were recovered from the customary rituals and celebrations associated with the equinox sabbat. Uriens came for me at sunrise and shuffled me away to the Isle of Stone where the trials would commence. We were met near the Fire Pit by Faelan, Ennis macDwyr, and Haseph, the three Druids who would judge and officiate the trials.

The Five Trials would take a single day to complete. The Trial of the Flames would come first, then the Trial of Protection, followed by the Trial of Faces, the Trial of the Fools, and, lastly, the Trial of the Gate. If I could succeed in all five to the satisfaction of my judges, it would mark my readiness and competence to enter the order. I was nervous about the whole affair, not because I doubted my abilities but because I was unsure I wanted to go through with the process. I was in love with Accolon but could barely see him. He dwelt on the Watch Hill with Cunamaglos and Bedevere while I lived alone in the House of Initiates. If I completed the trials and took my vows, I would move to the House of Druids and live alongside the ten other priests, including Faelan. Slipping away unnoticed would be next to impossible and my relationship with Accolon would suffer or even disintegrate as a result. There I stood, questioning my devotion, but there was no turning back. I had come too far.

"Are you ready?" asked Ennis macDwyr, stepping forward from where he was standing with Faelan and Haseph next to the edge of the Fire Pit. The last time I'd seen the pit was when Mab turned its flames against my mother, burning and blinding her and casting us both into Faerie, me for over a year. I tried to put that horrible night out of my mind as Ennis waved his hand over the pit and the wood at its bottom burst into flames. Within seconds, a roaring fire was reaching up from the pit to lick at the boughs of the fir trees growing nearby.

"In order to succeed in the Trial of the Flames, we do not ask that you start a fire, but that you extinguish it. A far harder task," said Ennis.

I moved to the edge of the pit opposite Ennis macDwyr and focused on the roaring bonfire. I pictured the air around the flames being replaced with a vacuum incapable of feeding the flames. I imagined the fire itself turning scarlet red before sputtering and slowly dying out, licking desperately at the lack of air for nourishment. I put my hands out, almost into the fire, and spoke an incantation in Ogham.

"In ýpno tóra fotiá kai óchi perissótero zoúme," I said and suddenly, as though doused with a massive bucket of water, the bonfire was reduced to nothing but ash and embers. Ennis macDwyr looked surprised, as if he expected the process to take much longer and then walked over to rejoin the others. They whispered amongst themselves for a few minutes before Faelan motioned for me to come closer.

"The Ritual of Protection will require you to invoke a Spell of Protection powerful enough to resist our hexes," said Faelan, "and we are very skilled in the uses of magick. If your spell crumbles, you lose, and you will never be a Druid."

Faelan smirked as he stepped back far enough for me to call forth the spell. I focused on expanding my brilliant, silver aura outward, to form a large cocoon, like a chrysalis guarding the caterpillar as it transforms into a butterfly. I thought about the aura becoming tangible, transmuting itself into a substance as hard as steel. Then, when I was sure I had done all I could to fortify my energy, I spoke loudly with an echoing voice.

"Prostatévoun mou theós kai theá," I said, "apó tin dýnami aftón ton ieréon tis velanidiás."

A sudden tingle rising up from my feet and erupting from the crown of my head ensured my spell was a success. Now to see if it would hold up against a barrage of hexes cast by the most powerful Druids left in the world, aside from Taliesin. Faelan was the first to act, throwing a hex meant to put me to sleep which rebounded off the invisible barrier of my impenetrable aura like a ball bouncing off a wall. Haseph and Ennis macDwyr then joined in, throwing bolts of electricity, balls of fire, and hexes to make me sleep, to confuse me, to cast my spirit from my body. For a moment it seemed my spell would dissolve. The more intense the assault became the more apparent it was effecting not only my spell but also my body. I was feeling fatigued and weak, not from the hexes but from my own exertion in maintaining the field of protection around me. Faelan was particularly ruthless in his assault, conjuring every form of hex he could think of in the hopes that he would shatter my spell and prove me inadequate. He was taking pleasure in my discomfort and I wondered how such a cynical, competitive man had risen to become the High Druid. Ennis macDwyr and Haseph also took note of how brutal Faelan was acting and it was they who judged the trial concluded.

"That's enough," said Ennis macDwyr forcefully, "I think the boy has proven he has the means of protecting himself from magical assault."

"I don't know about that," said Faelan before throwing one final hex, a powerful spell of sorrow meant to penetrate my mind and cause me to succumb to such pure grief I might entertain the idea of ending my life to escape the pain. I believed the trial was over and was unprepared for the assault. The hex pierced by auric field and hit me hard. I suddenly felt as though the whole world was a nightmare and I should end my life before Ennis macDwyr conjured his own protective shield to stop the hex dead in its tracks. He looked thoroughly displeased as he rounded on Faelan with Haseph at his side.

"That was completely uncalled for," barked Ennis macDwyr, "If you cannot control yourself, you have no place in these proceedings. I don't care if you are High Druid or not. It is not your place to overpower the boy and force him into failing. You are a judge. Make it a fair contest."

Faelan grunted something under his breath but he showed his consent to Ennis' request by stepping back, allowing Haseph to take control and usher in the next trial. This was the Trial of the Faces and required me to change my appearance six times, to assume six different identities in a manner convincing to the judges. Ennis macDwyr produced a large looking-glass from behind one of the nearby boulders and held it up in front of me so I could see my progress or lack thereof. My face was youthful and smooth, without blemishes or any real facial hair. I had fair skin but my hair was reddish black like my mother's and my eyes were sky blue. I thought I was attractive enough but was by no means a gorgeous specimen of manhood like Accolon or Madoc. I focused on changing my face to look like Madoc, to have golden blonde hair that shimmered in the sunlight and a strong, masculine jaw with perfectly symmetrical features.

"Kánoun to prósopó mou to prósopo tou fílou mou," I said and, to my utter astonishment, my face was instantly changed. I was no longer staring at myself in the mirror, I was staring at Madoc. Haseph looked please as he smiled when my face melted back into my own image. The next face I chose to focus on was that of my mother.

"Kánoun to prósopó mou to prósopo tou mitéras mou," I said and once again my face was transformed, this time to the likeness of Viviana, with the deepening wrinkles across her brow and her little button nose. After becoming Madoc and then Viviana, I decided to transform into Eogan, Morgana, and Uther. Finally, I went out on a limb and manifested a face totally of my creation, that of a middle-aged man of the Tribes with dirty gray hair and a long, wiry beard. Each time, I uttered a version of the glamour spell Taliesin taught me and each face was a complete success. So far I had finished three of the five trials and two of the three Druids serving as my judges seemed to be pleased with my progress.

"The Trial of the Fools will require you to evoke the most powerful of common hexes, one which renders its victim disoriented and dazed," said Ennis macDwyr. He was speaking of the Confoundent Hex. It was one I knew well. Taliesin demanded that I spend more time learning the Confoundent Hex than any of the others he taught me. Ennis macDwyr would be serving as my guinea pig. He moved a few yards away and stood proud, with his arms hanging at his side and a smile on his face. I thought about my intentions, about manifesting a wave of energy akin to a lungful of opium. Opium was capable of rendering a man's mind empty and confused so I required the same type of energy to manifest my hex. I put my right hand out before me, as though I was waiting to catch a ball pitched underhanded and then spoke the incantation.

"Kánei aftós o ánthropos," I said, "na xechásoume aftó to chróno kai ton tópo, pou egó prostázo."

As I finished the incantation I made a motion with my hand like I was throwing a javelin directly at Ennis' heart. For a split second it seemed nothing would happen. Then Ennis' eyes went glassy and he began looking around like an old man with dementia, searching for his long-dead wife, as though she would be standing there waiting for them to be married. Faelan and Haseph looked at one another and then back at Ennis macDwyr. They each pointed a finger and Ennis was restored to his normal, competent self, fully aware of his surroundings and what we were trying to accomplish. I was sure my hex was satisfactory, though the three Druids said nothing about my effort, whether they judged it a failure or a success.

The last trial was the Trial of the Gate and would require me to pass from the Unseen Vale into the outside world and then back again. The three Druids and I descended the stairway down the side of the Isle of Stone and rejoined our bargeman, Fishwalker. We set out across the Brackish Lake to the Isle of Glass, with the Stone Circle on the summit of the Tor Hill. The Maiden-Healers were absent from the island, either locked within the House of Healing or out on the other isles gathering wild herbs. The Druids and I mounted the Processional Way unopposed and were soon standing on the edge of the Stone Circle, the only accessible gateway between Avalon and the outside world.

"As your final test," said Faelan, "You must travel from here to the Christian's Isle and back again of your own accord. We will not help you. If you cannot return, you will stay in the outside world forever."

"Do you know the incantation?" asked Ennis macDwyr.

"I do," I said somewhat unconvincingly.

"You don't have to do this," said Faelan, "You can give up right now and return to the Watch Hill."

I wasn't going to let Faelan get the best of me. Ever since I came to Avalon, he'd been doing everything in his power to see me fail. I stepped into the Stone Circle alone and crossed to the largest of the monoliths, placing my hand on its smooth surface. I was familiar with the routine, having passed between the worlds before at Taliesin's behest but, the pressure was still mounting and my nerves wavered.

"Metakinoúntai mou me ton éxo kósmo," I said.

The world of the Unseen Vale melted away and the outside world materialized, as though it were a velvet curtain drawn down to obscure the stage existing behind it. I was standing on the hillside, but the Stone Circle and Processional Way were gone. The waters of the Fens were very low, exposing the trails connecting the islands to one another. The Christian monks were out and about, some on the grassy knolls near the edge of the Fens, fishing for whiting and trout. The others were out on the trails, gathering reeds and marsh-peat to burn in their fires. I wanted to seek out the older monks, the ones present when I was a boy living in the commune but I feared what they might think of me just appearing on the hillside after years without a word. Father Jimellus was long since dead, as was Eogan. Father Fortunatus and his Nicene Monks were the masters of the commune and had no love for me or the other Druids.

I was just about to leave the hilltop and go for a quick walk, despite my reservations, when one of the monks in the knolls below spotted me. He dropped his pitchfork and screamed to the others. It was clear he was young and new to the isle. He'd never seen a Druid before and, judging by his reaction, he was ready to believe what he was taught by Fortunatus, that I was a servant of the devil come to steal his soul. The other monks came running with their scythes and shears brandished high. I turned and put my hand back on the monolith with a sigh, wishing the outside world had remained as it was when I was a child.

"Metakinísete píso mou kai páli," I said. The angry monks moving towards me disappeared, replaced by the full Stone Circle and my three Druid judges looking at me sternly.

"What took you so long?" barked Faelan.

"Never mind," interrupted Ennis macDwyr, "Congratulations, Galahad. You've passed the tests."

☼　　☼　　☼

Faelan, Ennis macDwyr, and Haseph took me straightaway from the Isle of Glass back to the Isle of Oak, where the other seven Druids were gathered in the Sacred Grove, at the altar of Kernos, praying for my success. When they caught sight of us, they stood and silently formed a single filed line beside the altar. Faelan walked over to stand in front of the altar while Ennis macDwyr and Haseph took me by my arms and forced me out of my Initiate robes. Haseph pulled away my loincloth, leaving me to stand there naked and exposed. It was then that Livia, Adiane, and Rowa, the three greatest Maiden-Healers, stepped out from behind one of the larger oak trees. Livia was carrying a basin filled with essential oils, Adiane had a pitcher of water from the springs of the Sabine, and Rowa carried a jar of ink with a sharp instrument that sort of resembled a pen attached to a tiny hammer.

Livia used her hands to wash my body in oil, rubbing the glistening substance into every crevice. I was overwhelmed by the smell of roses, yew, and jasmine. For a moment, I was washed in a sense of euphoria, until Adiane approached and poured the cold spring water over my head, shocking my skin into forming goosebumps and snapping me back to reality. Faelan then took the little device from Rowa and held it to my head, painfully hammering the symbol of the rising sun into my forehead, the sacred tattoo worn by all sworn Druids. I tried not to grunt or squint as the little pen-like needle dug into my flesh again and again. I didn't want to give Faelan the satisfaction of knowing he was hurting me. When he finished he took the jar of ink and doused a cloth with it. He held the cloth up to my head for a second and then wiped away the excess ink, revealing a dark tattoo of the sun on my forehead. Faelan nodded and the Maiden-Healers retreated from the Sacred Grove back the way they came, headed to their home on the Isle of Glass since their part in the ritual was done.

"We are gathered here to witness the indoctrination of Galahad," said Faelan, "The newest member of our holy order in the service of mighty Kernos and the Dagda. Kneel."

I did as I was commanded and went down to one knee. I was less aware of my naked body as Faelan placed his hand on my head, though the cold of the night air was piercing me to the bone. I suppressed the desire to shiver and shake.

"Do you, Lord Galahad, swear to be always obedient to the will of Kernos, expressed through the Merlin and High Druids?"

"I do," I said.

"And do you swear to keep all our Mysteries a secret?" he asked.

"I do," I said.

"Do you swear to always remain loyal to us, your brethren in service to the Gods?" he asked.

"I do," I repeated.

"Do you swear to remain chaste, except when called by Kernos to surrender your flesh to another in the name of the divine?"

I hesitated for a fraction of a second.

"I do," I said.

"And do you swear to live a simple life free of earthly goods and pleasures?" he asked. I was the son of a king but we never had great wealth or prestige. The answer was simple.

"I do," I said one last time. The Druid, Gaius, stepped forward with a clean set of hooded white robes. He handed the fresh robes to Faelan who, in turn, held them out to me.

"Rise, Mon Galahad," he said, "You entered this space a mere Initiate but now, by the authority given me in the name of Kernos, you shall leave with the mark and manner of a Druid."

Chapter Nineteen
"Broken"

"Congratulations," said Uriens as the ceremony concluded. I was a full-fledged Druid and the others wanted to welcome me with open arms. Uriens was followed by Gaius and Bodon, Orin and Baelig, Sorin and Haman. Ennis macDwyr and Haseph were the last to shake my hand. Only Faelan remained at a distance, with his eyes fixed on the ground. He was still unhappy I was officially part of their fold.

"Now that you've earned the name of Mon, it's time for you to celebrate," said Faelan, "You may take this night to drink and dance with the Fenfolk if you desire. We will start your induction into the Mysteries tomorrow. But don't stray too far. Taliesin will want to see you."

The moment Faelan spoke I knew exactly where I wanted to go. With a courteous bow I turned on my heel and rushed away from the Sacred Grove, down the hillside, across the outer glade on the Isle of Oak, to the dock where a Fenfolk man named Fishwalker was waiting with a barge. Now that I was a Druid, I was afforded a new level of respect I hadn't yet known, starting with Fishwalker who refused to look me in the eye, keeping his head slightly bent, as the Fenfolk always did with Druids and Priestesses. I boarded the barge and took a seat near the stern while Fishwalker picked up a pole and pushed us away from the island.

"Take me to the Watch Hill, please, Fishwalker," I said and Fishwalker veered the barge towards the grassy hill in the distance, rising from the waters of the Brackish Lake.

I was so intent on reaching the Eponi encampment and seeing Accolon I failed to notice that another barge was being paddled across the water towards us. We reached the dock as the Fenfolk were gathering in the heart of their village for their evening meal. I smiled at Fishwalker, who bowed in reverence to my station, before I took off at a quick jog towards the Eponi encampment on the other side of the island.

I found Accolon inside his tent, laying on the bed naked, reading one of the Greek classics translated by the Christian monks living on the Isle of Glass in the outside world. Accolon was a bit of a contradiction in that way. He was a muscular, relentless warrior, hard and decisive, yet he was also kind and gentle, spending his spare time reading books and playing with his Caledonian wolves, Geharis and Bakka. In many ways, he was the perfect man and I felt lucky to have him as my own. There were many Eponi maidens, Fenfolk women, and even Priestesses, who would be glad to call Accolon their mate but he was mine and that made me feel more proud of myself than the trials I just mastered.

Geharis and Bakka were sleeping at the foot of the feather bed and didn't even raise their heads as I walked in. Accolon looked up from his book and smiled, flipping over to expose his torso and growing troth. He winked as I shed my new, bright white robes on the ground and jumped onto the bed next to him, wrapping my legs around him and pulling his manhood inside me. It had been more than a week since we had sex and I was hungry for it, like a starving peasant begging a rich aristocrat for a scrap of bread. We were so involved in our lovemaking, kissing and panting and calling out in lust, we didn't see the flap of Accolon's tent flip back. It wasn't until Taliesin was standing at the foot of the bed that I realized he was there. I jumped off the bed like a cat leaping to sit on the edge of a fence, grabbing my robes and pulling them over my head with my eyes fixed on the floor.

"I wanted to congratulate you on your success in your trials," said Taliesin, "and to let you know I found an incantation to counteract Mab's love spell pulling you towards Accolon. But it would seem I'm too late."

"How did you know I was here?" I said, still looking at the floor. Accolon was also avoiding Taliesin's eyes, wrapping himself in his fur blanket to cover his still raging manhood.

"We're in love," said Accolon defiantly, "And your spell won't change that, at least not for me."

"It won't change anything for me either," I said, "What he says is true, Taliesin. I love him. I'm sorry I didn't tell you, but I wanted you to trust me and to teach me about magick, about being a Druid."

"Clearly, there were some lessons you learned better than others," he said, "You say you love him. I can respect that, if it is real. There is only one way for us to be sure. Unless you are afraid things won't be the same after I break Mab's spell."

I looked at Accolon and nodded as he smiled back at me.

"Do it," he said.

Taliesin didn't hesitate. He put his hands up in the air, one pointed towards me, the other towards Accolon, and spoke his incantation with a voice that echoed through the tent and beyond.

"Spásoun apallagméno apó aftó," said Taliesin with a roar, "to xórki tis agápis kai afíste tis kardiés tous na periplanithoún."

All at once it was like something suddenly broke inside of me. I was still attracted to Accolon but that insatiable lust that drove us into each other's arms was gone. I could tell Accolon felt different too. He looked embarrassed. He jumped up from the bed and dressed in a tunic and breeches before whistling at Geharis and Bakka. The wolves jumped up and followed him out of the tent. He didn't stop to look at me or to say a word. With a flip of the flap on his tent he was gone and I began to doubt I would ever see him again. I was devastated. I was willing to give up everything because of my faith in my love for Accolon, a love that just faded in the blink of an eye, a love that was never real to begin with. Taliesin looked sympathetic but he also looked callous and hard. I'd seen him angry many times. He was prone to cursing and causing a scene. It was not in his nature to bottle up his emotions behind a veil of stoicism as he was doing in that moment. I was genuinely frightened. He was staring at me with the eyes of disapproving teacher and I felt like a teenager caught having sex in my parents' bed. I wanted nothing more than for him to speak, to yell at me, and to tell me how much I screwed up. But he wouldn't. He remained eerily calm as he spoke the words I dreaded hearing.

"I'm sorry Galahad," he said, "You will have to go before the Council. You've broken the law of the Druids. You have to be judged for your crime. I doubt they'll allow you to continue serving in the order, or even to stay in the Unseen Vale. I warned you when we started all this, there would be serious consequences if you broke the rules."

☼   ☼   ☼

Taliesin called the Council the next morning and, by the time the sun rose over the surrounding hills, I was standing at the center of the Stone Circle on the Tor Hill. For the second time in my life, I was waiting for the Council to pass judgment and decide the course of my future. The Council was smaller than I'd ever seen it. Viviana, Elaine, Maeve, and Asphodel were present, representing the Priestesses of Nimue. Faelan, Gaius, and Bodon were there on behalf of the other Druids. Livia, Rowa, and Adiane were there representing the Maiden-Healers, and Ector and Cunamaglos were there on behalf of the Knights of Avalon, having arrived in the Unseen Vale the night before with a message for my mother from the High King. Taliesin was also there, standing near the entrance of the circle, his eyes filled with shame.

"I can't believe this," said Elaine hotly, "Are we seriously going to sit here and debate passing judgment on Galahad when he was under the control of Mab's spell. He wasn't acting of his own accord."

"That's not entirely true," said Faelan, eager to put in his two sense, "Mab's spell would compound and amplify feelings only if they were already present. Galahad had to be attracted to Accolon before the spell was enacted in order for it to work. He wanted him and wasn't going to allow any law or rule stand in his way."

"You know this how?" asked Bodon.

"Have you ever been under the influence of a love spell?" added Livia in my defense.

Faelan grumbled something under his breath and then gave up his position by throwing his hands up in the air to signal his surrender.

Unfortunately, there were others in the Council who felt the same way as he and were all too willing to let their opinions be known.

"I think Faelan has a point," said Adiane, "it doesn't matter whether or not Galahad was attracted to Accolon before the spell was invoked, what matters is that he knowingly broke the rules as an Initiate and then again on his first day as a sworn Druid."

"Well stated, Adiane," said Asphodel.

"I think we can all agree Galahad has broken our sacred laws," said my mother, "we are not here to judge whether or not he is guilty but to pass judgment for his crimes. Taliesin has asked that we show mercy and allow Galahad to continue living here, with us, in the Unseen Vale as a sworn priest of the Druids. He has suggested that, as penance, Galahad be banished back to the Crossroad to live a life of solitude for the next full year. No disrespect to my father but I do not agree. I believe Galahad should remain here as a Druid but that he should come to live in my Tower on the Isle of the Font, so I may keep a closer eye on him and ensure he never steps out of line again."

"I don't believe this," laughed Faelan, "If this was anyone else, they'd be stripped of their place in the order and exiled from Avalon in a heartbeat but, because he is a blessed son of the fey, he is shown amnesties reserved for those of the bloodline alone."

"These are different times than the ones you are used to, Faelan," said Maeve, "Can we really afford to eject such a valuable member from our ranks when there are so few of us left?"

Maeve's declaration caused a stir as the Druids whispered amongst themselves and the Maiden-Healers refused to speak altogether. Viviana was listening intently and Elaine was looking back and forth from the Druids to the Maiden-Healers and the Knights, hoping someone would see sense and side with my mother in her proposal for my punishment. Faelan wanted me ejected and exiled but my mother was the more prominent figure with the greater authority.

"I believe Galahad should stay in the Unseen Vale," said Gaius, "but I think he's proven he cannot be trusted as a Druid. As a senior member of the order I want him stripped of his membership in our brotherhood. Send him to live on the Watch Hill with the Eponi. Let him be a warrior or a shepherd or a fisherman. But he won't be a Druid, not anymore, not as long as I draw breath."

It seemed the solution was clear as Adiane, Faelan, and Asphodel shouted in support of Gaius' proposed solution. Elaine yelled out no and Viviana remained perfectly silent. Taliesin was pacing back and forth, waiting for judgment to be rendered. I was sure my fate was sealed as the Council seemed to come to a consensus in favor of Gaius' proposal. Then, unexpectedly, Viviana jumped to her feet and dropped to her knees like a peasant catching sight of a king. She was followed by the other Priestesses and then by the Druids before I realized what was happening. The Viking woman with the blonde hair and piercing blue eyes I'd seen sitting with my mother the morning of Arthur's birth was standing next to Taliesin in the entranceway of the Stone Circle. She was wearing a long white gown, shimmering in the light of the morning sun and covered with a cloak of red velvet. Atop her head was a tiara of silver and her face was youthful and vibrant, free of wrinkles or blemishes. The Maiden-Healers seemed confused, as did the Knights, but they dropped to their knees as well, if only because my mother had set the precedent.

"You grace us with your presence, Goddess," said Viviana humbly and the situation became clear. This was not a mortal woman or even a lady of the fey. The Viking woman was the goddess, Nimue, descended from the Otherworld to enter the Stone Circle and make her opinion known to everyone gathered there. Last time she appeared, it was only me who could see her. This time everyone was aware of her presence. Her energy filled the circle with an electrical charge that made my hair stand on end and her voice was like a song.

"Lady of the Unseen Vale," she said, "Viviana, daughter of Taliesin, daughter of Rhiannon, I have come here this day to address you and you alone with these others bearing witness. I know the sorrow you feel in your heart at the loss of the mother you never truly knew and the son you loved more than life itself. Yet your still living son stands here before you, pleading for your approval and forgiveness. Do not turn him away the way your mother did you when you were a girl. Show him clemency. He is young. Let him make his mistakes without fearing reprisals from this Council formed to serve my will. It is my will that Galahad remain a Druid."

With that final word, Nimue vanished and the Stone Circle returned to the way it had been before she appeared. Viviana and the other councilors stood and returned to their seats, each disoriented, each in awe of what they had just witnessed, a goddess standing in their midst.

"I do not serve Nimue, I serve Kernos," said Faelan, "Unless he comes here to make his mind known, I will not change my opinion. Galahad deserves to be ejected from the order."

"I agree," said Gaius.

"Are you two insane?" added Bodon, "The Goddess has just made her mind known to us and you would ignore it. You may be the High Druid, Faelan, but your word is nothing compared to that of Nimue. I will do nothing that contradicts her wishes."

The majority of the other councilors agreed with Bodon, most vehemently Elaine and Maeve. Livia also believed in second chances and didn't need the Goddess to tell her what she already knew was right. I would remain a Druid. The question then became what my penance would be for my crime: would I be banished to the Crossroad to live in exile for the next year as Taliesin wanted, or would I come to live in Viviana's Tower as her personal servant and ward? The councilors debated both options for almost a half-an-hour and decided they didn't like either course of action. Instead, I would live on the Watch Hill, in the Fenfolk village, with the medicine woman named Stargazer for the next two years, to learn the ways of the Fenfolk medicine and shamanic rituals. I would have no interaction with the other Druids, except for Bodon and Ennis macDwyr who would come regularly to the Watch Hill to continue my training as a Druid. Taliesin would also come to teach me and, as far as I knew, I was still his apprentice and chosen successor. I left the Council that day with a relatively minor punishment. The harder pain to endure was the loss of Accolon, of what we had felt for one another.

I was confused about my feelings. I no longer felt that raw passion driving me to think of nothing but Accolon. At the same time, I was still fond of him, I still thought about his body, I still wanted to be in his arms. I realized that Faelan was right about one thing: I was attracted to Accolon before Mab's love spell took hold and I thought he was drawn to me as well. Maybe I was wrong or maybe I was right. Only time would tell.

☼　　☼　　☼

The little stilted hut of Stargazer sat over the waters of the Brackish Lake at the edge of the Fenfolk village. It was simply furnished with stick furniture and filled with strange smelling herbs gathered from the deep places of the Unseen Vale. Stargazer was as rundown as her hut. She was at least eighty years old, with sagging, wrinkling skin and only two teeth in her otherwise barren mouth. She was balding and the little hair remaining atop her head was as white as a snowflake. Stargazer was blind in one eye, deaf in one ear, and bent over from severe arthritis. She could speak the common tongue a little but preferred talking in the Fenfolk language which I could barely understand, let alone speak. I had no idea how I was going to learn anything from her and suddenly felt like a nursemaid sent to see that Stargazer was made comfortable until the imminent day when her long life would finally come to an end but Stargazer proved to be more vibrant than I initially thought. She had no problem carrying peat and wood in to fuel her fire and was an excellent cook. She made three squares a day from modest ingredients and was fond of taking a pipe on her porch after dinner while I strolled along the banks of the Brackish Lake.

I was on one of my evening walks when I was suddenly set upon by a man dressed in a black cloak with the hood pulled up to obscure his face. I was about to invoke a hex that would split his spirit from his body when he pulled the hood down to show me his face. It was Accolon.

"Are you crazy?" I said, "I could've fried you like a chicken on a spit. What are you doing here?"

"I wanted to apologize," he said.

I looked down at the water, avoiding his gaze, and frowned.

"Yeah, for what?" I asked.

"For running out on you when you needed me most," he said, "I was in shock. Taliesin's spell made me see things clearly for the first time and I needed to get away. Not from you, but from the situation. I've decided to leave Avalon for good. I'm going back to Camelot to join the other Knights. I wanted to see you before leaving."

"Well, you've seen me," I said, "Now you can go."

"Don't be like that," he replied.

"How should I be?" I asked, "You're leaving. Good for you."

Accolon turned around and started to walk away but he stopped a few feet away. He was staring at the Brackish Lake and he seemed to be crying. I wanted to run to him and put my arm around him, to console him in his moment of sadness and I realized the feelings I thought were gone when Taliesin broke Mab's spell were still there to a degree.

"Wait," I said and he turned around to look at me. I ran over to him and put my lips to his, pulling him into me like a man hiding a runaway beneath the folds of his cloak. I thought Accolon would rebuke my advance, that he would pull away and run off but he didn't. He wrapped his arms around me as we stood there by the lake, locked in one another's embrace. The kiss must have lasted for minutes. When we finally detached from each other, he smiled one of his heart-stopping grins.

"I do care for you, Galahad, in my own way," he said.

"That's better than nothing," I replied.

I expected Accolon to take my hand and lead me to his tent in the Eponi encampment but he didn't. He detached himself from me and, with a wink, resumed his course away from me down the banks of the lake. I knew without him saying it that he still intended to leave Avalon and rejoin the other Knights. We still desired each other but we had our duties. He was a

Knight and I was a Druid. Without the interference of Mab's spell, we were reminded of this and no longer willing to shirk our responsibilities to satisfy our desire for one another. Maybe one day down the line we would be able to settle down together and live a simple life as lovers but it would not be that moment. Accolon stopped only once to look back at me.

"Do me a favor," he yelled back at me, "Take care of Geharis and Bakka for me. They'll be happier here with you than in the fortress-city."

Accolon's wolves came running down from a nearby thicket of trees at the sound of their names but they didn't make for Accolon, they ran to me. I was so distracted by their licks and whimpers I didn't notice Accolon board one of the Fenfolk barges. By the time I looked up from the wolves, my lover was gone, leaving me to wonder if I'd ever see him again.

Chapter Twenty
"The Prodigal Priestess"

As part of my punishment for having sex with Accolon against the laws of the Druids, I was required to journey to the Isle of the Font weekly, to clean Viviana's Tower and the House of Priestesses. Every Day of Sun, Fishwalker would bring his barge and carry me across the Brackish Lake. The Priestesses once again treated me like a pariah and outcast, avoiding my gaze and refusing to speak to me. Elaine was the only woman living in the House of Priestesses that dared to approach me. She always sat near the hearth in the House of Priestesses while I scrubbed the floors with a brush or folded linens freshly laundered in the lake. When it was time to move to Viviana's Tower, Elaine followed me. It was as though she worried about my safety and wanted to ensure I would remain unscathed. Viviana was never present during my weekly duties. I started to think she might not be in the Unseen Vale at all, that she might've left to journey to Camelot and council Uther in matters of the Old Religion. After two Sundays cleaning, I finally built up the nerve to ask Elaine about something on my mind since the night the goddess, Nimue, appeared to us within the Stone Circle.

"Can I ask you a personal question?" I said to Elaine while I was running a broom across the floor of the entry room of Viviana's Tower.

"Of course," she replied kindly.

"What did Nimue mean when she told Viviana not to be the same kind of mother to me that Rhiannon was to her? Viviana seems so devoted to the memory of her mother."

At first it didn't seem Elaine would respond. She sat there staring out the nearby window at the House of Priestesses in the field below. Elaine was a beautiful woman but she looked tired and worn out, as though her time in the Unseen Vale aged her by twenty years. She was also extremely sad-looking, entering into a state of perpetual melancholia after her son, Madoc, decided to remain in Camelot and become a Knight of Avalon.

"Did Viviana ever tell you about our older sisters?" she asked.

I heard of them only once in passing but I didn't know their names. Neither Taliesin nor Viviana felt it necessary for me to know much about the other daughters of Rhiannon, or even how they lived and when they died. I knew they couldn't still be alive because of Viviana's position.

"Before my mother fell in love with Taliesin," continued Elaine, "when she first stepped into the Unseen Vale from Faerie, she gave her heart to another man, a Gael named Narain, and with him she had two daughters, Evena and Blathnaid. Mother knew Evena wasn't well-suited to life as a Priestess so she sent her away to Glevun, to live in the outside world with a foster family but Blathnaid had great potential. Mother always kept her close. When Narain died, mother retreated into her Tower and shut out the rest of the world, until my father came along and reignited her passion for a man. Viviana was the first daughter from that union, as you know, and I was the second. Since mother was already training Blathnaid, she decided to send both of us away to be fostered. Viviana was taken to the Isle of Mona and raised by a nice Welsh couple. I was sent to live in Dubrae with one of Taliesin's cousins, the man I knew as my father, a wonderful man named Llewellyn macKyric. Neither Viviana nor myself ever knew where we really came from or who our parents were."

"And Igerna's father was the King of the Dumnonii?" I asked.

"Exactly," she replied, "Mother laid with him during the rite of the Beltane Fires when I was just a little girl. Since Igerna had a father in the outside world, she was sent to live with him in Tintagel."

"So none of you knew about the others?" I asked.

"Evena and Blathnaid knew about each other and Blathnaid knew about the rest of us," said Elaine, "I didn't learn about my sisters until I was grown and a mother myself. I think that's why we've never felt like sisters, or even liked each other very much."

"What happened to them?" I asked, "Evena and Blathnaid?"

Elaine once again looked like she would be overcome with sadness, that she might burst into tears and sob uncontrollably, but she remained resolved to keep her emotions at bay.

"Evena died in childbirth when she was seventeen," she said, "And Blathnaid, Blathnaid was found murdered on the Isle of Stone a few years before Viviana grew into womanhood. Blathnaid's death hit my mother really hard, it changed her from a fun-loving, carefree soul to a bitter and short-tempered authoritarian with little love left in her heart. That was the mother I knew, the mother Viviana knew, a cold, callous, unfeeling woman who reminded us more often than not that we would always be inferior to her memory of Blathnaid. I tried to stay away from her as much as I could. I felt sorry for Viviana."

"Because she had to become Lady of the Unseen Vale?"

"Not so much that," she replied, "More that she had to come here and live with our mother in the Tower, to learn how to be a Priestess and the Lady of Nimue. She lived with our mother's constant abuse for almost ten years before mother decided to sacrifice her spirit to save the Holy Isles from the Christians."

Taliesin already told me about how Rhiannon died and, after hearing Elaine's story, that act became the one glimmer of heroism in an otherwise spiteful life. Almost twenty-five years before that day with Elaine in Viviana's Tower, the Christian commune on the Isle of Glass was controlled by a maniacal religious zealot called Lucius, a Saxon Sellsword turned Nicene Priest installed on the Isle of Glass by the tyrant, Vortigern. Lucius made it his sole purpose from the moment of his arrival to find a way into the Unseen Vale and destroy it. The Nazarene Christians of the Isle of Glass were traditionally peaceful and friendly with the inhabitants of the Holy Isles but, as Lucius took control, the atmosphere changed. Rhiannon warned her Priestesses not to leave the Unseen Vale. She'd seen a vision of the Priestesses being massacred, burned alive by Lucius and his Nicene followers. The Druids were bolder but even they remained mostly behind the borders of the Unseen Vale, watching from afar as Lucius destroyed everything they had built with the Nazarenes. Only the Merlin, Maponos, dared to face off against Lucius and his maniacs. He alone passed to and from Avalon, until he was unexpectedly captured and held hostage in one of the Christian cottages on the Isle of Glass. He narrowly escaped his confines but not before Lucius employed dark magick to ascertain the secret incantation that would allow him to pass between the worlds.

Maponos learned of what Lucius did and carried that knowledge to Avalon, to Rhiannon. Rhiannon knew there would be only one way to stop Lucius from invading the Unseen Vale. She would have to forcibly close the gateway between the worlds while Lucius was passing through it, she would have to take his life in order to ensure Avalon's survival. Unfortunately, the price for claiming a life with magick was the forfeiture of another life. As Lucius and his Nicene Priests-of-War began to cross from their commune to the Isle of Glass in Avalon, Rhiannon sacrificed herself to bring the gateway crashing down around Lucius like an avalanche of falling boulders wiping out an entire village. Lucius' followers were not hurt since they were still in the outside world. They disbanded and returned to the continent, leaving the commune on the Isle of Glass to be reclaimed by the Nazarenes under the leadership of Father Jimellus. Since fey are immortal and cannot die, Rhiannon's body remained in a state of eternal sleep atop the funeral pyre on the Crossroad but her spirit crossed into the Otherworld and never returned. Viviana was then proclaimed Lady of the Unseen Vale at only seventeen years of age.

"You didn't really answer my question," I said to Elaine as I finished my sweeping.

"I didn't, did I?" she laughed, "Nimue was telling Viviana not to be like our own mother, not to push you away but to embrace you, and Guinevere as her children, her future. I have cherished Madoc every day of his life, since the moment he was born. I try with all my might to make him feel important, to help him grow into the great man I know he will be. Viviana should've done the same with you. One day she'll regret being so much like our mother. That's what Nimue meant."

"Can I ask you something else?" I said.

"I suppose," she replied.

"What happened with you and Igerna? You really seem to have some issues with her," I said.

"You once lived with Morgause," said Elaine, "You know how selfish and self-absorbed she was, always thinking about herself regardless of the consequences to others. Where do you think she learned that behavior? It wasn't from Gorlois."

"But Igerna doesn't seem evil," I said.

"She's not," replied Elaine, "She's just snobby, snooty, selfish, and unkind, and she always treated her children like property. I don't think she shed a single tear at the loss of her sons or husband. At least not when she was in her right mind."

Elaine's explanations helped answer some questions I'd always been too afraid to ask, especially why she, Igerna, and my mother were such different people. Elaine was the kindest, no doubt learned from her years with Llewellyn macKyric. My mother was the most authoritative, likely a quality she inadvertently picked up from Rhiannon during her years training to become the Lady of the Unseen Vale. Igerna was the most immature and selfish, character flaws developed while she lived as a pampered princess in the distant Castle Tintagel. On the same note, the next generation was turning out to follow the same path as our parents. I was fostered with my father and only came to Avalon to learn with Taliesin after the death of my older brother, just like Viviana. Madoc was a kindhearted and dedicated warrior seeking to preserve the traditions of our ancestors, like his mother, my Aunt Elaine. Morgause was selfish like Igerna, Morgana was easily manipulated like her father, and Mordred was some mixture of those flaws yet to be seen. We were all set on our courses, once walking side by side, now at odds with one another. I felt a newfound level of respect for my mother after hearing the difficulties she went through in her own childhood, the battles she fought to overcome hating my grandmother.

"Where's Viviana?" I asked Elaine.

I was done with my chores and Elaine and I were sitting at the table just outside the door of Viviana's Tower, drinking apple mead and eating sweetbreads prepared by the Priestesses. The colors of the trees were changing from rich green to shades of brown, red, and yellow, heralding in the coming winter. We were only two weeks from Samhain, when the crown would pass from Nimue to Kernos for the remaining seasons of the year. The air was cooling with a bit of a chilly bite when the wind would start to blow and, each morning, the Brackish Lake was covered with a thick blanket of fog. It wasn't like Viviana to be absent at such a time. As the representative of Nimue amongst the druidesses, it was Viviana's responsibility to play the part of the goddess in the Samhain ritual.

"I'm not sure where Viviana is," replied Elaine, "She left the Holy Isles four nights ago on a secret mission. Ector and Cunamaglos are with her. They'll keep her safe."

"What if she doesn't return before the Samhain Feast?" I asked.

"She won't miss Samhain," smiled Elaine.

The outside world had become a treacherous place. Uther was working to reunite all the lands of the Britons under a single ruler but there were parts of Britannia that were less inclined to accept his rule than others. All of Valentia was lost to the Saxons while Caledonia was home of the natural enemies of the Britons: the Picts. The Dumnonii of Cornewall were loosely allied with Uther because Igerna was their queen but they had also not forgotten Gorlois' murder. The Iceni, who were naturally rebellious against any universal authority, were beginning to rise up in open rebellion and their close proximity to Camelot was proving a problem for the new High King. The Nicene Christians, living mostly in Londinium, Durovernum, and Dubrae, were following Bishop Sebastianus instead of Uther. Sebastianus was observant of the authority of Igerna, the Nicene High Queen, but he was skeptical of Uther's right to rule. Many of the lesser kings and dukes present at Uther's coronation were reneging on their oaths of fealty, while the smaller kingdoms east of the Armorica, including my home, Lodecran, had formally withdrawn from the alliance of the Britons, choosing instead to turn to the

Franks building a kingdom to the northeast. It seemed Uther's rule would fail before it began, and that wasn't the worst of it.

We were all aware Lot survived the ordeal when Taliesin sank his fleet off Witch's Point. As an act of cowardice, he slunk back to his distant Orkney Isles to lick his wounds. Viviana deployed her spies into the north to keep a close watch on Lot and his activities. What she discovered caused us all to shiver. Shortly after appearing in Camelot and cursing Igerna, Morgause took Morgana and Mordred into the north and fell on the good graces of Lot as a common ally dwelling in the darkness. Lot was a servant of Mab of his own volition, as was Morgause. It made sense for them to team together to further their ambitions. Lot decided fairly quickly that Morgause would be his queen and they were wed in a dark ceremony befitting their maniacal devotions. There was no word on Morgana or Mordred. The spies feared Morgause had killed them and quietly disposed of their bodies. I knew better. Morgause would never hurt Morgana, no matter how dark her soul became. It was more likely Morgause was keeping her brother and sister locked away in Lot's castle to prevent them from escaping. Morgana was a vowed Maiden-Healer, heir to the Ladyship of the Unseen Vale. I was sure she was being held captive under duress but I also had my doubts, like, for some reason, Morgana could no longer be trusted.

Wherever Viviana was, she was surely doing something of great importance. It wasn't often she left the Unseen Vale, where her power was at its strongest, so her absence had to be one of absolute necessity. I was not often in her presence but, living in the Fenfolk village, I was made privy to all the gossip of the Holy Isles. I knew Faelan was still advocating my immediate dismissal from the order of Druids, and that Taliesin was concerned at the lack of new Initiates and Virgins entering the orders of the Holy Isles. Four of the ten remaining Druids, and nearly all the bards, were in the last years of their lives. The majority of the Priestesses weren't much younger and the number of Maiden-Healers was constantly dwindling. There were only three Guardians with no one to take their place and the Crones were dying off like grapevines in a drought. If the ways of the Old Religion weren't restored in the outside world we wouldn't need to worry about Mab. There would be no one left to fight her.

Elaine and I finished our sweetbreads and mead before she returned to the House of Priestesses to resume her duties. I sat there for a while looking out over the waters of the Brackish Lake and thinking about how much of a home Avalon had come to be for me. I'd dwelt on all of the Holy Isles where men were permitted to live and even on the forbidden Crossroad. I knew each and every person living in the Unseen Vale by name and counted many of them as friends. The loss of the Holy Isles would be worse than an apocalypse. I would be homeless and lost. I said a silent prayer to Nimue and Kernos, begging them to bring new life to the Unseen Vale and ensure the Old Religion continued to flourish in Avalon.

☼   ☼   ☼

Another week passed and there was no sign of Viviana. The Priestesses were beginning to worry. Asphodel was the most Senior Priestess and in charge of the Isle of the Font in Viviana's absence. She was a capable druidess but her old age caused her to be cantankerous and easily irritated. She ordered the younger druidesses around like a dictator on drugs as they busied themselves preparing for the Samhain Feast.

Samhain was one of the two days of the year when all the orders of the Holy Isles came together to celebrate with festivities and a formal ritual signifying the passing of the crown from Nimue to Kernos. The Fenfolk women and Eponi maidens were responsible for cooking an enormous feast of folk foods to feed all those attending the Samhain celebrations. The Maiden-Healers served the others at the dinner, the bards entertained with songs and dance, while the Priestesses and Druids were honored guests. Viviana would sit on a throne adorned with heather wearing a silver mask in the likeness of Nimue. Faelan would sit on another throne showered with holly and he would wear a golden mask in the likeness of Kernos. They remained in their places as unapproachable and silent statues until after the conclusion of the feast, when Viviana would ceremonially pass the crown worn atop her head to Faelan to demonstrate the passing of rule over the earth from the goddess to the god. I'd never been to a Samhain Feast. Initiates were permitted to attend neither the Samhain Feast nor the Beltane Rites but I knew everything about both Sabbats from the endless stories told to me by Taliesin.

"I'm worried about my mother," I said to Elaine one afternoon as we sat on the dock of the Isle of the Font dipping our feet in the water of the lake. It was abnormally warm for a mid-autumn day and we were taking the opportunity to roll up our sleeves and drink in the sun's love.

"I don't think she's going to make it back for Samhain," I continued.

"I told you before, Viviana won't miss the Samhain Feast," said Elaine, "Can you imagine old Asphodel wearing the mask of Nimue? She'd look more like a Roman wearing a death mask than the mother of our faith and goddess of the earth."

I couldn't help but laugh at Elaine's joke. She had a way of taking my fears and turning them to joy. We'd grown especially close since Madoc decided to stay in Camelot. I think she missed him immensely and I was a way for her to fill the void. I didn't mind. She was more of a mother to me than anyone had been since Genovefa back in Lodecran. Elaine made sure I ate right, that I was sleeping enough, and that I did my chores promptly without complaint. She encouraged me to laugh and never to take life too seriously. She was a clear opponent of Faelan and his desire to disgrace me further by reliving that fateful night when Taliesin caught me in bed with Accolon again and again, telling the story to whomever would listen. Faelan was High Druid but there was nothing pious or sensible about him. I hoped he would find himself drawn away from the Holy Isle one day and replaced by a gentle soul like Gaius or Ennis macDwyr. Suddenly, as I thought about how much I despised Faelan, there came a gentle ring on the wind, heralding someone's arrival in Avalon. I was sure it was Viviana. Elaine and I stood and walked briskly towards the Stone Circle atop the Tor Hill, to see who it was that just came from the outside world into the Unseen Vale. By the time we arrived at the top of the Tor Hill, the Stone Circle was empty and there was no sign of anyone.

"I thought it would be Viviana," I said in disappointment.

"So did I," added Elaine, "But I wouldn't worry. She'll return soon."

"She already has," said a voice from behind us but it wasn't my mother's, it belonged to someone I never expected or desired to see in the Unseen Vale again, someone I knew very well and also feared, an inquisitive soul capable of accomplishing anything. Elaine and I turned around quickly but apprehensively to be greeted by my mother standing just feet from the entrance to the Stone Circle, dressed in a black cloak and riding boots, with her hand threaded through the arm of a tall young woman wearing a red cloak with the hood pulled over her head. I didn't need to see her face to know who it was that spoke. It was Morgana le Fey.

Chapter Twenty-One
"A Samhain Message"

I stood there in complete shock as Morgana pulled the hood from her head to reveal her young, fair complexioned face and her narrow brown eyes. She looked exactly the same as she had the night she accompanied Morgause and Mordred into Camelot to kill their mother. Morgana may not have been guilty when it came to casting the curse but she stood by and watched without trying to stop Morgause. Morgana always followed where Morgause led and I was suspicious of her sudden return to Avalon, without her psychotic older sister. Ever since I'd known them, they'd never been apart. Morgana clung to her sister like lint to cotton.

"Why are you here?" I asked abruptly.

"Don't be rude, Galahad," chastised my mother.

"It's alright, Lady," interrupted Morgana, "I don't mind answering for my actions. I only wanted to wake up my sister, Galahad. I didn't think she'd go crazy and force me to leave the Unseen Vale. She kept her magick a secret from me. I didn't know she knew such things. She turned her power against me and held me prisoner, forcing me out of the Holy Isles and back into the outside world. We made our way to Tintagel to find Mordred locked in the dungeon, starving and crying for water. Then we went to Camelot where she did that horrible thing to our mother. I told her I wanted no part of it but she didn't care. She treated me like a slave. After we arrived in the Orkneys and she married Lot, I finally found my opportunity. I used the power of the Sending to reach out for help and Viviana heard me. She risked her life to come to Lot's castle and rescue me. I owe her everything."

"And you believe her?" I asked my mother.

"I believe in her enough to have risked my own life to go and get her," said Viviana.

Viviana was a stern but compassionate person with a trusting heart, at least for those in her own family. She'd probably find it in her heart to forgive Morgause if she came and fell at Viviana's feet begging to be allowed back into the Unseen Vale and our family. I was more of a realist. Something didn't feel right about Morgana's story but I wasn't going to convince my mother with just words. If Morgana was up to no good I would need to prove it with irrefutable evidence before my mother would take me seriously. Viviana, Morgana, and Elaine made their way towards Viviana's Tower while I walked back to the dock and boarded a barge for the Watch Hill, to return home to Stargazer's hut, the whole time contemplating whether or not Morgana returned to rejoin us or to destroy us all.

✧   ✧   ✧

The night of the Samhain Feast came faster than I expected as I found myself in the company of the other Druids for the first time since judgment was passed for my crime of knowing Accolon intimately. Gaius and Ennis macDwyr came regularly to the Watch Hill to continue my training in the Mysteries of the Druids but the other eight Druids remained estranged. Even as we loaded on the barge to make our way to the Isle of the Font for the celebration, the others refused to speak to me, remaining abnormally silent as we flitted across the waters of the Brackish Lake. The air was cold and the sky dark with clouds. A misty haze hung over the water like a blanket thrown over a hypothermic child. It wasn't until we came within yards of the Isle of the Font that I caught sight of five small fires burning around enough tables to seat all the inhabitants of the Unseen Vale, except for the Guardians who never left their post on the Isle of Stone.

The two dozen Eponi and forty something Fenfolk villagers were already gathered around the tables, setting out extravagantly prepared dishes, everything from meat pies to raspberry cakes. There were pitchers of beer and honey mead, wine and fresh spring water. A large roast boar was situated at the center of the middle table and there were dozens of apple dishes, pies, tarts, and puddings. Samhain was the one night we were encouraged to eat as much as we could without thought to our normal lives of strict abnegation. The food was fit for a king.

The bards were seated at the edge of the tables, each holding a different instrument, ready to entertain the guests with ancient folk songs and vivacious music with harp, fiddle, and drum. The Maiden-Healers were lined up near the front of the tables, where two large wooden thrones sat, one adorned with heather, the other with holly. I followed the Druids to one of the front tables where we were seated and plied with beverages by the Maiden-Healers. The Priestesses of Nimue had yet to arrive and the Crones would remain on the Isle of Birds, staring into their Cauldron. The Old Religion taught that Samhain was the night when the veil between the mortal world and the Otherworld was at its thinnest, when the spirits of the dead were free to once again walk amongst mortals. The Crones saw their greatest visions during the darkest hour of Samhain night and refused to abandon their Cauldron in order to attend the festivities. Taliesin was also absent, likely in the outside world celebrating with the Knights at Uther's court.

Faelan wasn't seated with the rest of us Druids but continued on to Viviana's Tower to dress the part of Kernos. I purposefully took the seat between Ennis macDwyr and Gaius to avoid having uncomfortable conversations with the other less friendly Druids. I longed to be anywhere else but there and was seriously doubting my future in the order. I'd learned nothing of any real importance since taking my vows. Gaius and Ennis were attempting to indoctrinate me into the Mysteries but their lessons were less practical application and more textbook learning. I learned how the ritual circle works to amplify the magick of a practitioner and how to invoke the power of the celestials. I was taught the secret of conjuring light and how to bend time so that, to others it would seem I was moving at the speed of a swift wind when really they were slowed to the pace of a fatigued slug. However, I hadn't tried to apply that knowledge and actually work any spells. It was only theory that I'd be able to achieve the aforementioned tasks if asked to do so for the purposes of testing my knowledge. I almost felt I'd learned more from Stargazer, my quasi-foster mother I'd been living with in the Fenfolk village for just over a month. She taught me the practical uses of herbs, how to make healing salves and tinctures, and the necessity of burning sage to clean the energy found inside enclosed structures.

"How do you like living with the Fenfolk?" asked Ennis macDwyr as we were served green salad by Livia and Adiane.

"The experience has been very informative," I said, "I always thought the Fenfolk were simple people but their society is actually as complex as their language. They have their own clan council and decide everything democratically. I didn't expect that."

"The Fenfolk are an enigma," interrupted Gaius, "they've been living here for thousands of years. Taliesin says they are the last remnant of the Beakers who brought the ancient wisdom from the Drowned Lands but there are others who are certain their culture is far older. I think they are the original mortal inhabitants of Britannia and they once lived side by side with the fey and the giants in peace. I guess we'll never know who they really are or where they came from. Especially since none of us can even speak their traditional language."

I glanced over at Stargazer and smiled. She was seated with the other Fenfolk at the tables furthest from the ceremonial thrones, picking at a plate of food and conversing with the other elderly Fenfolk women in their native tongue. She was very old but still vibrant and witty. I spent many nights with her, laughing at her eccentricities while we sat on the porch of her stilted hut, drinking spirits brewed from a Fenfolk secret recipe and strong enough to burn the throat on its journey to the stomach. She called it Tuketna but refused to tell me what it was made from, or the process of its fermentation. Stargazer was like a warmhearted grandmother, concerned more with making me feel loved than ensuring I follow the rules and fulfill my responsibilities. I began to believe Viviana convinced the Council to send me to Stargazer because of what Nimue said about being a better mother. This was Viviana's attempt at giving me someone who would love me without any thought of payment or pride. I wished I was sitting with the Fenfolk where I could laugh at Stargazer as she tried to eat a steak without teeth or innocently flirt with Fishwalker and the other attractive young men. But it was my obligation to sit with the Druids. I focused on the food in front of me and the lively music of the bards and drowned out the men around me, except for Gaius and Ennis macDwyr.

☼　　　☼　　　☼

The formal portion of the Samhain Feast began when the doors of Viviana's Tower flew open and the Priestesses of Nimue marched single-file down the hillside towards the ceremonial thrones in front of our tables. The Priestesses had traded their usual light purple robes for those of silver silk sparkling in the light of the fires encircling the tables. Behind them walked Faelan. He was wearing the hide of a bear like a cloak and wore a golden mask over his face depicting the eternally youthful yet extremely masculine face of Kernos. He walked with his head held high and his energy seemed less obtrusive, as though the mask of Kernos imbued him with the sense and reason he normally lacked. At the rear of the processional walked my mother. She was adorned in a layered gown of silver and white with the silver mask of Nimue over her face and the Earthen Crown atop her head. The Earthen Crown was forged from bronze but bore an interweaving Celtic braid of gold and silver, signifying the union of the god and goddess.

The processional circled the perimeter of the tables twice by the widdershins before the Priestesses took their seats at the front table. Viviana sat upon the throne of heather and Kernos on the throne of holly. Unlike the rest of us who were gorging ourselves on all the wonderful delicacies prepared by the Eponi and Fenfolk women, the Priestesses, Viviana, and Faelan refrained from both food and drink. They were sworn to fast until after the ritual where Viviana would pass the Earthen Crown to Faelan, symbolizing the sleep of Nimue and the rise of Kernos. The music resumed and the festivities continued for another hour, all the while Viviana and Faelan sat on their seats as still as statues. It was only when the moon had risen to its apex in the night sky, visible through a small break in the clouds, that Viviana rose from her seat. The Priestesses also stood as Viviana came to stand in front of them.

"The year has turned once more around," said Viviana from beneath her mask, "And the time has come for me to rest. I have grown weary of the world and, just as the autumn turns to winter, I am now old and ready to die. I will come again, reborn anew in the spring."

Viviana reached up and removed the Earthen Crown from her head and handed it to Asphodel who carried it over to stand at the feet of Faelan, seated on his throne of holly.

"Let you, my sisters, bear witness as I turn over rule of this world to my consort and lover," said Viviana.

Faelan reached down, plucked the Earthen Crown out of Asphodel's hands, and placed it upon his own brow. He then rose from the throne of holly and moved to stand in front of me and the other Druids. He spoke with a voice that sounded vastly different than his usual gruff, apathetic tones and it seemed the earth shifted at the force of his words.

"I now rise from the deep places of the forests," he said, "to claim kingship over the dark time of the world, when the winter spreads to cover the land in its ice and cold. It is by the fire of my heart that you shall endure, safe here in the Unseen Vale."

It wasn't until the ceremony was concluded and the music resumed that I noticed Morgana was absent from the festivities. She'd been present at the beginning of the Samhain Feast, lined up with the other Maiden-Healers to serve food and beverage. I noticed her near the back of the gathering space when the processional of the Priestesses, Viviana, and Faelan came down from Viviana's Tower. Sometime after that she slipped away and I was unnerved at the thought of what she might be doing. My mother was willing to trust Morgana, to welcome her back into the folds and invite her to resume her duties as a Maiden-Healer. I was less convinced of Morgana's altruism. She'd been in the outside world too long, in the constant presence of Morgause. I had seen many times how Morgause was able to manipulate

Morgana, to bend her to her will, and I doubted very seriously Morgana would really abandon her relationship with her sister to come back and spend her life as a Priestess.

I decided I couldn't ignore my instincts any longer and decided to go search for Morgana. I looked in the House of Priestesses and Viviana's Tower. I walked up the hillside and back down to the narrow plateau opposite the druidesses' compound. All the Fenfolk were attending the Samhain Feast. If Morgana had left the Isle of the Font one of their barges would be missing. I started back towards the docks, moving swiftly along the banks of the Brackish Lake, and was just about to the docks when a sudden burst of cold wind caused goosebumps to rise on my arms.

"You are right to distrust Morgana," said a voice as two spirits appeared in front of me, hovering inches above the water of the lake. They were barely visible in the dark. I had to strain to make out their features. I thought I was daydreaming as shock settled in. I was looking into the ghostly faces of my father and our family friend, Eogan. They looked exactly as they had in the last moments of their lives except they were strangely opaque and translucent.

"Viviana does not see it but you do," said Eogan, "You know, in your heart, that Morgana is the one. She is Mab's earthly host. She has been the whole time she's dwelt within the Unseen Vale. It was she who cursed me and Elaine and Madoc to act on her behalf. It was she who coerced Morgause into the darkness. Even now she works to destroy you all. You must find her and stop her before it's too late."

"What does she want?" I asked.

"Revenge," replied my father.

"She means to make herself immortal," said Eogan, "If Mab finds an immortal host she will become unstoppable."

"There are no immortals here," I said, "There haven't been since…"

Then the answer dawned on me.

"She's come for Rhiannon," I said, "She wants to possess Rhiannon's body and become immortal in the flesh."

As the truth washed over me like the first drops of a spring rain I thought I heard the sound of a bell ringing on the wind behind the loud music of the bards and I knew it was Morgana. She was on the Isle of Glass, within the Stone Circle atop the Tor Hill, and she just let someone or something into the Unseen Vale. A shadow stretched out to cast the Holy Isles in its terrifying darkness. It didn't seem like anyone else at the party in the distance heard the bell. The apparitions of my father and Eogan began to fade as the clouds rolled in to conceal the light of the moon.

"Hurry, Galahad," said Eogan, "There's still time to stop her."

Then he and my father vanished.

I ran back to the party as fast as I could. Viviana was still seated on the throne of heather. She'd removed her mask and was bobbing her head back and forth to the rhythm of the music. I approached her as silently as I could, so as not to draw attention to myself and bent down to whisper.

"Mother," I said, "We have a problem."

I told her what happened down by the water, about the ghosts of Ban and Eogan, and about the revelation that Morgana was the host of Mab. Viviana remained calm as I urgently recounted what Eogan said before she stood and made her way into the crowd. Minutes later she returned with a small group consisting of Faelan, Elaine, Gaius, Livia, Ennis macDwyr, and Fishwalker. She took Fishwalker's arm and he led us quickly down to the docks where we loaded onto his barge.

"Where are we going?" asked Faelan as we set out across the water in the misty darkness.

"The darkness has come again to Avalon," said Viviana.

"Morgause is here?" said Elaine.

"It is not Morgause," said Viviana, "It is Morgana. She is the host of Mab and she means to destroy us all. We must be quick. We may already be too late to stop them."

Fishwalker paddled as fast as I'd ever seen a Fenfolk man move and our barge flew across the calm waters of the Brackish Lake towards the distant Isle of the Crossroad, where the eternally young body of Rhiannon sat upon its funeral pyre waiting for Mab to claim it as her own, to use its fey magick to doom us all.

☼   ☼   ☼

As our barge approached the Crossroad it was clear we were not the first to arrive. Three barges were already moored at the dock and no less than two dozen Saxon Sellswords were standing guard just beyond. Amidst there ranks stood Lot of the Orkneys, his scarred, ruddy face, aged by years of war and his graying hair falling out by the handfuls. Faelan leaned in and told Viviana about the small army already on the island but it didn't seem to change her resolve.

"Take us around to the secret stair, Fishwalker, and do so silently," said my mother, "Once we are ashore, Elaine, you must go at once into the outside world and call for father. Tell him to bring Uther and the Knights. I fear the fight for Britannia will begin here on this night."

Fishwalker maneuvered the barge as quietly as if it were a piece of driftwood floating along with the current. He stayed far enough from the shore to avoid the light cast onto the water by the Saxons' torches until they faded from sight altogether. Within a few minutes, we came around to the side of the island occupied by one of the two high hills forming the walls of the ravine where my friends and I built our cottage a few years before. I was expecting to be greeted by the sheer incline of the hill as the barge came to rest against solid ground, but instead saw a narrow stairway hewn into the hillside leading up to a small tunnel forty feet above our heads. One by one our group disembarked. I took Viviana's arm to guide her up the path but she refused my assistance, demonstrating she knew the way better than the rest of us. Elaine remained on the barge and, once we were all safely ashore, Fishwalker edged the craft away into the darkness.

The small tunnel led through the hillside and opened up behind one of the fountains spread across the gardens where I first met my grandfather, Oberon. We made sure to keep to the perimeter of the garden, concealing our presence with bushes and tall hedges as we inched closer to the funeral pyre where Rhiannon's body laid in its eternal slumber. It quickly became obvious there were three individuals standing around the pyre. Morgana, Morgause, and Mordred were looking down at Rhiannon's body. Morgana was smiling devilishly while Morgause and Mordred looked on in confusion.

"I still don't understand," said Mordred as we inched close enough to hear them talking.

"What's not to understand," sneered Morgause, "Rhiannon's body isn't really dead. Fey are immortal but, without her spirit, her body just lays here like a mummy. It's perfect, already unoccupied, just sitting here waiting for Mab to claim it has her own. And then we'll have our sister back."

"Is that all you care about?" hissed Mab from within Morgana, "I thought you were here to serve me. Remember, Morgause, you took vows to always act on my behalf, by my will, just like Morgana. She wouldn't be pleased if you tried to abandon me as soon as she is free. And neither will I. I would be very displeased, indeed."

"We won't leave you, mistress," said Morgause with a shaky voice, "We live only to serve you."

Viviana was no longer willing to wait in the bushes. She stepped out into the open and guided herself towards the funeral pyre, towards her sister's evil children. When they caught sight of her, Morgause and Mordred ducked behind the pyre, occasionally poking their heads up to see what Viviana was doing. Morgana remained standing and continued smirking as my mother came to stand in front of her, her walking stick held out like a sword ready to strike off the head of a treasonous rebel. Viviana was blind but, in some ways, she could see the world better than any of us.

"Step away from my mother, goddess of darkness," said Viviana, "You are not welcome here."

Morgana laughed a billowing, psychotic chuckle that carried across the water like the howl of a banshee. She didn't attempt to move away from the funeral pyre. Instead, she threw her hands up and a barrier of invisible yet potent auric energy extended outward to protect her and everything surrounding her, including Rhiannon's funeral pyre. Viviana thrust her walking stick out in front of her but it shattered into a hundred pieces as it came into contact with Mab's protective barrier, leaving Viviana without a weapon to use in her defense.

"You think you have the power to face me?" smirked Morgana, "You are nothing more than a mortal. You may have fey blood in your veins but you are no match for a goddess. You're all alone, Viviana, with no one to come to your aid. My pious sister, Nimue, has gone to her rests. Even if your prayers could reach her, they would fall on deaf ears."

Faelan, Gaius, Livia, and Ennis macDwyr jumped out of the bushes to join Viviana at the edge of Mab's impenetrable sphere of energy.

"She is not alone," said Faelan and then he began to chant the same incantation in Ogham again and again. When the others figured out what he was doing, they joined in and the power of the chant grew with every voice added to its mantra.

"Afíste tis fonés," they said, "mas na spásei aftó to teíchos kai as to pnévma na páei doreán."

Each time they repeated the incantation it had more of an effect. The barrier around Mab began to crack and weaken, as though it was a brick wall being pulverized by a giant. Mab didn't look the slightest bit alarmed. She was set on her course and she wouldn't let Druids or Priestesses or anyone else stand in her way. She waved her right hand, as though she was dismissing a servant, and a powerful wind came rolling in off the Brackish Lake with enough force to knock everyone except Viviana off their feet. I wanted to run to help my mother but I was frozen with fear. I only knew a few minor acts of magick. I was no match for a goddess and I knew it. Viviana stood her ground and continued chanting but, without the others, all now unconscious on the ground, her spell was having little effect. Morgana put her hand on Rhiannon's forehead and spoke an incantation of her own, one seething with hatred and malice.

"Metakiníste to pnévma," said Morgana, "mou apó edó ekeí kai na kánoun tin orgí mou gnostá."

There came a sound like the breaking of glass as Morgana hunched over, clutching at her stomach. She began making vomiting noises as her skin went as white as a freshly bleached sheet. With a terrible gagging, Morgana wretched all over the ground at her feet and then toppled over unconscious, just as Rhiannon's body opened its eyes as sat up on its pyre. She took a second to check out her arms and legs, her breasts and feet, before she turned and leaped off the stone slab. With eyes as red as rubies, she glared over at Viviana, smiling wryly with the expression of a madman finding innate pleasure in causing others slow, tortuous pain. Mab laughed sinisterly from within Rhiannon's body as she came to stand in front of my mother.

"What's the matter, Viviana, my darling?" she asked, "You look like you have seen a ghost."

Chapter Twenty-Two
"The Circle Burns"

"How dare you," screamed Viviana in pure rage, a side of my mother I'd never seen before.

Normally Viviana was stoic and calm, addressing every situation with the same commanding presence but seeing the body of her mother standing in front of her alive drove her over the edge. Mab mocked Viviana's anger by strutting around like a peacock, checking out every part of her new, immortal flesh. Viviana conjured hex after hex, hurtling them at Mab like rocks of ice falling in a hailstorm. Mab remained smug. She wasn't phased in the least by the barrage of hexes. She held up her hands as if she was signaling a carriage to stop and all Viviana's conjurations were rendered useless. Mab laughed as Viviana escalated her attack. But no matter how hard Viviana tried, she couldn't even come close to hurting Mab.

"I don't know about you, but I am growing tired of this," sneered Mab and, with a wave of her hand, Viviana was frozen in place, held in a state of paralysis by Mab's godly energy.

Faelan, Gaius, Ennis macDwyr, and Livia slowly came around, urgently pulling themselves up off the ground with the realization they were in serious danger. Faelan raised a Spell of Protection around him and the others but, when the energy of the spell reached out to cocoon Viviana it was repelled like water dripping down a window. Mab looked amused by Faelan's attempt, like a vain, unfeeling noblewoman watching a peasant be tortured. She barely even took note of them as she walked over to where Viviana was locked in place like a statue. Viviana's face was still twisted by rage but she was unable to counteract Mab as Mab reached out and placed her index finger on Viviana's forehead, like a magician meaning to distract onlookers with a slight-of-hand trick.

Faelan, Gaius, and Ennis macDwyr began summoning as much offensive magick as they could, calling for the trees to come alive and defend Viviana like giants swatting at an ant. They brought down the winds and conjured a storm that sent bolts of lightning crackling down from the heavens towards Mab. They threw hexes to make Mab sleep, to split her spirit from Rhiannon's body, to strike her dead where she stood but nothing worked. Mab wrapped herself in her own sphere of protection as she continued to hold her forefinger to Viviana's brow.

"You have been so devoted to your mother all these years," said Mab, "wondering what her life was like after her spirit was cast into the Otherworld. I think it only fair that I show you."

"Stï gi ton oneíron," said Mab with a maniacal tone and Viviana crumpled lifelessly to the ground. Mab stepped over her body towards the Druids and Livia with an evil smile on her face.

"What will you do now?" she sneered, "With Taliesin far away at Uther's court and Viviana dead, there will be no one here to lead you. Nimue has gone to her rest and Kernos has not shown himself in the world of the living for centuries. I am your only hope at salvation now. Join me or face my wrath. The choice is yours."

With a twisted grin, Mab turned around and walked back towards the funeral pyre where Morgana, Morgause, and Mordred were waiting, still cowering like scared children. Mab sneered at them and snapped her finger for them to join her. Together they walked away towards the narrow ravine leading down to where Lot and the Saxon Sellswords were still gathered awaiting orders from their dark queen. They boarded their stolen barges and disappeared into the darkness, leaving the Druids and Livia standing by the funeral pyre frozen in fear. Once I was sure it was safe, I launched myself out of the bushes and ran to my mother. She wasn't breathing and had no pulse. What Mab had said was true. My mother, the Lady of the Unseen Vale, was dead. I cradled her in my arms and cried, wailing like a banshee come to harvest a soul. Ennis macDwyr came over and put his hand on my shoulder, pulling me away from Viviana so that Faelan and Livia could examine her body more closely. I didn't know how we would be able to win against Mab. Inside Rhiannon's body, she was virtually indestructible and, without Taliesin or Viviana, we were down our two most powerful players.

"She's not dead," said Livia after finishing her examination.

"What?" I asked in shock.

"Mab cast her spirit into the land of dreams and placed her body in a state of perpetual sleep. She's not breathing and has no pulse but she still lives, or rather she is frozen in a state of death without decay until such a time as her spirit finds its way back from the beyond."

As we lifted Viviana's body and put it on the funeral pyre where her mother's own immortal but lifeless form laid for twenty-five years there came the sound of a single barge moving across the water. Faelan and Gaius instinctively drew a Spell of Protection around the five of us as the barge docked and the single passenger disembarked. The individual was wearing a brown traveling cloak and had his hood pulled up to conceal his face but I knew him by the way he was walking, leaning on a staff to take pressure of his failing knee joints. It was Taliesin. I ran down the path as fast as my legs could carry me and threw myself into his arms, sobbing on his shoulder like a man who just lost his wife. He ran his fingers through my hair and cooed, as though he was trying to tame a wild bird.

"There, there, Galahad," he said, "You must be strong now."

Taliesin took me by the arm and gently guided me back towards the others near the funeral pyre. When Faelan saw it was Taliesin he let out a dramatic sigh of relief while Gaius exclaimed praises to mighty Kernos for bringing the Merlin back to us in our hour of need. Taliesin seemed older and weaker than I'd ever seen him. He was having trouble breathing and, from the slight limp as he walked, I knew his joints were causing him immense pain. Yet his mind was as sharp as ever and he moved with the same determination that made me respect him so much. Livia was still standing beside my mother's lifeless body when Taliesin noticed his daughter on the pyre. He walked over to her and kissed her gently on the forehead, the act of a loving father seeing his child in distress, wanting to change her

circumstances, to take his pain as his own. It was the most tender I'd ever
seen Taliesin.

"Can you help her?" asked Livia.

"Her spirit has moved beyond my reach," replied Taliesin,
"Viviana's survival now depends solely on her determination to live."

"What about us? How will we survive?" asked Faelan, "Mab just
moved us around like pieces on a chess board. We don't have the power to
face her in open combat. Do you?"

"I don't have the power to defeat Mab," replied Taliesin, "The best I
can do is conceal our movements in a blanket of fog. We need to go to the
other isles with haste, gather up all those who are willing, and make for the
Stone Circle. Avalon is lost."

☼   ☼   ☼

The five of us followed Taliesin back down to the docks where
Fishwalker and another Fenfolk man I didn't recognize were waiting on their
barges. We boarded the barges, me, Taliesin, and Livia on the one manned
by Fishwalker and Ennis macDwyr, Faelan, and Gaius on the other. Before
we set out into the open water, Taliesin raised his hands into the air and began
to speak in Ogham.

"Afxísei tin omíchli gia na krýpsei tis kiníseis mas," he said.

At once a thick curtain of dense mists rose from the waters of the
Brackish Lake, concealing the Holy Isles in its impenetrable blanket. It
provided the perfect cover for anyone trying to move unnoticed across the
water. When the thick mists were fully formed, we pushed off into the lake
and made our way silently towards the other Holy Isles. I was fairly certain
nearly everyone would still be on the Isle of the Font celebrating the Samhain
Feast, except for the Guardians and the Crones who never attended the
festivities. It was likely the Crones would not be willing to abandon Avalon.
They were cloistered old women waiting until the last days of their long lives.
They had no fear of death. In fact, they welcomed it with every prayer spoken

in honor of Catsubodhva and every vision extracted from the depths of their smoking cauldron.

The barge carrying Gaius, Ennis macDwyr, and Faelan continued on towards the Isle of the Font while the barge paddled by Fishwalker veered off towards the Isle of Stone. I knew without asking what we were setting out to accomplish. The two greatest treasures of the Druids laid in the catacombs beneath the Isle of Stone: Tara, the Cup of Life, and Excalibur the Cursed. Taliesin would not abandon Avalon without first securing those treasures and transporting them away from the Unseen Vale with us. Without the treasures in the catacomb, the Guardians would have no purpose and would likely accompany us on our exodus. There were only three Guardians left: old Leawys, Tristram, and Ywain. I knew Tristram and Ywain well. We grew up together in the House of Initiates and I was confident they'd travel into the outside world with us.

"Livia," said Taliesin, "When we reach the Isle of Stone, go to the cottages of the Guardians and tell Leawys all that has happened. I don't think Leawys will come with us. He is old and the journey might bring him prematurely to his end. The younger ones must leave alongside the rest of us. Do not allow them to choose otherwise."

Fishwalker pulled the barge up to the stairs carved into the side of the jagged cliff rising high into the air on the Isle of Stone but, instead of mounting the steps, we followed the narrow bank towards the cottages in the distance. Livia did as she was commanded and disappeared into the home occupied by Leawys while Taliesin and I continued on into the catacombs. The journey to the heart of the labyrinthine caverns passed more quickly this time. It was a familiar course, one I walked with Viviana, and I found it less frightening as we descended into the heart of the earth. Within a half-hour we arrived in the secret antechamber where the statues of Nimue and Kernos stood holding their treasures. I instinctively moved towards Excalibur but Taliesin grabbed my arm and stopped me dead in my tracks.

"You mustn't touch the sword with bare hands," he said, "Remove your robes and wrap the sword inside them."

I stripped down to my loincloth and tossed my robes over Excalibur like a blanket, wrapping it securely within the folds of fabric before placing it under my arm. Taliesin retrieved the Cup of Life and tucked it into the deep pocket of his traveling cloak.

"No matter what happens," said Taliesin, "Do not let the sword out of your sight. It may be the only thing that can save us from Mab."

As Taliesin spoke I understood the inscription on the blade. The ancients called it Caliburn, the God-Killing Sword. If run through by the sword, Mab would perish. I could feel the power of the blade pulsing through the fabric of my robes as we ran back through the catacombs and out into the cool night air. Tristram and Ywain were already aboard the barge with Livia but Leawys was nowhere to be found. It wasn't until Fishwalker used his long pole to push us back out into the open water of the lake that I caught sight of the old man. He was hanging from the side of the cliff with a rope around his neck. I wanted to jump off the barge and swim back to him, to cut him down and breathe life back into his frail body but as the mists closed in around us, he vanished from sight, and I knew if I attempted to swim back to the Isle of Stone I'd be lost in the fog and drowned.

"What happened to Leawys?" I asked Tristram urgently.

"He said he was ready to enter the Otherworld," said Tristram, "and then he threw himself from the cliff. He was eighty years old. The prospect of leaving Avalon to start a new life was too much for him."

I stayed silent for the remainder of the ride across the Brackish Lake, cradling Excalibur in my arms and thinking about the losses we'd been made to endure by Mab. My father, Eogan, multiple druids, dozens of soldiers, a High King, Leawys, and my mother. I thought about her lying there on the funeral pyre, abandoned to be consumed by the darkness spreading from Mab to engulf the Holy Isles like a plague. I wanted to go back to the Crossroad, to wrap her in a shroud and carry her with us into the outside world but the urgency of our exodus made it impossible to turn around. Mab and her servants were still somewhere in the Unseen Vale. It was too dangerous for any of us to linger in Avalon any longer.

There were more than a dozen barges beached on the Isle of Glass with over sixty people standing on the field around the House of Healing. I could make out the faces of Faelan, Gaius, Adiane, and several others. The size of the group meant all the Eponi and Fenfolk were also present, ready to abandon their lifelong homes out of fear for their lives. Fishwalker poled us right up onto the shore. We disembarked to join the others and, together, we headed in mass towards the Stone Circle atop the Tor Hill but, just as we reached the Processional Way we were greeted by the full force of Saxon Sellswords led by Lot of the Orkneys, standing behind Mab and the Mors.

"You're not going anywhere," laughed Mab.

☼　　☼　　☼

We stood there in a standoff for what seemed like hours, Taliesin at the head of our group, Mab at the head of theirs. It was strange to see them there, so near to each other, since Taliesin was once the lover of Rhiannon, whose body Mab was wearing like a swimsuit. I wondered what he was thinking as he looked on the face of the woman he had loved. The mists were furling in around us, cutting the Isle of Glass off from the rest of the Holy Isles so it appeared to be an island floating within a cloud. There we stood, staring down our enemies, with our only means of escape lying behind them.

"Step aside, Mab," demanded Taliesin.

"Or what?" sneered Mab, "What are you going to do?"

In truth there wasn't much that Taliesin could do. He could draw Excalibur and lunge for Mab but he would most likely be surrounded and subdued by her warriors before getting close enough to deal a fatal blow. He could conjure some mighty force of magick but Mab had already demonstrated how easily she could reverse anything we threw at her. It seemed she maintained the upper hand and we were all doomed. Taliesin took a step closer to Mab and his expression was one of sadness, like a man mourning the loss of his one great love, deprived of that final moment to say his goodbyes.

237

"Please, Mab, let these people go free," he said, "It's me you want. You can have me. I will surrender myself to you this very moment if only you spare the others."

"Why do you make me out to be the villain," said Mab, "All I want is for the Old Religion to be renewed and for the Christian usurpers to flee from our shores. You Druids have remained cloistered here between the worlds for too long. You've let the hearts of men drift away and into the hands of the God of Abram, the Tetragrammaton, who is my only true enemy. We cannot endure without the prayers of men, not me, not Nimue, not even mighty Kernos. The Britons have lost their way but the Saxons, the Saxons are ready to stand by us to the death, to renew our power and allow us true rebirth in the mortal world. And you would stand against me?"

"You speak with such sincerity," said Taliesin, "But your words are like acid falling from the sky. You don't care about the Britons, or the Saxons, or even the Old Religion. All you want is to make Kernos and Nimue suffer. You thought you'd dealt with your sister, imprisoning her in a dungeon on the distant shores of the Otherworld but she escaped, with my help, and returned to the Unseen Vale unscathed. She may now slumber but she will awaken in the spring, unless you murder her before she has a chance to open her eyes again. And then, there's Kernos. He slighted you once, choosing to love your sister instead of you and you want to make him suffer. But you can't find him, can you? He has hidden himself in some place beyond even the confines of the Otherworld."

Mab's demeanor was immediately changed from the bitter woman feigning spiritual altruism to a psychopath reveling in the pain she was causing the world around her, the suffering induced with every breath from her stolen body.

"I should've known better than to try and sweet talk you, Taliesin," she smirked, "You are the Merlin of all the Britons, after all. Everything you said is true, except for one thing. I do know where to find Kernos."

"This is absurd, Mab," said Taliesin, "The only way you are going to stop us from leaving the Unseen Vale is to destroy the gateway. Then you would be trapped here as well and something tells me that's not a part of your master plan."

The Saxon Sellswords behind Mab looked to be growing restless, as if they were driven to kill by some unknown force, that the only way to satisfy their maniacal hunger was to shed innocent blood. They were just waiting for Mab to give them the permission and they would launch themselves forward with their swords and battleaxes to mow down the defenseless Fenfolk and Eponi making up the bulk of our party. The Druids stepped out in front of the innocent people behind them, forming a wall to protect them from the Saxons. The Priestesses also stood towards the front while the Maiden-Healers did their best to tend the children and elderly. Many of the Fenfolk were armed with kitchen knives and pitchforks while all the Eponi men were carrying a gladium sword. If battle ensued, there would be severe casualties on both sides. We'd be lucky if any of us walked away alive.

Mab and Taliesin seemed to understand the situation and both were reluctant to sacrifice their people. However, Mab's concern for the Saxon Sellswords seemed more of a formality than genuine caring. If Taliesin provoked her she wouldn't hesitate to unleash her forces on us before sitting back to watch everyone tear themselves apart. Morgause, Morgana, and Mordred looked villainous as they stood behind Mab, like tyrannical children seeking nothing but the love of an unfeeling mother. Mab had them in the palm of her hand with them pledged to her service of their own free will. I felt sorry for Morgause, knowing that she had always been a pawn of Mab and nothing more, and I was sad for Mordred. He was still a child and probably didn't understand what his devotion to Mab truly meant.

"You don't know the first thing about my master plan," laughed Mab, "And you are stupid to assume you do. Do you know why I am still standing here, Taliesin? Why I'm not already through the gateway and in the outside world seeking my revenge? It's because I don't need to leave the Unseen Vale. Everything I need, everything I want to see realized, is right here under our very noses. And the first thing I need is to see you dead, each and every one of you. There will be no escape."

Mab turned around and made a movement like she was throwing a rock towards the Tor Hill and the Stone Circle suddenly burst into flames, not the kind of fire that we cook with and use to warm our homes, an otherworldly demon-fire burning bright green and hot enough to melt stone. One after another, the monoliths forming the Stone Circle, gateway into the outside world, began to melt. Simultaneously, the Saxon Sellswords rushed forward, weapons raised, and lunged into the crowds behind Taliesin. Pandemonium ensued as the Saxons fought through the line of Druids and Priestesses and began hacking down the Fenfolk and Eponi, as though they were wheat being gathered during the autumn harvest. The Saxons were trained in the ways of war and employed all their skills to render us completely inefficient in defending ourselves. It seemed everything would be lost and we would all die there, locked in the Unseen Vale, until there came a loud ringing on the air and, with a flash, Elaine appeared in the burning Stone Circle with Uther and the Knights of Avalon.

Chapter Twenty-Three
"Murder in the Mist"

The arrival of Uther and the Knights of Avalon tipped the scales in our favor but the battle was far from over. The Saxon Sellswords were relentless in their assaults and seemed not to notice any wound inflicted on them. The Fenfolk were decimated with only twenty of the forty-four villagers standing. The Eponi fared better and nearly all of them still stood but many were wounded. Bodon and Orin were dead, as were Eamon and Dorien of the bards. The Priestesses all still lived, not because of their superior skills, but because the Saxons seemed offended by the prospect of murdering unarmed women. The Maiden-Healers were also still alive, standing behind the Priestesses in terror. I could see Tristram using a Saxon claymore against an enemy warrior and Ywain was laying on the ground at his feet, nursing a fatal wound to his abdomen. Morgause was fighting Faelan, Morgana was squaring off against Asphodel, and Mordred was cowering behind a rock. I was doing my best to evade the assault, still clinging to Excalibur. I wanted to draw the blade but Taliesin made me swear I would keep it covered and not allow it to touch my skin. I was so focused on protecting the sword I didn't notice as a Saxon crept up behind me with his sword raised to deal a fatal blow. As he moved to bring his blade down on my neck, one of the Knights leapt over the tall grass I was using as a shelter and drove his own sword into the heart of the Saxon. The Knight was wearing armor of red leather and a golden helmet but I knew him, not by any distinguishing feature but by the sword he held in his hand. It was Eregolan and the Knight was my cousin, Madoc.

"You need to be more careful," said Madoc, "We're in a battle, Galahad, now is not the time to hide in the bushes."

"I wasn't hiding," I said defensively, "I was keeping this safe."

I pointed to the lump of robes cradled under my left arm and Madoc looked at me as if I was crazy.

"Nothing is worth your life," said Madoc.

Madoc didn't wait for me to respond. He hurtled himself back into the battle, brandishing Eregolan against a pair of Saxons attempting to strike down Gaius. Uther and the Knights were moving through the Saxon ranks like a mower cutting down blades of grass but the Saxons were resolved they wouldn't be so easily defeated. As a result of some protection spell cast by Mab, the magick of the Druids was ineffectual against the enemy. Taliesin was the only one smart enough to redirect his energy from trying to hex the Saxons to using the elements and environment around him as a weapon, making him the primary target, to be eliminated no matter the cost. He was facing off against Mab near the wall of mists closing in on us from all sides. She was throwing powerful curses at him but he shielded himself each time and narrowly escaped defeat.

"I was expecting more from the Mistress of Magick," said Taliesin as he caused a boulder to fly through air towards Mab. Mab countered with a spell causing the boulder to explode into millions of miniscule particles.

"I'm just getting started," laughed Mab.

Mab began making a sound like a cat whose tail was just stepped on, filling the misty night air with her horrible wailing. Taliesin looked confused, as though he'd never witnessed such magick. Then he turned to the remainder of our forces and with a magnanimous tone of authority he screamed a single command.

"Run," he shrieked.

The Saxons, Eponi, Fenfolk, and Druids lying dead on the ground began to twitch, opening their hollow, lifeless eyes and standing one by one. They were devoid of any human characteristics, hollow shells of decomposing flesh answering only to the call of Mab. Our remaining forces did as Taliesin ordered and ran. I followed suit but remained close enough that I could still see Taliesin in the distance. The dozens of corpses ignored the rest of us and made their way towards Taliesin, slowly dragging their rotting feet across the field. Mab remained where she stood, smiling a sinister grin, eyes filled with psychotic satisfaction. The monster eclipsed the woman as Mab was consumed with rage.

Taliesin raised his staff in front of him, brandishing it like a sword, as the undead descended on him. I worried how he would fight something that had already perished but, to my relief, he was prepared. As his staff came into contact with the first reanimated corpse, it burst into ashes, as though placed in the heart of a fiery kiln. The other undead attackers hesitated for a split second but, with a wave of her hand, Mab compelled them to continue their assault. Taliesin moved like a martial arts master as he blocked and dodged each attempt to take him down, driving his staff into one corpse, then another, and another, rendering them nothing but steaming piles of ashes and soot. Seeing the ease of Taliesin's battle against the undead, Mab conjured another powerful spell. The Isle of Glass seemed to groan and shift as the mountainous boulders adorning the landscape suddenly came to life, fracturing into human-like giants of stone.

Faelan, Gaius, and Ennis macDwyr appeared to my right, no longer able to stand by and watch as Taliesin was overwhelmed by Mab's unholy supernatural forces. They ran with all speed towards the stone giants moving slowly to descend on Taliesin but Taliesin waved his staff and all three Druids were thrown backwards off their feet.

"I told you to run," screamed Taliesin with fury, "You cannot help win this battle. These creatures are beyond your strength to fight."

Taliesin dealt with the giants the same way he fought the undead, driving his staff into their rocky bodies, causing them to explode into thousands of pieces. Unfortunately, the sheer numbers of Mab's minions were beginning to overpower Taliesin. He kept them at bay with his magick but they inched closer by the second. When Morgause and Morgana joined in the foray, casting hex after hex at Taliesin's backside, I knew he wouldn't last much longer. It was a moment of instinct for me. Without thinking, I reached into the folds of my robes and unsheathed Excalibur, drawing it from its scabbard like a solider preparing for war.

I sprinted with all my might towards the cluster of undead and giants with Excalibur held aloft. I could feel the power of the sword coursing through my veins, as though it were an extension of my own flesh, as if it had always been a part of me. It made me feel strong and alive in a way I'd never felt before. The whole world seemed to become less complex and the battle itself seemed little more than a minor inconvenience. I moved like a great warrior, like Achilles rushing into Troy with his spear brandished proudly. Excalibur slashed through the undead of its own accord, guiding my hand as though it had a spirit of its own. As the blade drove into them, the corpses exploded into ash and the rock giants crumbled to dust. When Taliesin saw me, I thought he'd be relieved I'd come to help him, but he looked angrier than I'd ever seen him.

"I told you not to touch the sword," he yelled but his voice was drowned out by the sound of the Druids, Knights, Eponi, and Fenfolk returning to the battle at the foot of the Tor Hill armed with whatever they could wield as a weapon.

I kept cutting through the enemy with Excalibur until I reached Taliesin. As Mab caught sight of the sword she screamed, as though she'd looked upon the face of that which frightened her most. Up until that point, Taliesin was in control of the mists encircling the Isle of Glass but, with another wave of her hand, Mab caused the mists to invade the island itself, drowning us all in its thick vapors and making it impossible to see more than four feet in front of your face. All I could see was Taliesin. He struck down the last few corpses trying to attack him and then approached me with a vengeance. He tore off his cloak and threw it over Excalibur, yanking the sword out of my hands and concealing it within the folds of fabric. The moment the blade left my possession all I could think about was touching it again, holding it in my hands and being washed in its power. I almost attacked Taliesin before I remembered who he was and my own purpose in the battle. Taliesin expected my response. He slapped me hard across the face, as though he meant to wake me from a fantasy before he stepped back and regained his composure.

"You will never be free of it now," he said, "The sword will call to you every moment of every day for the rest of your life."

Taliesin was focused on me and I was staring at the ground, allowing Mab to creep up behind us unnoticed in the fog. While Taliesin stood there chastising me for my actions, she leapt out of the mists with a dagger in her hand and ran it across Taliesin's neck, slicing his throat open from ear to ear. I was paralyzed in shock as Taliesin coughed blood and then fell to the ground, dropping his staff and Excalibur at my feet. He twitched a few times and sputtered as he struggled to breathe before his body went still. He did not move again. I lunged for the sword and pulled it from Taliesin's cloak, holding it high in Mab's face. She cowered in fear and, as she vanished back into the mists, she yelled with a demonic voice.

"Prostatévoun mou," she screamed and Morgause, Morgana, and Mordred emerged from the dense fog cutting me and Taliesin off from the rest of our forces. I could hear metal hitting metal and the sounds of men engaged in the heat of battle. I knew the Druids and Knights were close but I couldn't see them through the mists.

Morgause and Morgana each carried a gladium and war-dagger. They looked like Iceni warrior women ready to join their men protecting their homes from vicious invaders. Morgause attacked first but I didn't even have to think about how I would defend myself. Excalibur leapt to life and collided with her gladium hard enough to split blade from handle. Morgause jumped back to avoid a swipe of Excalibur aimed at her stomach while Morgana tried to jump me from behind. Excalibur caused me to swing around on my feet just in time for the sword to impale itself in Morgana's shoulder. Mordred held a small war-dagger but he seemed frozen in fear. Morgana screamed as Excalibur drove itself deeper into her flesh while Morgause conjured a hex meant to render me unconscious. Excalibur deflected the spell and then once again rounded on Morgause while Morgana dropped to the ground, cradling the wound in her shoulder and sweating from shock. Morgause tried to conjure another hex but Excalibur deflected it as well. All I could think about was Taliesin lying there motionless on the ground. He was my mentor, my grandfather, and my closest friend. I wanted to make Mab and her servants suffer, starting with Morgause and Morgana.

"We can't win this fight," screamed Morgana in pain.

"I won't stop until Galahad is dead," spat Morgause. She leapt high into the air and then rounded on me with her war-dagger held out like the tail of a scorpion but she was too slow. Excalibur shifted to match her movements and, as she descended on me from above, the sword drove itself through her torso, impaling her on its blade. Morgana screamed in agony as Morgause gagged, choking on the blood rising in her throat. She fell to the ground as I withdrew Excalibur from her chest. She continued to gaze at me with malice as the light left her eyes, replaced by the absent lifelessness of all those passing into the world of the dead.

Morgana was in a rage and, even with the bleeding wound to her shoulder, she was determined to have revenge. If it hadn't been for Mordred grabbing her and dragging her off into the mists, she would've met the same fate as her sister. I felt compelled to run after them, to catch them and cut them down with Excalibur but, as I took off in pursuit, a strong arm reached out from the mists and grabbed me by the arm. I turned around to see Accolon staring me in the face.

"Let them go," he said, "The battle is over."

A loud ring carried on the air confirmed what Accolon already knew. The mists receded at once, revealing the full scope of the Isle of Glass, a battlefield littered with bodies and burns. Our losses were great. The Druids, Baelig, Sorin, and Haseph, the bards, Tovin, Jareth, and Llewellyn, the guardian, Ortheon, and the Knights, Neithon, Gwynedd, Gnaeus, and Mareth were all dead. Nearly thirty Fenfolk had been cut down, and only seven Eponi males still stood. Uther was wounded but still alive, tended by Ector and Cunamaglos near the edge of the island. The Stone Circle was no longer aflame but all that remained of it were a few little stone stumps where the great monoliths had stood. Mab, Morgana, and Mordred were gone while the rest of their forces were lying dead and bleeding on the ground, moaning for a quick release from their agonizing pain.

No longer able to contain the weight of the loss, I let Excalibur go limp at my side and collapsed into Accolon's arms. He bore my weight as he dragged me away from the bodies of Taliesin and Morgause, down the hill and passed the burning remnants of the House of Healing. The Priestesses and Maiden-Healers, who were mostly unscathed, were running around tending to the wounded and dousing the fires burning wildly in several places across the island. The mists had completely receded, revealing the waters of the Brackish Lake and the other Holy Isles, untouched by the violence of that day. I barely noticed as Accolon pulled me onto one of the barges and we set out across the water. It wasn't until he tried to take Excalibur that I snapped out of my shock. I yanked the sword back from him defensively and buried it in Taliesin's brown traveling cloak, still hanging off the handle of the sword where it was snagged by a thread on the ruby. As I wrapped the fabric around the sword I felt a lump in the pocket of the cloak and remembered what laid within it. It was Tara, the Cup of Life. I had in my possession both the great treasures of the Druids.

☼   ☼   ☼

The remaining inhabitants of the Holy Isles spent the next four days cleaning up the carnage of the battlefield on the Isle of Glass. The dead were burned in the funerary rites of the Old Religion and a somber energy settled in over the Unseen Vale. Taliesin was the last to be burned and was given the greatest honors of any of the dead, not only because he was Merlin of all the Britons but because of his final acts of heroism, protecting us from the vile machinations of Mab and her servants. I chose not to attend any of the funerals. I stayed locked away in Stargazer's hut on the Watch Hill with Accolon. Stargazer stayed on the Isle of Glass to help the Maiden-Healers replenish their stores of herbs and rebuild the House of Healing. I hid Excalibur and the Cup of Life, beneath the floorboards of Stargazer's hut and made Accolon swear to never reveal to anyone where the treasures of the Druids were hidden. Then I took to my bed and remained there for seven days and nights, exhausted from the losses and the battle, in a state of shock over the loss of Taliesin.

Accolon stayed by my side the whole time, bringing me food and water, and lying beside me in the evenings with his arms wrapped around my torso. He was as loving and nurturing as I remembered him. It was as though Taliesin never broke Mab's love spell and nothing had changed between us. We made love in the early hours every morning and allowed ourselves to fall into one another completely. His time away from the Unseen Vale had changed him. He was no longer unsure of our love. This man I never thought I'd see again. My only lover. I was confused about everything, except my feelings for Accolon. I knew I wanted him and I was no longer willing to let anything come between us.

Elaine came to the Watch Hill every day to look in on me. She was concerned about how I was taking the loss of both Viviana and Taliesin. She would sit at the table in the corner of the room where I slept and sipped tea while I stayed in bed with the covers drawn up to my nose. She brought me news of the rest of the inhabitants of the Unseen Vale and what was being decided about the future.

"Faelan wants to abandon Avalon," she said one of the mornings she came to see me, "The winter is coming and he is worried about our survival. The food stores are dangerously low and, without the Eponi to tend the pastures, the sheep have disappeared onto the hillside. There are no more Fenfolk men to fish and the Druids are beleaguered by wounds received during the battle. Without your mother or my father, Faelan is the supreme authority of Avalon. I doubt anyone will speak up against his plan."

"We can't leave Avalon," I said, "Life won't be any simpler in the outside world and here we are protected from the harshness of winter. We may have little food but it beats starving to death in the snow."

"I agree with you," replied Elaine, "The trouble is no one else will. They're scared. Mab is still alive in the outside world and they think it's only a matter of time before she returns with fresh forces to wipe us out."

"She won't return here," I said.

"How do you know that?" asked Elaine.

"I just do," I said.

I didn't explain further because I didn't want to reveal the location of Excalibur to anyone, not even Elaine but I knew from the way Mab looked at the sword in fear that she would rather forfeit her new body than face Excalibur again. She proved herself untouchable by almost every form of weapon we could muster, both physical and magical, but Excalibur was the God-Killing Sword and it alone could strike her dead. I wanted to keep the sword close. If Faelan learned it was in my possession, he might try to claim it as his own or make me return it to the hidden antechamber in the catacombs beneath the Isle of Stone.

Excalibur called to me, it sang a mesmerizing song urging me to pull it out from its hiding place and hold it in my hand. I dreamt about the sword, I yearned for it like a man hungering for human contact. I was happy to have Accolon back in my life, at my side again, but the insatiable lust I once felt for him had been replaced by the call of Excalibur. With each day that passed it became harder and harder to resist taking up the sword.

"I wish I had your confidence," continued Elaine, "or that Faelan would listen to reason but he is determined. He has called a Council for tomorrow to make his intentions known. I do hope you'll find the strength to attend the meeting. It's being held in what's left of the Stone Circle."

"I don't think I'll be there," I said.

"Come one, Galahad," interrupted Accolon, "You've been laying in that bed long enough. The world is moving forward as it always does and you're in danger of being left behind."

I didn't want to think about the future. Without my mother or Taliesin it didn't seem we had much to be hopeful about. There had always been a Merlin in Britannia, since the days when the Beakers brought the ancient wisdom from the Drowned Lands, just as there was always a Lady of the Unseen Vale. Now both were gone forever and I felt strangely like it was my fault. If I had just died that day on the Isle of Glass when I was poisoned by Eogan, none of the other terrible events would've happened.

"There is still a chance Viviana will awaken from Mab's curse," said Elaine, "If we do end up leaving Avalon, we will take her with us. No matter what Faelan says about it. Will you help me carry her?"

There was a chance Viviana could wake up. She was still technically alive, her body locked in an everlasting sleep, her spirit exiled into the land of dreams. If she had the fortitude to navigate those strange shores and the determination to live again, she might find her way back. But I wasn't holding out hope. As far as I was concerned, she was as dead as Taliesin and my father and Eogan. There were so many casualties to be saddened by. The only death I did not mourn was Morgause. I was satisfied justice had been done when Excalibur cut her down. I wanted Mab but I was willing to settle for the satisfaction I felt from Morgause's death. My only regret was that she didn't suffer, that her fall was swift and painless.

That night, as Accolon and I laid intertwined together, naked in my bed, I thought about my distant childhood, about the simple days spent studying the Vulgate with Brother Jonas, the evenings eating sweets in Genovefa's kitchens. I missed Eogan and his determination to protect me no matter the cost. I even longed for my father. Ban of Lodecran was anything but loving and that was not what I missed about him. It was the fact he didn't get to see me grow into the young man I'd become, that I never had the opportunity to earn his respect. I started to cry, lost in the sadness of my memories, as Accolon pulled me closer to him.

"I wish I could take away your sadness," he whispered.

"I don't," I replied, "If you took my sadness, you'd take all my memories with it. It feels good to cry about the ones I've lost. It feels like I'm giving credit to who they were with each tear."

"That's a good way to think about it," said Accolon, "I can't imagine what you're feeling."

"Actually, right now I'm feeling angry," I said as my sadness gave way to frustration at the thought of leaving Avalon, the only real home I'd known since Lodecran.

"Angry about what?" asked Accolon.

"Faelan," I grumbled, "He thinks he has the right to dictate orders to the rest of us without even asking the consent of the Council. The Council rules the Unseen Vale. It always has. There can be no king here. Not if the Druids are meant to endure."

"It sounds like you want to attend the meeting tomorrow, after all," smiled Accolon.

"I think I will go," I said confidently, filled with a new feeling of empowerment. There was yet one more battle to wage in Avalon, and it was against the High Druid, Faelan.

☼   ☼   ☼

The Council began just after sunrise within the remnants of the Stone Circle. Most of the monoliths forming the perimeter had melted to nothing but stumps, resembling little more than simple boulders fallen from a nearby mountainside. Only a single stone remained intact, rising into the air like a giant standing guard. I couldn't be sure but I was fairly positive it was the exact stone that remained standing on the Isle of Glass in the outside world. All the Priestesses and Maiden-Healers were in attendance, as were the remaining Druids and Knights of Avalon. There were no more Bards but Tristram was there, the only remaining Guardian. Faelan sat in the seat usually occupied by Viviana, with Gaius and Ennis macDwyr at his sides.

"We must abandon the Holy Isles if we hope to survive," said Faelan from his seat, "It is the only way."

"It's not the only way," interrupted Elaine, "We can stay here, in the Unseen Vale, and try to rebuild our lives, our community. What do you think Viviana and Taliesin would want us to do?"

"Viviana and Taliesin are dead," said Faelan. It was clear Faelan felt very little emotion at the loss.

"And with them the wisdom of the Merlin and Lady of the Unseen Vale," added Gaius, "As much as I hate the thought of leaving Avalon, I must agree with Faelan. We have a better chance in the outside world, where there are still men of the Tribes who will help us. Here we are nothing more than frightened deer waiting for Mab to return and cut us down."

"Mab will run away and lick her wounds," I said, "She won't return here, not while we remain."

"And you can be sure of this, how?" asked Faelan cynically.

"He understands what the rest of you should already know," interrupted Tristram, "Caliburn, the God-Killing Sword, is still somewhere within the Unseen Vale. It is the only weapon with the power to destroy Mab and, as long as she thinks we have it, she'll be too afraid to come back."

"That sword is cursed," said Faelan, "I wouldn't risk unsheathing it for any reason, not even to murder Mab. We cannot rely on the reputation of the sword to keep us safe."

"If only the Merlin were here," said Livia in almost a whisper, "He would know what to do."

"The Merlin is gone, and he will not rise again," said Faelan.

"There is still a chance Viviana will wake from her sleep," said Elaine, "I think we should remain here and wait for her. Without Taliesin, she is the leader of both Druid and Priestess. We owe it to her. We cannot leave her behind to awaken alone."

The Council was divided. Uriens, Haman, and Gaius were clearly in support of Faelan's desire to leave Avalon, along with Adiane, Rowa, and Asphodel. Elaine had the support of the rest of the Priestesses and Maiden-Healers, as well as Ennis macDwyr and Tristram. Madoc and Accolon also agreed with Elaine but the rest of the Knights sided with Faelan. We were clearly divided and it was obvious there would be no resolution. I feared the order would split in two, with those following Faelan departing the Unseen Vale and those in support of Elaine remaining behind to rebuild their community of Avalon without the others, splintering the Old Religion into factions like the Christians. I felt it went against the memory of Taliesin to allow his religion to die with him.

"Perhaps we should allow each man and woman to make their own choice," said Gaius, "To go or to stay."

"I don't think it's a good idea for us to split up," said Elaine, "It will be easier for our enemies to destroy us if we break into factions. It should be one order standing strong against the tide."

"How can we be one order when it's clear we'll never come to a consensus?" asked Livia.

"We stay here until everyone agrees." said Gaius, "Although I feel we should do as the High Druid commands. Without the Merlin and Lady of the Unseen Vale, Faelan is the voice of authority here and none can contest that. Such is the law of the ancients."

Elaine looked like she was ready to contest the law in an attempt to claim leadership of Avalon herself. She was next-in-line to Viviana and a daughter of Rhiannon. Her opinion mattered greatly, especially to the Priestesses of Nimue. Elaine could take ownership of the title as Lady of the Unseen Vale if the Merlin was there to endorse her claim. As it stood, she could only assert her opinions as a Senior Priestess and nothing more. I wanted her to succeed but it didn't seem like a possibility as more of the Council sided with Faelan. They were afraid and Faelan's suddenly seemed to be their only savior.

"I value your wisdom, Elaine," said Faelan, "You are a daughter of Avalon but you have not been a Priestess for many years. You cannot truly understand the importance of our survival. In the Unseen Vale, we are useless. How can we turn the hearts of the Tribes back to the Old Religion when we segregate ourselves from them?"

It was a good question and the only reason I would be willing to leave Avalon. Many of our numbers were killed in the battle on the Isle of Glass. There were no more Bards and the few Druids that remained, aside from myself, Uriens, and Orin, were rapidly approaching the last days of their lives. If we didn't find others to come and learn the Mysteries, the Old Religion would be lost to the decays of time. Nimue and Kernos would be left without worship and their power would fade. I was not willing to let that happen but I also wanted to remain in the Unseen Vale. It had always been home to the Druids.

"Since there can never be another Merlin," said Faelan, "There can never be another Lady of the Unseen Vale. It is the responsibility of the High Druid to ensure the survival of our order, my responsibility. We must leave the ghosts of this place in the past."

"You are wrong," said a voice from the entrance of the Stone Circle and everyone turned to see Oberon, the Faerie King, standing proudly wearing a loincloth and bear hide. It was true that the hierarchy of the Druids deemed Faelan our new leader and voice of reason but Oberon was beyond such distinctions. When he spoke it was our duty to listen.

"There will be another Merlin," he said.

Chapter Twenty-Four
"Merlin of all the Britons"

"What do you mean there can still be another Merlin?" asked Faelan from his seat at the head of the circle.

The King of Faerie saw Faelan for what he was, a desperate man fearing displacement from his new position of power. Faelan didn't want another Merlin to rise or Viviana to wake up from her eternal sleep. Either outcome would result in him once gain becoming nothing more than the High Druid, with authority only on the Isle of Oak. Instead of addressing Faelan, Oberon spoke to the Council as a whole.

"Taliesin's spirit rests awhile in Faerie," said Oberon, "He waits for Galahad to come and find him, on the distant shores where once he dwelt for a single year."

I couldn't believe what I was hearing. Taliesin was still within my reach. I could go to him that instant, see his face, know his warm embrace but I would have to return to Faerie, something I swore I'd never do after my long absence the last time, when Mab threw me into that world between the mortal coil and the everlasting beyond. I trembled slightly as I thought about the days I spent alone by the river. Accolon noticed my trepidation and stood suddenly beside me. He was extremely protective of my needs in that moment, demonstrating the truth of his feelings. I desired him more in that instance than I ever did before, like a she-wolf in heat, lusting for a mate to copulate under the light of the full moon.

"Galahad cannot go alone," said Accolon, "He endured that nightmare once. I won't have him trapped there for another year. If you will not allow the Druids to accompany him into Faerie, you will at least let me. Either that or Galahad stays here while Taliesin moves into the Otherworld and beyond all of us forever."

I was genuinely touched by Accolon's demand, that he would be willing to face long exile in another world in order to protect me from harm. Mab's love spell was gone but we were no less in love. It just took a battle with the forces of darkness to realize it. Oberon looked less inclined to think highly of Accolon's bravery.

"You are needed here," Oberon said to Accolon, "To keep safe that which must stay hidden."

I knew what Oberon meant. Excalibur and the Cup of Life were still hidden beneath the floorboards of Stargazer's hut in the Fenfolk village on the Watch Hill. If Accolon accompanied me on my journey to Faerie, there would be no one in the Unseen Vale with knowledge of the treasures' location and, more importantly, no one to keep them from being discovered and stolen. It was Tristram's duty to guard the treasures but, for some reason, I was hesitant to let him in on their secret whereabouts. I was having a hard time trusting anyone. Mab's carnage left a cold void in my heart, a place yearning for revenge. I wanted to return to the days of my innocent youth, when the only thing I worried about was how to avoid Brother Jonas and his lectures. I longed for Genovefa's sweet cakes and pumpkin liqueur. For the first time since leaving, I was homesick for Lodecran and the familiarity of my father's villa. The hardening of my heart was indicative of my growing older and more jaded from the constant hurts of the world. I thought I saw Accolon looking at me from the corner of my eye, reading my expressions, recognizing my discomfort.

"I have another companion in mind," said Oberon and he walked over to where my cousin, Madoc, was seated beside Uther, Ector, and the other Knights of Avalon.

When Madoc realized Oberon meant him, he stood and bowed, honored by the Faerie King's request. Oberon placed his hand on the crown of Madoc's head and Madoc fell to the ground unconscious. The other Knights apprehensively jumped to their feet, thinking Oberon had done something sinister to render Madoc incapacitated, but I stood and moved to stand between them and the King of Faerie. The Knights wouldn't raise their weapons against me. I was still a Druid Priest and the Knights were forsworn to never wield a weapon in my presence.

"Madoc isn't hurt," I said, "His spirit was transported to Faerie."

"And now it is your turn," said Oberon and, with a touch of his hand to my forehead, the world around me suddenly went dark.

☼   ☼   ☼

I awoke to the sound of a river, its water rushing by on its journey down from the mountains, and I knew I was back in Faerie. My suspicions were confirmed when I opened my eyes to see the roof of the mossy shelter Viviana and I built around a fallen tree when we were exiled into Faerie by Mab the night Viviana sought answers in the Fire Pit. The sky was its usual clear blue with only a soft glow to illuminate the scenery. I could hear the sound of a fire crackling and smelled fish cooking. As I extricated myself from the shelter, I was greeted by Madoc. He was sitting on a large rock, watching a few filets of river trout as they crisped.

"There you are," he said when he caught sight of me, "I was beginning to think you weren't coming."

In Avalon, my transport to Faerie took place mere seconds after Madoc's but time worked differently in the land of everlasting twilight. From the look of him, Madoc had been in Faerie for at least two days. His five o'clock shadow was turning into a scruffy little beard and he smelled of musk and manly odors. He was wearing only a loincloth and his muscles were covered with dirt and dust. He looked like a savage Pictish warrior waiting to assail a group of Britons traveling across the river or a painted gypsy seeking to live a life of fundamentalism.

"How long you been here?" I asked him as I sat down by the fire.

"A week," he said, "Seven days alone with no sign of you or anyone else. I've done a lot of exploring. There's nothing here. Not one spirit, not a single fey. Taliesin's gone, Galahad, if he was ever here to begin with and now we're trapped in Faerie."

"Oberon wouldn't send us here if Taliesin had already moved on into the Otherworld," I said,

"How do you know?" replied Madoc, "Do you know the King of Faerie? I know he's our great-grandfather but how do we know we can trust him? Didn't your mother warn you about his motives?"

Viviana told me once not to trust Oberon. That everything he did was self-serving but, in this instant, I had to believe he was telling the truth, that Taliesin was somewhere in the great expanse of Faerie. I was desperate to see his face again, for him to tell me everything would be alright, that something would change and peace would return to the world. I knew he was there. He had to be.

"I never saw another person when I was here the last time," I said, "Maybe a cloaking spell lies over Faerie, preventing us from seeing the other people who call this place home."

I didn't know if it was day or night but I was well rested and ready for an adventure. Madoc and I ate the fish he'd cooked and then set out, walking away from the river towards the rolling hills in the distance. I never ventured that far when I first came to Faerie. I was afraid if I walked there alone, I would lose my way and never wake up in the Unseen Vale. This time, with Madoc by my side, I was braver. I knew we could reach the hills, I just didn't know how long it would take. I was in Faerie a week the last time and it turned out to be a year in Avalon. If we remained in Faerie too long, our entire lives could pass us by and we'd never be the wiser.

I was grateful for the opportunity to spend time alone with Madoc. We were once very close but, since he left the Unseen Vale to join the Knights of Avalon, he'd become a different person, stronger and more confident. He was more of a man now, twenty years old and full of energy. In another life we might've been closer. He was very attractive, with soft, blonde curls falling down to his shoulders and the muscled form of a Greek statue. If Accolon was not a part of my reality, Madoc might be the one to share my bed. He was with Morgana for years when we were young but I heard stories of his dalliances with Fenfolk men. He was impartial in his sexual tastes but he was a sensible gentleman who would never let you know about his bisexual nature if you weren't someone he counted as a close friend.

"Tell me about life in Camelot," I said as we continued on towards the rolling hills on the horizon.

"It's amazing," he replied, "I've been there less than a year but it already feels like home. Don't get me wrong, I love Avalon but it's a place filled with memories and attachments. In Camelot I'm free to be who I want to be. I follow both Kernos and the God of Abram. I make friends with people who should be my enemies. There's such a cosmopolitan feel to Camelot. Not like Londinium, with its merchants and lenders. It's more British. Uther insists on returning to the ideals of the Tribes and orders all things Roman to be dismantled and destroyed. There are only a few Romans left in Britannia but there are plenty of other foreigners to make Camelot feel like it's a part of the world, like it could one day become the heart of its own great empire."

"And have you found anyone to share your bed with?" I asked.

"More than one," laughed Madoc.

"Be serious, is there anybody that you love?"

"Not yet," he replied, "I haven't really found anyone who makes me feel like Morgana did. But that doesn't mean I'm giving up hope. What about you? I saw you and Accolon together on the Watch Hill."

"I don't know what's happening with Accolon," I admitted, "One minute we were in love, the next he was running out on me, then he comes back and it feels right but can it be right? I mean, our whole relationship started with a love spell. Somehow that makes it feel hollow."

"Take some advice from your cousin," said Madoc, "If you think there's even a glimmer of love between you, hold onto it and never let it go, no matter what happens in the future."

We reached the very edge of the hills sooner than I would've expected and were greeted by something that came as a total surprise. There seemed to be a large stone archway standing in the middle of an open field, as though there has once been a great fortress rising to look out over the plains but all that remained was this one simple gateway. Madoc looked at me with an expression of curiosity and I knew we were thinking the same thing. We had no choice but to enter.

In all my explorations within the land of everlasting twilight, I'd never seen a single sign of civilization, not one ruined foundation, not one crumbling road. Now there stood an archway in front of us. It felt like it was magically placed in our path for a reason. I decided we had no choice but to pass through it and see if it would make a difference. Madoc was wary of trusting my instincts but I took him by the hand and dragged him along with me as I walked slowly through the archway. Suddenly, it was like a light was turned on above us to reveal what had always been there in the shadows.

There were hundreds if not thousands of people surrounding us and we were standing at the heart of an extraordinary city the likes of which I'd never seen before. The buildings seemed to be forged from pearl and the streets were gold. The people were a mixture of dark-skinned men and women who resembled the Fenfolk, those I knew to be fey, and others of varying ethnicities and backgrounds. We were standing in a garden with the archway at our backs and, there on a stone bench, dressed in radiant robes of sparkling white, sat Taliesin. He was smiling and his face was free of the wares and wrinkles inflicted upon him by his years of battle and stress. His hair was no longer white but a shade of reddish brown and his eyes were filled with life and youth.

"I've been waiting for you," he said.

I started to cry as I ran to my teacher and grandfather. I wanted to pull him into a hug and use my lifeforce to bring him back into the world of the living, to reunite him with his body so that he might breathe again and help me turn the tide against Mab. I wasn't ready to face what I had to become, not without Taliesin to guide me.

"I missed you too, Galahad," he said softly.

"You look fantastic," said Madoc, "Will I look that good too when it's my time to die?"

"We all reflect the true nature of our soul here in the realm between life and death," said Taliesin, "What you see is merely a manifestation of the deeds of my life. If you remain true to yourself, you will enter the Otherworld with beauty and youth."

I wondered what I would look like after death. If my soul would remain untinged by base human emotions. I already bore a dark spot on my spirit from my desire to seek vengeance against Mab and my readiness to cut down Morgause without flinching. Taliesin seemed to know what I was thinking, as if he'd used the power of his third-eye to reach into my mind and see my troubled thoughts.

"Now to the matter at hand," said Taliesin nonchalantly.

"I don't know if I can be what the world needs me to be," I said in a moment of weakness.

"You have to be," said Taliesin, "There is no one else capable of bearing the burden of being Merlin. I didn't choose you as my successor because I thought you stronger or more alert than the other Initiates. I chose you because I could feel your heart, your love for the world around you. The Merlin is protector of all Britons, it is a duty that only the most compassionate spirit can hope to endure."

"I'm frightened," I admitted.

"I was too, when Maponos died and I took the power of the Merlin into me," he said, "but that power made me stronger and gave me a clearer understanding of the world around me. There is magick that only the Merlin knows, a magick that goes beyond the Mysteries. You will be made aware of the powers that animate and move the world. I know you're ready."

I wished I was as sure as Taliesin but the truth was, whether I was prepared or not, this was the moment I'd been waiting for since I was a little boy. Through all my trials and all my mistakes, I never gave up hope that I would one day become the Merlin, that I would take Taliesin's place as the greatest of all the Druids and protector of the ancient secrets of Britannia. It was my time to be the hero. I just didn't think it would come so soon, that I would still be so young when Taliesin died. I wanted to have him there to teach me and guide me towards becoming the man he saw me to be, the man I didn't know I could be.

"You must promise me something," said Taliesin, "Promise me you will watch out for Arthur. He is the True King. He will save our people and our way of life but he'll need guidance. He'll need a friend. There will be many who seek to harm him as he grows into manhood. Right now, he is nothing more than an infant, suckling at his mother's breast. Men do not fear babies. When he becomes more intelligent and grows closer to maturity, he will be faced with many enemies. He will need your help."

"I will help him, Taliesin," I said, "and I will keep him safe."

Taliesin took a deep breath and then stood. He looked up at the sky for a moment, as if drinking in the freshness of the air and the beauty of the heavens. Then he turned to me and pulled me into him, wrapping his arms around me as if he meant to give me a bear hug. With a flash of soft sparkling light and a smile, Taliesin was transmuted into pure energy, an energy that entered my body and joined with my soul.

☼ ☼ ☼

My head ached with information overload as the memories and minds of the 215 Merlins before me came flooding into my brain. It was as though I was standing at the base of a great dam cracking from the weight of the water pressing against the other side. The water was the former Merlins and the breaking dam was the energy of Taliesin and the others bonding with every fiber of my being, merging with my body and spirit. I collapsed onto the ground from the weight of the transference. I was only slightly aware of Madoc as he leaned over and grabbed my arm to pull me back to my feet. I was somewhere else, someone else, living lives that were not my own.

I was a balding man with a little strip of a beard called Akaret, standing in the heart of a massive golden pyramid with incense hanging thickly in the air. I was worrying about someone called Kalyra-Assat, and the future of a world called Lemuria. I could see the waters of the sea rising up from a window near where I stood as it formed a giant tidal wave crashing down on the city surrounding the pyramid. With a final breath, Akaret was washed away by the force of the wave, drowned in its heavy saltwater, crushed by the weight of the tide.

Then I was a beautiful, ageless woman wearing a decadent silver gown and strange tiara. I was called Numessa and revered by a group of bizarre looking men and women with dark skin and long features calling themselves the Mi'ta'mareta. As I pondered the name, its meaning was revealed to me. Mi'ta'mareta meant the Last Survivors in the tongue of Lemuria. They were the people the Britons called the Beakers, who came from the Drowned Lands with the wisdom of the ancients, a wisdom I finally understood to be greater than anything I'd ever imagined. The Beakers were migrating across the lands of Africa and I, I was their queen. I knew I would live a long life, long enough to see my people arrive in the Mediterranean and to settle the Golden City of Troy. I would die in my bed, a crippled old woman losing my grip on reality and surrounded by family. That thought made me content, it made me feel loved.

I became an olive-skinned man with bushy black hair, dressed in a simple leather tunic and brandishing the God-Killing Sword. I was named Gideon and living in Troy. It was the time of the Great War when the Greeks assailed the golden city relentlessly, hoping to reclaim the fair Helena from the hands of her lover, Paris. I watched as the Greeks brought their machines of war against the Trojans, as they lost battle after battle. I wielded Excalibur against them and killed my fair share. I yelled with joy when they finally loaded onto their boats and retreated across the Aegean. Then the city elders brought their gift, the Great Horse, into the city and, in the dead of the night, the Greeks hidden inside broke free and killed us all. I died with Excalibur gripped in my hand, unable to pass my wisdom on to my successor. There was a sound like the cracking of a stone and I felt cold. The world went blurry and I worried how the sword would find its way to safety or how the world would endure without the Merlin. Then I died.

I died Gideon and awoke Maponos, Taliesin's mentor, a huge bear of a man with hair from head to toe. I was a man of the east but I carried myself like a Briton. I wore my hair and beard in braids, I spoke the language of the

Tribes. I fought against the Romans and warned the elders about the imminent arrival of Vortigern, first servant of Mab. The elders didn't heed my advice and Vortigern brought the Saxons down upon Britannia in full force, driving the sons of Constantius from our shores and establishing his tyranny. I was an old man by the time the darkness descended on Britannia. I'd seen the fall of the Romans and the rise of the White Dragon but I wasn't destined to witness more. My heart gave out as I laid in one of the Fenfolk huts on the Watch Hill, within the Unseen Vale, with my youthful apprentice sitting beside me, waiting to take the power of the Merlin.

And then I was the apprentice. I was Taliesin, my own teacher, a rambunctious young man with a special place in my heart for the ladies and a desire to bend all the rules. I knew my purpose and was proud to be the Merlin but not as proud as I was to be a father. I was so protective of my daughters, Viviana and Elaine, and even little Igerna. As I traveled the countryside, living nomadically with the Tribes, I would stop and watch the girls from afar, Viviana on the Isle of Mona, Elaine in Londinium, Igerna at Castle Tintagel. I watched them grow up from a distance, saw the women they grew to be, the children they themselves would come to create. I was there when my grandson, Madoc, was born, the first to hold him in my arms. I was there when my other grandson took his first breath and, even in those first minutes of his life, I saw in him the light of a future Merlin, my little prince, my little Galahad.

At the sight of me being held in Taliesin's arms, I once again came to know myself as Galahad, the living Merlin, meant to carry the secret knowledge back into the mortal world. The secret knowledge of how to rob men of their freewill, to call down the celestials like an army of light to combat the darkness. I learned the secret ways between the worlds and how to entreat the supernatural creatures of the cosmos to do my bidding. I knew how to use fey magick, to be an extension of the environment and allow the energy of every living creature to flow through me. All the Mysteries of the Druids were revealed to me in the fraction of a second. I was more knowledgeable than any living man and my power was such that only a god or goddess could challenge me. I could rewrite reality at a whim and reshape others into a better likeness of what man should be, yet all this magick came with prices I knew I'd never be willing to pay.

The call of Excalibur I'd felt since I raised the sword to protect Taliesin did not fade when the power of the Merlin flowed into me. If anything it was only compounded. I wanted the sword, I needed the sword, and I was willing to do anything to get my hands on it. I was washed in a primal need, a dark and foreboding realization that the sword would always have a hold on me. It was a bane I couldn't escape. All the knowledge of all the magick that was or is made me feel more powerful with each passing second but I also understood the importance of never using certain magick without knowing the grave consequences it would reap on me and the world in general. It would take a far stronger man than me to wield Excalibur, just as the secret magick would have to wait for a greater Druid to use it. I would maintain Taliesin's philosophy, of which I was made aware only after he transferred the power of the Merlin into me. He believed that only the magick that works in cooperation with the natural world should be utilized, only the spells of the Druids and Priestesses, of the ancients and the greats, of the Beakers and their successors.

I struggled to find myself amidst all the voices speaking in my head. I could hear every Merlin, all 215, speaking as though they still lived, as if my body was their own to do with what they will. I was them more than I was me. It would take absolute, unyielding concentration for me to remember who I was in that moment but, in truth, Galahad was gone. I was changed by the minds of the other Merlins, shaped into someone with an entirely different personality. What was once important to me seemed to be trivial and things I'd never even pondered were now at the forefront of my thoughts. I knew who I was, the son of Ban of Lodecran and the Lady Viviana, that Madoc was my cousin, and Accolon my lover but they seemed to be nothing more than a few trivial individuals in lifetimes of love and relationships. I was no longer Prince Galahad of Lodecran, Druid of the Unseen Vale. I had become Merlin of all the Britons.

"Are you alright?" asked Madoc, snapping me back to reality, to where we were standing next to the bench in the courtyard of the fey city. I looked at him for a moment and then spoke with a voice that didn't seem to be mine, though I knew it was.

"I'm just fine," I said, "At least I will be. I think it's time for us to go home and face the others. They'll be eager to know we're unharmed."

I grabbed Madoc by the hand and focused my mind on the Ogham incantation revealed to me during the transference of Taliesin's power, the spell I knew would instantly return us to our bodies in Avalon. With a rush of wind and a feeling like dropping from a cliff, Madoc and I were whisked away from Faerie and back to the Unseen Vale.

☼   ☼   ☼

Unlike my first visit to Faerie, when a week there was a year in the mortal world, the second visit was the opposite. Madoc was there for eight days and me one but only a matter of seconds had passed in Avalon. We awoke to find the Council still gathered in the remains of the Stone Circle, each sitting on the edge of their seat, waiting for me to awaken. I could feel their eyes on me as I stood from where I'd fallen on the ground. Madoc also rose to his feet, brushing off his clothes and looking around, clearly disoriented. Faelan was glaring from where he sat on Viviana's chair and the others looked bemused by my short trip to Faerie.

"Well?" asked Faelan, "Are you changed into our salvation?"

"I think you should remove yourself from my mother's seat," I said boldly, "And remember your place, Faelan, son of Forn. You may be High Druid but you are not a king. There has never been a king in Avalon and there never will be, not as long as the Merlin remains in Britannia to remind us of the order of things."

"You are him," said Elaine with wonder, "You are the Merlin. I can see it in your eyes. You're changed into someone different. You're not the little boy who left this world moments ago."

"I am that which I am," I replied without having to think about my answer. I wasn't the frightened seventeen year old who went to find Taliesin but I wasn't the salvation of the Britons either. I was something in between, a new person in a strange body. It wasn't until I saw Accolon that I felt like myself. His love grounded me and made me Galahad again.

Faelan was reluctant to rise from the seat beneath the one remaining monolith of the Stone Circle. He would hold onto his little portion of power as long as he could and wasn't going to take the word of a teenager turned immortalized collection of lives as anything more than suggestion. It wasn't until he heard the tapping of a stick on the hillside just beyond the demolished entrance of the circle that he rose and hurried off to join the other Druids, hiding his face in shame. He knew what that sound meant, it was the sound of hope and renewal.

"It seems a stowaway crossed through the gateway opened by Oberon when he sent me and Madoc into Faerie," I said.

The Council turned their eyes towards the noise growing stronger with each passing moment, their faces filled with wonder and dread. Slowly, the form of a woman rose over the slope of the Tor Hill and the Council breathed a sigh of relief. It was Viviana, limping her way blindly towards the Stone Circle with a walking stick to guide her. Elaine stood and ran to her sister, pulling her into arms with a cry of happiness and Viviana smiled with joy. I was happy to see my mother but not as a son. I was glad she was returned to reclaim her seat as Lady of the Unseen Vale. Elaine took Viviana by the arm and guided her into the circle, leading her to her seat beneath the monolith vacated by Faelan. Viviana sat with a sigh before she turned her head towards me, her blind eyes seeing something the others could not perceive, something hanging in the air around me.

"You are transformed," she smiled.

"I am," I replied, "and you are returned just in time to lead your people through these troubling times. Remain here in the Unseen Vale, away from the hurts of the world, and rebuild the Holy Isles we have called home for generations. More children will come in time and the numbers of the faithful will be restored. I've seen it. They will need you to guide them and keep them safe, Lady."

I didn't wait for Viviana to respond. I turned around and walked towards the Processional Way, ready to face my destiny and make the sacrifices of those I loved worth something. I would do as Taliesin always wished, I'd become the man to stand against the darkness and hold back the tide of evil threatening to engulf us all. I knew Mab's mind in a new way since merging with the power of the Merlin, I could see her suffering and understand her woes. She was a goddess but her heart was like that of a human. She was hurt and, like me when I struck down Morgause, she had allowed that pain to transform into a need for vengeance. I pitied Mab, not for the things she had done, but for the being she'd allowed herself to become, and for the future hardships she would face. No matter how much she fought to realize her revenge, she would never attain it, not while I drew breath or while Viviana ruled in Avalon. We would keep the world safe until the day the Pendragon would rise again as the True King.

"Where are you going?" asked Viviana as I moved beyond the entrance of the Stone Circle and I turned around to smile.

"I made a promise to Taliesin I mean to keep," I said. I left the Unseen Vale that same day, to make my way to Camelot, to Arthur, the True King, to teach him and keep him safe.

Excerpts from

The Crimes of Camelot

Legends of Avalon
- Book Two -

Epilogue
"The Crimes of Camelot"

"There is no way I will do what you ask," hissed Igerna from her seat. I was asking a lot of her, I knew this, but there was no other way.

The Saxons were massing just north of Camelot, under the leadership of Mab and her minions. The city was no longer safe, especially for a boy of five. Uther would remain to lead the Knights and his armies. Igerna would stay by his side, praying relentlessly to the God of Abram for her husband's victory against the barbarians. They were adults and, if they chose to remain in the line of fire, there was nothing I could do. But Arthur was different. I could hear Taliesin's voice inside my head driving me to fulfill my promise. I would keep Arthur safe, even if that meant taking him far from Camelot and his loving parents.

"I would not ask this of you if it weren't of the utmost importance," I said, "Arthur's future is written in the stars. His life is too important to risk here in the face of battle. I will honor you with the respect due your station but I am not asking. Arthur leaves with me."

Igerna seemed like she would leap off her throne and start pummeling me with her bare fists but Uther maintained his composure.

"Where will you take him?" he asked.

"Far from the heart of your kingdom." I replied, "Somewhere his enemies won't think to look for him. Make no mistake, my Lord, there are many who wish Arthur dead."

Uther knew I spoke the truth. In the five years since Arthur's birth on the Isle of the Font, Mab's influence over the outside world had grown considerably. When she failed to turn the hearts of the Britons, she began sowing seeds of darkness and delight in the hearts of the Saxons flocking to the shores of Britannia from their own sinking homeland. No longer were they Sellswords in the service of Vortigern or Lot. They were a violent, barbaric people, but they were also smart. They understood the small parcel of land gifted to them by Vortigern as reward for their service in his name would never sustain their rapidly growing numbers. In order to ensure their own security, they were willing to turn on the Britons and invade our sovereign lands. In order to succeed, they would need to destroy Camelot, execute Uther, and assassinate his only son and heir.

"You may take him," said Uther, "but be quick about it."

☼　　　☼　　　☼

"Are you taking me to Avalon?" asked Arthur as we rode west along the Welsh Road, away from Camelot and towards the wilds of Whales. He was only five years old but he seemed so mature, with the natural regality of a prince born in the purple and an inquisitive mind not unlike that of his half-sister, Morgana. He had dirty blonde locks and eyes the same striking blue as his mother's, and mine. He favored Uther in the rest of his features, from his pale, freckled skin, to his long, skinny legs.

"What do you know of Avalon?" I teased.

"My mother says it's a place of evil, where the devil steals souls to use as his servants," he replied, "but father speaks of the Unseen Vale like a place of wonder, where the last of the Druids live and use magick. And he says there's a sword there that could save us all from the Saxons."

The mention of Excalibur caused spasms in the pit of my stomach. I yearned to touch the sword like a man addicted to alcohol, desiring nothing more than one more drink. Several months after I left Avalon behind, to journey to Camelot, I was compelled by the force of my dreams to return to the Unseen Vale and remove the sword from its hiding place beneath the floorboards of Stargazer's hut in the Fenfolk village. Accolon was meant to remain on the Watch Hill and keep the location of the sword a secret but he was soon after called away to the Isle of Wight to resume his duties as king. I feared the sword would be discovered, at least that's what I convinced myself. In truth, I was hungry to hold it again, to grip the cold steel in my fingers and feel its power coursing through my veins. I held Excalibur aloft and, for a moment, thought about taking it with me to the outside world, giving myself over to its call to wield it as champion against Mab.

"I thought I might find you here," came the voice of my mother, Viviana, as she entered Stargazer's hut, "The call of Caliburn is too strong to resist, even for the Merlin."

"You knew the sword was here?" I asked.

"And the Cup," she added, "I decided to leave them lie because I knew you'd return to seek out the sword again. I wanted to see you, in the moment of Excalibur's greatest hold, to shock you back to reality. Excalibur is cursed, Galahad. It cannot be trusted to assist us in our fight. It will betray us at the first opportune moment and will leave its wielder broken and infirmed. You think the sword is giving you energy but, really, it is feeding on your lifeforce. It must be put somewhere it cannot be sought out again, not until Arthur is old enough to safely claim it as his own. Only the True King can wield Excalibur without threat of the curse."

As Arthur and I entered a small glade of yew trees growing around the Welsh Road, I was drawn back to the present with the affirmation that Excalibur was beyond Uther's reach, and my own. It laid at the bottom of the Brackish Lake, in the hands of Nimue, where I threw it that day with my mother, the day I began to break the sword's spell over me. It would remain in its watery tomb until Arthur journeyed to Avalon to take ownership. The Cup of Life also dwelt in the depths of the lake. Viviana feared what might happen if it fell into the wrong hands. Giving it over to the protection of Nimue was the only way to ensure it would be there for use by future generations of Druids.

"I don't think Avalon is the best place for you, my young prince," I said to Arthur, bringing the conversation back to where it started.

"Then where am I going?" he asked.

"To the Lake Country in the north," I said, "to the town of Deva. There is a man there I know very well. He can be trusted to protect you and keep your true name a secret. He is Lord of the Corvanii Tribes and was once a warrior of significant skill before he was wounded in battle with the Saxons at Hadrian's Wall."

"And does this man have a name?" asked Arthur.

"He is called Ector," I said.

☼   ☼   ☼

After I was sure Arthur had acclimated to his life in Deva, as the orphan, Wart, I decided to go back to Camelot to assist Uther in his battle against the Saxons but I arrived to find the city deserted. The Saxon armies were camping just across the River Metaris, with enormous bonfires fed by the flesh of captured Britons. The sky was covered in a haze of clouds dyed red by the blood of the innocent men and women sacrificed on the fires in the name of Mab. I sought out the few people remaining in Camelot, those too poor or old to escape in time, and the story they told was one of heartache. It took me by complete surprise.

Just days following my departure from Camelot with Arthur, Uther disappeared. It was rumored he fled the city dressed as a peasant in the dead of night. I couldn't believe the great Uther who fought to claim the throne of Britannia would slink away like a coward at the first sign of trouble. If he did indeed abandon Camelot, he must've been driven to it by dire need. Igerna remained in the city and effectively became its ruler from that day forward but, she deferred her royal authority to Archbishop Sebastianus and Bishop Nikko of Mycenae. The Nicene Church had come to wield near absolute power over the Romanized Britons of the southeast, though a great division of culture still existed between the Christians and the rural Tribes. Sebastianus and Nikko were convinced the city would be lost and, just nine days before my arrival, the city's elite abandoned the peasantry as they departed Camelot in a mass exodus. I was deeply concerned for the wellbeing of those remaining in the city. The most I could do was provide them time to escape. I would invoke the magick of the Blood Oath to delay the progress of the Saxons and ensure the poor masses of Camelot would have time to leave the city unopposed.

I ascended the walls of Camelot, moving with great speed to the tallest parapet looking out over the River Metaris and the Saxon armies beyond. I'd only seen the power of the Blood Oath once, when Taliesin used its might to sink the warships of Lot of the Orkneys during the battle for the throne of Britannia. Every Merlin was bound to the land of the Britons, and the Tribes themselves, by blood, allowing them to access the deepest magick of the land in a manner unattainable by other practitioners. However, the cost was great. Taliesin nearly died from loss of blood. If I hadn't been there to drag him back to Camelot, he would've died on the Witch's Point. I had no one to watch me, or save me if the spell were to bring me to the bitter and inescapable gates of death.

I drew my ceremonial dagger from its sheath on my belt, the same bronzed blade carried by Taliesin, and closed my eyes. I ran the blade across one wrist, and then the other, allowing my blood to spill onto the stones of the parapet beneath me. The pain was overwhelming and I felt sick but I focused my mind on the task at hand, at what I meant to accomplish, and pushed the pain to the back of my mind.

"Afxísei to neró tou potamoú," I said with a voice that echoed across the meadow towards the Metaris and unaware Saxons.

Suddenly, the waters of the river swelled, rising up like a great tidal wave to wash out the only bridge crossing from the lands of the Iceni into the meadow surrounding Camelot.

"Blokároun ton ouranó me mávra sýnnefa," I said.

Dark clouds appeared in the sky above us, as if from nowhere, and began pelting the countryside with pouring rain. Thunder clapped and lightning struck as the wind kicked up into a mighty howl, bearing down on the Saxon encampment like the weight of a book pressing a flower.

"Férei ti gi na trémei," I commanded.

All at once, the ground beneath us began to tremble as an earthquake unleashed its damaging effects upon the Saxons, causing their horses to spook and run away, bringing their tents down on top of them, and sparking a panic amongst their superstitious ranks.

"Prokalései tromeró pónous tis peínas," I screamed.

I understood this last incantation couldn't be witnessed from the parapet on which I stood, bleeding out on the stones. But I knew it was working, inducing terrible pains of famine and hunger in the stomachs of the Saxons, flaring their bowels with dysentery. They would succumb to fevers and hives, their bodies would betray them. It was the final command. The fate of the Saxons was temporarily sealed and the poor people of Camelot would have time to escape. I didn't think I'd be so lucky. I was feeling lightheaded and dizzy. My strength was leaving me with every drop of blood flowing out through the wounds on my wrists. I fell to my knees with a dramatic exhalation and then hit the ground with a thud. My vision began to blur as I moved towards unconsciousness, but not before I caught sight of a man emerging from the nearby doorway onto the parapet.

"You're not going to die today," he said.

"How did you find me?" I asked.

"I will always find you," he smiled and, in my moment of weakness, I was glad to be in the arms of my lover. For the sixth time in the last five years, Accolon had come to save me.

☼   ☼   ☼

"What's happened to you, Uther?" I asked as Uther rounded on me with his sword brandished high.

We were standing on the very edge of the Brackish Lake, on the Isle of Glass. The Maiden-Healers, fearing for their lives, were locked inside the House of Healing while Uther's mercenaries remained near the foot of the Tor Hill, waiting for orders from their High King. Uther looked changed. His normally ruddy skin was as pale as fresh milk and his eyes were bloodshot, as though he hadn't slept in days. He was growing thin and his hair was graying prematurely. He didn't look like the High King crowned by Taliesin six years before, or even the man whom I visited often in Camelot, to advise and council about how to keep the British people safe. He had abandoned his seat of power and entered the Unseen Vale with a spell he was never meant to know. Now he was ready to strike me down in order to accomplish his goal of attaining absolute power.

"Why did you abandon Camelot in its hour of need?" I asked.

"I did not abandon the city out of weakness or cowardice," replied Uther, "I did so to make Camelot stronger. I've come for the sword, the one you've kept hidden from me all these years. I know your mind, Galahad. You wish to keep the blade for Arthur, you think he will be the great king to save us all from the darkness. But the darkness is already upon us. I must have Excalibur, to save my people from the Saxons."

Uther lunged at me with his sword but I invoked a power to slow time long enough for me to move out of the way. To Uther, it seemed I teleported from one place to another and he recoiled from the power of my magick, though his determination was not deterred. He lunged again, only this time he came at me from the side, cutting off my ability to move around him, even with time marching more slowly. I used a spell of transmutation to change the flesh on my arm into the substance of steel, using it to prevent Uther's sword from penetrating my torso. While I stood there locked in a moment of battle with Uther, a dark figure emerged from the Stone Circle, dressed head to toe in red, her maniacal eyes emblazoned with a desire to cause pain and undue violence.

Morgana used the same magick I just invoked to slow time, so that it seemed she moved from the Stone Circle to the banks of the Brackish Lake in mere seconds, coming to stand beside Uther, tall and fierce, with her face locked in a permanent, malevolent scowl. She pointed her hand at me and I was lifted off the ground, thrown backwards through the air like a leaf carried on a powerful wind. I used my own magick to prevent a collision with the water but, by the time I regained my composure, Morgana was already working the magick needed to retrieve the sword from the bottom of the lake. She invoked the power of Mab and used it to part the waters like the Red Sea, revealing the sword and Cup resting at the bottom. Morgana pointed her fingers at the treasures and muttered something under her breath but it seemed she was struggling against an invisible force. The sword was the first to break free. It came hurtling upward from the bottom of the lake and into Uther's waiting hands. The Cup was more reluctant to become dislodged and Morgana was forced to give up. She wasn't strong enough to face off against the power of Nimue for any length of time, for it was Nimue holding the treasures in their watery tomb and she was reluctant to give them up.

"We have what we came for," yelled Uther, "Get us out of here."

Before I could intercept them, Morgana grabbed Uther by the shoulder and, in a split second, they were returned to the Stone Circle. With the sound of a bell ringing gently on the wind, Morgana, Uther, and his mercenaries were transported back to the outside world. I stood there in complete shock. Morgana and Uther were working together. Excalibur was now in the hands of the corrupted High King and there was no telling what the consequences would be, for the world and for us.

"What's happened?" said Livia, head of the Maiden-Healers, as she ran out of the House of Healing to meet me, having watched the whole altercation from the window.

"The High King has fallen to the darkness, to the influences of Mab" I said, "And Excalibur is lost."

Legendary Timeline

413 AD: *The Romans withdraw their forces from Britannia. Most of the Roman citizenry departs the island with the soldiers but a few remain to organize Romano-British society into its own autonomous empire under the leadership of the Roman Prelate, Constantius, ruling from the Great Hall in Londinium on the River Thames.*

418 AD: *The tyrant, Vortigern of Valentia, invokes the dark power of Mab in order to gain a large army of Saxon Sellswords and the power to invade the south, killing Constantius, and forcing his sons, Constans and Ambrose, into exile. Vortigern establishes himself as High King and begins suppressing both pagan and Christian Britons, declaring war on the Unseen Vale and seeking to extinguish the wisdom of the ancients once and for all and bring about Mab's desired age of darkness.*

438 AD: *Vortigern sends his agents against the Unseen Vale in an attempt to wipe out the Druids but they are stopped by the Queen of Faerie and Lady of Avalon, Rhiannon, who sacrifices herself to prevent Vortigern's mercenaries from crossing into the Unseen Vale. Her lifeless, yet eternally young, body is placed on a funeral pyre on the Isle of Stone to be revered as the savior of Avalon and the Druids.*

439 AD: *Viviana, Lady of Avalon, and Taliesin, Merlin of all the Britons, unite with Oberon, the King of Faerie, and the goddess, Nimue, to banish Mab back into the Otherworld. Without Mab's dark power supporting his claim, Vortigern is soon forced to retreat back into the north, where he lives out the rest of his days in perpetual exile. The sons of Constantius return from exile and Constans is named High King.*

442 AD: *Constans dies suddenly from a mysterious illness and is replaced by his younger brother, Ambrose, as High King. Ambrose proves to be a well-tempered ruler who respects both the Christians and the Druids for their wisdom. He governs in the Roman fashion from Londinium and ushers in several years of peace.*

459 AD: *War breaks out between the Britons and the Picts who dwell in the highlands of Caledonia. The Picts begin raiding the southern coast on warships provided by their Saxon allies. The elders in the Unseen Vale begin to suspect the darkness of Mab is returning as the raids escalate into a full-blown war.*

461 AD: *The war between the Britons and Picts ends in favor of High King Ambrose. The lesser kings sworn to serve Ambrose journey from their homes to Londinium to celebrate the British victory. Ban, King of Lodecran, makes the journey with his son, Galahad, as Galahad is meant to go to the Unseen Vale and meet his mother, Viviana.*

465 AD: *Arthur is born on the Isle of the Font and it is prophesied that he will rise to become the True King, the Pendragon, savior of the Britons and the Druids.*

466 AD: *The battle between the light and darkness comes to a head as Mab's forces gain strength and the power of the Druids ebbs. The only hope for the Old Religion and the Briton people rests in the last Merlin and his ability to keep the darkness at bay while the infant Arthur grows up to become the savior of Britain, the Pendragon.*

About the Author

R. Matthew Jocks-Warren is an independent author of fantasy fiction, supernatural mysteries, and poetry. He earned his BA in English from Portland State University in 2008 before going on to pursue a Master's in Secondary Education. Matthew is a registered democrat with moderately liberal views and writes a successful blog on politics/religion in America. Matthew is the author of a full-length novel, collection of short stories, and two poetry collections, published under the pseudonym R.J. Pommarane. When he's not writing his next great work of fiction, Matthew enjoys camping, hiking, reading, swimming, and sitting in the sun. He currently resides in Portland, Oregon, with his partner, Kevin, and their two cats.

www.ingramcontent.com/pod-product-compliance
Lightning Source LLC
Chambersburg PA
CBHW031111030726
47496CB00002BA/491